LEATHER & LIES

Tarnished Angels Motorcycle Club Book 7

EMMA SLATE

©2024 by Tabula Rasa Publishing LLC
All rights reserved.

No part of this publication may be reproduced, distributed or transmitted in any form or by any means, including photocopying, recording, or other electronic or mechanical methods, without the prior written permission of the publisher, except in the case of brief quotations embodied in critical reviews and certain other noncommercial uses permitted by copyright law.

This book is a work of fiction. Names, characters, places, and incidents are the product of the author's imagination or are used fictitiously. Any resemblance to actual events, locales, or persons, living or dead, is coincidental.

Leather & Lies
(TARNISHED ANGELS MOTORCYCLE CLUB BOOK 7)

"There's nothing I wouldn't do for you, Hayden. Nothing."

All I wanted was to be home in my pajamas…instead, I'm at a club with my best friend.

When she bets me I won't talk to the leather-wearing snack on the dance floor, I hop off my high-horse to prove her wrong.

The next thing I know, I'm kissing a bad-boy biker in the dark.

Bones makes me want to throw out my good-girl rulebook…and my panties too.

He doesn't belong in my world, but when I see Bones in a tuxedo charming my upper-class, matchmaking mother, I start to think he and I could have a future together.

But then there's an attempt on my life. Now I'll have to marry a man from the wrong side of the tracks for protection...

I never asked him to make the ultimate sacrifice, but to keep me alive, that's just what my Tarnished Angel is willing to do...

Chapter 1

"What are you staring at?" I asked.

"The hottest guy I've ever seen." My best friend brought a flute of Prosecco to her bright red lips, her eyes locked on a man across the club floor.

I grinned. "Are you going to talk to him?"

"And leave you sitting here all by yourself? What kind of a friend do you think I am?"

"The horny kind."

She winked at me. "The night is young and so are we. He might be hot, but I'm not willing to forgo all my other options just yet."

I rolled my eyes.

"You haven't even asked who I'm talking about. Aren't you at all curious?"

"Not really." I grabbed my rocks glass and took a sip of my clear, bubbly drink.

"You're no fun."

"I came out with you tonight, didn't I?"

"I had to beg…"

I pointed to her. "Extrovert." And then I pointed to myself. "Introvert."

She pointed to herself. "Embraces life." She pointed to me. "Reclusive shut-in."

"Okay, fine. If I check out the hot guy you're talking about, will you leave me alone?" I demanded lightly.

"Sure." Charlie gestured with her chin. "Ten o'clock. Leather vest."

"A leather vest? Seriously?"

"Not *that* kind of leather vest," she assured me.

My curiosity was piqued. I swiveled on the bar stool, my eyes sifting through the people in the direction Charlie had motioned.

The lights of the club were low and the music was soft enough that I didn't have to yell at Charlie to be heard. The hum of conversations faded away when I finally saw exactly who Charlie was talking about.

He was tall, towering over nearly everyone around him. His height wasn't what made me pause, though. Those who moved in his sphere gave him a wide berth, like there was an invisible forcefield around him that people bounced off. His presence alone was commanding.

"Told ya," Charlie said with a knowing laugh.

"He doesn't even look like he belongs here."

Chaos was an upscale club—more like a wine bar atmosphere, but with a dance floor. The bar was made of marble and the floor was polished oak. Everyone was perfectly coiffed and presented, each of them hoping to find the perfect stranger to fill the void we all lived with but pretended we didn't have.

"Here." Charlie handed me a bar napkin.

"What's this for?" I asked.

"Your drool."

"Oh, shut up." I laughed and threw the napkin back at her.

"You should go talk to him," she suggested, taking another sip of her Prosecco.

"What? No. You were the one who saw him first. And he looks like he's just your type."

"The kind of man my parents would hate if I brought home? Hmm. Yeah. Normally, I'd be all about that, but that's what they expect of me. I have to keep them on their toes. If I bring home a clean-cut suit, they'll be so confused."

"You've got issues."

"Definitely," she agreed. "I bequeath him to you. Go talk to him."

"I'm not gonna talk to him. What would I even say?"

"Say nothing, just pet his leather vest."

"Pass."

She sighed. "I didn't want to have to do this, but you leave me no choice."

"What?"

"If you go talk to him, I promise I'll show up at the gala your mother is organizing."

I raised my eyebrows. "You never go to those things."

"Well, I will. For you. But only if you go up and talk to him."

"All I have to do is talk to him?" I asked.

"That's all."

I peered at her for a moment and then suddenly smiled. "Okay."

Charlie blinked. "Okay?"

"Okay," I repeated. "I'll go talk to him."

"You have to say more than *hi* to him. Otherwise, no deal. If you spend five minutes over there, I'll even wear the backless dress I've been saving for a special occasion. The dress will make my mother blow a gasket."

"Why do you want to torture your mother so badly?" I asked.

"Don't take her side," Charlie said. "Now go."

I set my drink down and slid off the stool. I grabbed my phone, shot Charlie a wink, and then with feigned confidence, approached tall, dark, and Bad Decision.

Capital B. Capital D.

Bad Decision was standing by himself and the closer I got to him, the more I realized I hadn't seen him clearly at all.

He was taller than I originally thought, at least ten inches over my five four. His jaw was covered in stubble and his gaze surveyed the floor.

Electric blue eyes glanced in my direction before drifting away. "I'm not interested, Jailbait."

His deep voice washed over me and despite his words, goosebumps arose along my arms.

"I'm not jailbait," I blurted out.

He turned his attention back to me and raised a dark brow. "Yeah? Prove it."

"Prove it?"

"Show me your ID."

"I'm not showing you my ID. I got into the club, that's proof enough I'm legal."

"IDs can be faked. You must have a fake ID. Now, if you don't show me your ID, I'll have to escort you out."

"You can't escort me out."

"I'm security," he said lightly. "So either show me your ID or I take you outside and put your underage ass in a cab home."

I glared at him, but his body was alert, ready to move.

It wasn't fair that I found him attractive.

"I'm waiting."

With a sigh, I pulled my license out from the slit in my phone case and handed it to him. Our fingers brushed when he took it from me.

I inhaled sharply, but otherwise made no sound.

He studied my ID and then lifted his eyes to mine. "Hayden Spencer. Twenty-five years old. I stand corrected. You're not jailbait. You're not jailbait at all."

Suddenly he smiled.

Danger, abort mission, fall back.

With a frown, I focused on the man in front of me and filched my license from his fingers and shoved it back into my phone case slit.

"You know what? Winning the bet isn't worth it," I said.

"Bet? What bet?" he asked.

"My best friend bet me I wouldn't talk to you for five minutes. But no amount of winning is worth this. You're insufferable, arrogant—"

"Your eyes are gorgeous."

The way he was looking at me made my stomach flutter and my long dormant libido crackle to life.

He held up two fingers and I turned around to see who he was gesturing to. The bartender inclined his head and began making drinks.

"I don't need a drink," I told him.

He flashed another libertine grin. "You're right. You need a few. Relax, Duchess, let me take care of you. You'll like it, I promise."

My brows snapped together. "Duchess?"

"You've got that expensive look about you."

Before I was able to stutter a reply, the music cut off and so did the lights. Darkness swamped the club. A murmur of collective confusion swelled throughout the room.

Panic swirled in my belly, a breath of terror escaping from between my lips.

A large hand settled on my hip and pulled me forward until my chest was flush against Bad Decision's leather vest. Another hand came out of nowhere and gently clasped the back of my neck and before I knew it, his lips covered mine.

My alarm immediately receded as I was consumed by the man kissing me. He wasn't forceful, nor was he tender. He was an expert kisser. He sipped at my lips, a connoisseur of pleasure. The flutters in my stomach quickly turned into a swarm of excitement.

My free hand had a mind of its own and pressed against the solid warm chest of the man whose real name I didn't know.

The overhead lights flared to life—not the dim, sensual glow of club lights, but the garish, everyday fluorescent bulbs.

With the illumination of the club, my senses returned.

I yanked my hand away from his chest—his firm, muscular chest—and slid it up between our mouths.

My vision swam and I stumbled on my heels.

Bad Decision's hands quickly grasped my upper arms to steady me. "I had no idea my kiss was going to make you faint."

I inhaled a deep breath and met his eyes in the light.

Dear Lord, he's even better looking than I thought.

"I'm not the fainting type," I sassed.

"Glad to hear you're made of stronger stuff. So," he continued, "you want to go somewhere and pick up where we left off?"

"Nope." I shook my head. "I want no part of this.

You're trouble, and I don't go home with men I've just met."

"Sex in the bathroom, then?"

I glared. "Good night, Bad Decision."

He flashed a sexy grin. "My name is Bones, but close enough."

"I didn't tell you to kiss him," Charlie said as she climbed into the Uber after me.

"Will you hurry up?" I demanded. "I want to get out of here."

"Worried about your leather snack coming out and finishing what he started?" She closed the door and the car pulled away from the curb outside of Chaos.

I let out an internal sign of relief. "No."

"Yeah, right. Color me surprised. The moment the lights came on, I saw you pressed up against him and I was kicking my feet, squealing and giggling like a teenage girl."

"I was just supposed to talk to him, not kiss him." I leaned my head back against the seat and closed my eyes. Unfortunately, all that did was make me relive the kissing scene.

"I didn't think you had it in you," she teased. "That was such a me move. You're my hero."

I looked at her. "I won, you know. You have to go to the gala."

She smirked. "I was gonna go anyway."

I gasped. "*You were?* You beast! So, what was with the bet?"

"Just wanted to see if I could get you to do something outside your comfort zone. I didn't think you'd actually *do* him."

"I didn't do him," I negated. "Though he was amenable about continuing down the path of carnal sin—in the club bathroom, no less."

"Classy."

"Very." I wrinkled my nose.

"So, tell me about him."

"Nothing to tell." I shrugged. "He said he was security for the club."

"Ah, no wonder he didn't look like he belonged."

"Yep. His name is Bones."

"Bones? That's not a name."

"Doesn't really matter what his name is. He's trouble. And it's done now. I'll never see him again."

Charlie didn't say anything for a moment and then she said, "I'm proud of you."

"For kissing a stranger? You already said that."

"Not that. I mean for actually coming out. Thank you. I needed the distraction." Charlie fell silent and looked out the window.

"You want to talk?"

"When have I ever wanted to talk?"

"It's why you chose a club versus a coffee shop," I said. "If you wanted to talk, you would've insisted on going to a coffee shop."

She didn't reply.

"You want to sleep over at my house?" I asked.

"Will you promise not to try and talk to me about what I don't want to talk about?"

"Uh, I think I followed that. Sure."

"Will you make me waffles in the morning?"

The Uber turned into the gated community of Vernon Estates and wound down the curvy road toward my house.

"I'll make you waffles," I said as the Uber pulled into my driveway. "But you have to learn how to operate the waffle maker. One of these days, I'm not gonna to be around to make you waffles, and you're gonna have to learn how to do it for yourself."

"But that's such an adult thing to do. Adulting: zero out of ten, do not recommend."

Chuckling, I waited for Charlie to get out first. She was already punching in the key code to the front door by the time I climbed out of the car.

"You know what I love about your house?" Charlie asked as she stood in the foyer and kicked off her heels.

"What?" I closed the front door and locked it.

"That it's your house." She grinned.

"I told you that you could move in," I said. "It's kind of lonely living by myself."

"Liar." She chuckled. "You love it."

"I do love it," I admitted. "But it's too big for one person. *Almost.*"

"Arnold still giving you grief about moving out?" She followed me toward the wooden stairs.

"Not nearly as much as my mother. Which is weird, considering she spends most of her time traveling with my stepfather. They're always at some resort spa, or at a charity luncheon or something. She's rarely home, so I don't understand why she's so upset that I live on my own."

Six months ago, I'd bought a house. It was modest, but only in relation to the house I'd grown up in. There was no marble fountain in my front yard and I lived in a gated community instead of on private property surrounded by wrought iron fences and a guard post worth more than most people's homes.

I flipped on my bedroom light and immediately went to the walk-in closet with custom-built cherry wood shelves and a matching dresser. I opened the middle drawer and pulled out a pair of sweats and a T-shirt to hand to Charlie.

"I won't move in. But maybe I should finally bring over some clothes to keep in the guest room," she said with a smile.

"That makes sense for as often as you're over here."

Charlie lived in her parents' pool house. For all her acts of rebellion, she hadn't yet cut ties and moved out. She loved her parents, even if she wanted to drive them to insanity.

"I'm gonna shower real quick," I said. "And then I'm going to bed."

"You mind if I watch a movie?"

I shook my head. "Tear it up. Stella restocked the popcorn before she left town."

Charlie flashed a wobbly grin. "You take such good care of me."

"We take good care of each other." I reached out and took her hand to give it a little squeeze.

She headed for the door of my bedroom, but then she stopped. "I'd never try and change you, you know."

I frowned. "I know."

"I think you're perfect as you are. I know you don't like going out. I appreciate that you did it anyway. For me."

"I'd do anything for you, Charlie. You get that, right?"

"I get that," she murmured. Her eyes were glassy, but I knew it wasn't from the Prosecco.

"I'll see you in the morning. For waffles."

Chapter 2

"Welcome home, Miss Hayden," Stanton greeted in his crisp English accent.

The aging butler had been with my family for as long as I could remember. My parents had met him on their honeymoon in London. When they returned home to the States, they had Stanton with them—along with me, though they didn't know my mom was pregnant at the time.

"I've missed you, Stanton," I said as I hugged him.

Despite his aloof exterior, I had no issue showing him affection.

He pulled back and stood straight, his spine showing no signs of age, unlike his lined face. "Your mother and stepfather are in the salon."

"Cocktail hour?" I asked in amusement.

He inclined his head and closed the door behind me.

I looked around the foyer and my eyes narrowed. "Mom redecorated again?"

"She did."

I held in a sigh.

Six different reiterations in the last three years. It was as though the moment she finished one redecoration she started all over again.

My heels clacked across the gleaming dark mahogany floors that were original to the house. My mother sat on a cream-colored couch, her spine erect as she sipped a martini, her blonde hair pulled back into a neat chignon. At her ears and throat were the pearls that had belonged to my grandmother.

Marilyn Edith Corbin Spencer Walsh was beautiful, elegant and petite, and she exuded a natural friendliness. She was neither standoffish nor snobby. Her every move indicated she was old money, yet most people seemed to forget that fact after a few minutes in her presence.

I took after my mother in stature, but I hadn't escaped my father's genetics. Same dark hair, same brown eyes. It hurt Mom to look at me sometimes.

"Hayden," she greeted, a warm smile drifting across her face.

"Hi," I said, meeting her smile with one of my own. I walked over to the couch and sat down next to her. I brushed my cheek against hers and noticed it was still smooth in spite of her age.

When I pulled back, she gently cupped my face and peered at me. "You look tired."

I rolled my eyes. "I went out with Charlie last night. I'm fine."

"You went out?" Her brows rose and wrinkled slightly, despite the delicate work she'd had done.

"I went out," I repeated. "Where's Arnold?"

"He had to take a call. He'll be back in a bit. So, you and Charlie went out."

"Still on that, are we?" I asked as I rose. I went to the

antique liquor cart near the unlit stone fireplace and filled a rocks glass with ice.

"It's just out of character for you, that's all."

"She begged." I unscrewed a bottle of club soda and poured it into my glass and garnished it with a lime.

"Dina's worried about her," Mom said.

"Dina worries about everything," I said. "It's her nature."

"So, there's nothing for her to worry about?" Mom pressed.

I loved my mother, but we did not share confidences. Anything I said to her would get reported back to Charlie's mom—a woman I loved dearly, and not just because she was my godmother.

"There's nothing to worry about," I lied. "She stayed with me last night."

Charlie had snuck out before I'd even gotten up. She knew I'd bug her into talking if I fed her.

"Hmm." My mother lifted the martini to her lips and took a small sip. "Anything else interesting to report? Anything new?"

I shook my head. "No, nothing new."

My stepfather entered the salon. His dark hair was still full, even if half of it was gray. Arnold Walsh was tall, commanding, and dressed casually in a pair of khakis, a crisp white polo, and the finest loafers money could buy. He looked ready for lunch at the club.

"Hayden," he said, flashing a grin and showing off his perfect veneers.

"Hi, Arnold."

He walked over to the drink cart and embraced me. "Sorry I wasn't here. Business call."

I waved away his excuse. "No worries. Mom and I were just catching up."

"Ah." He poured himself three fingers of single malt scotch and then took his drink to the couch and sat down next to Mom.

"Hayden and Charlie went out last night," Mom explained, a devilish twinkle in her blue eyes.

"Hayden went out last night? Voluntarily?" Arnold teased.

"Okay, me going out isn't that big of a deal. Can we please talk about something else?"

Before Mom or Arnold got a word out, Stanton appeared in the doorway. "Paula wanted me to inform you that dinner is ready."

"Good, I'm starving," Arnold stated.

We took our drinks and moved into the formal dining room that could seat twelve. The three of us sat at one side of the table.

It wasn't until the lobster in cream sauce entrée was served that my mother turned the conversation to the charity gala she was organizing.

"You're coming, aren't you?" Mom asked. "I don't want to hear any excuses. You've got a few weeks to find a dress."

"I already told you I was," I said absently.

"And you're not dating anyone, are you?"

I lifted my gaze from my plate. "Who is he?"

"He who?" Her eyelids fluttered as she feigned innocence.

"*Mom.*"

"Walker Lawton Anderson." She paused. "The Third."

I frowned. "Why does that name sound familiar?"

"His father is Walker Anderson the Second," Mom supplied. "*Senator* Walker Anderson."

I groaned. "Mom, no. No senators' sons."

"What about a judge's son? Too poor? How about the son of an oil tycoon?" Arnold asked with a stamp of amusement across his mouth. He reached for his glass of scotch.

"Worried I'm approaching spinsterhood?" I asked, pointing the question to my mother.

"Well, you haven't dated anyone since Tyler," she said. "And that's been, what? Two years?"

"Closer to three," Arnold corrected.

"Right." Mom nodded as she cut another bite of lobster.

I rubbed the spot over my right eyebrow. "I know you mean well, but I'm happy with my life. So please stop trying to set me up with men in your circle."

My mom shot Arnold a look. He raised his brows.

"What?" I demanded.

"Your mother already told Walker about you," Arnold said.

I groaned. "*Mom.*"

"What? I want grandchildren."

"I'm twenty-five. I have plenty of time to have children."

"Let's say you meet a man and you date for a year before you get engaged. It'll take another year to plan the wedding. And then another year to really set up your home. And then it'll be a year after that before you get pregnant. That's *four* years! You'll be almost thirty. How much time do you think you have?"

"Old-fashioned much?" I asked, trying to hold in my laughter and anxiety. My mother did *not* like to be laughed at.

"Geriatric eggs are a risk. For you *and* the baby. And you won't just want one child…"

"You and Dad only had me," I pointed out. "I don't see any siblings running around, do you?"

"That's different."

"Why?"

"We wanted more children, but nature said no. What if it takes you a long time to get pregnant? You might have to do IVF."

"IVF is invasive. Just like this conversation," I said pointedly.

"Don't listen to your mother," Arnold said. "There's no rush. You're young. You should be enjoying life, not worried about getting serious and having a family. Plenty of time for that."

"If you got married, you'd be able to take your seat on the board."

"*Marilyn*," Arnold warned.

"What?" My mother batted her eyes with sham innocence.

My stepfather looked at me and sighed. "I'm sorry, Hayden."

"It's not your fault," I assured him.

"Just so you know, there's no rush." Arnold shot me a commiserating smile. "I'm happy to oversee things until you're ready."

I liked the direction of this conversation even less than the one discussing marriage and babies. I dabbed my mouth with my cloth napkin and gently set it next to my plate before rising.

"Where are you going?" Mom asked.

"I have an early morning," I said.

"You're leaving? Before dessert? I had Paula make pear tarts with homemade vanilla bean ice cream."

"You know I don't eat dessert. And I really do have an early morning."

I walked around to the other side of the table and kissed the top of my mother's head. "I love you. I'll call you later. Bye, Arnold."

"Bye, Hayden." Arnold looked at my mom. "I told you, Marilyn."

She sighed. "Yes, you did."

I headed out of the dining room, the sound of their conversation drifting away as I walked down the immaculate hallway to the foyer.

Stanton waited at the door with my purse. I arched a brow. "How did you know?"

"I know all." He cracked a smile. "I can't remember the last time you stayed through an entire dinner."

"My mother is in rare form…"

"She is," he said.

I kissed his cheek. "It was good to see you, Stanton."

"You too, Miss Hayden."

I was halfway home when my phone rang. I pressed a button on the steering wheel, answering the call.

"How did I know you escaped Sunday dinner early?" Charlie asked.

"Because I am nothing if not predictable," I joked.

"What did she do?"

"We talked about my geriatric eggs. She's concerned I'll never get married or have children. So she told a senator's son about me. He'll be at the charity gala."

"Yikes. Good thing I'll be your wingwoman. You don't even sound mad about it though."

"I'm not. She's persistent, but harmless. I take it for what it is."

"Want me to have sex with the senator's son in a coat closet? Can't go after you if he's busy getting laid, right?"

I laughed. "I'm not telling you *not* to do it…"

"Green light. What's his name?"

"Walker Anderson the Third. He's Senator Anderson's son."

"Okay, let me look him up. He may not be attractive at all. And if he's not attractive, I rescind my offer in full."

I smiled. "A senator's son would be the perfect man to bring home to your parents. Just remember that."

"Damn it. Not only are you right, but he's also hot."

"Yeah?"

"Yeah. Like an All-American football star from the 1950s who wears a red letterman jacket and goes to Rydell High."

"Does he look like Lorenzo Lamas, too?" I teased.

"Yep."

"Are you weak in the knees?"

"No. I'm wet in my panties."

"I'm hanging up now."

"Introduce me," she begged. "And I'll do the rest."

"Bye, Charlie."

"Bye."

I hung up with my best friend, laughing, knowing the charity event wouldn't be nearly as boring because Charlie would be there.

God, I loved her.

Chapter 3

"Are you sure you want to do this?" I asked as Charlie parked her Mercedes AMG SL 63 in the parking lot of a tattoo shop.

"Damn sure," she stated as she engaged the parking brake. "I've wanted a tattoo forever."

"Yes, I know. But you've never known what tattoo to get. I don't think walking into a tattoo shop and letting the wall of generic designs decide what to permanently ink on your body is the best idea."

"They have tattoo removal lasers these days. If I regret the tattoo, I'll get it blasted off."

"That process is more painful than the tattoo."

She looked at me with an amused grin on her face. "Hayden, I say this with all the love in my heart for you—stop being a stick in the mud. Let me have my rebellion."

"Get something pierced instead," I suggested.

"Already thinking about getting my hood pierced," she said, shooting me a wink and climbing out of her nearly two-hundred-thousand-dollar car.

I scrambled from my seat and closed the passenger side

door. I immediately lifted the collar of my jacket so I wouldn't feel the late autumn chill on my skin. "You're joking."

"I can't win with you, can I?" Charlie teased.

"I don't know if you're kidding or not."

"I'm kidding. Maybe. Come on, I don't want to be late."

"Late?"

"I have an appointment with Roman."

"Roman? Who's Roman?"

"Only the hottest tattoo artist in town. He and his two brothers own Three Kings Tattoo Parlor," she replied as we trekked across the parking lot. "They do amazing work."

"If you say so," I muttered.

Charlie opened the front door and I walked in behind her. A redhead was at the counter on the phone, but she met us with a smile. While Charlie waited to speak to her, I ambled around the space.

It wasn't at all what I expected. The walls weren't covered with standard tattoo designs, but photographs of finished custom work. Each one of them looked like a true piece of art.

The young woman behind the counter hung up the phone. "Sorry about that. How can I help you?"

"Hi, I'm Charlie Beaufort and I have a one o'clock appointment with Roman."

"Wonderful," the redhead said with a smile. "He's just finishing up with a client and he'll be right out."

Charlie wandered over to me. "Cool, right?"

I was staring at a photo that showed off a completed back piece. "Very cool."

"I'm sure Roman could squeeze you in if you wanted something small, like a butterfly or a heart," Charlie said.

"Roman's booked solid for the next three months," the redhead chimed in. "So you won't be able to get your butterfly or heart tattoo today."

"Tragic," I said with a bite of snark.

The redhead grinned. "Not a fan of the butterfly or heart tattoos?"

"Not a fan of needles," I said.

She shook her head. "Ah, same. I'm the only Jackson sibling not to have ink."

"Oh!" Charlie exclaimed. "You're Brielle!"

"I am," the redhead confirmed.

"Roman mentioned you," Charlie said. "It's nice to finally meet you."

"Mentioned you," I repeated. "Mentioned you when?"

"In one of our other appointments," Charlie explained. "I've been meeting with Roman for a few months to finalize a tattoo. Today, I actually get it."

"You've been thinking about this for months and you didn't tell me? You tell me everything."

"I wanted it to be a surprise," Charlie said. "And I didn't want you to accidentally tell my mother."

I opened my mouth, but Charlie turned her attention back to Brielle. "Why are you working reception? Roman said you work at a bakery."

"Agnes got sick, so I'm filling in," Brielle said. "And I decorate wedding cakes. But right now, that's kind of on hold. My business partner—the one who actually bakes the cakes—just had a baby and is on maternity leave, so my schedule is pretty open right now."

"Which bakery?" I asked.

"Pie in the Sky."

Heavy boots clod across the floor, pulling my attention away from Charlie's conversation with Brielle to the two men who appeared from the back hallway.

My mouth dropped open. "What are *you* doing here?"

Bones raised a brow. "I'm a biker and I'm in a tattoo shop. I think the answer is fairly obvious."

"Biker," I repeated quietly. "Now the leather vest makes sense."

He grimaced. "It's called a cut, sweetheart."

Bones was better looking than I remembered. "Did you grow?" I blurted out. "You look…taller."

A slow grin appeared on his lips. "All cats look the same in the dark, huh?"

I flushed.

"You two know each other?" the other man asked as he ran a hand across his jaw. He had brown hair and his army green T-shirt showed off his muscles and ink.

"We met at Chaos the other night," Bones said. "Hayden had her way with me and then ran off."

"Had my way with—*you* kissed *me!*"

"Glad you remember, Duchess. So, would you like to have your way with me?"

Bones winked and I was suddenly lightheaded.

"Hi," Charlie interjected, holding out her hand to Bones. "I'm Charlie, Hayden's best friend."

Bones took Charlie's small hand in his massive paw and shook it. "Nice to meet you."

"So, you're a biker," Charlie said, dropping her hand. "Which club?"

"The Tarnished Angels," Bones said. He slapped the man next to him on the back. "My club comes here to get our ink done. Roman and his brothers are the best."

"Aww shucks, Pa, you'll make me blush," Roman joked.

"Roman," Brielle called. "I spoke to Slash. I penciled him in for tonight."

"That's fine," Roman said. "I told him I'd squeeze him in and I don't mind staying late. Charlie, are you ready?"

"Hold on," she said. "I want to see how this plays out."

"How what plays out?" I asked.

She gestured between me and Bones. "I'm completely entranced."

"I kind of am, too," Brielle added.

"We're standing right here," I stated.

"Yes, there you are," Charlie said with a grin.

Bones sauntered to the reception counter and picked up a black marker. He walked back over to me, and without a word, he took my hand, removed the marker cap with his mouth, and then wrote something on my palm.

He dropped my hand and then put the cap back on the marker. "You left Chaos in such a hurry I didn't get a chance to give you my number."

I glanced at my palm. "I'm not gonna call you."

"You'll call."

"No. I'm really not going to," I assured him.

"Hello, you're so in love with me already. Of course you're gonna call."

"Okay, this charming arrogant thing isn't going to work."

Bones looked at Roman and grinned. "She called me charming."

Roman smiled back. "I heard."

"He's definitely charming," Charlie said.

"Again, I'm right here!" I snapped.

"We know," Roman said.

I pointed at Bones. "You're trouble. You're a bad decision wrapped in trouble. You're trouble cubed."

"You're not wrong," Bones said lightly. "But I'm also a lot of fun. And I'm really good at removing sticks from asses. So, if you need help removing yours, give me a buzz."

He chucked me under the chin and swaggered out of Three Kings, the door closing behind him.

I looked at my best friend. She opened her mouth to say something, but I quickly covered her lips with my non-numbered palm.

"You will not make an anal joke at a time like this," I said in warning.

Brielle let out a wheeze of laughter and even Roman cracked a smile. Charlie's green eyes sparkled with wicked humor.

"Will you be good and not say anything?"

She nodded.

I slowly removed my palm.

"Let's get you in the chair," Roman said to Charlie.

"Is it okay if Hayden holds my hand for moral support?" Charlie asked.

"Fine by me," Roman said.

"I'll hold your hand," I said, "on one condition."

"What?" Charlie asked.

"You don't mention Bones or that conversation, *ever again*."

She wrinkled her nose. "I think you should call him. That stick has been up there so long it's bound to petrify."

"And you say this as my best friend," I remarked blandly.

"With all the love in my heart for you," she replied.

Roman looked at his sister. "They remind me of you and Jazz."

"Don't they?" Brielle shook her head. "It's like looking in a mirror."

"Tell me it's not gorgeous," Charlie said as Roman slathered moisturizer on her new shoulder ink.

"It's gorgeous," I admitted truthfully.

"Gorgeous enough that it's convinced you to a get one?" Charlie asked.

"Nope," I said. "I'm good."

I wouldn't dare admit to Charlie that the incessant buzzing of the needle had given me a low-level headache or that watching Roman wipe away the blood had made me a touch queasy.

"You're looking a little green," Roman said to me.

"Oh come on now, I thought I was hiding it so well," I said with a laugh.

Roman flashed me a grin. "Why don't you head up front, ask Brielle for a bottle of water and sip on it while I cover Charlie's tattoo and go over some things with her."

Charlie released my fingers. "Thank you for your moral support."

"My pleasure."

I stood and headed to the front. Brielle was perched on her stool behind the reception counter. She was doodling on a blank page of an artist sketchbook.

She looked up. "They're all finished?"

"Just about. Roman said to get a bottle of water."

"Ah, yeah." She hopped off her stool and crouched down below the counter. "We have a mini fridge back here. You want water or a soda?"

"Actually, a ginger ale would be great if you've got it."

"The sight turned your stomach, huh?" Her smile was sympathetic as she rose and handed me the bottle of soda.

"Just a little bit," I admitted. I unscrewed the top and took a sip of the carbonated drink. I gestured with my chin. "What are you working on there?"

"Nothing," she said. "Just messing around. Trying not

to go out of my mind with boredom. I prefer decorating in frosting over ink. But my brothers keep asking me if I want to learn the ropes and have my own chair. But I'm not into it. Plus, they'd have to change the name from Three Kings to Three Kings and a Queen. Doesn't really have the same appeal."

"Not really," I agreed.

"So, you and Bones…"

I rolled my eyes. "I thought we weren't going to talk about that."

She shook her head. "You made Charlie promise. I do not abide by the same rules. So, you and Bones met the other night…"

"Yep." I clamped my lips shut.

"You really had no idea he was a biker?" she pressed.

"The club was kind of dark," I said in defense. "He stood out, like he clearly didn't belong there. But I had no idea he was a biker."

"And now that you know?"

"I have even more resolve to stay away from him."

"More resolve than I'd have," she said with a grin. "He's hot."

"Yeah, and he knows it." I rolled my eyes.

Roman and Charlie came out from the back hallway and Charlie settled up with Brielle.

"Now that you're a total badass," Brielle said to Charlie, "make sure you hit Leather and Ink."

"What's Leather and Ink?" Charlie asked.

"A boutique with leather pants, body suits, killer boots," Brielle explained. "And sexy-as-hell lingerie. I bought a bustier there last week."

"Brother," Roman grumbled as he pointed to himself.

"Sorry," Brielle said with a wide grin.

"You're not sorry at all," Roman replied.

"Nope," Brielle agreed.

"Thanks for the tip," Charlie said. "I'll check it out."

We said our goodbyes and headed out to the parking lot.

"You wanna hit Leather and Ink?" Charlie asked as she put her key into the ignition.

"Can't. I promised Mr. Clancy I'd visit. You want to come? He's not in the hospital anymore. I know how you hate hospitals."

"Who loves hospitals? I don't know anyone who loves hospitals."

"I think doctors love hospitals," she said.

"Fair point."

"Okay, I'll visit Mr. Clancy with you."

"We just have to make one stop first," I said. "But we should probably take my car."

Chapter 4

"This is the ugliest looking dog I've ever seen." Charlie sat in the passenger seat of my car and stroked a hand down John Milton's scraggly, furry back. "What kind of dog is he, anyway?"

"A terrier mutt of some sort."

John Milton had wiry black fur that hadn't become any softer despite a bath. At least he smelled like an oatmeal cookie instead of like sweaty dog.

I glanced at my best friend who looked a bit put out that she had to be the one to hold him on her lap.

But then the ten-pound mutt with a beard, underbite, and one ear that flopped, nuzzled his face underneath her chin.

"Damn it," Charlie muttered, hugging the dog tighter to her, no longer caring that the dog was shedding fur all over her black sweater.

"Don't get attached, he's not for you," I warned.

"I might make a run for it." She rubbed her chin against the top of John Milton's head. "You sure Mr. Clancy wants a dog?"

"Mr. Clancy doesn't *want* a dog at all," I informed her.

She frowned. "I don't understand."

"You will," I promised her as I pulled into the parking lot of Rose Hill Retirement Community.

John Milton, in all his scruffy mutt glory, scrambled from Charlie's lap and placed his paws on the passenger car door, eager to go out and explore.

I grabbed the leash and clipped it to his collar and then I opened the driver's side door. The cute mutt immediately came to my side of the car and jumped down, his little tail wagging in excitement.

"You're really not going to tell me what we're doing?" Charlie asked, grabbing her purse and then shutting the car door.

"Nope." I grinned. "It's more fun this way."

"If you say so."

We walked John Milton along the sidewalk, letting him do his business. I cleaned up after him and dumped the plastic bag into the designated trashcan labeled *dog refuse*.

"Yeah, never mind. I don't want a dog." Charlie shook her head.

"It's just poop," I said with a laugh.

"Ew."

"What happens when you have kids? They poop too," I reminded her.

"Now you're sounding like your mother," she warned.

I grinned. "My mother would also add on that there's no shame in a nanny."

"Exactly," Charlie said. "If I ever decide to have children, I'm not changing diapers. You can't make me."

She rushed ahead of me and opened the door. John Milton and I strode through.

The lobby of the retirement center was warm and inviting. There was a front room sitting area with blue couches and wooden bookshelves and the dining hall was just off the lobby.

A middle-aged woman sat behind the counter, a bright smile spreading across her face when she saw me.

"Good afternoon, Hayden," she greeted.

"Hi Beatrice." I leaned down and scooped up the mutt and presented him to her.

"Who is this handsome guy?" Beatrice asked, reaching out to touch his ear.

Charlie snorted.

"His name is John Milton," I explained.

"And who's he for?" she inquired.

"Mr. Clancy."

"Perfect."

"How's Mr. Clancy feeling today?" I asked.

"Grumbly." Her brown eyes twinkled.

"Even better," I said with a chuckle. "See you in a bit."

I headed through the lobby, Charlie keeping pace with me. "So even Beatrice knows what you're doing with this dog? Come on, I'm dying here."

"For the last couple of months, I've been matching shelter dogs with elderly companions," I explained. "It kind of happened by accident. I was volunteering at *Puppy Paradise Rescue* and I was taking one of their dogs for a walk. And while I was on my walk, an elderly woman named Mildred was doing her stroll around the neighborhood. We stopped to chat and Mary Shelley took an instant liking to Mildred. By the end of the day, Mary Shelley was in her new home, and Mildred had a new companion. It happened again when I took out Victor Hugo. Within a day, he was re-homed from the shelter and I just kept going."

"Well, now I understand the naming convention," Charlie said. "And actually, that's really sweet."

I nodded. "They need each other, and it just makes sense. It keeps everyone active and moving."

"How many dogs have you rehomed?"

"At this point, about fifteen," I said.

"Wow. That's actually pretty incredible. You should start a charity," Charlie said.

"What?"

"Yeah, a charity." She nodded. "Make this a bigger thing. You clearly have a talent for this. And you seem to love doing it."

"Something to think about," I murmured.

We arrived at Mr. Clancy's door. I knocked. There was no answer. I knocked again.

"Stop yer knockin' and come in!" called out a craggy old voice.

"He sounds fun," Charlie muttered.

"Watch, and be amazed," I whispered to her. I reached for the knob and turned it.

Mr. Clancy was sitting in a leather recliner, the TV on with some sporting event playing on mute.

"What's that?" Mr. Clancy asked gruffly as his eyes drifted over John Milton.

"This is John Milton," I said. "And this is my best friend, Charlie."

"Hello, Mr. Clancy," Charlie said.

Mr. Clancy barely looked at Charlie. "You brought a dog into my home? He probably has fleas."

"Actually, he just had a bath. He smells like cinnamon and oatmeal." I lowered John Milton to the floor and unleashed him without asking for permission.

John Milton wasted no time. He ran to Mr. Clancy, jumped up onto his lap, laid his head on Mr. Clancy's thigh, and closed his eyes for a nap.

Mr. Clancy harrumphed, but his hand lifted and settled onto John Milton's head, his face softening ever so slightly.

Nailed it.

"How are you feeling?" I asked him as I waved Charlie over to the loveseat.

"My incision hurts," he remarked.

"Hmm, I'm sorry to hear that," I said, not offended by his tone. "But I'm glad you're on the mend. Has your son visited?"

"Few days ago," he said. "Brought the grandkids. Little heathens. Henry feeds them too much sugar."

He pushed the recliner footrest down, scooped up the dog underneath one arm, and stood. Still carrying John Milton—who wasn't at all protesting at being carried like a football—Mr. Clancy wandered into the kitchen.

He opened the refrigerator and pulled open a drawer.

"The dog have a name? Or should I just call him *mutt*?" Mr. Clancy asked.

"His name is John Milton," I repeated.

"What kind of name is that for a dog?" Mr. Clancy asked.

"That's what I'm saying," Charlie piped up.

"Well, what's he look like to you?" I asked lightly.

Mr. Clancy paused for a moment and then said, "Oscar."

"Oscar is a great name," I said, biting my lip to stifle a smile. I looked at Charlie who rolled her eyes and then shot me a grin.

"Here we are," Mr. Clancy said. "What do you think, Oscar? You want to try some bacon?"

∼

"Just sign here," I said, pointing to the line at the bottom of the pet adoption papers.

Mr. Clancy hastily scribbled his signature and set the pen aside. "Anything else?"

"No," I said.

"No adoption fees?"

I shook my head. "It's been taken care of. I hope you two will be very happy together. Would you like me to run to the pet store for you?"

"No, I've got it. Oscar will ride shot gun with me. I'll take care of him from now on."

Charlie and I said goodbye to Mr. Clancy and I stopped off at reception to give Beatrice the good news.

"I wouldn't say Mr. Clancy had a change in personality," I said with a soft smile. "But I think the dog will go a long way in improving his overall mood."

"Glad to hear that," Beatrice said. "See if you can do anything for Mrs. Stevens when you can, will you?"

"Next time," I promised.

Charlie and I stepped out into the late autumn sunshine. The cold of the early afternoon had burned off and it was fairly temperate.

"Unbelievable," Charlie said to me. "You really do have magical powers."

"We all have magical powers, it's just about finding them," I said.

"Hmm." Charlie frowned. "I'm still looking for mine."

"Mexican for a late lunch?" I asked softly.

"Oh definitely," she said. Her phone rang. She dug around in her purse for her cell. "Mommy dearest."

"Are you going to answer her?" I asked.

"I just spoke to her this morning," she said.

"On purpose or by accident?"

"Well, she came to the pool house. My territory. She

wanted to remind me not to go through the house this afternoon because the floors are getting waxed. What does she think I'll do? Slide across the floors in my socks? I only did that once."

With a sigh, she answered her mother's call. "Hello?"

We walked across the parking lot to the car as Charlie talked to her mother. "I have plans that night," Charlie said. She paused for a moment and then said, "Well, you can't just assume I'm going to be available. My plans? Hayden and I are working on a thing. Yes, *Mother.* I used the word *work*. Fine, I'll be there."

She hung up as we got to the car and I unlocked it with the remote clicker. It beeped and we stood there a moment.

I could practically see the steam coming out of her ears. Her face was flushed and she clenched her cell so tightly I wondered if she'd bend it.

"What was that about?" I asked as I opened the driver's side door.

"My parents are throwing a party this Friday, and she demanded that I be there. Naturally, I balked."

"Naturally," I said as I got into the car and latched my seatbelt.

Charlie threw herself into the passenger seat and huffed. "She's constantly trying to pull me into her world and I'm doing everything I can to leave it."

"Not everything," I said, pressing the Start button on the dash.

"Meaning?"

"Meaning you still live at home. Meaning you've done nothing to forge your own way."

She blinked. "Are you talking about—wait, are you saying I need to get a job and move out?"

I shrugged. "They can't pull strings if you cut them."

"But I like my life."

"Of course you like your life." I turned to face her.

"Oh no," she said. "You've got that look."

"What look?"

"The *tough love* look. The, *you're going to lecture me* look."

She reached for the door handle, but I quickly engaged the child-lock.

"Evil!" she yelled.

"You're my best friend. You get that, right?"

"I get that," she muttered.

"You tell me stuff I don't want to hear, and I'm going to do the same for you."

"Fine." She crossed her arms over her chest in a posture of defense, but her eyes were on me.

"You were accepted to some of the best business schools in the country, but you didn't go. You're proficient in languages you don't bother to speak. You're a gifted pianist but you don't play. Are you getting what I'm saying?"

"Yeah, I've got ADHD and I never finish anything."

"You could do so many things, Charlie. And yet you're content to just shop your life away and rebel against your parents because you have no reason to be unhappy, but you are."

She ran her hands all along her body. "Nope. Not bleeding out."

"You have all these doors open to you and you won't walk through any of them."

"That's easy for you to say. Your parents are just happy if you're happy."

"Hmm. My mother isn't completely happy until I get married and have babies."

"But for the most part, she leaves you alone. She loves you."

"Your parents love you too."

"I don't know why I'm like this," she said quietly. "It feels ridiculous. Money solves all problems. And I've got that. So, what's my damage?"

"I don't know," I said.

"Can we still get Mexican?" she asked.

"Sure. But guacamole won't fix your problems either."

"No," she agreed. "But it definitely won't make them worse."

Chapter 5

"Son of a monkey-cock sucking fluncha-munch!"

"Colorful," Charlie said as we stepped into Leather and Ink.

"Where's the angry pirate?" I looked around the boutique, my eyes skimming over the racks of clothes in an attempt to find the owner of the vocal, creative cursing.

"I think it's coming from the dressing room."

We headed toward the back of the boutique and sure enough, the grumbling and growling grew louder.

"Hello?" I called out.

"*Fuck*," the woman muttered and then she raised her voice to a louder caliber. "Be out in a sec!"

Charlie and I exchanged a look and she raised her brows.

A moment later, the black curtain of the dressing room whooshed open and a tall, angry blonde stood with an assortment of clothes hanging over her arm.

She flashed a smile. "How are you ladies doing today?"

"Uh, good," I said. "Are you okay?"

"Okay?" The blonde sailed past us and began hanging the clothes up on the racks.

"We heard you cussing like a drunken pirate who had his peg leg stolen," Charlie said.

"Oh." The blonde shot us a sheepish look. "Sorry about that. I was kind of stuck in a pair of pants. They didn't fit and my sister went next door to the sandwich shop to grab us food so I had no help to get out of them. I can't even begin to tell you about the wiggle I just did to get them off."

"Do you own the boutique?" Charlie asked.

The woman shook her head. "No. My name's Willa. I used to work here, but now I just fill in from time to time when Laura—the actual owner—has an appointment or errands or something."

"Ah," Charlie said, looking around.

"How'd you find us?" she asked. "Social media? The internet?"

"Word of mouth, actually," Charlie said as she picked up a black leather halter top. "I just got a tattoo at Three Kings and Brielle said we had to check this place out."

"Brielle!" Willa exclaimed. "I love Brielle! Who did your tattoo? Virgil?"

Charlie shook her head. "Roman."

"Oh. Roman." She grinned. "He's hot, isn't he?"

"So hot," Charlie agreed.

"Can I help you find anything in particular?" Willa asked.

"More clothes that will show off my shoulder tattoo," Charlie said.

"Well you've already found that halter, which is one of our most popular items, but come this way." Willa waved Charlie over, but I stayed put and perused at my own speed.

The front door to the boutique opened and a redheaded teenager walked in.

"Congratulations," the teenager said as she approached the counter. "The most disgusting calzone award now belongs to you."

"I'm with a customer," Willa called back. "Maybe try and rein it in?"

"No offense," Charlie drawled, "but we heard you say *son of a monkey-cock*. I'm so stealing that, by the way."

Willa laughed.

"The pants?" the teenager asked.

"Yep," Willa said.

"I told you to wait to try them on."

"Waverly," Willa said. "I'd like you to meet—oh sorry, I didn't get your names."

"I'm Charlie." Charlie waved.

"I'm Hayden," I added.

"The redhead is my sister, Waverly. If you think I have a potty mouth, Waverly outperforms me ten to one."

"Thank you," Waverly said, her blue eyes shining with amusement.

"You guys okay to look around while I eat?" Willa asked. "I'm starving."

"Have at it," Charlie said.

"Uh, Willa? You might want to eat it in your car," Waverly said, her nose wrinkling.

Willa sighed. "It's gonna stink up the place, isn't it?"

"And make me vomit." Waverly made a face and pinched her nose. "A calzone with meatballs, anchovies, and banana peppers? I understand pregnancy cravings, but dear Lord. Don't take us down with you."

"You're pregnant?" Charlie asked Willa. "Oh, the pants situation makes a little more sense now."

"Second trimester. Where all of a sudden, my pants no

longer fit. Like, even getting them up my thighs is an ordeal. I've succumbed to wearing yoga pants or my husband's sweats. Sadly, they fit me now."

"That sounds not at all fun," Waverly said.

"Right?" Charlie agreed.

"You guys okay if I eat real fast?" Willa asked. "I'm not being super professional, but if I don't eat I'm gonna get mean."

"Eat," I urged.

"I'll ring them up," Waverly said. "I got it."

"Thanks. Give me ten minutes. Fifteen tops," Willa said as she grabbed the bag with the calzone and left.

Waverly's phone chimed in her back pocket, and she fished it out of her pants. She looked at the screen and then hastily typed a reply.

"What do you think of this?" Charlie asked as she held up a strapless leather dress. "Think this'll look good on me?"

"Everything looks good on you," I said with a smile. "And it'll definitely show off your tattoo."

"Tattoo?" Waverly asked, looking up from her phone. "You got a tattoo?"

"Yeah." Charlie nodded. "A few days ago."

"Cool! Can I see it?" Waverly asked. "I want a tattoo, but Willa won't let me get one until I'm eighteen."

"You're not eighteen?" Charlie asked. "I could've sworn you were at least eighteen."

"You're my new best friend." Waverly grinned. "If I thought I could get a fake ID and go get a tattoo, I'd totally do it. But I'd only get my tattoo at Three Kings because they're the best. And they all know I'm only fifteen. So, they won't ink me." She rolled her eyes.

"What kind of tattoo would you get?" I asked Waverly

as Charlie headed to the dressing room with a few hangers of clothes.

"I don't know yet," she said. "I talked to Roman about designing something for me and Willa to get together. Sisterly bonding and all that."

My phone trumpeted from the bottom of my purse. I fished around and found it. The name flashing across the screen caused anxiety to churn in my stomach.

"Charlie! I've got to step outside and take this call," I said.

"Okay! I won't make a decision without you!" she yelled back.

I walked toward the front door of the boutique, my phone already to my ear. "Hello, Oliver."

"I didn't think I'd get you," he said after a brief pause. "Usually when I call you let it go to voicemail. I leave a voicemail and then you call me back after the board meeting."

A blast of cold air hit my cheeks and I huddled in on myself. "Usually that's the way of it, yeah."

"But you answered this time."

"I did."

"Why?"

"Momentary insanity."

The old man chuckled. "Will you have another lapse in sanity and come to the next board meeting in a few weeks?"

"Doubtful," I said. "I'm not on the board."

"Not yet. But your father would want—"

"Thanks for calling, Oliver. I'll read the minutes when they're available."

I hung up and closed my eyes.

My throat tightened; my eyes filled with tears. I hastily turned my head and swiped at my cheeks. When I felt in control again, I turned toward the boutique. A silent gasp caught in my throat as I saw a man with pale skin pointing a gun at me.

He reeked of sweat and onions. "Give me your fucking purse!"

My limbs were frozen with terror.

"Do you want me to shoot you, bitch? Hand over the fucking purse!"

He lifted his aim to my head as I held out my purse with wobblily arms.

A gunshot sounded and my would-be attacker screamed as he pitched forward and slightly away from me, grabbing his shoulder and momentarily lowering the gun away from my face. In a rage, he swung his arm back toward me, pointing the pistol at my forehead. Before I could process what was happening, there was another gun shot. It went through his neck and he dropped to the ground, gurgling and gasping for air. In a few short seconds, he fell silent.

I looked in the direction of my savior. Willa was poised with both hands wrapped around her pistol. She lowered it slowly and looked at me. "Are you okay?"

My head was full of static as I glanced at the prostrate dead body on the ground, blood leaking from his wounds as he lay there.

The front door of the boutique blew open and Waverly and Charlie ran outside.

"What the fuck!" Waverly yelled.

Charlie was wearing a strapless leather dress and goosebumps erupted across her shoulders and chest. "Oh my God!"

"Hayden," Willa barked. "Are you okay?"

My gaze found hers. Bile churned in my belly. "No. I'm not okay," I said, right before I turned my head and puked.

Chapter 6

After I'd emptied the contents of my stomach, I stepped away from the mess at my feet.

"Both of you," Willa commanded, "back inside. I'm calling the cops."

Charlie and Waverly both ducked into the boutique, the front door slamming behind them. I burrowed my face into the collar of my jacket. My head felt heavy, but cloudy, like I couldn't form a thought.

Willa's voice filtered in and out as my gaze continued to stray from her to the body on the ground. I hastily turned around to avoid it altogether so I wouldn't be sick again.

"Cops are on their way," Willa announced.

I nodded and faced her, about to ask her what the hell had happened and how she wasn't falling apart. I was on the verge of collapsing but somehow, I was still standing.

She put the phone to her ear and waited.

"Who are you calling now?" I asked.

She held up a finger, instructing me to wait.

"It's Willa," she said to the other person on the phone.

"I'm in trouble. No, I can't say over the phone…" She paused. "Cops are already on their way." She closed her eyes a moment and exhaled a shaky breath. "Okay. I won't. See you in a few."

She hung up.

"Who was that?" I asked, my voice growing weaker with each question.

"My attorney." She met my gaze. "*Our* attorney."

"Attorney." I shook my head.

"Unless you want to call your own?" she offered.

"No, I—I wouldn't even know who to call." In order to get a name, I'd have to involve my mother and she couldn't know about this.

She can never know about any of this.

Willa made a move toward the boutique.

"Where are you going?" I asked, hysteria suddenly rising to the surface.

"Inside to get my coat," she explained. "It's cold out here."

"Oh." I nodded. "Okay. I thought you were leaving me."

She took my hand and gave it a squeeze.

"Willa, I—if you hadn't…"

"I know." Her blue eyes were suddenly bright. "Do you feel like you're moving in slow motion and the air is thick around you, and you can't get enough of it into your lungs?"

"Yeah. That's exactly how I feel."

She squeezed my hand again and let it go before stepping around the corpse and heading inside the boutique.

A man had pulled a gun on me.

And Willa had killed him.

She'd *killed* him.

I was a stranger to her and she hadn't even hesitated.

What if she hadn't been in her car?

What if she—

I would be—

With a wave of nausea, I bent over to catch my breath for a minute.

The rumble of motorcycles in the distance was a momentary distraction.

Once the nausea had passed, I stood up straight. Willa came out of the boutique wearing a blue jacket that was already zipped up to keep her neck warm. She held two bottles of water and without a word, she came to stand next to me and handed me one.

I was in the middle of taking a sip when three motorcycles roared into the parking lot.

Willa sighed. "My husband Duke is here."

"Did you call him?"

She shook her head. "Vance—our attorney—told me no phone calls, not to anyone. Vance must've called him…"

Three tall men in jeans wearing heavy leather motorcycle boots and leather cuts pulled up beside us and got off their motorcycles.

"You've got to be kidding me," I muttered.

"What?" Willa asked.

"Your husband is a biker?" I inquired.

"Yeah. Why?"

"Well, Duchess," Bones drawled. "If you wanted to see me, all you had to do was call."

~

The cops and Vance showed up within a few minutes of each other. It was pure pandemonium.

Questions were being asked, voices were being raised, and my head swam.

Bones took a step toward me and wrapped an arm around me. It took all of my willpower not to collapse against him.

"I need to speak with Willa and—" The attorney's eyes found mine and he raised his brows.

"Hayden," I supplied.

"Hayden," Vance repeated with a nod.

The attorney was tall and imposing, but the cops recognized they weren't going to get any answers until Vance had spoken to us.

I looked up at Bones, but his gaze was trained on the now covered dead body in front of the boutique. Finally, he dragged his attention to me, curiosity brewing in his eyes.

He wanted to know what happened. But he remained silent.

Vance spoke to Willa's husband in quiet tones. The dark-haired man nodded. He looked at the third biker who'd come with him and then at Bones, and gestured with his chin to the boutique. The blond biker whose name I didn't yet know strode inside.

"Savage will keep Waverly and Charlie company," Bones explained, "while this whole mess gets sorted."

I was overwhelmingly grateful for all the people that would help us navigate this insane situation.

"Hayden? Willa?" Vance asked.

I nodded.

Bones released me slowly and I immediately regretted losing his warmth. I walked with Willa and Vance to the side of the building, out of ear and eyeshot of the cops.

"What happened?" Vance asked bluntly.

I told him that I'd gone outside to take a phone call

and when I'd hung up, there was a man holding a gun to me, and that his intent had been to rob me.

"And while I was about to hand over my purse, Willa shot him. Twice."

Vance looked at Willa. "Now you."

"I was finishing lunch in my car. I saw the guy approaching her. He looked nervous. Maybe a tweaker? I don't know. When I saw what was happening, I grabbed my pistol from the glove box and like she said, I shot him twice."

"All right. The boutique has security cameras?"

Willa nodded.

"We'll need to see the footage to corroborate the story before you say a word to anyone. They're going to get that video regardless, and what you say has to match what's on it. What about Waverly and Charlie?"

"They were inside the store," Willa said. "I don't know what they saw."

"Okay, I'll speak to them," Vance said.

I took Willa's hand in mine, wanting to offer her some support. She'd saved my life.

"Let's get back there," Vance said. "The sooner we clear this up, the sooner you both can go home."

Willa's blue eyes were filled with concern. "Vance, I'm—"

"I know," he interrupted. "Just one step at a time. This could have been a lot worse. You did good."

"Yeah?" Willa asked. "You sure?"

"I'm sure." He gave her shoulder a squeeze. "Now we really do need to get back there. Your husband doesn't want to let you out of his sight."

Willa cracked a smile, but I could tell she was on the verge of tears.

Emotions were catching up to both of us now.

We kept our hands clasped like two close friends instead of what we were—near strangers who were now linked by a traumatic event.

My vision rippled, but I blinked, and I could see again. Only, when we got back to the scene a black curtain slid down over my eyes. My knees buckled, I dropped the bottle of water, and everything went dark.

Chapter 7

I WOKE up to a pair of electric blue eyes staring at me in obvious concern.

"What happened?" I asked, my tongue heavy.

"You fainted," Bones said. "Vance caught you before you hit the ground."

I turned my head and looked at the attorney. "Guess you're my savior in more ways than one."

"No one has ever called me a savior before," Vance said. "I kind of like that."

Bones whipped his gaze to Vance and glared.

Vance raised his brows.

Bones helped me sit up and handed me the bottle of water I'd dropped.

"Can we get this shit sorted?" Bones demanded. "So I can take her home."

"You don't have to take me home," I announced. "I can have Charlie drive me."

"I'm taking you home, Duchess," Bones commanded. "Now sit there, sip on your water, and give your statement to the police."

It took longer than I thought. There were dozens of questions and I had to repeat myself several times. Eventually, Vance had the security feed pulled and we were released from questioning.

"I'll have the paperwork taken care of and be in touch," Vance said.

Duke held out his arm to shake the attorney's hand. "Appreciate ya."

Vance nodded. He reached into his breast pocket and handed me his business card. "Call if you have any questions. And not a word of any of this to anyone who wasn't here today, okay?"

Nodding, I pocketed his card.

"God, I'd kill for a drink," Willa said, her hand covering her stomach.

"You get hot tea, a blanket, and a foot rub," Duke said as he pulled her into his side. He looked at me. "We didn't get a chance to officially meet."

"No, we didn't," I agreed.

"I'm Duke. Willa's husband."

The door to the boutique opened and Savage held the door for Waverly and Charlie. Charlie had put on her clothes, but she carried a brown shopping bag.

She bee-lined to me and quickly enveloped me into a hug. "This has been a shit day."

"Yeah," I sighed. "It has."

"You ready to go?" Charlie asked.

"I'm driving her," Bones stated.

Charlie looked at Bones and then at me. "You okay with that?"

I nodded. "We can drop you off at home first."

"I'll take her," Savage offered.

"On your motorcycle?" I asked.

"Yeah." Savage looked at Charlie. "We could get a drink first. You look like you could use a drink."

"I could," Charlie replied. "But I really need to go with Hayden. She's gonna want to talk about this and—"

"I don't want to talk about it," I insisted. "I just want to go home and go to sleep. Sleep this entire day off."

"I'll still come with you. I won't say anything, I'll just be there."

"Charlie—"

"Excuse us a second." She grabbed my hand and hauled me away, out of earshot. "You shouldn't be alone. What if you have one of your episodes?"

"*If* I have one of my episodes, I'll be at my house. I'll be safe."

"Are you having any symptoms?" she inquired.

"No." I had fainted, but it was more from shock than anything else. I didn't have any of the other signs that an episode was impending.

"It doesn't feel right that I leave you alone," she muttered.

"I just want to be by myself," I stated.

"Are you sure?" She bit her lip in uncertainty.

"Yeah. Go have a drink with Savage."

I embraced my best friend and she whispered in my ear, "If you change your mind, you can call me. Anytime. Doesn't matter. Even if it's two in the morning."

"Okay, I'll call you if I change my mind," I lied. "Do me a favor, though."

"What's that?"

"Today stays between us. None of this to the parental units."

"Say no more." Charlie pulled away and we headed back to the group. She looked at Willa. "I would say it was nice to meet you, but that seems like the wrong thing to say after what happened."

"I get it," Willa said. "But for what it's worth, I'm glad you were inside with Waverly."

Charlie glanced at Waverly. "You. I'm calling you."

"You better," Waverly said.

With a frown, I looked at Charlie.

"I'll explain later." My best friend hugged me one last time and then she walked with Savage to the parking lot.

Bones hung up his cell phone. "You ready?"

"I'm too shaky to ride on your bike," I explained.

"A prospect is coming for it. We'll take your car."

"Okay," I said, feeling like a doll being moved around. "Willa, I—"

"You're welcome," she said with a soft smile.

I said goodbye to Waverly and then Bones took my hand in his. "You're pale," he said when we got to my car. "You need a shot of bourbon to put some color back in your cheeks."

I shook my head. "I don't want a shot of bourbon."

He opened the passenger side door and waited until I was settled before closing it.

Bones went to the driver's side and slid into the seat. His legs were scrunched up because I had it set for my small frame. He got situated, adjusted the mirrors, and then held out his hand. "Keys."

I dropped the keys into his palm. Before I could pull away he took my hand and turned it over.

"Just as I suspected," he said, letting go of my hand and sticking the key into the ignition.

"What?"

"You scrubbed your palm free of my number," he said.

"It took half a bottle of rubbing alcohol to remove it," I informed him. "You really thought I was going to call?"

"I had hopes, but no, I didn't expect you to call."

He backed out of the space and I stared through the window. "Thanks for driving me home."

"Sure thing."

"Why did you show up here?" I asked. "I mean, I know why Duke came. He's Willa's husband. And Savage…well, I'm not sure why he came either."

"Savage, Willa, and Duke have been friends since they were kids. But the three of us were finishing lunch together when Vance called."

"What did Vance say?"

"He told Duke he needed to get to Leather and Ink because Willa was in trouble."

"Oh. Well, I'm glad Vance came." I fell silent for a moment. "I hope she's going to be okay. I mean, she killed a man for crying out loud."

"Better him than you," Bones said, his tone dark.

I closed my eyes. "I can't think about it. If I think about it, I'll…"

"What's your address?"

I gave it to him. "You want me to put it into my phone?"

"Nah. I know where you live." He glanced at me and grinned. "Not in a stalker sort of way, I just meant I know that part of town. I got it."

"Is Charlie going to be okay with Savage?" I asked.

"Yeah, she'll be fine. Better than fine."

"What's that mean?"

"It means Savage knows how to distract a woman from her troubles."

"Charlie has enough troubles," I muttered.

Bones chuckled. "What about you?"

"What about me?"

"Do you need to be distracted?" He took his eyes off the road for a moment to glance at me.

"Yes, I do need a distraction," I said, meeting his gaze.

His eyes heated.

"Tell me a joke," I stated.

"Tell you a joke?"

"Yes. That's all the distraction I'm interested in."

"Not nearly as fun as getting naked and letting me distract you that way. A joke is no substitute for a few orgasms."

"A *few* orgasms?" I raised my brows. "Aren't you the optimist."

He grinned. "I'm confident I could give you a few. It would blow all that static out of your head. Nothing like a good fuck after what you've been though. But if it's a joke you want, it's a joke I'll give you. Lemme see. I gotta dig for one…"

After a moment, his brow unwrinkled. "Okay, I got one. A three-legged puppy walks into a saloon and says, *I'm lookin' for the dog who shot my paw.*"

The laugh started small, almost like a chuckle. But for some reason, Bones' terrible dad joke hit me at just the right spot and my chuckle became a full-on belly laugh. I laughed so hard I couldn't breathe, tears of humor streaming from my eyes.

I wasn't sure when it happened, but the humor turned into something else, something akin to my body realizing I'd almost died, and it was processing it the only way it knew how.

My chest filled with pain. Sharp, like a knife was slicing through my lungs and heart.

His hand settled onto my thigh, but he said nothing.

It only made me cry harder.

By the time Bones was pulling into my driveway, my

tears had turned into sniffles and hiccoughs. Bones parked and turned off the ignition, but we just sat there, his hand on my leg as I slowly came back to myself.

"Sorry," I muttered.

"What are you sorry for?" he asked.

"For losing it."

"Duchess," he said softly, "you had a gun pulled on you and you watched a man die. The fact that you're not doing more than crying actually has me a little worried."

I reached into my purse for a tissue. "What would make you less worried?"

"If you yelled, wanted to punch a wall. Anything. But tears?" He shook his head. "I don't know how to handle tears."

I gave him a watery smile. "I think you handled my tears just fine."

"Maybe," he agreed. "Why didn't you want Charlie to come home with you? And why didn't she fight harder to be with you? You're best friends, right?"

I dabbed at my eyes, wondering if the waterproof mascara was living up to its advertising. "Best friends. Yes. But I—I don't know. It's been so heavy between us lately. I didn't want to burden her with this."

"Is she a true friend?"

"Yes."

"Then you should want her to see you like this. And she should want to be here for you."

"It's complicated," I said slowly.

"It's not. Not really. Is she your first call when you're in trouble?"

I didn't even have to think about it. "Of course she is."

"And are you her first call when she's in trouble?"

"Charlie's always in trouble," I joked.

Bones didn't crack a grin. "You pushed her away. And she let herself be pushed."

"I appreciate the drive home," I said, unlatching my seatbelt. "But I didn't ask for a therapy session."

"I threw the therapy session in for free." He handed me back my keys.

"How are you getting home?" I asked pointedly.

"I'll call a prospect to come get me."

"What's a prospect?"

"Someone who wants in the club but is going through the hazing ritual before they become a full brother. They have to prove themselves by doing the grunt work first."

"I see." I sighed. "Well, why don't you come inside. You can wait for your prospect while sitting on my couch and watching TV while I shower."

"Okay."

"One condition though," I said as I reached for my door handle.

"What's that?"

"No more therapy sessions."

He smiled slightly. "Deal."

Chapter 8

"You live alone?" Bones asked as I punched in the code to the digital lock on the front door.

"Yeah." I pushed open the door and stepped into the foyer, trying not to think about the heat radiating off the man behind me.

"Big house," he commented. He looked around the foyer, his gaze darting up the stairs.

"It's not that big. Not compared to the house I grew up in."

"Hmmm."

"Shoes off," I stated.

"What?"

I crouched down to unzip my boots. "Shoes off."

"Bossy." He smirked.

"My house, my rules," I said. "Or you can wait outside for your prospect. Your choice. But my couch has a built-in recliner."

His blue eyes twinkled. "How's your sound system?"

I bit my lip. "State of the art with surround sound, installed by a pro."

"Definitely worth taking the boots off," he said. "Am allowed to sit on the stairs?"

"Yes."

Bones slid past me and plunked down on the third wooden stair from the bottom and began unlacing his boot.

"Do you live alone?" I asked.

"No."

When he didn't elaborate, I asked, "Do you live with a woman?"

"You think I'd kiss you in a club, then drive you home after today and be taking my shoes off in your house if I lived with a woman?"

"That's a no then."

"That's a fuck no. That's an *I don't fuck around like that* kind of no."

"Touchy," I remarked.

"You just basically accused me of being a cheating pig."

"I did no such thing," I said in exasperation. "I asked if you lived with a woman because you said you didn't live alone."

"Would it bother you if I lived with a woman?"

"Uh, kind of, yeah."

He grinned.

"Not because I'm jealous—which I'm not—but because it would most definitely make you a cheating pig."

"You're *so* jealous."

"Of a fictional woman you don't live with? Oh please." I rolled my eyes.

"I live at the clubhouse. I don't have a lot of shit. I don't have a family." He shrugged. "It works."

"Now, was that so hard?" I asked, trying to stem a smile from appearing across my lips.

He rose from his spot on the stairs and neatly placed his boots by the front door. "You gonna show me the place?"

I gave him a brief tour of downstairs with the living room, kitchen, and bathroom.

"Help yourself to anything in the fridge. I should be out of the shower before your prospect arrives."

He groaned.

"What?"

"Now I'm gonna think about you in the shower. Naked. Wet. Are you sure you don't need someone to wash your back?"

"I have a loofa," I said, even though I felt my cheeks flush with the idea of wet, naked Bones; water sluicing down his muscled chest…

Clearing my throat, I reached over and grabbed the remote off the coffee table. "Entertain yourself."

"You're no fun."

"I'm a lot of fun."

"Yeah? Not sure I believe you, Duchess."

Smiling, I headed up the stairs, taking them two at a time.

It wasn't until I was alone in the shower, halfway through conditioning my hair that I moaned in embarrassment. The man had seen me cry. Not just cry, but ugly cry. I'd completely fallen apart and I'd had no ability to stop it.

But he hadn't given me any grief over it. On the contrary, he'd comforted me while I cried out my storm.

My hands shook when I lathered my body with soap.

I could've died today.

I could've died today, but I didn't.

Bones was waiting on a prospect to come get him and then I'd be alone. Alone in this big house with nothing but my thoughts.

I got out of the shower and quickly threw on a pair of leggings and a comfortable oversized Notre Dame sweatshirt.

My feet were cold, so I put on a pair of thick wool socks before tying up my hair into a damp knot and padding downstairs into the living room. Bones had made himself comfortable, his feet up on the recliner. He'd removed his leather cut and slung it over the back of the couch.

"Hey," he greeted, pulling his eyes away from the TV to look at me. His gaze started at my head and slowly inched down.

I swallowed. "Hey."

"Feel better?"

I nodded and took a seat on the couch. I grabbed the blanket folded in the corner and flung it over me.

"You look dazed," he said, not taking his eyes off me.

"I feel like I've been beat to hell." I grimaced. "My body hurts."

My soul hurts.

"You fainted."

"Hmm. Yeah."

"That takes it out of you."

"No doubt," I agreed.

"We should talk about it," he said. "You went through something traumatic today. If you don't talk about it—"

"I'm not ready to talk about it," I interrupted. "It's too fresh, too…*raw*. I fell apart in the car; I don't want to fall apart again."

"You mean you don't want *me* to see you fall apart."

I sighed. "No. I just—it's hard to rein it in. If I let it all out…"

"You're afraid you won't be able to pull it together again."

I nodded. "So can we please just…you know. Do anything else?"

"Anything?" he asked with a suggestive raise of his brows.

I rolled my eyes. "What are you watching?"

"Haven't decided. You know you have three streaming services?"

"Yeah, and I spend an hour at a time trying to find something new to watch, only to watch a comfort movie I've already seen a hundred times."

He handed me the remote. "I'll watch your comfort movie."

"Really?"

"Really."

"And you won't say anything about it?"

"I won't say anything about it."

I looked at him for a long moment and then finally I nodded. "Okay. Not a word about Mr. Darcy's hand flex."

"Mr. Darcy's what?"

"Just watch."

During the first twenty minutes of *Pride & Prejudice* with Keira Knightley, I snuck various glances at Bones, wanting to gauge his reaction to the film.

With a sigh, he grabbed a couch pillow and set it down next to him. "I can't enjoy this movie with you watching me."

"I'm not watching you," I lied.

"I'm interested in the film, okay? So lay down and let's watch it."

He patted the pillow.

I bit my lip in momentary indecision and then decided to rest my head. I still had a clear view of the TV, but my top knot made it uncomfortable. After a few minutes of fighting it, I sat up and took my hair down before placing my head back on the pillow.

Mr. Collins complimented the boiled potatoes and then Bones put his hand on my neck. He began to sift his fingers through my hair and rub my head. My eyes closed, the cadence of English accents and Bones' warm, easy touch lulling me to sleep.

∼

I woke up in my own bed.

Groggily, I rolled over. On my nightstand was a glass of water. The alarm clock read seven AM.

I sat up and reached for the glass, downing it in a few gulps. The last thing I remembered was falling asleep on the couch.

There were the faint sounds of kitchen cabinets opening and closing.

Is Bones here?

My cell phone wasn't plugged in or resting on the nightstand.

I got up and went into the bathroom, did my business, and quickly brushed my teeth. I did a bodily inventory—I didn't feel like I normally did before having an episode, so I hoped that meant I wouldn't have one.

Bones was barefoot. His dark hair was askew and he needed a haircut. He was rooting around in the kitchen, looking confused as all hell.

"Uh, morning," I greeted.

He crouched down and opened the cabinet that contained the pots and pans. "Morning. Where the hell is your coffee maker?"

"I don't have one," I replied. "And what are you still doing here? And how did I get up to bed last night?"

"I carried you," he said. "You didn't even wake up when I moved you. I stayed because I didn't think you being alone was a good idea. And what the hell do you mean you don't have a coffee maker?"

"I don't drink coffee," I explained. "Where did you sleep?"

"Are you even human?" he asked in shock. "Everyone drinks coffee. And I slept on the couch."

"Not everyone drinks coffee," I announced. "I don't like coffee. And you should've slept in one of the guest rooms. It would've been more comfortable than the couch."

"The couch was fine," he said.

"You hungry?" I asked.

"Yes. But I already went through your refrigerator last night. You've got nothing in there. I ordered take out."

I frowned. "I really must've been conked out if I didn't hear the doorbell."

"Dead to the world."

I flinched at his choice of words. "What do you mean I've got nothing in the refrigerator? There's tons of stuff."

"You have kale."

"So?"

"So, kale is like…spinach's bitchy cousin."

"Kale is good for you."

"I notice you didn't say you *liked* it. If I'm staying for breakfast and you have no coffee, you gotta offer me something better than kale. Especially since I watched your favorite comfort movie with you."

I smiled. "How'd you feel about the movie, by the way?"

"That Darcy is a real dreamboat."

I laughed, causing him to smile.

His smile made my heart flutter in my chest.

"All right, I'll make waffles. Sound good?"

"Sounds great. You mind if I borrow some toothpaste? Maybe some mouth wash?" He scrubbed a hand across his stubbled jaw.

"Sure. You can use my bathroom upstairs. Toothpaste is on the counter."

"Thanks."

He went upstairs and I went to find my phone, which was still in my purse by the door. I had several missed texts and calls from Charlie, and I was about to text her back when my phone rang.

It was my mother.

"Good morning," I greeted as I walked back toward the kitchen.

"Good morning," she replied. "I didn't wake you, did I?"

"No. I was awake. What's going on?"

"I'm about to walk into my yoga class, but I wanted to tell you that we had dinner with Senator Anderson and his son last night."

"That's nice," I said, not rising to the bait.

"I'm donating to his re-election campaign."

"I imagine you would. Is that all you called to tell me?"

"Walker asked about you."

"Why would he ask about me? He doesn't know anything about me."

My mother was silent.

"Mom, what have you told him?"

"I might have given him your number."

I ground my teeth in frustration. "I was not put on this planet so I could enter into a marriage of alliance."

"A marriage of alliance?" she repeated. "That's not what I want for you."

"No? I don't see you giving my number out to the plumber's son who fixed your toilet three months ago."

"Think what you want of me, but I want you to be happy."

"I *am* happy."

"You're not happy! You fill your days volunteering and spending time with Charlie, but what else do you do?"

Bones came down the stairs, and my eyes met his.

"I don't share everything I do with you, Mom."

She sighed. "I don't want to argue."

"Then why do you push my buttons on purpose?"

"I just want you to have what I had with your father. Life is better when you're sharing it with someone."

"And you think Walker Anderson the Third is the someone I should share my life with, huh? You've met him, what? A handful of times. You don't really know him. You just know his pedigree and the family he belongs to. I love you, Mom. I do. But you've got to stop this match-making business."

She fell silent again. "Will you come to Sunday dinner?"

"Only if my love life is off the table. I mean it. I'll walk out before dessert again if anyone starts talking about—"

"I'll keep my mouth shut," she vowed.

"No, you won't," I said lightly, my anger diffusing. "But I'll be there anyway. I love you."

"Love you, too, darling."

Chapter 9

With a sigh, I gripped my phone. "Sorry about that," I said to Bones. "I haven't started on the waffles."

"So, your mother…"

"My mother."

"You didn't tell her about yesterday." His blue eyes surveyed me. "Why not?"

"It's complicated," I said slowly.

"I'm a pretty smart guy. I think I can follow along."

I sent him soft smile and gestured with my chin toward the kitchen. "You know how to crack eggs?"

"I'm better at cracking skulls."

I blinked, but when Bones didn't rescind his comment, I realized he wasn't joking.

There's a badass biker in my house.

"No time like the present to learn."

We headed back to the kitchen and gathered everything I needed to make waffles.

"So, your mom," Bones pressed.

"My mom can't handle stress," I said.

"Can't, or won't?"

I plugged in the waffle iron. "Can't. When life gets too stressful for her, she checks out. It's not like she goes into a state of depression or anything. Nothing like that. But she's…she has to be protected."

"You're making her sound fragile."

"She *is* fragile."

"She's your mother. You really don't think she would want to know what happens in her daughter's life?"

"Oh, she wants to know what happens in my life. She's even trying to manufacture a marriage for me." I shook my head.

"With a senator's son."

"You heard more than you let on." I whisked the ingredients together and then ladled the batter into the hot waffle iron.

"Why's she so determined to fix you up?"

"She was really happy with my dad," I said absently. "And she wants that for me. Only her approach is sort of lacking. I'm supposed to meet this guy at the charity event Charlie and I are going to in a few weeks. But now he's gonna call and I'm going to have to level with him."

"Level with him about what?"

"That I'm not interested."

"Senators' sons aren't your type?"

I shrugged.

"What is your type?"

His tone had lowered, and I looked up to meet his intense, focused gaze. My eyes skittered over his tattoos, his strong jaw, the breadth of his shoulders.

"What's *your* type?" I fired back.

"Big tits, big hair, big attitude."

I wrinkled my nose at him. "I think I'm going to burn your waffle on purpose."

"You can burn my waffle any time you want."

"Okay, how did you make that sexual?" I asked.

"That wasn't sexual. You just read into what I said as being sexual. Are you thinking about sex?"

"No."

"You ever think about sex?" he asked.

"For someone that needs caffeine in the morning, you're far too on-the-nose for this conversation."

Bones slid off the stool and sauntered toward me.

"What are you doing?" I demanded as he glided up behind me, pressing his strong chest against my back.

"I want to learn how to make waffles."

"You were learning fine from over there."

His large hand went to my hip, and I felt him turn his head so that his nose brushed against my hair. "I have bad eyesight."

"Then get glasses…"

"You like men who wear glasses? You're into hot nerds, aren't you? I know the quadratic formula."

"You do not," I said with a laugh.

"I do. My math teacher taught it to us in a song. I still know the song, I still know the formula, but I have no idea what the fuck to use it for. By the way, your nipples are hard."

"They are not!" I lied.

"They *so* are. If I'd known that math turned you on, I would've mentioned it sooner."

I arched my back just a bit and bumped my ass against him.

He sucked in a harsh breath.

"Prove it," I stated.

"Prove what? That being near you makes me hard?"

His words sent a shiver of pleasure down my spine. "No, I mean prove that you know the quadratic formula."

"X is equal to negative b plus or minus the square root of b squared minus 4ac all over 2a."

"You could've made that up," I said.

"Jesus, Duchess. Will you give me one?"

I turned in his arms so that I was flush against the counter. We stared at one another and then his lips met mine.

My hand went to the back of his neck, sinking into the dark hair at his nape.

I felt him everywhere. I was surrounded by his heat, his scent. His tongue slid into my mouth and he pressed against me.

"It's burning," I murmured against his mouth.

"What's burning?" he asked as he glided his lips to my cheek. "Your loins?"

"The *waffle*." I laughed.

He pulled away from me, but I was in danger of saying *screw it* and demanding he go back to kissing me.

Bones stayed close as I removed the waffle from the waffle iron. It was dark golden brown, and I placed it on the plate and set it down on the island in front of the stool he'd vacated.

"Eat," I commanded. "Before it gets cold."

"I'd rather eat you…"

The ladle fell from my hand and clanked into the mixing bowl. "You can't say things like that."

"Why not?" Bones asked as he walked to the stool and took a seat. "It's the truth."

"Because you can't," I said in exasperation. "People don't…that's not how people talk."

"If they don't, they should. We should all be more honest about what we want, don't you think?" Bones slathered his waffle with butter and maple syrup.

"There's such a thing as decorum."

"Fuck decorum. When the senator's son calls you, are you gonna be polite and brush him off, or are you gonna tell him that your mother is trying to set you up and you're not interested?"

"I don't have to hurt his feelings," I replied as I closed the waffle iron.

"No, you're just willing to be a pawn in your mother's schemes. Do you have any real boundaries? Or have you been a people pleaser your entire life?"

"Are you trying to be an ass?" I snapped.

"No. I'm genuinely curious." He raised his brows as he waited for me to answer. When I didn't, he went on, "Even if you tell this guy you're not interested and you've told your mom to back off, do you really think she will?"

"No. She won't back off until she sees that I'm dating someone," I replied. "That's the only thing that'll get her to stop."

"Okay. I'll do it."

I frowned. "Do what?"

"I'll be your date to this charity, ball-gala or whatever."

His statement rendered me speechless. My eyes took in his appearance. Sexy as hell, rough around the edges, and those tattoos…

He wasn't from my world.

I could only imagine him striding into the gala wearing jeans and his leather cut.

"You don't seem to hate the idea," Bones said with a raise of his brows.

"Ah, don't take this the wrong way, but—"

"Everything you just said before the *but* is bullshit. Spit it out, Duchess. You worried I'm going to embarrass you? Worried I'm too crass to hang with you and your crowd for the night?"

"Worried is the wrong word," I admitted. "But these people…they expect a certain appearance."

"Okay."

"You'd have to wear a tux."

"Fine. James Bond is cool as fuck."

My lips twitched. "There are forks."

"So, I can't eat with my hands? Damn."

"It's a sit-down dinner. There are appetizer forks, dinner forks, salad forks, dessert forks. There's a way to set your napkin on your lap. I learned all these things at various cotillions over the years."

"You're right, I've never seen a fork. I'm a spork guy all the way."

"*Bones…*" I sighed.

"Duchess," he said in the same tone. "I don't like the idea of senators' sons sniffing around you. You want to stick me in a tux and teach me about forks, then go ahead. I'll do it. Your world doesn't scare me."

"Does anything scare you?"

"No," he brazened. "I don't have the DNA for fear."

"Hmm. This is either the worst idea or the best idea ever," I murmured.

The front door opened and a moment later, Charlie popped into the kitchen. "Thought I smelled waff—" She stopped and looked at Bones. "You're still here."

"I'm still here," Bones agreed.

"Wait," I said. "How did you know he was here?"

"I called you like an hour after you got home and you didn't answer. When I couldn't get a hold of you, I asked Savage to call Bones. Bones told me you were already asleep and that he was staying the night."

"I was going to call you back this morning," I said, plating the waffle and handing it to her. "But I got sidetracked by my mother's phone call."

Charlie glanced at Bones, looking like she wanted to say something but was hesitant to voice it aloud.

"Bones knows we don't tell my mother things," I said, giving her a pass.

"Oh, okay."

"Bones is going to go with me to the charity event," I explained.

Her grin was slow. "Seriously?"

"Seriously."

"I'm so glad I get to see that. Please tell me you're introducing him as Bones only, no last name."

"I'm still in the room," Bones said as he polished off the rest of his waffle.

"Well, can you leave so we can talk about you?" Charlie demanded. "I want to gossip with my best friend."

"He can't leave yet," I stated. "He has to wait for a prospect to pick him up."

"A prospect dropped my motorcycle off last night," Bones explained. "You didn't hear it?"

I shook my head.

"You really sleep hard," Bones said with a laugh. "Gimme your phone. I'm putting my number in it."

I unlocked my cell and handed it to him. While he punched in his number, Charlie and I looked at each other. She raised her brow and I shook my head.

Bones handed my phone back to me. I glanced at the name he'd put in.

"You didn't."

"I did," he said with a smile.

"What?" Charlie asked.

I let out a laugh. "He put his contact in as Bad to the Bones."

Bones took his empty plate to the sink, rinsed it off, and put it in the dishwasher.

When he turned around, he saw both Charlie and me watching him.

He raised a brow. "What? I know what a dishwasher is. For the record, I'm house trained."

"I like you more and more," Charlie said, shoveling a bite of waffle into her mouth. "Thanks for taking care of her last night."

"Happy to do it." Bones met my gaze. "You'll call me?"

I nodded.

He stalked toward me, grasped the back of my head, and kissed me. A noise of surprise escaped my mouth, but the kiss was over as soon as it started. Bones pulled back and grinned. "Later, Duchess."

Chapter 10

The front door closed and Charlie let out a vocal sigh. "Okay, wow. You're dating a biker."

"I'm not *dating* a biker."

"He kissed you goodbye."

"That doesn't mean we're dating."

"He's willing to suffer through an evening of blue bloods in multi-thousand-dollar tuxedos just to spend time with you. That's dating."

"Charlie—"

"*He stayed the night.*"

"On the couch."

"The *whole night*...just to make sure you were okay."

"That's not—you would've stayed the night, too," I pointed out.

"I should've stayed the night," she said quietly. "I should've insisted."

"Honestly, I really didn't want you to," I admitted.

"Why not? I'm your best friend."

"I don't like asking for help and I—I fell apart when

Bones drove me home. It was embarrassing and weird…I was vulnerable, and I didn't want you to see that."

"That's stupid. That's literally what best friends are for."

"Yeah. I guess so," I said.

"The moment I got to the bar with Savage, I had second thoughts about not being there for you. I started calling and texting and you didn't answer."

"My phone was on silent," I admitted. "And I fell asleep watching a movie. I didn't even wake up when he carried me to my bed."

"I should've come over."

"There was nothing for you to do."

"I could've just been here for you." She frowned. "I'm sorry, by the way. What you said the other day—about me not finishing things. You were right. And I didn't like that you were right. Maybe I was punishing you for the truth. Which is stupid. You always have my back and you're my biggest cheerleader."

"Sometimes we don't like the truth, even if it comes from the person we love most in this world."

"You love me most?"

I smiled. "Sisters. In all ways but blood."

She swallowed and I knew she was trying to keep her emotions in check. "So…how are you?"

"I don't know," I admitted. "It's surreal. What happened yesterday. I haven't had much time to think about it because I passed so out early last night. Just kind of checked out, you know?"

"Yeah."

"And when I woke up, he was still here. He occupied my physical space as well as my brain space. I kind of appreciated it, actually." I pointed to her empty plate. "Another waffle?"

She shook her head. I ladled in the last of the mix into the hot waffle iron and closed it. "Okay, I told you everything that happened with Bones. Now I wanna know what happened with you and Savage."

"Well, he took me to a bar and we had a drink. After I spoke to Bones, I was still feeling shitty about not being there for you…so Savage made me feel *not-so-shitty*."

I blinked. "You had sex with him?"

She nodded. "Of course I had sex with him. Acrobatic, yoga-inspired, brain-melting sex."

"How very nice for you," I quipped.

Charlie grinned. "You should try it."

"What? Sex with Savage?"

"Not Savage. *Bones*. Sex with Bones. Pretty sure he's amenable to that idea."

"Yeah, I know he is." I snorted.

"You're not going to do that thing, are you?"

"What thing?"

"That thing of waiting for feelings to develop before sleeping with him? It didn't work so well the last time you did that. Tyler was a terrible lay."

"It's because he was repressed," I stated. "And dare I say, frigid."

"It's because he's a WASP. WASPs are frigid."

"You're a WASP," I said with a laugh.

"Exception, not the rule," she retorted.

"You don't think I'm frigid, do you?"

"I've never had sex with you, so I don't know."

"*Charlie*," I pleaded.

"Even if you are, which I'm not saying you are, but even if you are, based on that goodbye kiss, I don't think Bones will let you be frigid much longer."

I pictured myself in bed with Bones. Our limbs

tangled, our bodies slick with sweat, his lips between my legs…

"Frigid my ass," Charlie said with a laugh. "You're thinking about Bones naked, aren't you?"

"Yep." I sighed. "So, taking him to Mom's charity gala…thoughts on that?"

"Is he going to wear his biker garb or a tux?"

"Tux."

"Hmm. I think it'll be a night to remember. That's what I think."

"Also, what were you and Waverly talking about yesterday? Why did you say you were going to call her?"

"Oh. She flips furniture. Pretty cool stuff actually. She also said she's interested in dollhouse restoration. I didn't even know that was a thing. Apparently, there's money there."

"I had no idea."

"I have that dollhouse from my grandmother. I was thinking Waverly could do something with it. The wallpaper is yellow, the paint is chipping. I don't know. I thought Waverly might be able to restore it."

I paused. "Doesn't your mom love that dollhouse?"

"Yeah."

"And you're thinking of having it restored for her?"

"Don't think too much about this," she said.

"Okay." I hid my smile as I removed the waffle from the iron. "I hope Willa's all right. Yesterday was…yeah. Hard to even process."

"Savage called her when we were out together. Just to check in. He's a good dude."

"A good dude," I repeated.

"And good in bed." She smirked. "So, tell me the truth…"

"About?"

"Bones. Did he love *Pride & Prejudice*?"

~

Charlie and I hung out for the rest of the day. We vegged on the couch, watched movies, and every now and again I looked at my phone.

"Call him," Charlie said, not taking her eyes off the TV as she dug into a bowl of popcorn.

"Call who?"

"Don't play dumb."

"I don't have a reason to call him."

"Even better. You like him. The first step is admitting it."

"Did you stay out all night with Savage?" I asked.

"Yes."

"You didn't invite him back to the pool house?"

"Nope. Now stop redirecting the conversation. If you're not gonna call Bones, at least text him."

"And say what?" I asked.

"Thank him for staying over."

"I already thanked him."

With a sigh, she muted the TV and then held out her hand. "Phone."

"No." I held my cell to my chest in a protective gesture.

"Hayden, give me your phone so I can text something dirty to him, or you text him yourself and thank him. Ten bucks says his reply is instant."

"He's not gonna reply right away. He's busy. He's a guy."

"First of all, Bones is a man. Second of all, when a man really likes you, it doesn't matter how busy he is. He'll reply. He won't make you wait. You'll know where you stand with him."

"That's what has me worried," I muttered.

But I unlocked my phone, found his contact, and sent him a text.

> ME
> Thanks for staying the night with me

My phone chimed not ten seconds later.

> BAD TO THE BONES
> Thanks for the waffle. You still set on me wearing a tux?

> ME
> A tux is a must.

> BAD TO THE BONES
> Where the hell do I get one

> ME
> I know a guy. You free tomorrow afternoon?

> BAD TO THE BONES
> I could be free tomorrow afternoon…

> ME
> 1pm

> BAD TO THE BONES
> Fine

> ME
> Text me your address. I'll pick you up

> BAD TO THE BONES
> Why don't you give me the name and address of the place and I'll meet you there?

> **ME**
> When you're in my world we play by my rules. Address.

> **BAD TO THE BONES**
> That's how it's gonna be, huh?

> **ME**
> Yup.

> **BAD TO THE BONES**
> Okay. But turnabout is fair play…sure you're ready for that?

I didn't reply to him for the rest of the night.

∼

"Hayden, wake up!"

I opened my eyes, my heart in my throat. I didn't remember falling asleep on the couch, but apparently I had. Now Charlie was staring at me with fear in her eyes.

While I gulped air into my lungs, I sat up. The lamps on the end tables were aglow, but the main light of the living room had been turned off.

"Nightmare?" I guessed.

She nodded. "Not like your other ones, though."

"Oh." I ran a hand across my face. "What time is it?"

Charlie picked up her cell phone off the coffee table and looked at it. "Three fifteen."

I swallowed, my tongue heavy and dry. "When did I fall asleep?"

"Two movies ago."

"I need water," I said, throwing my legs off the couch.

"I'll get it for you."

"Okay."

She got up and headed toward the kitchen.

"How are you still awake?" I asked.

"Unlike you, I survive off caffeine and spite. No crashing for me."

I fell silent and Charlie returned with a glass of water and held it out to me.

"Thanks." I took it and gulped the entire thing in a few swallows.

"So, what were you dreaming about?"

"He pulled the trigger," I said quietly. "And then I floated out of my body, so I was staring down at the scene. And I watched him run away with my purse while my brain was splattered all over the cement."

She blinked.

"Wishing you hadn't asked?"

"Kinda." She took a seat next to me. "But I'm definitely glad I stayed tonight. You shouldn't be alone for a while."

"You can't stay with me all the time," I pointed out. "What about tomorrow or the next night? Or the night after that?"

"You told me I could move in. Remember?"

"I remember."

"But I don't think I want to move in now that you're dating a biker. Because I know I'm not gonna wanna hear you guys going at like primates in the jungle."

I snorted out a laugh, causing Charlie to crack a grin. "I knew that would get you to laugh." Her smile dimmed. "Maybe you need to see a shrink."

"Maybe."

"You won't, will you?"

"I won't," I agreed.

"Why not?"

"Why won't *you* see a shrink to talk about your issues?" I threw back at her.

"Okay, fair." She cocked her head to the side. "Think you can go back to sleep?"

"Not any time soon."

"Want to watch another movie?"

"No."

"Want me help you pick out an outfit for tomorrow, so you look effortlessly amazing but not like you're trying to look hot for Bones?"

"Absolutely."

Chapter 11

I PARKED in front of Pie in the Sky and cut the engine. With a deep breath, I looked in my rearview mirror, checked my appearance one final time, and then climbed out of the car. Under-eye concealer only did so much when your sleep was erratic, and you'd had a slumber party with your best friend.

The bakery was warm and inviting. A woman with a long, dark braid wearing a pair of glasses stood behind the counter. She handed a man his change and a cup of to-go coffee.

Another customer stepped up to order.

I looked around the bakery for Bones. He was sitting at a corner table, his back facing the wall, his blue eyes locked on me.

His chin lowered ever so slightly, and I knew he was checking me out in my tight black jeans, ankle boots, and designer black and white chenille sweater.

As the customer waited for his drink, it was my turn to step up to order.

"You must be Hayden," the woman at the counter said.

I was momentarily taken aback, and then I nodded. "I'm sorry, have we met?"

The woman shook her head. "Nope. But Bones said when a well-dressed, gorgeous woman with your physical attributes ordered I was supposed to put it on his tab. I'm obsessed with your boots, by the way."

I grinned. "Thank you."

"My name is Jazz."

"Jazz," I repeated in confusion and then understanding dawned. "You're best friends with Brielle."

"You know Brielle?"

"I met her at Three Kings a few days ago. Roman tattooed my best friend."

"It's a small world after all," Jazz quipped.

"It is."

"So, you and Bones?" Jazz pressed.

"Oh gee, can I get a cup of your strawberry hibiscus tea and a plain croissant?"

"Plain? Are you sure you don't want chocolate? It's one of our best sellers," Jazz said.

"No thanks. The plain one is fine."

"The tea needs a few minutes to steep. I'll bring it over to you."

"Thanks."

I opened my wallet and pulled out a few bills and stuck them in the tip jar before heading to Bones.

He folded his legs back and rose slowly. "Duchess," he greeted, placing a hand on my hip and leaning in to kiss my cheek. His mouth was warm and his breath smelled faintly of coffee mixed heavily with cream.

I suddenly wished his mouth would move a few inches over and graze my lips, but I was too chicken to turn my head so our mouths could meet. Plus, I could feel Jazz's eyes boring holes into my back.

Bones dropped his hand from my waist, and we sat.

"You been here long?" I asked.

"About an hour."

"An hour! But we said 1 PM."

"I came early."

"But why?" I asked.

"Because Brooklyn wanted to stop by and Slash wouldn't let her come alone, and I needed to speak to Slash. Made sense for me just to come early and wait for you."

I frowned. "Am I supposed to know who these people are?"

"Brooklyn owns the bakery," he explained. "Brooklyn is Slash's Old Lady."

"Oh, right, Brooklyn. Brielle mentioned Brooklyn just had a baby so the wedding cake part of the business is on hiatus for now."

"We'll see how long that lasts. Brooklyn can't stay away from the bakery. Even though it drives Slash crazy and he tries to get her to slow down."

"What's an Old Lady?" I asked. "Is it like, a biker wife?"

"Sorta, yeah. But an Old Lady is more than that. If something were to happen to Slash, the club would make sure Brooklyn and the baby were taken care of. We're family."

"Oh." I nodded. "Well, that's nice."

"Nice. Yeah."

Jazz brought over my croissant and tea, her gaze bouncing back and forth between us. "Need a refill, Bones?"

"No thanks. I'm good." He sent her a smile.

"So, what are you guys doing today?" Jazz asked.

I broke apart the buttery croissant as I waited for Bones to reply.

He flashed a grin. "I'm getting fitted for a tuxedo."

"You're getting fitted for a tuxedo?" Jazz repeated. "Why?"

"Because I'm going to a charity gala with Hayden. As her date."

"Well, that's…weird."

"I get why you and Brielle are best friends," I said with a laugh.

She grinned. "Let me know how you like the croissant when you're done."

"I will."

Jazz headed back toward the counter as the front door opened and a few customers came inside.

"So, do you hang out here often?" I asked, taking a bite.

"Not really, why?"

"Because Jazz seems to know you well enough to tease you."

"Jazz hangs with the club sometimes." He adjusted his seat. "I haven't fucked her, if that's what you're getting at."

I made a noise in the back of my throat. "That wasn't what I was getting at."

"Okay." He lifted his cup of coffee to his lips. "Speaking of fucking—are you fucking anyone? Because if you are, you need stop."

"*Can you lower your voice?*" I snapped, feeling my cheeks heat. "We're in public."

"So?"

"So, can you not drop the F-word so casually?"

"The F-word? You're adorable. And your face is red."

"You need to be put on a leash," I muttered.

"The only one getting collared is you."

"Okay, whoa. If you can't behave, I'm leaving." To back up what I said, I stood.

"Relax, I'm just kidding. Sit down. I'll be on my best behavior, I promise."

I shot him a look.

"I promise," he said again.

"This is a good segue into discussing the gala. Clearly, I'm going to have to give you some pointers on appropriate topics of conversation."

"If you make me talk about stock portfolios the deal is off," he joked.

"I'm serious," I said. "I appreciate the fact that you're doing this for me, but people are going to talk. They're going to wonder who you are, where we met, your pedigree, all of it."

"People? Or your mother."

I closed my mouth.

"Has the senator's son called you yet?"

"No."

"Good. Which brings me back to my original question. Are you fucking anyone?"

"Bones," I groaned, burying my face in my hands.

"Just answer the question."

"*You* answer the question," I fired back with a glare. "What was it you said? Right… Big tits, big hair, big attitude? Got any of those hanging around?"

"Nope."

I raised my brows. "Really?"

"Really." He leaned forward. "Now answer the damn question."

"No, there's no one else."

The corner of his mouth twitched.

"What?"

"You might not have big hair, but your big attitude gets me hard."

"I noticed you didn't say anything about my other attributes."

"That's because you don't have big tits."

I glared.

"You've got *perfect* tits."

"There must be something wrong with me, because I'm far too flattered by your crass compliment."

"I'll give you five bucks if you say *fuck*."

"Finish your coffee, Bones. We have somewhere to be."

∾

"You look tired," Bones said as we walked to my car.

"Your compliments need work."

"Thought we established that I give good compliments." He winked. "Seriously, Duchess. Did you sleep at all last night?"

"I slept. Kind of."

I unlocked my car and Bones opened the driver's side door for me. "What do you mean *kind of*?"

"I mean I fell asleep on the couch and the next thing I remember Charlie was waking me up from a nightmare. And instead of going back to sleep right away, we stayed awake for a while. I crashed again around seven this morning."

Before I could climb into the seat, Bones reached out and cradled my cheek in his hand, his thumb stroking my skin. "You ready to talk about it?"

I shook my head.

"Okay." He leaned forward and brushed his lips against mine. It was deeper than a hello kiss. It was an *I-want-you-but-I'm-going-to-tease-you-into-wanting-me* kiss. It was a kiss I wanted to fall into. It was a kiss that made me forget he wore leather, rode a motorcycle, and had tattoos.

It was a kiss that made me want to ask him to spend the night with me, so I didn't have to be afraid of the dark.

I gently pressed my hand against his chest and pushed him away. "We're going to be late."

"I don't mind being late," he whispered huskily.

A shiver danced down my spine and desire pooled in my belly.

"My world, my rules. And in my world, we are punctual to appointments."

He stepped back and waited for me to get into the car before closing my door. Then he went around to the other side and climbed in. He adjusted his seat to give his long legs room to stretch out.

"You never texted me back last night."

"I didn't?" I buckled myself in.

"You know you didn't."

"Should we go over these rules?" I asked him, shooting him a flirty look.

His gaze dropped to my mouth. "Nah. I think I'll let you surprise me."

The temperature in the car felt like it suddenly spiked.

I cleared my throat. "We need to go."

"You're the one driving, Duchess. Unless you want me to drive because you're so flustered you can't see straight?"

"I'm not flustered."

He laughed. "Okay. Just don't crash. I actually want to see what I look like in a tux."

∼

Bones looked majestic in a tux. Even a tux off the rack that didn't fit him properly.

"Not too shabby," Bones said as he looked at himself in the mirror. "I might pass for a gentleman."

"God, I hope not," I blurted out.

I met his gaze in the mirror.

"I mean, I like the way you look," I amended. "The tux is a nice change. I was correct though. You're going to need a custom tux."

"You're right," Mr. Ambrose said. "His arms and shoulders are too muscular for that coat. I can take material away, but I can't add it and keep the bespoke look."

"And the pants don't hang correctly," I added. "We have an event in two weeks. Will we be able to make it happen?"

"Anything for you, Ms. Spencer," the aging tailor said, gripping my hand and giving it a squeeze. "I'll have his tuxedo ready in time."

I kissed his cheek. "You are, and always will be, the best."

He flushed with pleasure. I continued to speak with Mr. Ambrose while Bones changed back into his street clothes.

Bones came out of the dressing room and met us at the counter. He reached into his wallet and pulled out his credit card and handed it to the tailor.

Mr. Ambrose held up his hand. "It's been taken care of, sir."

Bones looked at me.

"My rules."

His expression remained passive, but his jaw clenched. He stuck his credit card back into his wallet.

The shop phone rang and Mr. Ambrose sent me a smile as he went to answer it. "Hello? Oh, hello, Mr. Buchanan. Yes, your tuxedo is ready. I'll have it sent over to The Rex. You're welcome. Goodbye." Mr. Ambrose hung up the phone and returned his attention to us. "I apologize for the interruption. I need Mr., ah…Bones' phone number so I can call for the final fitting and adjustments."

Bones rattled off his phone number to Mr. Ambrose.

"Give your mother my best," Mr. Ambrose said.

"I will."

Bones and I left the Dallas shop that had been worth the hour-long drive. Mr. Ambrose was the best tailor in the state. His family of expert tailors and seamstresses had emigrated from England to New York City in the 1940s and set up shop in the Garment District. After decades in Manhattan, Mr. Ambrose had moved to Dallas to service the oil tycoons that were invited into polite society despite their new wealth.

He was in his eighties now, but the man still cut the best suits.

"You're not paying for my tuxedo," Bones said as we walked down the street. "And don't you fucking say *your world, your rules*."

"Custom tuxedos are expensive," I said.

"And you think I can't afford it."

"You want to spend fifteen thousand dollars on a tuxedo?"

"*Fifteen-fucking-thousand*? Are you insane? For a God damned custom-made tuxedo?"

"Look," I said, pulling him out of the walkway to stand in the doorway of a furniture store. "This isn't your world. But for me, this is everyday life. Fifteen thousand dollars for tuxedos and charity functions at two thousand dollars a plate is the norm. That's the world I live in. Please don't let this be a pride thing. Let me pay for this, because I can't in good conscience ask you to spend that kind of money knowing you'll wear the tuxedo once and never have to put it on again. Okay?"

Bones stared at me. "I still don't like it."

"I know."

"You're rich."

I sighed. "Yeah."

"I mean, *really* rich…"

I nodded.

"Rich like they name buildings after your family kind of rich."

"Only universities," I joked.

Bones didn't smile. "Fine. One condition though…"

"Name it."

"When you're in my world, you don't get to ask questions. You just have to go along with whatever I say. Can you do that?"

I nibbled my lip while I debated.

"Duchess?"

"I guess I don't really have a choice, do I?"

He cracked a smile. "Not unless you want to dodge the senator's son all night on your own."

"Okay, Bones. In your world, I won't ask questions and I'll go along with whatever you say."

"You hungry?"

I nodded.

"You eat seafood?"

I nodded again.

"Good, I know a place."

Chapter 12

The restaurant was less of a restaurant and more of a hole in the wall. You wouldn't find it on a map or in the Zagat guide. It was the kind of place my mother wouldn't be caught dead in.

I loved it.

It smelled like the ocean and the tables were covered in brown paper. The walls were decorated with dusty black and white vintage photos of fishing boats and rough, weathered dock men.

Bones placed his hand at the small of my back as the hostess led us to a tucked away corner table.

"Your server will be right with you," she said before disappearing.

"What's good here?" I asked as I reached for the menu.

"Everything," he said. "But I think we should start with two pounds of crab, potatoes, and corn. It sounds like a lot, but trust me, we'll get through it."

I nodded. "Sounds good to me." I set my menu aside and picked up a folded plastic square. "What's this?"

"A bib."

"A bib? Why do I need a bib?"

"Because the crabs splatter when you crack them open."

"We're cracking our own crabs?" I asked.

"Have you never cracked your own crab legs?"

I shook my head.

Bones leaned back in his chair. "This'll be fun."

The server came by our table and Bones put in our order.

"And to drink?" the server asked.

"Water's great, please," I said. "Thanks."

"Pilsner on draft," Bones said.

I gathered my hair into a high ponytail and then tied the bib around my neck. Bones looked at me with amusement. "What?" I asked. "I'm just getting ready."

"You'll probably have to get that sweater of yours dry-cleaned after we're done."

"Then I'll get it dry-cleaned." I rolled up the sleeves, ready for when the crabs came to the table.

"Been meaning to ask you something," Bones said.

"Shoot," I replied.

"You wore a Notre Dame sweatshirt."

I raised my brows. "That's not a question."

"That your Alma Mater?"

I paused for a moment and then shook my head.

"You just wear a random university's sweatshirt even though you didn't attend? That's kind of weird."

"My dad went there," I clipped.

"You haven't talked about your dad before."

"You haven't talked about your family at all," I fired back.

Bones didn't seem offended by my tone, and his expression remained passive. The server returned with our drinks, brought us mallets and metal crab claw crackers before leaving us alone.

Bones smiled slightly and then said, "My parents live in Florida. They own an HVAC company. My dad likes to fish and my mom likes to needlepoint. I don't have any siblings and I grew up with a dog that looked more like a wolf than a dog. Me and my friends used to build log cabins in the woods behind my house, dam up creeks and shoot each other with bb guns. Just a normal Saturday afternoon for young boys. Anything else you want to know?"

"No, that's a pretty clear picture," I said with a smile. "Wild boy even then, huh?"

"It was a good childhood," he said softly. "Happy."

"And you joined the club when?" I asked.

"Twenty years ago."

"Wow. So you're…"

"Old?"

I bit my lip to stifle a grin.

"I'm thirty-nine, Duchess. Hardly old."

He picked up his beer and took a large gulp and I played with the straw in my water.

"Your mom remarried, then," Bones said, setting his beer down. "After your parents split up?"

I frowned. "My parents didn't split up."

His brow furrowed and then straightened. "Oh."

"Yeah." I sighed. "I don't like to talk about it."

He reached for my hand across the table, but I recoiled, quickly placing my hands in my lap.

"So, you're a dog person?" I asked.

"A big dog person, not a little dog person. You?"

"I love dogs."

He leaned forward and smiled. "Yeah?"

I nodded.

"Then why don't you have one? You have that big empty house. Seems like a dog would be a good idea. Something to come home to."

"I'm not ready for that kind of commitment," I said, boldly looking him in the eye.

Our server returned to our table, carting a huge steaming pot. He dumped it over onto the table. Crabs, corn on the cob, and potatoes hit the brown paper. The aroma made me salivate in anticipation.

My eyes widened at the sight.

"Another beer, sir?" the server asked Bones.

"Nah, I'm good, thanks."

"Okay, well enjoy." The server retreated, leaving me to stare at the food, unsure of where to start.

Bones handed me a claw cracker and a mallet. "Don't stop eating until you get the sweats."

∽

"That was *so* good," I announced as I took a wet nap and wiped my hands.

He chuckled. "Yeah, I knew you liked it when we ordered a second round."

"The crabs were small and a lot of work. But definitely worth it." I tossed the wet nap onto the soiled brown paper and pile of corn cobs.

"How are you feeling about dessert?" he asked. "They have a decent key lime pie. As a native Floridian, I know good key lime pie when I have it."

"I'll pass," I said.

"Health nut," he teased.

"Not a health nut. I feel better when I don't eat sugar, so I don't eat it."

"No coffee, no sugar. What else don't you eat?"

"Red meat."

"You just stabbed me in the heart."

"And I don't drink."

"Do you have any vices?"

I tilted my head to the side. "No."

"Do you have any fun?"

"Okay, now you're starting to sound like Charlie," I mocked.

Bones raised his hand and gestured for the check. "What do you do to blow off steam?"

"I don't want to tell you. You'll make fun of me."

"Oh, come on. Now I have to know."

"I go horseback riding."

"Why would I make fun of you for that?" Bones asked.

The server brought the check and set it down in front of Bones, who glanced at it and then reached for his wallet to throw down some bills.

"I don't know. Because it's another reminder that we come from very different worlds."

"Me standing in a bad fitting tux didn't remind you of that?" he asked lightly.

"What are we doing here, Bones?" I asked quietly. "Why are you spending time with me?"

"I could ask you the same question. You clearly don't want to be with a man from your own world who likes the same things you do, who'll ride horses with you on the weekends, who won't balk at dropping fifteen k on a tuxedo. I like you, Duchess." He leaned forward. "I like touching you, I like kissing you, I like talking to you. You're…not what I'm used to."

"What are you used to?"

"Easy."

My gaze narrowed.

He shot me an unapologetic smile. "You're not easy,

Duchess. You don't give an inch. But that's okay. I like working for it. So, there it is. I'll let you show me your world, and I'll show you mine. And maybe we'll meet somewhere in the middle."

∽

I drove us back to Pie in the Sky, the lunch conversation heavy between us. I parked out front of the bakery and idled the car.

"So, I'll see you Wednesday," Bones said.

I frowned. "What's happening on Wednesday."

"You're going to show me how to eat with the proper forks. And then on Saturday, I'm taking you to this club thing that's going on."

I blinked. "Wait, what?"

He grinned. "Admit it. You want to see me again really soon."

"What's this club thing you want to take me to?"

"A wedding."

"A wedding? A biker wedding?"

He nodded. "One of the brothers is getting married to his Old Lady. So, you teach me not to eat like a neanderthal this week and then this weekend I'll take you to the best party you've ever been to."

"That hardly seems fair," I pointed out.

"You think this exchange is a bit uneven? Then how about we even the score?"

Before I could ask what the hell that meant, he clasped the back of my neck and was drawing me close.

"No!" I pulled away. "Don't kiss me."

"Why? You afraid you'll maul me in the car?"

I glared at him. "I smell like butter and Old Bay."

"Aphrodisiac." He brushed his lips against mine and then pulled back. "I'll see you, Duchess."

He let me go and then he got out of my car. Bones walked into the bakery and disappeared.

I pressed a button on my steering wheel to call Charlie. She picked up on the first ring.

"Hello?"

"I'm so freakin' screwed."

She paused for a second. "I'll be at your place in twenty."

Chapter 13

"You brought wine," I stated.

"I did," Charlie said as she came into the living room.

"But I don't drink wine," I pointed out.

"It's not for you. It's for me. I can't have girl talk without wine," she said. "Um, it smells like a seafood boil in here…"

I groaned and buried my face into the arm of the couch.

"What? What did I say?"

"Bones took me to a seafood restaurant and I cracked my own crabs."

"That sounds dirty."

"It was. I got crab splatter all over my sweater. I even wore a bib, but it clearly didn't help."

"No, I meant it actually sounded *dirty*. Like, sexual." She set the bottle of wine onto the coffee table. "Tell Dr. Charlie the problem. On second thought, you might want to shower first."

By the time I got out of the shower and my clothes

were in the dry cleaner's pile, Charlie was already half a glass into the bottle of wine.

"Okay, tell me everything that happened. But also, how does he look in a tux?"

My shoulders sank. "Even in a tux that doesn't fit, he looks perfect."

"Oh no," she murmured.

I nodded. "I'm going to be a puddle of hormones when I see him in the bespoke tux."

"Will you jump Bones' bones?" She sniggered.

I rolled my eyes.

"So, what's the problem?"

"He invited me to a wedding."

"Huh."

"Right? Like, that's weird. I mean, we kind of have this thing going on where for every date we spend in my world, then I have to respond in kind."

"Date?"

"Not a date exactly. But the tux fitting thing. My world. Seafood restaurant where I cracked crab with my bare hands. His world."

"Like a tit-for-tat situation."

"Kinda, yeah. This Wednesday, I'm teaching Bones about forks."

"As in which one to stab himself with the night of the charity gala?"

"As in which one to eat a salad with."

"Ah. How engrossing. How will he stay awake during dinner? Wear something plunging, that's my recommendation."

"Charlie," I warned.

"Fine. Okay. You want my professional opinion on this?"

"Professional opinion? What are you a professional at?"

"Getting involved with the wrong men."

"Oh. Yeah, you are kind of a pro at that," I teased.

She grinned back. "I think you should see this through."

"See what through? He's going with me to this charity event, but we have nothing in common. Nothing to bind us together long term. What's the point?"

"That's *exactly* the point," she insisted. "You don't want Walker Anderson. You don't want Tyler, so what the hell do you want? Sounds like you need the complete opposite. Shake it up, Hayden. You'll be better for it."

"I wish I didn't like him," I muttered. "It would be so much easier if I didn't like him."

"That's your mistake," she said. "You gotta be like a rolling stone. Or Teflon. Or a Teflon rolling stone that enjoys men but doesn't keep them."

"So, you're not keeping Savage?"

"Nope. I'm not interested in keeping Savage. Not like you want to keep Bones."

"What? I don't want to keep Bones. I don't even know Bones."

"But you're going to get to know him because you're going to spend time with him. The only time you won't be talking is when you're doing it. And even then, he looks like the type to talk dirty."

"Can you be quiet now?"

"Hmm. Maybe. Got any food?"

∽

"You sure you don't want me to stay," Charlie asked three hours later.

"For the hundredth time, no. Please don't stay."

"What if you have nightmares?" she asked.

"Then there will be no one to hear me scream."

"God, you have a dark sense of humor." She shook her head. "Now I *really* think I should stay."

"Go. Go out. Have fun. Have some fun for me."

"I'll have a lot of fun. I just texted Savage asking if he wants to take me on a ride on his motorcycle."

"Be safe."

"I always use protection."

"I meant wear a helmet," I laughed.

"I will." She hugged me. "I've only had like a glass and a half of wine and I won't drink any more tonight, so if you call, I'll be available."

"That's sweet. But I'm fine. I swear."

We were standing in the foyer and I was about to open the front door for Charlie when I heard the rumble of a motorcycle down the block.

"Did you tell Savage to pick you up here?" I asked.

She slid into her boots. "No."

"Then who—Bones? No. There's no way it's Bones."

"You know anyone else who rides a motorcycle who's been to your house?"

"But why is he here? And we don't even know for sure if it's him."

The rumbling of the motorcycle drew closer until it sounded just outside my house. Charlie opened the front door.

"It's Bones," she said to me. "Seems like someone else is catching feelings."

"Oh, go away," I groused.

Charlie stepped out as Bones was coming up the walkway, carrying a plastic grocery bag. The porch light illuminated his tall, rugged form.

"Charlie," Bones greeted.

"Bones," Charlie returned in the same tone.

"You don't call?" I asked him. "I could've been out."

"I took a shot that you were home." He shrugged. "Plus, I was worried that if I asked to see you tonight even though we spent all afternoon together, you'd make up an excuse because you like me and you don't want to like me."

Charlie looked at me. "He's got you pegged."

"Not yet, but here's hoping," Bones quipped.

Charlie laughed. "You're good for her. I approve."

"Okay, *bye* Charlie. Have fun tonight," I said.

"I always do." She saluted and then skipped to her car.

"I like her," Bones said. He looked over his shoulder at Charlie who was still sitting in the driveway, the car not even turned on. "Is she going to leave?"

"She's waiting to see if I let you in."

"She and I both."

With a sigh, I reluctantly stepped back and waved him inside. I closed the door behind him. He held out the plastic bag to me. "This is for you."

I took the bag and peered into it. "You brought me loose leaf tea?"

"It's supposed to help you sleep. Logan has trouble sleeping and swears by this tea."

I swallowed. "Oh."

He rubbed the back of his neck. "Anyway. I'll see you Wednesday, then?"

"Wednesday." I nodded.

Bones made a move to leave.

"Wait," I called out.

He looked at me over his shoulder.

"You want to stay? For a bit?"

"Do you want me to stay because you're afraid to fall asleep alone, or because you actually want me here?"

I lifted the bag. "You've done this before."

"Done what before? Brought a woman tea to help her sleep? I haven't done that before."

"No, I meant—never mind."

"Never mind what?"

"You've done this before. The relationship thing."

"We're in a relationship?" Bones raised his brows.

I sighed. "Thanks for the tea. You can go now."

"Nope. You asked me to stay. And I'm still waiting on the answer to the question I asked you."

"Which is?"

"Do you want me to stay because you're afraid to fall asleep alone, or because you actually want me here?" he repeated. "I get it, Duchess. You've got walls and you're trying not to let them come crumbling down. But I came here with the tea because I care about you. So just tell me the truth."

I sighed. "You're a good sport, Bones. What you're doing for me…I want you to stay because I want you to stay. I like being around you and that's very unusual for me. I don't…with men and I…I like you."

Bones' smile was slow. "Was that so hard?"

"Like pulling teeth," I muttered.

He let out a laugh as he stepped away from the door toward the stairs. He sat down and began to remove his boots.

"Where was Charlie running off to?" Bones asked, rising.

"She was going to meet Savage."

"You sure that's a good idea?"

"What's that supposed to mean?" I walked to the kitchen, Bones trailing me. "I'm hanging out with a biker. She can't hang out with a biker?"

"Savage is…*Savage*."

"Yeah, I don't know what that means."

"It means that if you don't want Charlie to get hurt, you won't let him near her."

"Charlie won't get hurt," I assured him. I set the grocery bag onto the kitchen island and then went to fill the kettle with water. "And why are you warning Charlie away, but you're not warning me away?"

"If you wanted to cut and run, you would."

"We're not even together," I said in exasperation.

"We're not?" He frowned. "How do you figure?"

"Because we barely know each other."

"We're getting to know each other," he pointed out. "And we both said we're not sleeping with other people."

"That doesn't mean we're sleeping with each other."

"Yet."

I sighed. "I'm too tired for the mental gymnastics."

"Mental, now there's a word."

I glared at him.

"We're taking it slow, Duchess."

"Taking it slow…but we've both admitted that we're not sleeping with other people. That basically means we're monogamous."

"You don't want to be monogamous?"

"Of course I want to be monogamous."

He let out a long sigh. "Do you think I volunteer to wear tuxedos for just anyone?"

"I don't know what you'd volunteer to do because I don't know you."

"Back to that, huh?"

"You're a biker."

"We've established that, yeah. I think your excuses for keeping me at arm's length are getting kinda flimsy. You want me. Just admit you want me. I'll wait."

"There's that arrogance I remember from the night I met you."

"And I remember the moment the lights turned on, you high-tailed it out of there."

"Play this forward for me," I said. "After this charity event, how do you envision this continuing?"

"Well, I imagine I'll like you even more then because I'll have spent more time with you, and so far, I really like what I've seen."

I moaned. "Bones."

"What? I was being honest."

"I haven't even met your friends yet. And you're talking like you want to keep me around for a while."

"You're meeting them at the wedding this weekend. You'll like them. Especially the Old Ladies. You already met Willa. You've got nothing to worry about."

"Odd choice of words," I said.

I opened a drawer and pulled out a loose-leaf tea strainer.

"Do me a favor, would you?" he asked.

"What?"

"Stop worrying about everything."

"Easier said than done."

"Well, try this. Just for tonight, drink your tea, we'll sit on the couch and you can make me watch one of your other favorite comfort movies. And then I'll put my boots back on and go home."

"Why do you like me, Bones? I mean, honestly. Don't you want to be around someone easier?"

"I've done easy."

I arched a brow.

He rolled his eyes. "I didn't mean it the way it sounded. I think about you when I'm not with you. You're different than I'm used to. Your world is different than I'm used to. I like a challenge."

"Oh, I see. It's the chase, right? As soon as I give in and sleep with you, you'll no longer be interested?"

"You're going to sleep with me?" He grinned. "*Hot dog.*"

My lips wavered and I finally cracked a smile. "Okay, okay, I take everything too seriously. I'll try and relax about…this."

"Orgasms help with relaxation."

I reached into the cabinet and pulled out two mugs. "So does tea."

Chapter 14

"Sit," Bones commanded, holding both cups of tea in his hands.

I sat on the couch and covered myself with a blanket and then Bones gave me a mug. He nestled in at the other end. "You can stretch out if you want."

My legs were curled up and I eased them out, my sock-clad feet grazing his jeans.

He took a sip of his tea and made a face. "That's disgusting."

"I added honey." I sipped on the tea. "What are you talking about? It's delicious."

"I'm not drinking this." He leaned over and set the mug onto the table.

"Charlie opened a bottle of wine earlier," I said. "It's the only alcohol I have, but you're welcome to it."

"Red or white?"

"A cabernet."

"That means nothing to me."

I grinned. "Red. Try it. See how you feel about it."

"Ah, I see. More rich people education?" He was teasing, but he did get up. "Fine, I'll try the wine, but I'm putting it in a mug out of principle."

A laugh escaped my lips. While I was queuing up a movie, Bones came back from the kitchen and sat down on the couch.

"Well?" I asked.

"I haven't tried it yet." He lifted the mug to his lips and took a sip. "Huh."

"Huh?"

"Not bad. Maybe I like wine."

"Maybe you do." I smiled. "And I know our next date isn't until Wednesday, but I'll give you a piece of advice when it comes to wine."

"I'm all ears."

"Make it up."

"What?"

"Make it up. You know when people swirl and sniff and taste and then pretend they know exactly what they're talking about? *Make it up*. Like cherry with hints of leather and tobacco and a subtle note of oak."

"Leather and tobacco? Seriously?"

"See? Ridiculous, right?"

"Rich people also eat a bunch of weird foods in weird sauces. Am I gonna eat weird foods in weird sauces at this restaurant you're taking me to on Wednesday?"

I fell silent as I tapped the rim of my mug.

"What?" he asked.

"I just had a thought."

"What's your thought?"

"Why don't we have dinner here," I said. "On Wednesday."

"Ashamed to be seen with me in public? I promise not to put the napkin in my shirt like a bib. Though we did that this afternoon and you were fine with it."

"No, I'm not ashamed," I assured him. "It's just—well, the places I'd take you to with all the silverware and china, you have to wear at least a sport coat. I'm guessing you don't have one of those in the back of your closet?"

"No, I definitely don't."

"Plus, it might be better to have our first dinner in private. You know, so if I have to correct you—"

"*When*. When you have to correct me."

I inclined my head. "I have the dining room. I have my grandmother's china. We can be informally formal."

"Fine by me. This is your rodeo." He took another sip of wine. "You sure I'm going to be ready for this thing? It's only a couple of weeks away."

"I have faith in you."

"I told my brothers about what I was doing…Viper said I should read Pygmalion. That mean anything to you?"

I grinned. "Yeah. It means something to me."

"Do I want to know?"

"Hmm. Hand me the remote. We're watching *My Fair Lady*. How do you feel about musicals?"

"Shoot me."

"How do you feel about Audrey Hepburn?"

～

"Hayden."

"Hmm," I murmured, my eyes closed.

"I'm gonna go," Bones said.

"What? Why?" I opened my eyes and found the movie paused just as Eliza Doolittle was regally coming down the stairs in her epic Edwardian dress.

"Because you're falling asleep. You'll be more comfortable in your own bed."

"But the movie…"

"We'll finish it another time."

"Stay," I blurted out.

He peered at me with bright blue eyes and ran a hand across his jaw. The rasp of his fingers against his stubble made my insides quiver.

"Stay," I repeated. "The night."

"If I stay that means I'll be here when you wake up," he warned.

"I know."

"It means I'm gonna see you in your pajamas."

I smiled slightly. "I'm already in my jammies."

"It means I'm gonna know if you snore."

"I don't snore!"

"Hmm. We'll see."

I got up off the couch and locked up the house and set the alarm. Bones followed me up the stairs. I didn't even consider offering him a guest bedroom.

My heart kicked into high gear when I pushed open my bedroom door and flipped on the light. The room was decorated in grays and greens. It was expansive, with a custom-built walk-in closet and a master bath that had a luxurious hotel feel.

"Nice," Bones said as he looked around.

"You want the bathroom first or—"

"Hey," he said.

I paused. "Hey."

"Nothing's gonna happen."

"Nothing's gonna happen?" I repeated with a frown. "What do you mean?"

"I mean we're brushing our teeth and getting into bed. And if you let me spoon you, I'll spoon you. That's it."

"I'm even more confused."

"You thought by asking me to stay, we were gonna fuck."

"No. I mean, yes. Maybe? I don't know, I just assumed that you'd want to—"

"I *do* want to. Fuck yeah, I want to." He took a step closer to me and gently cradled the back of my neck in his hand. "But until you're jumping into my arms, wrapping your legs around my waist and trying to climb me like a tree, then all we're doing is spooning."

I exhaled a shaky breath and nodded.

He leaned down and gently kissed my lips. "You use the bathroom first, yeah?"

"Okay."

I went into the bathroom and closed the door. I was behaving like a shy virgin, spooked every time she was touched. I wasn't a virgin, but I wasn't that experienced either.

And Bones…

He kissed like a man who had experience.

He kissed like he knew how to pleasure a woman.

He kissed like a conqueror who wanted his conquest to fall apart and shatter beneath him.

I would never be the same after I went to bed with him. Something inside me knew that. And if let him in, if I truly let him in, it would change me. And I wasn't sure I was ready to be changed.

After I did a quick nighttime routine, I opened the bathroom door. Bones was sitting on the edge of the bed, leaning over so his elbows rested on his thighs. He'd taken off his leather cut and his shirt.

"It's all yours," I said, flustered at the sight of his bare chest.

He unfolded himself and rose. "Thanks." He flashed a grin and sidled past me.

I walked to the bed and climbed into it and turned on the lamp. I pulled the covers up to my chin and stared at the ceiling for a moment, trying not to think about the big biker in my bathroom.

My gaze eventually wandered while I listened to the sound of the faucet. It landed on the nightstand on Bones' side of the bed.

It landed on his pistol.

An involuntary noise escaped my throat.

The bathroom door opened and he loomed in the doorway. He leaned against it, propping his forearm along the doorjamb.

"You look terrified," he stated. "The idea of me sleeping in your bed terrifies you?"

I shook my head. "No. It's…" I gestured with my chin to the pistol. "I wasn't expecting that."

His expression was passive. "The other men you've dated didn't have pistols?"

"I don't know. If they did, I didn't know about them. They certainly didn't sleep with them on the nightstand."

"If you need it, it doesn't do you any good in a drawer."

I paused. "That's a good point."

Bones pushed away from the doorframe and then killed the light. The lamp glow gilded him in shadow and amber.

He lifted the covers and slid in next to me.

I leaned over and turned off the lamp.

It was quiet except for the sounds of our breathing.

"My dad took me duck hunting once," I voiced.

"Did he?"

"Yeah. He taught me to use his shotgun and then we went a few days later."

"Yeah?"

"Yeah." I paused for a moment. "It's not about the pistol."

"It's about me."

"It's about you," I agreed.

"I am who I am, Duchess."

"And who is that, Bones?"

He was quiet for so long that I thought he might have fallen asleep, but his voice was a whispered promise. "A man who protects what's his."

Chapter 15

My cheek was pressed against something warm and hard.

Something unfamiliar.

My brain was mush, but my hand moved of its own volition and began exploring what was beneath me. I glided my fingers across skin and muscle, and yet I still refused to process the truth.

It wasn't until my hand came into contact with an erection and Bones let out a low groan that I realized I'd been groping him.

I flung myself off him, but in my state of panic I didn't realize the covers were tangled around me and I hit the floor with a resounding thud.

"Duchess? Are you okay?"

It was my turn to groan. "Yeah, I'm okay."

Morning sunlight streamed through the windows. I'd forgotten to close the curtains the previous night and now I was seeing Bones on display. Inches of rippling muscle and ink.

"Stop looking at me that way," he said, his voice husky and his eyes darkening with desire.

I bit my lower lip. "What way?"

"Like you want to lick me from head to toe."

A vivid picture formed in my head and refused to dislodge.

"Uh. Sorry about the groping. I forgot you were in bed with me."

"Never apologize for groping me. You can grope me anytime, anywhere." He raised his brows. "You getting up off the floor any time soon?"

"Oh. Yeah." I scrambled up, wincing when I put weight on my knee. "So, uh, did I have any nightmares last night?"

His gaze was intense. "Two. Do you remember what they were about?"

"Don't remember," I admitted. "Probably about the…" I made the sign of a gun. "Did I scream? Yell? Kick you?"

"You whimpered. You finally slept soundly around four when you threw yourself across my body and cuddled close to me."

I covered my mouth in embarrassment.

"Don't sweat it, Duchess. I liked being your emotional support animal." He flashed a grin, but it suddenly died.

"What?" I asked.

"You don't have any coffee."

"Oh. Yeah, I don't."

"I'm not gonna survive the day without coffee."

"Right. Well, thanks for…whatever this was. I'll see you Wednesday."

"You got plans today?"

I blinked at the rapid change in conversation. "Yeah, I have plans today."

"Cancel them. I'll take you for a ride on my motorcycle."

"Tempting, but I can't cancel plans."

"It's not work," he said. "So, blow it off."

"How do you know it's not work?"

"You didn't set an alarm."

"So?"

"So, if it was work, wouldn't you set an alarm?" he asked.

"I have a good internal alarm clock."

"*Do* you work?"

"I—no. I don't work," I admitted.

"What do you do with your days? How do you fill your time?"

"Lots of ways. I brunch, I shop, I—"

"Bullshit."

"Bullshit? Why are you calling bullshit?"

He still hadn't moved from the bed and instead of getting up, like he had originally intended, he fell back against the pillows and situated his forearm underneath his head. "I call bullshit because in the short time I've known you, you've never pretended to be shallow. So, I know you don't fill your time with useless shit. Be honest, what do you actually do?"

"What do *you* do?" I demanded. "You didn't set an alarm either. Doesn't seem like you have anywhere to be."

"I work at night."

"Doing what?" I pressed, my hands on my hips.

"Security for Chaos…and a few other things."

My gaze narrowed. "What *other things*?"

"Things."

"You want me to blow off my day to spend time with you, but you can't be honest about what things you're involved in?"

"Club things."

"Vague things." I sauntered past the bed toward the bathroom. "I'm taking a shower. I'll see you Wednesday."

Before I could get two steps, Bones launched himself off the bed, grasped my arms and hauled me toward him. I landed on top of his hard, warm body, but he wouldn't let me stay there. Instead, he rolled us over, pinning my arms above my head. He stared down at me and then his gaze landed on my mouth.

"How can you be this sassy without any caffeine?" he asked.

"Practice."

His lips crushed mine in a devastating kiss.

My fingers curled and my body softened. I cradled him in the V of my thighs.

He was hard and ready, and it made my blood pump though my veins. All rational thought fled my brain and my hormones were suddenly in control.

And they wanted Bones inside me.

Deep.

Hard.

Now.

Bones lifted his mouth and pressed his forehead to mine. He gently released my wrists, freeing me.

My hands wandered down his toned back and then rested on the curves of his ass. I urged him closer, and he shifted. And even with my layer of clothes between us, I felt him at the juncture of my thighs.

"Duchess," he growled.

"Bones," I whispered, lifting up and peppering his jaw with tiny kisses.

"We can't."

"Why not?"

"Because you're not ready."

"I'm ready," I insisted.

I thought he was going to kiss me again, but disappointment ricocheted through me when he lifted himself off me.

"Take a shower," he instructed. "You'll feel differently after you shower."

I looked at him in confusion.

His gaze softened as he leaned forward and cradled the back of my head. "I know you don't understand. And that's why we're not doing this. Not yet. You just went through something traumatic and you don't trust me."

My eyes drifted to his erection. "I trust you."

"Fuck, you're killing me, Duchess. What's changed from last night to this morning?"

"I don't know."

"Then nothing's actually changed. And when your head clears, you'll realize that." He kissed me briefly. "It's probably a good idea if you don't blow off your day to spend time with me. I won't be able to keep my hands to myself."

"This better not be a game," I said quietly. "You'd better not be stringing me along, playing hot and cold until I beg you to sleep with me and the moment I do, you're gone."

"This isn't a fucking game, Duchess. And if it was all about fucking, it would've happened the night we met."

I glared at him. "Arrogant."

"Confident." His gaze narrowed. "This isn't a game."

"Then what is it?"

"Something more," he muttered.

I swallowed. "Maybe you *should* go."

"Yeah, I should." He rose from the bed.

I curled my knees up to my chest and watched him slowly

put on his clothes and pick up his pistol. With each piece of clothing, he donned the armor of being a biker. Gone was the man who'd held me through nightmares I didn't remember.

"What time Wednesday?" he asked.

"Seven."

He nodded once and then he was gone.

∼

After I made another love match between a terrier mix and a sweet elderly widow, I met Charlie at our favorite sushi restaurant.

"I think I'm in over my head," I said to her the moment we sat down.

She frowned. "Why's that?"

"He shows up on my doorstep last night with tea to help me sleep. And then he stayed the night because I asked, and this morning he said he wasn't going to sleep with me until I was ready."

"Normally, I'd say steer clear because this is like total love-bombing. However…"

"However?"

Before she had a chance to reply, the server arrived. We ordered quickly, getting the same thing we always got. As soon as the server left, I repeated, "However?"

"However, Savage said something to me last night—and I don't think he knew what he was saying. It was a throwaway comment, but it kinda stuck with me."

"Well, don't keep me hanging," I said, reaching for my decaf green tea.

"He said his brothers have been falling like dominoes," she said slowly.

"I don't follow."

"Like, falling in love or whatever. Finding their Old Ladies. And Old Ladies? Who wants to be called old?"

"Okay," I said. "That's not really anything to be concerned about."

She sighed. "I know. But it was like, the *way* he said it. Like one day his brothers were all going along, happy as you please, nailing anything that walked, and then the next moment they were in love and making commitments and stuff. He said he didn't think he'd live to see the day that Bones would fall for someone and then he started singing 'Another One Bites the Dust.'"

"It's not love," I insisted. "That's crazy. This is infatuation on both ends."

I thought about how intense it had gotten this morning. Bones had been wrong, though. After my shower, I'd still wanted him. But it was definitely a relief that he hadn't been there when I'd gotten out.

My head was all screwed up over it.

"Yeah, infatuation," she drawled.

"Don't say it like you don't believe me."

"I've never seen you this way."

"What way is that?"

"When you were with Tyler, it was like you were there, but you weren't really *there*. You weren't invested. Not the way you are with Bones."

"Invested how?" I demanded.

"I don't know. You just look…you look like you can't stop thinking about him. Like you're thinking about the next time you're going to see him even though we're having a conversation."

"I'm seeing him Wednesday night for dinner."

"And then he's taking you to a wedding. A *wedding*. He's a biker, Hayden. Do you think bikers take random women to weddings of their club brothers?"

"I don't know what they do."

"Savage didn't ask me to go," she said.

"Are you upset about that?"

"No. Because I don't *want* to go to a wedding with him. And he has no interest in going to one with me."

My phone rang and my stupid heart leapt. I hoped it was Bones.

Damn it.

I fished the cell out of my purse and saw a number I didn't recognize. I immediately silenced it.

"Not Bones?" she asked.

I sighed. "Not Bones."

"You seem sad about that."

"Shut up, Charlie."

Chapter 16

"Wasn't there a time when we didn't talk about boys?" Charlie asked as she polished off the last of the spicy tuna sashimi.

"Yeah, I think we were in diapers," I muttered.

"Kingston Caldwell. My first crush," Charlie said. "I was five. He told me to eat dirt and then I tackled him on the playground."

I thought about Bones tackling me this morning and my blood instantly heated.

Not much had changed through the years, I realized.

"Have you given it any more thought?" Charlie inquired. "The charity, I mean."

"Charity? What charity?"

"The one you're going to start," she stated. "Find your furry soul mate, or whatever."

"That sounds like a weird, kinky hook-up app for furries."

"Don't knock it until you've tried it," Charlie said.

I looked at her. "*Really?*"

"I'm an explorer." She shrugged. "I've actually been thinking about it a lot."

"The furry thing?"

She rolled her eyes. "You make *one* joke. No. About your charity."

"It's not my charity."

"I know, but it should become one. And I've been noodling on a business plan."

"You have?" I asked in surprise.

She nodded. "Yeah. It's like a puzzle I'm trying to put together. Still surprised my brain isn't entirely useless mush, but the oddest thing happened. When I fed my brain a piece of information, it jump-started like a computer. Fascinating stuff, the brain."

"You downplay it so well, Charlie," I said with a laugh.

"What do you think, though? If I could get a plan together, would you at least look at it?"

"I definitely will."

Bones had asked me what I did for work. And I didn't have a good answer for him. I spent my time how I wanted. It was a luxury most people never had. I realized that.

It did make me wonder what he did, though. There were so many things we didn't know about each other, things we'd eventually learn if we chose to continue spending time with one another.

And that line of thinking brought it all back to what Charlie had mentioned.

Most people I knew didn't marry for love. They married for convenience, money, and business. My mother and father had married for love, but they'd come from a similar background. They weren't fighting an uphill battle to be together.

"Are your parents happy together?" I asked her suddenly.

"I think so. Why do you ask?"

"Just thinking."

"About…"

"About marriage. And love. And how it's hard even if you don't have the deck stacked against you."

"The divorce rate is close to sixty percent now if you're twenty-five or under," she said.

"That's a lot."

"It's not very comforting, that's for sure." She paused. "Your parents were stupidly happy."

"Grossly happy." I smiled softly. "They definitely were not the norm."

"Your mom and Arnold are happy, though. Right?"

"I think they are. But I wonder sometimes, you know? They've known each other for a long time. Maybe it's just familiarity."

"Maybe," she agreed. "You're thinking about Bones, aren't you?"

"I guess."

"And you're wondering if you have a shot in hell of making this work long term."

"There is no shot in hell," I said quietly. "There's no way at all this actually works. And it's too soon to even be thinking about something like that."

"It's never too soon," she said. "This is what we do. You get that, right?"

"I didn't think about it with Tyler. I mean, I guess I didn't really have to because it was supposed to work out. It was supposed to be graduation and a ring on the finger, a big house, and babies for my mother. My life was supposed to look so different than it does now."

"Regrets?"

"No." I frowned. "I thought we were solid and sure. I thought he was steadfast. I thought he'd be the rock the ocean waves crashed against in a storm." I let out a small laugh.

"What?"

"Nothing, just—with enough force, rock turns to sand."

∾

The scent of sugar and caramel hit me the moment I stepped into Pie in the Sky. I took a deep breath and savored the aromas. Normally, I didn't begrudge my inability to partake in sweets, but today, I resented the hell out of it.

It was my own fault, for going into the land of temptation.

"We just got Fluffernutter to stop peeing on the bathmat. You really think we're ready for another dog?" Jazz asked Brielle as she moved the glass jar of espresso beans and cleaned underneath it on the counter.

"I think our dog needs a dog," Brielle insisted as she closed the bakery display window. She looked up and saw me. "Hayden!"

I smiled. "Hey."

"Are you meeting Bones here?" Jazz asked.

I shook my head. "Willa, actually."

"Oh. Well, great. What can I get you?"

"Just an herbal tea. Surprise me."

"That's it?" Jazz asked. "I just took the goat cheese, lavender, and fig galettes out of the oven. If you wait for them to cool, I'll be glad to bring you one."

"I just had sushi with Charlie," I said. "So I'm full. But thanks for the offer."

Brielle went for a tin canister of tea leaves. "So, how's it going?"

"It's going well," I said.

"I mean between you and Bones." She grinned.

"It's…going."

"That doesn't sound very exciting," Jazz said as Brielle handed her the tea ball. Jazz placed it in a mug and filled it with hot water from the electric kettle that rested on the counter.

"Why is everyone obsessed with my love life?" I asked. "My mother, Charlie, now you guys."

They exchanged a look and then Jazz ventured to say, "Well, because it's kind of fascinating."

"Definitely fascinating," Brielle agreed. "You're you, and Bones is *Bones* and we're all just curious how this is going to shake out."

"We all *who*?" I demanded.

"Well, us," Jazz said. "And the Old Ladies. The club. Everyone, really."

"Wait," I began. "The Old Ladies know about me? The club knows about me?"

"Bones asked you to go to the wedding. Of course they know about you," Jazz said.

"How do you know about the wedding?" I asked.

"We're catering it," Brielle responded.

"So, everyone knows my business?"

"Kinda," Jazz said. "But not really. Not details. So, give us the details!"

I snorted. "So you guys can talk about it when I'm not around?"

The door to the bakery opened and Willa strode inside.

"Is everyone talking about me and Bones?" I asked Willa in way of greeting.

"Of course," Willa said.

"What do you mean *of course*?"

Willa looked at Brielle and then Jazz. "Hi guys."

"Hello," Jazz said. "Usual?"

"Please." Willa removed her jacket. "It's hot in here."

"Oven," Brielle stated.

"Hmm. What do I smell? Fig?"

"Yep," Jazz said. "Brooklyn's newest addition."

"I thought she wasn't coming back for a few more weeks," Willa said.

Brielle re-tied her apron. "She didn't. She made the recipe at home. We went over to her house the other day and she showed us how to make it."

Willa laughed. "I wondered how she was going to get around not being involved. She still balking at hiring someone in the interim while she's out?"

"Kind of," Brielle said. "But I'm putting the screws to her. I want to get back to decorating wedding cakes. Being an administrative assistant and appointment girl for my brothers is not doing it for me."

"Hmm," Willa murmured.

"Your tea's done brewing," Jazz said, handing me my mug.

"I'll bring over some goodies for you," Brielle said to Willa.

"Thanks." Willa looked at me. "Corner table?"

I nodded and followed her toward the back window. The café was quiet this time of day. She sat and I set my mug down before I removed my jacket and hung it on the back of the chair.

"So, people are talking about me and Bones," I said, wanting to pick up the thread of our earlier conversation.

"Yes. Well, the brothers aren't. I mean, they might be…I don't know. Duke and Savage are gossips." She grinned. "But the Old Ladies and I are taking about it. They can't wait to meet you at the wedding."

"Why is that?" I asked.

"Because the idea of you is utterly fascinating," she said. "The new girl is always the talk of the town."

"New girl?"

"Yeah." She paused. "How do I say this without freaking you the fuck out?"

"Well, that's not a good way to start," I huffed.

She smiled softly. "These men, they kind of…do things their own way."

"Okay?"

"When they see something they want, they go after it."

"Okay."

"They *know*."

"Know what?"

"They know when they've found the woman they want for the rest of their lives."

"Oh," I said quietly. "Yeah, Charlie might've mentioned that to me."

She raised her brows. "Charlie did?"

I nodded. "She's been…hanging out with Savage."

"I know."

"You do?"

"Savage is my best friend. I've known him and Duke since we were nine years old. Savage tells me everything. Well, not *everything*. He doesn't kiss and tell. He's actually a gentleman in that area. Anyway, Savage told Charlie?"

"To tell me," I said. "Almost like a warning about Bones."

"Huh."

"Charlie and Savage aren't anything but casual. She has no interest in falling in love."

"Good." She let out a sigh of relief. "Because neither

does Savage. Frankly, I'm not sure he's even wired for it. He's left a lot of women brokenhearted thinking that they'll be the one to change that. They're always so surprised when he lets them down. They're usually not even mad at him when he does it because he's honest about his intentions. It's crazy, actually."

"Crazy," I agreed.

"Well, I'm glad then. For Charlie's sake. I wouldn't want her to get hurt."

"Her heart is coated in steel," I stated. "She's not interested in love."

"Are you interested in love?"

"Oh, and look at that. We're back to talking about me."

Jazz briefly interrupted by bringing Willa a huge coffee with whipped cream and caramel syrup and a plate of assorted baked goods.

"Delish," Willa said with a sigh.

"I made it decaf," Jazz said.

"Thanks." Willa shot her a smile.

Jazz looked at me. "You good?"

"I'm good."

"The tea?"

"Still too hot to taste."

"Let me know," she said, and then left.

"You didn't call me to talk about Bones," I said.

She shook her head. "No, that's just a fun little byproduct. You still haven't answered though."

"About what?"

"About what I said. And how these men, these bikers, know quickly if they want a woman to be *their* woman."

"So, his behavior," I said slowly. "Can I trust it? Can I trust him? He's not love-bombing me?"

Willa shook her head. "No."

"So, when he says he's not playing games, he really means it?"

"He means it."

My brow furrowed. "You've given me a lot to think about."

"I'm going to say one more thing and then I'll hold my tongue, okay?"

"Okay."

"I know you guys come from different backgrounds. You're, well…ya know."

My lips flickered. "Yeah, I know."

"And he's…not. I know on the outside it looks like this'll never work. But don't let that be the reason you don't give this a shot. If you don't see him in your future, well, that's a different story. But don't look for reasons to say no."

"There are so many reasons to say no," I said quietly. "And not just because of the background thing. How would we even build a life together? I couldn't even figure out how to do that with someone from my own world— and that made sense."

"Did it? Because if it did, you'd be with that guy. Right now."

I let out a long breath. "Insightful."

"I don't know you. Not really. But if you pay attention, people show you who they really are. And I think you're one of the good ones. So is Bones. Sometimes we have to stop looking at our lives through the lenses of what *makes sense*. Has making sense made you happy?"

She placed her hand on her belly.

"No. It hasn't made me happy. It hasn't made me *unhappy*, but I've definitely been in limbo."

"Only you can decide if you're ready to let someone in and see you."

"It's terrifying."

"Yep."

"It's a huge risk."

"Definitely. But if your life looks just like it does now for the next fifty years, will it be enough for you? If the answer is no, then you have to decide if you're willing to chance heartbreak for the gamble that it all might pay off."

I swallowed. "He sleeps with a pistol on the nightstand."

"He carries it on him during the day," she pointed out.

"Yeah. But I saw it last night. And it…it was a realization."

"That he's not playing at being a biker, he's an actual biker?"

I nodded.

She smiled. "Yeah, they're not playing at being bad boys."

"Bad boys," I repeated. "I've never dated a bad boy."

"The trick is to find a bad boy who will fuck up anyone that tries to hurt you, but one who'd never hurt you himself. A bad boy that sees you as the center of his entire world." Her eyes grew misty. "A bad boy who promises you everything and actually delivers. That's the secret to falling in love with a bad boy."

"Scary enough to slay dragons and demons, but not become something I have to slay myself."

"Something like that," she said.

"I'm glad you called."

"I tried to give it a few days. I didn't want to crowd you while you sorted through stuff."

"I haven't sorted anything at all," I replied.

"I meant about the gunman."

"Right. Wow. That happened, didn't it?"

"It did."

"How are you doing with it all? I mean, you were the one who…"

"I pulled the trigger. I did the right thing. But it doesn't mean I sleep soundly." She shook her head. "But I've got a man who pulls me into his arms and holds me while I fall apart. And then he helps me pick up the pieces. And that is truly priceless."

Chapter 17

There was a shift change at the bakery and Jazz and Brielle grabbed two cups of coffee and joined me and Willa.

"You guys were talking about getting another dog when I came in," I said.

"We found this rescue," Brielle explained. "And we kind of time share him with my brother Homer who lives in the same building. But with the hours we work, I don't think Fluffernutter should be home by himself. It just seems mean."

"He's never alone longer than four hours," Jazz said. "Another dog is a lot of responsibility. Can't we get a cat?"

"No," Brielle stated. "No cats. Kittens are cute, but they turn into cats eventually, and cats jump up on counters and you have to spray them with a spray bottle."

"And they claw up furniture," Willa added.

"Fine, no cat. But we need to discuss why you want another dog," Jazz said.

"I told you. Our dog needs a dog," Brielle said.

Jazz raised her brows. "I think we need to dig a little deeper here."

Brielle rolled her eyes. "We don't have to dig deeper. I'm shallow. There's nothing to this."

"A puppy is not a substitute for a romantic relationship," Jazz said.

"I know that." Brielle sighed. "Although I would *very much* like a boyfriend…"

"Are there any single bikers?" I asked.

"A few," Willa said. "Raze, Kelp, Crow, Acid, and Savage. But don't go there with Savage. I love him, but I love you too. So don't do that."

"Plus, he's kind of hooking up with Charlie—or something. Not sure exactly what's going on there, but… yeah…" I said.

"I will not be going there with any of them," Brielle said, looking from me to Willa. "No offense."

"None taken," Willa said lightly.

"Why did you look at me?" I asked.

"Because you're with Bones," Brielle stated. "And before you say you're not, you *so* are, so let's just move on, okay?"

"Brielle has this thing against bikers," Jazz added.

"Not a thing *against* them per se, but my brothers don't want me getting involved with the club," she said. "Which is stupid since they tattoo all the Tarnished Angels anyway. *Okay for me but not for thee* kind of thing."

"Willa says a bad boy is the way to go," I said with a smirk at her.

Brielle groaned. "Don't tell me that. I'm already trying to talk myself out of the idea."

"Why talk yourself out of the idea?" Jazz asked. "They're both clearly satisfied with their bad boys. You should get one of those for yourself."

"Whoa." I held up a hand. "I'm not satisfied. We haven't even slept together yet."

The table fell silent.

"Damn it," I muttered. "You baited me on purpose, didn't you?"

Jazz had the grace to look sheepish. "I really wanted to know."

"We're taking it slow," I muttered.

"We?" Brielle asked.

I glanced at Willa who was sipping on the remainder of her coffee. "Feel free to jump in here?"

She shook her head. "I'm just part of the peanut gallery."

"The peanut gallery always has something to say," I pointed out.

"So, he slept over," Jazz said. "And nothing happened?"

"Do you really think I'm going to have this conversation out in the open?" I asked.

"Bones taking it slow," Brielle said quietly. "Didn't think he had it in him."

"Yeah, he seems kinda…" Jazz trailed off. "What's the word I'm looking for?"

"Hungry?" Brielle supplied.

"Yeah, hungry." Jazz nodded. "Definitely *hungry*."

"Hungry for a Hayden snack. Yup." Brielle finished off the last bite of her fig galette.

"Are your coffees spiked?" I inquired, feeling my cheeks heat.

Maybe I was a frigid prude after all.

"Don't get embarrassed," Jazz said.

"This is what they do," Willa said. "Call it initiation."

"Initiation into what?" I asked warily.

"Our friend group," Brielle said.

The cold feeling in my chest suddenly morphed into warmth. I sighed. "Initiation, huh?"

Brielle nodded.

"You're in the club," Jazz said. "Might as well go with it."

My throat constricted and I wanted to focus on something else. "Show me a picture of your dog."

∼

Willa's words chased me all the way home.

But it didn't matter what she'd said.

I had to listen to my own gut instinct.

And my gut instinct was telling me that Bones was showing me exactly who he was. He'd brought me tea to help me sleep. He'd stayed the night because I asked, and he hadn't taken advantage of me even though this morning he absolutely could have.

But he'd been right. I hadn't been ready.

I hadn't been ready in three years, but I was ready now. I wanted him. I wanted to feel the weight of him on top of me. I wanted to feel him slide into me and make me moan.

No longer concerned about how it would come across, I pressed a button on my steering wheel, enabling the Bluetooth call function on my car.

"Call Bad to the Bones."

I snorted.

"Calling Bad to the Bones," the automated voice chimed.

It rang twice and went to voicemail.

"Bones, hey. It's—uh—Hayden. Hi. Yep. Said that already. Okay, well, call me."

I hung up.

"Seriously?" I muttered to myself.

I pulled into my driveway and pressed a button to open my garage door. As I was parking, my phone rang.

It was Bones.

My heart immediately tripped with nerves. Which was stupid. I needed to get out of my head.

"What kind of coffee do you drink?" I asked in way of greeting.

He paused. "Anything dark and bold. You okay, Duchess? You sound a little…"

"A little what?"

"Frazzled."

"I'm not frazzled. I was just wondering if…"

"Wondering if…what?"

"Wondering if you were coming over tonight?" The words felt stilted and stuck in my throat.

He paused again. "Are you asking me to come over tonight?"

"Can't you answer a simple question?" I demanded.

"Can't you?"

"Are you smiling? I can hear you smiling."

He chuckled. "I can come over, but it'll be late. I've got some business to handle tonight."

I thought of his pistol on the nightstand.

"What time will you be done?" I asked.

"Not sure. Late. After midnight."

I bit my lip. "Then maybe I'll just see you tomorrow night. For dinner."

"All right," he said easily.

"Bones," I muttered.

"What? I'm being agreeable. What is it you want? Ask, Duchess."

"Bring a toothbrush tomorrow." I hung up quickly, my heart pounding hard enough I felt it in my neck.

I waited to see if he'd call back.

He didn't.

I backed out of the garage and went to buy a coffee maker.

Chapter 18

I straightened a salad fork just as the doorbell rang.

My heart leapt into my throat and excitement swirled in my belly.

I straightened my spine and went to answer the door.

The sight of Bones packed a punch to my stomach.

He seemed taller and broader every time I saw him.

He was devastating.

His blue eyes raked over me as a slight smile curved his lips. "Duchess."

"Hi," I greeted, stepping back to let him in.

He entered the foyer, standing close enough that his leather cut brushed my chest. Without a word, he grasped the back of my neck and lowered his mouth to mine.

My hands gripped his lapels and I sank into him.

His tongue slid between my lips and with his other hand, he clasped my hip and pulled me closer.

Sparks of desire erupted between my legs and just as I was in danger of collapsing and saying to hell with dinner, Bones released me.

My eyes fluttered open and Bones was staring down at me.

"You hungry?" I asked.

"Starving," he rumbled.

Yeah, we both know he isn't talking about food.

I licked my lips. "Shoes off, please."

The heat of his desire banked into embers. It would take very little to stoke it into flames once again.

Bones sat on the stairs as he removed his boots.

"You can take off your cut, too," I said. "Get more comfortable. If you want."

He rose and without taking his eyes off me, slowly removed his leather cut. Now that his lips weren't on mine, I noticed what he was wearing. A black button-down shirt, and a pair of jeans that weren't faded or molded to his body from years of being worn.

"You look nice." I took his leather cut and walked to the coat closet and hung it up.

"You don't like it."

"Like what?" I asked.

"How I'm dressed."

"I just said you looked nice," I pointed out. "But I was expecting you how I always expect you. A bit more relaxed. That's all."

He fell silent.

"This is the part where you tell me I look nice," I said, trying to lighten the mood, wondering why it had darkened to begin with.

"You don't look nice."

"Well, that's rude—"

"You look sexy as fuck," he stated. "And I don't know how I'm supposed to keep my hands off you during dinner."

Heat bloomed on my cheeks.

I was wearing a pair of perfectly fitted Japanese denim jeans in dark blue with a purposefully oversized green Vicuña wool sweater that fell off one shoulder. I'd dressed down, even though the dinner was a mockup of what the charity gala would be like.

"Okay that's a better compliment than the one I gave you," I admitted with a smile.

"You have the whole dinner to make it up to me. Maybe you can start by paying homage to my fine attributes."

"Fine attributes. Give me a few ideas about what these fine attributes are," I teased.

"First, I have the jaw." He rubbed his chin. "And my hair. Have you seen my hair?"

"I've seen your hair. If we slowed down a video of you shaking your head from side to side, you'd be a regular shampoo commercial."

"Let's not forget my manly pecs." He puffed out his chest. "You should feel them. I can make them dance."

I couldn't hold it in anymore. I started to laugh, and the tenseness I had felt earlier began to dissolve.

Bones looped an arm around me and hugged me to him. "There she is."

"There who is?" I asked.

"The woman I'm getting to know. You were so formal when you answered the door. I didn't know if you were playing a part for the evening, or if you were hiding behind a veneer."

"Hmm. You're a good judge of character," I stated. "It'll come in handy the night of the gala. Come on, I promised I'd feed you."

"Did you cook?" he asked.

"You're asking if I cooked a three-course meal?"

"Yeah, that's what I'm asking."

"You're adorable." I grinned up at him. "No. I hired a chef and server for the evening."

He raised his brows. "You did?"

I bit my lip. "Now might be the time to tell you that I normally have a chef, but that she had a family emergency. So, really the only reason you haven't met her yet is because she's been gone and I've been on my own for a little while."

"A private chef," he repeated slowly.

I swallowed. "I have a housekeeper, too."

"What, no butler?" he joked.

"Stanton still works for my mother."

He paused. "You're serious? You grew up with a butler?"

"Yeah."

"And his name is Stanton?"

"Yep."

"He's British, isn't he?"

"Yeaaaaah."

"Fuck, you really are out of my league, aren't you? I mean, I guess a fifteen-thousand-dollar tux should've tipped me off, but this makes it really sink in for some reason." His tone was light, but it was just another reminder of the worries that I had about having a long-term relationship with him.

"Let me show you to the dining room," I said finally.

He dropped his arm and followed me. There were two place settings, one at the head of the table and the other just to the right of that setting.

"Damn. How many glasses do rich people need?" he joked.

I smiled. "You'll want this many glasses, trust me. The wine helps the conversation go down."

"Okay, I'm ready to learn how not to be a heathen."

Bones wiped his mouth with the black cloth napkin and set it in his lap. Celeste cleared away the salad plates and took them into the kitchen. The swinging door closed, giving Bones and I privacy.

"Not bad," he said.

I arched a brow.

"Fine, I liked it, okay?" He grinned and reached for his glass of white wine.

"I knew you would."

Even though Bones was rough around the edges, I liked having him at my formal dining room table. He wasn't put off by anything I was throwing at him. In fact, he was attentive and had listened intently, nodding along, answering correctly when I'd quizzed him on something I'd taught him.

"So, what were you doing last night?" I asked. "You were kind of vague on the phone."

"I was vague on purpose."

"Oh." I frowned. "Why?"

"Your world has rules, and so does mine," he began slowly. "And I was handling some business for the club. I can't tell you what it was because we don't involve our women in our business."

"Our *women*?" I asked.

He cocked his head to the side. "You know what I mean."

"No, I don't actually. I mean, I think I get where you're going with it, but maybe you should be more specific."

"Don't get caught up on what I said. We don't include women in club business. Our women or other women."

"All right. But what does club business even mean?"

"It means when I say club business, you don't ask questions."

"Uh, that's not gonna work for me."

The swinging door opened, and Celeste entered with our entrees, a filet mignon for Bones and scallops for me. Lisa poured Bones another glass of white wine and the two of them discreetly left.

Tension loomed in the air between us.

I couldn't take my eyes off him.

"We don't include women in club business for their own protection," he said finally.

"Hold on, let me see if I can piece together what you're really saying. You don't include women in club business for their own protection because that means you're involved in something that they need to be protected *from*."

He sighed. "This is the problem with dating a smart woman."

"Don't," I clipped. "Don't joke. This is serious. You've got to give me something here. Some sort of explanation that I can wrap my head around."

"Duchess, I'm sitting at your dining room table, letting you school me on napkin placement and which fucking fork I need to use so I don't embarrass us at this charity event. The least you can do is not bust my balls and ask about what the hell I'm involved in. When I say it's for your own best interest not to ask questions, you need to trust that."

Blood roared in my ears. "First of all, I didn't ask you to go to the charity event. You volunteered. You're here of your own free will. Second, no woman in their right mind would just accept a blanket statement of *we don't include women in club business for their own protection* and call it a day. I've got to be out of my mind for ever entertaining this idea. Thank God I've come to my senses." I rose. "I'll go to the gala alone."

"You don't know what the hell you want, Duchess. One minute, you're begging me to fuck you. The next you're ready to shove me out the door because you don't like being reminded that I'm a biker."

"I didn't beg you to fuck me."

"Revisionist history." He rose from his chair with such force that he knocked it to the floor. "You know what the fuck I think?"

"No, and I don't care," I snapped. "You can leave."

He ignored me when he placed his large hands on the table and leaned forward. "I think you know exactly what you want, but you're too damn chicken shit to admit it. I think you're tired of men from your mother's circle. I think if they really knew how to fuck you, you wouldn't be slumming it with me. But I make you *feel* and that scares the ever-loving shit out of you. And I think you don't have the balls to admit that I'm all wrong for you and that's exactly what you're looking for."

"Oh, so you have me all figured out, do you? Bones, the Hayden Whisperer, huh? Is that your new title?"

"Duchess, you need a good fuck to clear out all the cobwebs. You're so damn in your head, you don't even know how to lead with your heart."

We stared at each other, the words we'd hurled hanging between us. He was breathing hard and his cheeks were flushed.

And then I was suddenly in his arms, my legs wrapped around his waist. His lips were on mine and his tongue plunged into my mouth.

He carried me to the other end of the table and lay me down on top of it. He bent over and kept kissing me, the anger and fear turning into molten lust.

"I've got to touch you," he murmured against my mouth. "If I don't touch you, I'm gonna go insane."

"Yes," I whispered. "Touch me. Please."

His hand slid down between us to rest at the apex of my thighs. His eyes were lit with hunger and determination.

Just as his fingers began to play with the button of my jeans, the door to the dining room opened.

"Oh!" squeaked Celeste. "I was coming to see how you liked your dinner. I'll just…yeah. Leave you to it then." She immediately departed.

We froze and looked at one another, and then suddenly we both laughed. Bones lifted himself off me and gave me space.

"Guess we both lost our heads," I said.

"Guess so." He reached for his glass of wine and brought it toward his mouth.

I nibbled my lips.

He stopped. "What is it?"

"Your knuckles. They're raw."

Bones paused. "Yeah."

"I noticed them earlier, but didn't want to say anything."

He took a long drink and set his wine glass down and held out his hand to me. "Come on."

"Where are we going?" I took his hand and hopped off the table.

"You want to see my world? I'll show it to you. Grab your jacket and let's go."

Chapter 19

"I've never been on a motorcycle," I said as we walked toward his bike in the driveway.

"I'll keep you safe."

His promise reverberated through the air.

He handed me the helmet resting on his seat. After he ensured it was tight, he straddled his bike. He turned the key in the ignition, the growl of the steel and chrome beast dominating my senses.

"I gotta warn you though... You're not gonna be able to keep your hands off me after this ride," he said, throwing me a sinful smirk.

"We'll see about that," I quipped as I climbed on behind him.

"Closer. You need to be closer. Wrap your arms around me."

I did as he commanded, pressing the heat of my thighs against him.

Excitement danced in my veins as I enclosed my arms around his muscular form. Before I knew it, we were zooming down the road, the night air cold against my cheeks, my body alive and warm with exhilaration.

I didn't know where Bones was taking me, and I didn't care.

By trying to control every outcome of my life, I'd shut myself off from experiencing it to its fullest. And yet life had thrown me into the orbit of a man who lived in a different world and who followed his own rules.

Time had no meaning on the back of his motorcycle. Underneath the stars with pavement stretching out in front of us, we could ride until dawn, and it would feel like no time had passed.

But eventually, Bones turned onto a gravel road, slowing down only when we approached a gate. Two men were standing watch. They opened the gate and waved as we passed through.

Bones parked on the gravel lot near the other motorcycles. A few cars were there, too. He cut the engine and my ears buzzed from the sudden quiet.

I slid off the bike, my legs familiar with the sensation of coming to stand on solid ground. Years of horseback riding were ingrained within me.

I unlatched the helmet and shook out my hair.

"Well?" Bones asked. He was still straddling his bike and didn't seem in a hurry to move.

"It was incredible," I breathed.

He smiled. "Yeah, it was."

I handed him the helmet and then looked around. "Where are we?"

"The clubhouse."

"The clubhouse?" I asked in surprise. "Why did you bring me here?"

"Because you wanted to see what my life is all about. This is my life."

He climbed off his motorcycle and set his helmet onto the seat. He then wrapped an arm around my waist and guided me toward the clubhouse steps.

"Who were those guys at the gate?" I asked.

"Prospects."

"Do they have names?"

"Yes."

"What are they?"

"Prospect Three and Prospect Four." I looked up at him and he was smirking. "It's better than Grunt Three and Grunt Four."

"I guess." I rolled my eyes.

I wasn't sure what to expect when Bones opened the front door of the clubhouse and urged me forward, but to say I was surprised was an understatement.

"It's clean," I blurted out.

"We have housekeepers too," he said with a wink.

"Seriously?"

He nodded. "Yep. This is the living room and kitchen. We've got a theater and game room downstairs in the basement. The clubhouse is three stories. Down the hall is the back door that leads outside, which is where we're going."

He clasped my hand and marched down the hallway.

"I thought it would be a friggin' mess," I stated. "I'm pleasantly surprised that it's not."

"It probably was back in the day," he said. "But a lot of the brothers are married and starting families. Can't be a shit-show here when we've got younguns learning how to walk and shit."

"Younguns? How many younguns are there?" I asked in amusement.

"Too many to keep track of," he said absently. He pushed open the back door.

People were sitting around a huge bonfire and old

school country music was playing from a sound system with speakers mounted on the back of the clubhouse.

"Hayden!" a woman yelled.

I squinted, trying to decipher who'd recognized me. It took me half a second to realize it was Willa.

"You're in it now," Bones said, hugging me to him as he led me toward the fire.

As we got closer, I saw a group of women sitting in camp chairs while a cluster of men in leather cuts stood nearby.

"He finally decided to show you off," a man said, taking a drink from his beer bottle.

"Here," a woman said, thrusting a glass bottle into my hands. "You're gonna need this."

"What is it?" I asked, sniffing the contents, which immediately made my eyes water.

"Apple Pie Moonshine," the woman said. "Boxer's secret recipe."

"Oh, thanks," I said handing it back to her. "But I—ah—don't drink."

There was a moment of silence and then the blonde said, "Damn. Booze would make this easier for you. Can I get you something else?"

"Water's fine," I assured her with a smile. "Thanks."

She lifted the cooler lid and fished out a bottle of water and handed it to me.

"Ready for some introductions?" Bones asked.

"Hold on, let me get a pen so I can write it all down," I said.

Willa chuckled. "Yeah, this isn't even the whole gang."

"You'll meet the rest of them at the wedding," Bones said. "If this lot doesn't scare you off first."

"If she's not scared off by your ugly face, then she can handle us," a man said.

"Hush," the blonde who'd handed me the bottle of moonshine said. "He likes her. We're supposed to speak of his wonderful qualities."

"Thanks, Logan," Bones drawled.

"Logan?" I frowned. "You're Logan?"

The blonde nodded. "I'm Logan."

I looked at Bones. "*That's* Logan?"

"Please don't tell me you thought I was a guy," Logan said with an eye roll. "I've heard it all before."

"Well, Bones didn't clarify. I assumed Logan was one of his biker brothers."

Logan grinned. "Nope."

"I guess I have you to thank for the tea."

"Tea?" Logan frowned. "What tea?"

"The tea Bones brought me to help me sleep." I frowned. "He said you recommended it to him."

Logan looked at Bones. "Did he, now?"

"Logan is Smoke's Old Lady," Bones explained, diverting my attention momentarily.

Smoke raised his beer bottle to me.

"Willa and Duke, you already know," Bones said. "Where's Sutton and Viper?"

Logan cleared her throat. "Occupied."

I laughed. "Got it."

"You'll meet them if and when they decide to resurface," Bones said with a grin. He pointed to two other men who looked to be in their late thirties. "Raze and Kelp."

The back door opened and three more bikers strode outside.

"You're here," Savage said to me in surprise.

"I am," I agreed. "Holy hell, what happened to your face?"

His eye was bruised, and his lip was split.

"Sparring at The Ring. It's the club's gym." He frowned. "What?"

"Nothing, just—Charlie told me she was hanging out with you and that's why she couldn't meet me tonight."

"I'm sorry, I don't know anything about that," I said.

"Wait, a woman blew off Savage?" a pint-sized brunette asked. She then took the bottle of moonshine from Logan and downed a huge swallow.

"She didn't blow me off," Savage muttered.

"Kinda sounds like she did."

"Shut up, Tavy," Savage growled.

Tavy smirked. "Hi, I'm Tavy. I'm Logan's best friend and Smoke's daughter."

I blinked. "Wait, you're…"

"Yep." Tavy nodded. "Logan's gonna be my new mommy."

Logan tugged on a lock of Tavy's hair. "Ignore her. She has no filter."

"How are you doing with names?" Bones asked.

"I don't need name tags yet," I quipped.

"Then here's two more to add to the list." He gestured to the two younger bikers who'd come outside with Savage.

"Acid and Crow."

They gave me a couple of chin nods.

"Okay, so you guys can go away now," Tavy said. "We want to talk to Hayden."

Bones looked at me.

"I'm good. I swear." I leaned closer and lowered my voice. "So far, none of this has scared me off."

"I'm still easing you in, Duchess." He kissed me briefly, swiped the bottle of moonshine from Logan, and followed his boys to the other side of the bonfire.

Savage held back for a moment.

"You want me to text Charlie?" I asked, reaching for my phone only to realize that I'd left the house without my purse or cell.

"Nope."

"Just as well, I don't have my phone on me."

Savage turned and headed toward the other bikers.

"Sit," Willa commanded.

"Yeah, sit," Logan urged.

"So, there are more of you," I said as I settled my bottom into a vacant chair.

"A lot more," Willa said. "We're fruitful and we multiply."

I laughed.

"We didn't think we were going to get to meet you until Viper and Sutton's wedding this weekend," Logan said. "So, this is kind of a surprise."

"It's a surprise for me too. This was kind of impromptu," I admitted.

"Bones looks dressed up," Tavy said. "I mean, dressed up for a biker. Were you guys out on a date?"

"I—we—" I sighed. "It was a date, but it was as my house."

"Oh, *really*," Tavy said with a grin.

"Yes, really." I laughed. "He's doing this favor for me. My mom is having this event soon and she's trying to foist me onto a designated bachelor. Bones volunteered to be my date and I'm hoping it will help keep my mom at bay. She's determined to see me married."

"Hmm," Tavy said. "Logan, hand me a beer, would you? Bones took the moonshine."

"On it." Logan lifted the lid of the cooler again and fished out an ice-cold beer, popped the tab, and handed it to her friend.

"Okay, so Bones was at your place for dinner wearing his nice shirt," Logan said. "I'm still not sure why, though."

"The event is a charity gala with a bunch of wealthy people…"

"Let me guess: etiquette lessons?" Logan asked.

"Yeah. I just want him to be prepared," I said. "So he's not a fish out of water."

"He'll be a fish out of water anyway," Willa said. "It'll be okay though. Bones has enough confidence not to care what other people think."

I glanced in the direction of Bones who was laughing at something Smoke had said. His eyes caught mine and we shared a moment.

"Yeah, he's got the confidence down. I just didn't want him to walk into the lion's den without at least a little bit of weaponry in his arsenal, you know? My mother's circle can be…"

"Cold, cruel, snobby?" Tavy supplied helpfully.

"All of that and more," I said. "When you're an outsider, they don't let you forget it."

"That doesn't sound fun," Willa said.

"Definitely not," I agreed. "But I promised my mother I'd be there for this event and for whatever reason, Bones agreed to go with me."

Logan snorted.

Willa giggled. "She still doesn't get it."

"It seems that way," Logan agreed.

"What don't I get?" I demanded.

"That once a Tarnished Angel commits, he's *committed*," Logan said. "Smoke committed early and fast, even if I was a little slower to get with the program."

"If you're going to talk about you and my dad, then I'm leaving," Tavy said lightly.

"I'm done," Logan promised, taking a sip of her beer. "By the way, I never told Bones to bring you tea. That was all on him."

"Then why did he tell me it was you?" I asked.

"You'll have to ask him," Logan said.

"I'll do that. What were you saying about a Tarnished Angel being committed?" I asked.

"They move fast, when they've found the woman they want to be with," Willa replied.

"That's intense," I muttered. "What am I supposed to do with that?"

Logan and Willa exchanged a look but didn't say anything.

"So...did you guys do it on the dining room table?" Tavy asked.

"*What?* No."

Almost.

"We—ah—got into a fight," I admitted softly.

"About what?" Tavy wondered.

"Things," I said evasively. "His world. My world. All the obstacles in the way of us being together."

"Ah," Logan said with a nod. "He's a biker and that comes with a lot of stuff."

"What kind of stuff?" I asked. "He won't tell me. But I'm not stupid...his knuckles are raw, like he punched someone in the last couple of days. What's the deal with *club business*?"

"Party line," Logan muttered.

"Totally," Willa said.

Neither of them went on.

Tavy broke the silence. "Let me guess...I'm not an Old Lady so now you're all going to clamshell." She rose. "I'm going to the bathroom. When I get back, can we please talk about something that includes me? I hate being out of the loop."

Tavy headed inside and I looked to Logan and Willa.

"Well?" I asked. "What can't I know?"

Chapter 20

"Technically, you can't know anything," Willa said. "You're not an Old Lady, and only Old Ladies are privy to information about the club. And even then, you'll never know as much as you want."

"I don't belong here," I murmured. "Do I?"

"That depends," Logan said slowly. "Do you *want* to be here?"

I looked at Bones again. I watched him laugh and joke with his brothers. He made my stomach flip with lust, but what the hell was I doing?

"My head says no, I shouldn't be here. But my body…" I sighed.

"Yeah." Logan nodded. "I get it. I *so* get it."

"Doc really should be the one to talk to you," Willa said.

My attention shifted to her. "Doc? Why?"

"Because she's like you. She comes from money. She's from the opposite side of the tracks, but she fell in love with Boxer anyway. And she stayed."

"But she's not here. You two are. And I need…I don't

know. I need insight. I need to know I'm not completely crazy to even entertain this idea."

"You take this one," Logan said to Willa. "You've been around longer."

"By like, only a few months," Willa said. "This is really something for Mia or Darcy to talk about."

"They're not here," Logan said. "Tick tock."

"Fine," Willa said with a sigh. "The men in this club… they're loyal and protective. They want families. And there isn't anything they wouldn't do for each other or for their women and kids. But they also live life in the gray area."

"I gathered that," I drawled. "The fact that he carries a pistol and came to my place tonight with raw knuckles kind of gave it away."

"It used to be that Old Ladies weren't involved in club business at all," Willa continued slowly. "We didn't know what the club was doing, like, in any way. It was a way to protect us in case…in case things went south."

"Okay," I said with a nod. "That makes sense. I guess."

Willa looked at the men who were busy talking and not paying us any attention. "They didn't tell us so we couldn't testify against them, if it came to that."

I blinked. "Wait, are you saying they're involved in—"

"Not anymore," Willa hastened to say. "The club was involved in some bad stuff, but they're not anymore. They're moving in a different direction."

"That doesn't ease my fears," I said. "It just makes it sound like they moved from morally black to morally gray."

"I get it," Logan said. "It was hard for me to wrap my brain around it as well."

"So how did you?" I asked.

"I chose to focus on how Smoke treated me and how he made me feel over anything else," Logan explained.

"It's not easy. Choosing to be with a man like Smoke. I didn't grow up in this world. It was like traveling to a foreign country where I didn't speak the language. It had me questioning what I was doing several times. On paper, my ex was *the* guy. He checked all the boxes. He said the right things, knew the right people. But in the end, he was a piece of shit."

I knew what that was like. Being with the *right* man. And when the chips were down, he'd left me.

"These men won't lie to you," Willa said. "They're going to be evasive; they're not going to include you in what's going on with the club. That's just how it's been done for as long as anyone can remember. But with them, what you see is what you get. Bones spending time with you the way he is…it matters. It means something. And if you let it, it can be real."

"Things are changing, though," Logan said. "With the club, I mean."

"How so?" I asked, intrigued even though I knew I should run far, far away.

"The club has moved in a different direction, so how they treat the Old Ladies has changed too. Not a lot. I mean, they don't run business ideas by us. We're still not included in that kind of stuff…but recently, when things affect the entire club, we've all been informed. We're a family and we operate like a family business."

I took a sip of water to bathe my parched throat.

"But if you're not an Old Lady, things are buttoned up even tighter. So where you are in your relationship with Bones…you won't know anything because he's not allowed to discuss it with you. Hell, Duke doesn't discuss stuff with me either, but sometimes he can and then I'll know."

Logan nodded. "It's the same with Smoke."

"It's like the mafia," I murmured. "They keep their women out of it."

"Yes," Willa agreed.

"So, Bones won't ever tell me anything. Not unless I become an Old Lady."

"And there's no guarantee that he will then, either," Logan said.

"But there's more of a chance that he *could* if you were his Old Lady," Willa said.

"It sounds complicated," I stated.

"It's not. It's a trust thing," Willa said. "He's not gonna tell a woman who's not committed to him and his way of life if she's going to bail."

"I see," I said slowly. I was turning over their words, trying to compute them.

"And you're not all-in because you're not sure about Bones and the club," Logan said.

"I'm not all-in because this will affect my life in ways I can't even fathom. I don't do things like this. I've never done anything like this in my life."

"Anything like what?" Willa asked. "Spend time with gutter trash?"

I flinched. "No. I didn't mean it that way. Not even a little bit. But you've got to understand…my world is tuxedos and trust funds, glitz and galas…not guns and bloody knuckles."

"Your world sounds cold," Willa said. "No offense."

"None taken. I just…how do I even explain this? I've always done the right thing."

"How's that worked out for you?" Logan asked.

"I'm alone and unhappy," I said quietly.

"It's hard," Logan said, shooting me a smile of commiseration. "I've been where you've been. I've had to leap without looking. It was the best thing I ever did, though. I'd do it all over again."

Bones slapped Raze on the back and then he began to walk toward us.

"Ladies," Bones greeted. "What are you talking about?"

Logan and Willa were awkwardly silent, and I jumped in with a smile. "The wedding. I asked what the heck I'm supposed to wear to a biker wedding."

"I told her something in leather," Willa said, picking up what I'd laid down.

"With a rockabilly hairstyle. Like a pinup girl," Logan added.

"Please God, tell me this is true," Bones said.

"I'll see what I can do," I said with a laugh.

He held out his hand to me and helped me stand. "I'm gonna take Hayden and show her around."

"Show me around? It's dark," I stated.

"Trust me," Bones said.

"Whew, I know what that look means," Willa said with a laugh.

"You know nothing," I said to her.

"Hmm." She rubbed her belly. "How do you think this happened? Just be careful, that's all I'm saying."

I groaned. "Let's go."

Bones escorted me away from the bonfire and party.

"Where are we going?" I asked.

"The club bought the land behind the clubhouse with the intention of expanding," he explained, his hand clasping mine. "I'd like to show you what the future holds. The clubhouse didn't have enough space for all of us. Not to mention when the Idaho boys come down to visit, quarters are tight."

"Idaho boys?"

"There's a Tarnished Angels chapter in Coeur d'Alene," he explained. "Anyway, they visit us down here from time to time and there just wasn't enough space for everyone. So, we built some tiny homes."

"Where?" I asked.

"Just up here. We wanted to keep them close to the main clubhouse, but at enough of a distance so that we're not all on top of each other."

He stopped and gestured to several tiny homes that looked newly completed. "We have more land that way." He pointed. "And that's our private shooting range."

"You have a shooting range?" I asked in surprise.

He gave me a look. "Where do you think Willa learned to shoot?"

"Oh," I said quietly.

"I could teach you. If you wanted. Get you comfortable with a pistol."

I bit my lip. "Yeah?"

"Yeah." He rubbed the back of his neck. "The Old Ladies have competitions. It's fun, actually."

"Sounds fun," I admitted.

"So, you'll learn how to shoot a pistol?"

I nodded. "It's not completely foreign to me."

"Right. Your dad, the duck hunter."

"Yeah." I looked at him. "I appreciate you bringing me to the clubhouse and everything, but this isn't what I had in mind."

"What did you have in mind?"

"I don't know. I just—never mind."

"Tell me." His hands found my hips and he pulled me toward him.

"I thought you'd take me around town on your bike, show me where you hang out."

"This is where I hang out."

"Isn't there like, a biker bar or something you could show me?"

He laughed. "What, like the one Arnie walks into at the beginning of *Terminator 2*? That kind of biker bar?"

"Yes. Exactly like that. Don't laugh at me."

"I'm not. I swear I'm not."

"I'm serious, Bones. You want me to be in your world. So show me a biker bar."

"First of all, you being in my world doesn't mean you have to hang out in a biker bar. I don't even hang out in biker bars."

"You really don't?"

"No."

"Why not?"

He sighed.

"Where did you go to pick up women?" I prodded.

"Yeah, like hell I'm actually having that conversation with you."

"Tell me," I said.

"Well, I picked up a woman at Chaos once."

I pressed my hand to his chest and attempted to push him away, but that only made him tighten his arms around me.

"You tried to pick me up. It didn't work that well," I quipped.

"Where are you standing right now?" he asked.

"In your arms. At your clubhouse."

"Then it worked pretty damn well."

"I approached *you* that night."

"Yeah. That doesn't mean I wasn't aware of you before then."

"Wait, what?" I pulled back just enough so that I could stare up at him. The flames of the bonfire danced in his eyes.

"You think if you hadn't approached me, I wouldn't have approached you?"

"You called me jailbait the first time we met."

"Of course. How else was I going to get you to show me your ID so I could get your name," he said with a slow smile.

My entire body softened, and his hand wormed its way down from the small of my back to the curve of my ass. He pulled me against him, showing me how much he wanted me.

"I'm not asking for you to meet me halfway," he said as he stared down at me. "I know you're not ready for halfway. But maybe a quarter of the way?"

"What does a quarter of the way look like?"

"More nights like tonight," he said.

"Which part?" I asked. "The dinner part, the fighting part, or the back of your motorcycle part?"

"All of it. And I like you on the back of my bike, Duchess." He angled his head down.

"I liked being there," I whispered just before his mouth covered mine.

We kissed in the darkness, the bonfire behind us, the stars above us, the budding promise of a future ahead of us.

"So tell me the truth," I said against his lips.

"Hmm?"

"Are your biker parties always this tame?"

He cradled the back of my neck. "Truth?"

"Yes, the truth."

Bones pulled back to stare down at me. "When it's us single guys, no, it's not always this tame."

I swallowed. "Women with big hair, big tits, big attitude?"

"Yeah."

"Have you…ah…been to one of those types of parties since we, you know, started this thing?"

"No."

"I mean before we told each other we weren't sleeping with other people."

"The answer is still no," he said.

"Seriously?"

"Yeah, seriously.

"But why?" I asked in confusion.

"Because I didn't want anyone else after I met you."

"Sentiment like that will ruin your street cred," I joked lightly.

"Hayden," he began.

"You just called me *Hayden*."

"Because this is important, and I want you to hear me."

"Okay, I'm listening."

"I've got nothing to prove by hooking up with a bunch of women. I've been there. I've done that."

"How great for you," I said snarkily.

"Listen," he said, not rising to the bait. "I'm not fucking around. I can't get you out of my head. I can't go five minutes without thinking about you. I don't want anyone else. I don't want to fuck anyone else. So until you're ready to fuck me, I'll use my hand and fantasize about you. Okay?"

"Okay." I was glad he couldn't see me blush. But I was blushing.

Hard.

I stood on my toes and sank my fingers into the hair at the nape of his neck. "Bones?"

"Yeah, Duchess?"

"I'm almost ready for that too."

"Yeah?"

"Yeah."

He brushed his lips across mine, sliding his tongue into my welcoming mouth. He kissed me until I was drugged with pleasure and my body wanted more.

"Hmm, I have a really good idea," he said after he lifted his lips from mine.

"What?"

"I'm now the one holding out."

"Huh?"

"We're not crossing that line until you beg me for it."

I let out a screech of outrage. "*Beg* you for it? What makes you think I'll beg you for it?"

"Oh, Duchess." He shook his head and gave me a wicked grin. "You begged me when I nearly had you splayed out on your dining room table. So I don't *think* you'll beg for it. I *know* you will."

"Challenge accepted," I said loftily, pushing away from his warm embrace. I trailed my hand softly down the front of his shirt to lazily glide against the fly of his jeans. I could feel the straining outline of him. "We'll see who begs."

Chapter 21

WE HEADED BACK to the bonfire, hand in hand.

"Well, she doesn't look satisfied," Raze announced.

"So clearly he didn't have his way with her," Kelp teased.

"They were only gone a few minutes," Smoke added. "So that leads me to one of two conclusions. One, he got off in less than—"

"Fuck you all," Bones said. He pointed to Smoke. "*Especially* you."

"Relax, it's just pay back," Smoke said with a grin. "For all the shit you gave me over Logan."

"Without Bones, we might not have gotten together," Logan said to Smoke.

"Hmm. Maybe you're right. Maybe I should send him a fruit basket instead."

"Tropical fruits only, please," Bones said. "I'm dating a rich girl. Rich people eat tropical fruits."

"Is that true?" Kelp asked.

"I'm allergic to tropical fruit," I deadpanned.

Bones looked at me. "Really?"

I rolled my eyes. "No. Not really."

Raze laughed. "I like her."

"Where's Willa?" I asked, looking around. "And Duke?"

"Waverly and Sailor were in a car accident. Not a big one. Someone rear-ended Sailor, so Duke, Willa, Savage and Acid left," Logan explained.

"Who's Sailor?" I asked.

"Sailor lives with Duke and Willa, but she's not related. It's a long story," Logan said. "We'll catch you up later."

"Okay, there seem to be a lot of stories," I said, taking a seat. "I'm glad they're okay."

"Still no Sutton and Viper," Tavy remarked.

"I think it's safe to say that they've hunkered down for the night," Raze stated.

"How are you going to pull him away from Sutton for his bachelor party tomorrow night?" Tavy asked.

"The same way you're going to pull Sutton away," Kelp said. "By kidnapping her and taking her to her bachelorette party."

"You're coming, right?" Tavy asked me.

"Oh. I hadn't—"

"Of course she's coming," Logan said.

"I might have plans," I said with a laugh.

"Cancel them," Tavy said. "We're fun. Even if most of the Old Ladies can't drink at the moment. But then again, you don't drink, so you'll be in good company."

"Way to put me on the spot," I said. "Shouldn't you clear this with Sutton? I mean, she's never even met me."

"The more the merrier," Tavy said.

I looked at Bones and then the others. "A little help?"

"You could just say no," Bones said.

"I don't think they'll let me."

"Then I think you should go out with them and have fun," Bones said wryly.

"If I do that, I'm going to ask a bunch of questions about you," I warned. "I'm going to ply them for information."

"They don't know anything about me to use against me," Bones said.

"Hmm. You sure about that?" Logan asked.

There was a moment of silence.

"Shit," Bones muttered.

We burst into laughter. Even the guys.

"I'll go to the bachelorette party," I said as the laughter died down.

"Yay!" Tavy yelled. "It's going to be so much fun."

"What are we doing?"

"Sutton used to work at Spurs," Logan said. "So we're all dressing up and having dinner. And seeing who can stay on the mechanical bull the longest."

"And there might be line dancing," Tavy said.

"Okay, this I can definitely get on board with," I said, looking at Bones. "What are you guys doing for the bachelor party?"

"Sorry, Duchess," Bones said. "We can't share that information with you."

"They don't have anything planned, do they?" I asked Logan.

"Hmm. It's not looking like they do," Logan said with a smirk.

"We've got it planned," Smoke said.

"Oh yeah? What are you guys doing then?" Logan asked.

The two of them began to playfully tease each other.

Bones looked at me. "You wanna see my room?"

"Sure."

"Great," Kelp muttered. "My room shares a wall with yours. I can hear it already."

My cheeks heated and I shot up from my chair. "Nice meeting all of you."

"See you tomorrow for the bachelorette party," Tavy said.

Bones placed his hand at the small of my back and urged me toward the clubhouse.

"Don't listen to Kelp," he said.

"Kind of hard not to," I remarked.

He opened the screen door and let me through first. He stepped in behind me and we headed for the stairs. We got to the second floor and he opened a door, waving me inside. He flipped the light and closed the door behind us.

It was a sparse room with a full-sized bed, a three-drawer dresser and a single nightstand. I took off my jacket and hung it on the back of the door.

He reached into his leather cut and pulled out a red toothbrush still in its plastic packaging. "This is the one I was going to use at your place, but you can have it."

I took it from him. "Thanks."

"So?"

"So what?"

"What do you think? Of what I showed you tonight?"

"I think my head is crammed full and I'm tired of thinking. Can we just brush our teeth and go to bed?"

"Yeah, Duchess. We can do that. But before we do that, I have to tell you something."

I groaned. "Not another bomb, please."

"No bomb," he promised. "I just thought you should know my name. My real name. It's Royce. Royce Garrett Dalton."

"Royce," I whispered, and shook my head with a tiny laugh. "Of course that's your name."

It was unique.

He was unique.

As we stood next to each other, brushing our teeth in the small bathroom down the hall, I realized that sex and intimacy weren't the same.

It was intimacy I was truly afraid of.

Chapter 22

Minty fresh and entirely uncertain, I followed Bones back to his room.

He first removed his leather cut and hung it on the hook by the door. His pistol was next and he set it on the nightstand. He took a seat on the edge of the bed and took off his heavy motorcycle boots.

Nerves skated through me as I watched him undress. He wore a pair of army green boxer briefs and his legs looked like massive tree trunks. His skin was decked out in tattoos.

He was a gorgeous vision.

"You're next, Duchess," he drawled. "I can't get into bed until you do. I sleep on the outside."

"Afraid I'll sneak out in the morning before you wake up?" I joked.

"And go where?" He smiled.

"Maybe I'll swipe the keys to your motorcycle and drive myself home."

We both knew I was full of bravado.

"I sleep on the outside because if I have to get up, I won't wake you. So, you sleep here."

He patted the spot next to the wall.

"Okay." I took a deep breath and bent over to unzip my boots. I used the dresser to help me balance. Next came my green sweater.

I wore a flimsy white camisole that did nothing to hide my jutting nipples.

My shaking fingers went for the button of my jeans. I slid them down my legs and took them off. I folded them and put them on top of my sweater.

I looked at Bones.

He was staring at me with darkening eyes. His jaw was clenched.

It didn't take a genius to know what he was thinking about.

"Come here, Duchess," he growled.

I padded barefoot toward him.

Bones reached out and grasped my hip. He gently lifted my camisole to expose my belly.

His warm lips grazed my skin and I shivered.

"Get into bed." He released me and I scrambled into the spot by the wall.

He got up and turned off the overhead light. The lamp was still aglow, but after Bones crawled in next to me, he cut that too.

The room was bathed in darkness.

I swore he could hear my heart trying to leap out of my chest.

"Roll over, Duchess. I'm going to spoon you."

"Won't that just torture you?" I teased.

"The best kind of torture. Now roll."

I did as he commanded and then I was suddenly pressed against his firm, warm chest.

One of his hands wormed its way underneath my tank and settled on my lower belly.

"Good night, Duchess."

"Good night."

I closed my eyes.

Adrenaline was rushing through my veins. Desire punctured every thought of sleep. A low throb pulsed between my legs and I knew all I had to do was roll over and meet his waiting mouth with mine.

But then I was reminded of our standoff.

Who's going to beg first…

And suddenly, the idea of slowly torturing him until he had no choice but to cave had me smiling to myself.

I glided my fingertips across the back of his hand that was resting on my belly.

"Duchess, what are you doing?"

"Hmm. Nothing." I shifted so that my ass grazed his erection.

He sucked in a breath. "Go to sleep."

"This game between us," I began. "We never did establish any rules."

"The rules are, there ain't no rules." His hand was suddenly sliding into my thong. "For example, I can touch you. I can push my fingers into you. I can get you so hot and bothered and leave you on the verge of coming and then I can stop while you're writhing against me, begging me to make you come."

"Or I can let you get me to that point. That point where I know exactly where I need to be touched and I can do it myself. I can come without you. How would you feel about that?"

"I'm gonna make you scream. Do you want our first time to be in my room at the clubhouse with thin walls, or do you want the privacy of your own home? Be sure of your answer."

I sighed. "Stand down, Bones."

He ground his erection against me.

"I meant get your hand out of my panties."

"Hmm, I thought that's what you meant." He slid his hand out of my thong and settled it back on my stomach. "Truce?"

"Truce."

∼

I woke up in a compromising position.

My cheek was pressed against Bones' muscular stomach, and my hand was down his briefs.

With a startled squeak, I gently released him.

"Don't stop," he rasped.

I shoved away from him but couldn't go far because I hit a wall.

Literally.

The wall was behind me.

Bones looked at me with heavy eyelids and his cheeks were flushed.

"I was groping you in my sleep," I said aghast.

"You hear me complaining?"

"Why didn't you stop me?"

"Well, you were sleeping soundly. I didn't want to disturb you."

I rolled my eyes. "That's considerate of you."

"How about *you* be a little more considerate and finish the job you started."

"As much fun as that sounds…" I surveyed the room.

"What are you looking for?"

"A clock."

"Don't have one."

"I'm not surprised," I drawled. "But I really need to know the time and I forgot my cell phone at my house."

With a sigh, he reached for his phone. "It's seven forty-five."

"Crap. I'm late." I rolled over him with the intention of hitting the floor, but he grabbed my hips and stopped me. "What are you doing?"

"Tollway," he said with a smirk.

I pecked his lips.

"Just for that, the toll has doubled." His hand cradled the back of my head, and he urged me closer.

As our lips met, I settled on top of him. With his hands in my hair and the hard feel of him beneath me, it was tempting to stay right where I was.

One of his hands left my hair and skimmed down to grasp my ass.

He squeezed it and then he gently patted me.

I pulled back, dazed.

"Sufficient," he said. "Get dressed. I'll drive you home."

I climbed off him just as his phone chimed. He grabbed it and read the message. "Damn."

"What?"

"Something came up. I can't take you home right now."

"But I have to—"

"I'll find you a ride, I promise." He launched himself out of bed. Despite his earlier desire to lounge and pick up where we'd left off, he was suddenly full of energy.

I got dressed as quickly as I could and took some extra time to go to the bathroom and brush my teeth. Bones was waiting for me in the hallway when I opened the door.

He sidled past me. "I'll meet you in the kitchen."

Kelp and Raze were already awake and they were sitting on the couch with cups of coffee.

"Morning," Kelp said.

"Hi," I greeted.

"You're not walking funny," Raze stated. "You shut my boy down?"

"Huh. How old are you?"

"Thirty-eight," Raze said. "Why?"

"When's the last time you read an etiquette book?" I quipped.

Raze let out a good-natured laugh. "Coffee?"

"No, thanks, I've got to get home. Bones can't take me, though. He's got to do something." I hated the vague statement, and it only reminded me of what we'd fought about the night before.

It was still tangled in my head, but my body was clearly leading the way in my decision-making process.

"I'd offer to take you," Kelp said, "but I'm going where Bones is going."

"Where are you and Bones going?" a slim brunette asked as she came into the room. She looked to be about my age.

"Where your fiancé is going," Kelp said. "Nice of you to make an appearance, Sutton."

Sutton grinned, clearly not bashful. "My private party with Viper was more fun than a party with all of you. No offense."

"None taken," Kelp said.

Sutton's eyes slid to me. "Hey, we haven't met yet."

"Hayden Spencer," I said with a wave.

"Ah, Bones' Old Lady. Nice to meet you."

"I'm not his Old Lady," I protested.

She raised her brows. "Sure. Whatever. You're coming tonight, right? To my bachelorette party?"

"Oh. Yeah. How'd you know I was invited?"

"Logan texted last night. I saw the message this morning."

"Ah. Is that okay? That they invited me and informed you after the fact?"

"Absolutely." She grinned. "It's gonna be a hoot and a half."

"How about just a quarter hoot?" A huge man with a fierce expression across his face stalked into the room and threw his arms over her shoulders.

"I'm not telling you how to have fun at your party, don't tell me how to fun at mine," she stated. "Besides, it might be a full-on hootenanny."

"Viper doesn't know how to have fun," Smoke said as he sidled around Sutton and Viper. He went immediately to the coffee maker and poured himself a mug.

"Which is why we're forcing him to have fun," Raze said.

"I just need a few hours of girl time before he crashes my night. He can't stand to be away from me." She looked up at her hulk of a man and smiled. "Isn't that right?"

He grunted, but I swore his eyes softened with affection when he looked at her.

"Where's Bones?" Smoke asked. "We've got to get going."

"He'll be down in a minute," I said. "Where's Logan?"

"She left already," Smoke said. "She had an early meeting."

The tramp of heavy boots on the stairs preceded Bones' appearance. "Hayden has to get home, but I can't take her."

"Neither can we," Raze said. "We're going with you."

"I'll take you home," Sutton offered. "I drove my car last night."

"You don't mind?" I asked her.

"Not at all. It'll give me a good time to pester you with questions."

I laughed. "I hate to be that person, but I kinda need to go. Like now."

"Sure. Let me run upstairs and grab my keys real fast. Be back in a jiff." She lifted Viper's arms from her shoulders and ducked out of his hold.

"I need to suck down some coffee," Bones said. He passed by me. "You good? You need anything?"

I shook my head.

Sutton returned and looked at me. "Ready?"

"Ready," I said.

"Hey." Bones marched over to me with a cup of coffee in his hand. "I'll call you later."

"Okay," I whispered, mindful of all the eyes on us.

Screw it.

I stood up on my toes and kissed the hell out of him.

Hoots and hollers erupted around us.

When I pulled back, I shot him a smug look.

"See ya, boys," I called as I headed for the front door.

Sutton dogged my heels.

"That was awesome," she said.

"What was?" I asked.

"The look you put on Bones' face. You're running circles around him, aren't you?"

"Trying."

Chapter 23

"Whoa," Sutton remarked.

"Whoa, what?" I asked.

"Whoa, your house...sorry, I said that out loud, didn't I?"

"Yeah, but I get it. Let's not make it a thing though. Deal?" I asked with a smile.

She grinned. "Deal. So tonight, seven-thirty at Spurs. Bring your honkey-tonk."

"Consider it brought." I smiled. "Thanks for the ride."

"Anytime."

I climbed out of her car and headed up to the front porch. I punched in the code to the door and unlocked it. While my hand was on the knob, I turned and waved to Sutton. She waved back and then pulled out of the driveway.

Charlie's shoes were in the foyer. "Charlie?" I called out.

She appeared like an apparition. "Where have you been, young lady?"

"Sorry, Mom. I went to the drive-in with Scooter and lost track of time."

"Hmm. I see no hickeys on your neck. I'm disappointed. I thought you were having a romantic night with Bones."

"Change of plans," I said as I headed for the stairs. "We can talk, but I have to shower. I'm running late as it is."

"I ate the left-over filet," she said as she followed me up the stairs.

"You had steak for breakfast?" I asked in amusement.

"Absolutely. I left the sweet potato puree though. Why do chefs always puree vegetables? Is it to make them more palatable?"

"Not for you, apparently. By the way," I said as I walked into my bedroom. "Savage said he asked you to hang out last night but you told him you were spending the evening with me. And I didn't know I was supposed to be your alibi, so when he saw me at the clubhouse last night, he put two and two together and knows you lied to him. So that might be a mess."

I stripped out of my jeans and sweater, tossing them on the bed before I went into the bathroom.

"So, are you going to tell me what you were really doing last night?" I asked.

"Only if you tell me why you weren't doing what I thought you'd be doing last night." She followed me into the bathroom and sat down on the closed toilet seat and waited.

I turned on the shower and let it steam for a moment. "Bones came over for the fork lesson and we were going to have a sleepover."

"You've already had a sleepover."

"A *naked* sleepover," I clarified.

"Ah." She smiled. "So, how did it go?"

I tested the water with my hand and once I was satisfied, I quickly stripped out of my tank and thong before hopping in. Charlie and I had known each other since we were infants and neither one of us was modest around the other.

"There was no naked sleepover," I replied.

"What happened?" Charlie asked.

I told her what had occurred at dinner and how we'd wound up at the clubhouse.

"Oh, wow," she said.

"Oh, wow? That's all you've got to say to me." I closed my eyes as I rinsed my hair of shampoo and then I added conditioner.

"What do you want me to say?"

"Is he right? Am I right?"

"Both of those things can be true," she said. "You can be wary about getting involved with a biker, and he can be treading softly about what he's involved in so as not to scare you off."

I rinsed one final time and then turned off the water. I reached for a fluffy white towel and wrapped it around me.

"If you were seriously dating Savage, would it bother you not knowing what he's involved in? And when you ask, he'd just say 'it's club business'."

"But I'm not seriously dating Savage."

"But if you were," I pushed.

"What does it matter what I think?" Charlie said. "You clearly don't like that Bones won't tell you stuff. What I think doesn't matter."

I wrung out my hair. "I'm at a crossroads. I know I am. I've never felt this way before. I want him. And every time I try to step back and take space, he shows up, reminding me that my life has been lackluster…empty. I don't want empty, Charlie. I want something real."

"You do?" she asked quietly.

I nodded. "I really do. I've made the right choice so many times and where has it gotten me? Nowhere. I kind of…want to make the wrong choice and see how that goes."

"I think that's incredible," she said. "I think you've been hiding from life for far too long, so I support this one hundred percent."

"How do I let him in, Charlie?" I stepped out of the tub onto a white bathmat. I curled my toes into the plush surface as I stared at her.

"I don't know how to answer that," she said quietly. "I think the fact that you want to says it all. Even with your head telling you it's a bad idea. What's your gut telling you?"

"That he means what he says and that I can take him at his word. That this isn't about the chase for him."

"That's hard to find. Background be damned."

I moved over to the sink and began to comb out my hair. "Now, tell me why you lied to Savage and told him you were hanging out with me last night."

"Because I didn't want to see him."

"Why didn't you want to see him?" I asked.

She looked at me.

I looked at her.

"Charlie, *no*."

"Yes."

"You caught feelings for him?"

She sighed. "Yeah. And I don't even know how that happened."

"You sure it's not just really great sex? I hear that clouds the mind."

"It wasn't just the really great sex. I know what it is. God, I'm such an idiot."

"What is it?" I asked. I slathered on my face lotion and then walked out of the bathroom to get dressed.

"It's the fact that he's completely unavailable. Like, *completely* unavailable. And I thought…"

"You thought you were the exception, not the rule."

She followed me into the bedroom and flopped down onto my bed.

"Are you sure he doesn't feel the same way about you?" I asked.

"Like I'd even admit it to him so I can find out if he feels the same. So he can call me Cling-on Barbie or something? No thanks."

"Maybe he has feelings for you, too," I said gently.

"He doesn't," she insisted. "I know he doesn't."

"How do you know?"

"The same way I knew Eden Swinton was hooking up with the married varsity coach when we were seniors. I just knew." She rubbed her forehead. "So instead of hanging out with him and falling even more for the wounded bird I want to fix, I lied and said I was hanging out with you."

"I don't get you," I said from the confines of my walk-in closet.

"What do you mean?"

"I mean, you're fully in support of me opening up to Bones. To letting him in. But you won't do the same thing with Savage?"

"There's one major difference between Bones and Savage."

"Which is?"

"Savage isn't capable of falling in love. Bones is."

"You thought you yourself were incapable of falling in

love," I pointed out. "And now you're clearly going down that road."

"I never said I was incapable. I just purposely avoid it. There's a difference. I know I can fall in love. I just didn't expect it to actually happen. Not like this. *Damn it*."

I quickly pulled on a pair of jeans and grabbed one of my favorite sweaters.

"So, girls' wallowing night tonight?" she asked.

"Ah, I have plans."

"Cancel on Bones. Chicks before dicks. Hoes before bros."

"It's not with Bones," I admitted. "I was invited to Sutton's bachelorette party."

"The Old Lady who's getting married?"

"Yes."

"Well, isn't *that* an interesting turn of events. The Old Ladies inviting you to the bachelorette party is them bringing you into the fold."

I took a deep breath. "I'm going to be late."

Charlie nodded. "Yeah. Okay. I wouldn't want to talk about it either. Not if my whole life was about to change and I wasn't ready for it."

"Are you ever ready for something like that?" I asked quietly. "My entire life changed three years ago and it's never felt…you can't go back. No matter how much you want to. I'd give anything to go back to before. But I can't. And living in the past, wishing reality was different…I've wasted enough time wishing for something that can never be."

"You're going to tell him. Aren't you?"

I nodded slowly. "I think so, yeah. I have to. If I want…"

"If you want…"

"Him," I finished. "If I want him."

Chapter 24

My phone rang just as I was putting on my red cowboy boots. I saw Bad to the Bones flash across the screen and a smile immediately graced my lips.

I answered and put him on speaker.

"How many beers in are you?" I asked.

"Zero," he said. "We're still getting a game plan together."

"A game plan? It's a bachelor party. Shouldn't there already be a plan?"

"Savage suggested renting a few cabins and tripping balls on a shitload of peyote, but the rest of us nixed the idea."

I chuckled.

"Viper's a chill guy. He wasn't gung-ho for a party anyway. Mostly, he's stewing, wondering what trouble Sutton will get into."

"She won't get into trouble," I stated. "She'll be surrounded by her friends. We'll make sure she's safe."

"Sutton is…Sutton. Trouble has a way of following her."

"I promise not to let her drink until she blacks out and forgets the night."

"I'll tell Viper. I'm sure he'll appreciate that."

"Hmm. Well, I'm about to run out the door."

"Now? You're going to be late."

"I started my day behind and it's just snowballed," I commented.

"You'll tell me about it later," he said. "Tonight."

"Tonight?"

"Yeah, tonight. When I come over."

"You're coming over?" I asked. "You're not going to be partying until the wee hours of the morning?"

"We'll have a few beers, we'll haze Viper, then we'll probably work on a motorcycle engine or two and call it. Most of my brothers have wives and families now. The landscape of bachelor parties has changed. Plus, I'm not twenty-five anymore. Hangovers fuckin' suck."

"You're right. You're like, what, thirty-nine? When I told you to bring over a spare toothbrush, maybe I should've told you to bring a pair of slippers and a robe to go with it."

"Not funny," he said, but his tone was light.

"So…later tonight?" I asked.

"Later tonight," he agreed. "Keep in touch, yeah?"

"I will," I promised.

I hung up with Bones, grabbed my purse and jacket, and was out the door.

The Spurs parking lot was nearly full and I had to park in the back. By the time I opened the front door of the restaurant, it was seven forty-five.

A cacophony of noises hit me at once. The loud clanging of the dinner bell to alert the servers that a table's food was ready, the steady hum of conversation, the cheering of men at the bar watching some sporting event.

I stepped up to the hostess stand and told them who I was meeting.

"Most of your party is already here," the hostess said. "Let me take you to the table."

We wound our way through the restaurant, passing large booths that could seat six. The Old Ladies were sitting at a long rectangular table in the back.

"You're here!" Sutton yelled, hopping up from her seat at the head of the table. She wore a plastic crown with the word *bride* blazed across the prongs.

She hugged me to her.

"Sorry I'm late," I said.

"It's fine," she assured me. "Doc is running late too, but that's Doc." She gripped my hand and looked me up and down. "I said bring your honky-tonk. You didn't bring your honky tonk."

"I wore cowboy boots," I said, lifting my leg and pointing to my foot to show off my red cowboy boot. "And jeans."

"No hat." Sutton pouted.

"Well, I think you look great," Willa said to me. She winked. "Nice flannel."

"Thank you," I said, beaming.

"Let me introduce you to everyone," Sutton said.

She went around the table. There was a range of women who looked like they were in their mid-twenties to early forties.

"We'll periodically remind you of who we are," Mia said, lifting her pint of beer and taking a sip.

"Thanks," I said. "Where should I sit?"

There was an empty seat between Logan and Willa. Willa patted the chair. "Here."

"Are we waiting until Doc gets here before ordering a

round of tequila?" Darcy asked. "I'm kid-free and I want to party."

"Count me out. I've got two hours before I have to get home to the baby," Brooklyn said.

"I'll do a shot," Joni said.

"Me too," Tavy added.

"Show of hands," Sutton said.

"What about you?" Mia asked Sutton.

"What about me, what?" Sutton asked.

"Do you want a shot?"

"No, I don't want a shot," Sutton remarked.

"You don't want a shot of tequila at your own bachelorette party?" Rach piped in. The pretty brunette's eyebrows rose to her hairline. "Why not?"

"Tequila and mechanical bull riding doesn't really seem like a good idea, does it?" Sutton asked. "And I really want to ride that bull."

"Oh my God, you're pregnant!" Mia yelled from the other end of the table.

There was a momentary lull in conversation, but it quickly dispelled, and everyone began talking again.

"Are you?" Logan looked at Sutton.

Sutton nodded, a little smile creeping across her face. "I haven't told Viper yet."

Chairs were pushed back as the Old Ladies got up and swarmed Sutton. I smiled, watching everyone laughing and talking, batting tears away from their eyes.

A blonde with a pixie cut rushed at the table. "Sorry I'm late. What's going on?"

"Sutton's pregnant," Mia announced.

The woman smiled. "I know."

"You know? How did you know?" Mia demanded.

"She came to the clinic," the woman said.

"I guess Viper really doesn't have to be worried about you drinking too much tequila tonight," I said with a laugh.

"I'll tell him at the wedding," Sutton said. "But everyone is sworn to secrecy until then. Now, let's order some food. I'm starving."

∼

"Bathroom," Willa announced.

"Oh, same." Logan stood up.

I wiped my greasy fingers on my soiled paper napkin and rose. "I'll come."

"I love that we go to the bathroom in packs," Mia said.

"Hurry back," Sutton said. "They're going to start the line dancing soon."

The four of us wove our way through the restaurant and found the bathroom.

There were four stalls and all of them were unoccupied. It wasn't until we were washing our hands that Mia asked Logan, "How's the new house?"

"Not at all unpacked," Logan said with a laugh. "Smoke's parents are coming for a visit in the next few weeks, so we need to get a move on."

"You just went to visit them," Mia said. "And they're already coming down?"

"Want to make up for lost time, I guess." Logan shrugged. "And spend more time with Tavy, too."

Mia looked at me. "How are you doing, Hayden? Have we overwhelmed you yet?"

I laughed. "No."

"We've been on our best behavior." Mia winked.

I checked my hair, but I'd used half a can of hair spray

to keep my big curls intact and I didn't need to do anything.

"How's Waverly? And Sailor?" I asked Willa.

"They're fine. A little shook up, but they're okay. Thanks," she replied.

"What happened to Waverly and Sailor?" Mia asked.

"They were in a minor fender bender last night. They were rear-ended. They're okay. So is the truck."

"That truck is indestructible." Mia chuckled. She looked at me and said, "Duke bought my old truck for the girls to share. It was the truck my grandfather used to drive."

"And it's still on the road," Willa said. "Despite teenagers behind the wheel."

We got back to the main floor. My attention was immediately drawn to the two men at the bar who hadn't been there when I came in. They wore leather cuts, but they were turned sideways so I couldn't see their club name written on the back.

"Hayden?" Willa called.

I turned to look at her. She and Mia had taken a few steps toward the direction of the table, but they'd apparently noticed I hadn't joined them.

I walked to them. "Sorry, I just—there are two men at the bar wearing leather cuts. Are they Tarnished Angels I haven't met yet?"

Mia's gaze narrowed as she took in the men. She looked away from them to Willa. "Why don't you guys head back to the table."

"Sure," Willa said, looping her arm through mine and tugging me away.

Mia stood rooted in her spot, but I watched her pull out her phone.

"Those men," I said to Willa. "They're not supposed to be here, are they?"

Willa clenched her jaw. "No. They're not."

"Who are they?"

"No clue."

"Really?" I asked. "Or is this one of those things where you're pretending not to know?"

"I really don't know," she said. "This is Tarnished Angels' turf."

"Turf? Like, the Jets and the Sharks? Turf like that?"

She nodded. "*Exactly* like that. Spurs isn't a Tarnished Angels bar, but it's in Tarnished Angels territory. So, the fact that there are other bikers here…"

"Oh," I said quietly.

"Yeah. *Oh*. Don't say anything to the girls, okay?"

"I won't," I promised.

"There you are," Sutton said when we got back to the table. "Where's Mia?"

"She had to make a call," Willa said. "She'll be here in a bit."

"Delilah brought another round of drinks," Rach said. "And told us the dancing is gonna start in about ten minutes."

"Which is probably my cue to go," Brooklyn said. "I have to relieve Slash of baby duty so he can get to the bachelor party."

She went around the table and hugged everyone goodbye, including me. She saved Sutton for last.

"Thank you for coming," Sutton said to her. "I know it was hard to pull yourself away from Palmer."

Brooklyn's smile was beaming. "Thanks for understanding." She hugged her tight again. "And congratulations. Tell Mia goodbye for me."

"I will. See you at the wedding."

Brooklyn grabbed her jacket off the back of her chair and waved goodbye.

Old school country music suddenly blasted through the sound system.

"Get your kit shickers ready," Sutton said. "We're about to have some fun."

Chapter 25

Three songs in and I was hooked. I was laughing, clapping, and having the time of my life.

And then I felt a pair of hands at my waist.

I tensed and nearly tripped.

"Didn't think you had two left feet, Duchess." His lips were close to my ear and his warm breath bathed my neck.

I immediately relaxed and then I shook off his hands. "You're not supposed to be here." I quickly got back into the rhythm of the dance, but when I looked around, I quickly realized that several of the Tarnished Angels were now at Spurs.

"Come to the bar with me, Duchess," Bones urged.

With a sigh, I let him take my hand and we walked off the dance floor. "What happened to the bachelor party?"

"Viper wanted to check on Sutton, Smoke wanted to check on Logan, Boxer wanted to check on Doc, Torque wanted—"

"I get the picture." I discreetly glanced around, wondering if the two bikers I'd seen were still here, but it looked like they'd cleared out. "You wanted to check on me, too, didn't you?"

Bones raked his eyes down my body, and I suddenly felt naked. "I'm liking the outfit, Duchess. Big hair. Very Miss Texas."

"Hmm. What do you think? If I sing 'Delta Dawn', do you think I have a chance at winning the talent contest?"

He grasped my hip and pulled me close. "Can you sing?"

I looked at him through the sweep of my lashes. "No."

Bones laughed. "Please tell me I didn't miss you riding the mechanical bull."

"You didn't miss it." I leaned forward, pressed my hand to his chest and whispered, "I know something else I can ride."

"Yeah?"

"Save a horse, ride a biker."

His laugh echoed off the walls. "I don't think that's how the saying goes."

"You don't want me to save a horse?" I shrugged. "All right. I won't."

Bones took a step closer to me. "Why do I have this vision of you right now straddling me, wearing nothing but your cowboy boots?"

"Because you're filthy," I said, breathless.

"You wanna get out of here?"

"We can't leave. It's a bachelorette party."

"Look around, Duchess. My boys are convincing their women to give up the good fight and go home with them as we speak."

I glanced around the dance floor. Bones was right. Smoke had Logan in his arms and he was whispering something in her ear. The other Old Ladies were in similar states with their men. All of them except for Rach and Darcy.

"No!" Darcy yelled from the edge of the dance floor closest to the bar. "This is bullshit! This was supposed to be a girls' night! And now everyone is leaving!"

"Let's go outside," Rach said, trying to take Darcy's hand. Darcy flung her arm back to prevent Rach from grabbing it, and when she did, she clocked a woman dancing near her right in the face.

"Ow!" the woman yelled as her hand went to her nose.

The guy next to her, her boyfriend no doubt, immediately jumped to her defense. "What the hell? Watch it!"

Darcy whirled and glared at him. "*You* fucking watch it!"

"Bones—"

"On it." He pushed away from the bar and stalked to the floor and immediately placed himself in front of Darcy, but gave her his back so he could address the woman and her boyfriend.

In a few minutes, he'd diffused the situation entirely and offered to buy them a round of drinks. The couple wandered over to the end of the bar and waited, clearly shrugging off the moment.

My attention slid back to Bones, who was now speaking in low enough tones to Rach that I couldn't hear him. Rach nodded and the two of them walked toward the exit with Darcy in tow.

Bones returned a few minutes later.

"You just broke up a potential bar fight," I said in amazement.

He sighed. "Yeah." He gestured to the bartender and pointed out the couple. Bones reached into his pocket for his wallet and pulled out a few bills. "Buy them a round, or two on me. The rest is yours."

"Thanks." The bartender took the cash and then left us to tend to the couple.

"So, what was that about?" I asked. "With Darcy, I mean?"

"How much did she have to drink tonight?"

I thought back over dinner. "She ordered a few rounds of drinks. And she did a few shots. Why?"

"Darcy lost her husband a few months ago," he said softly. "And she's not handling it well. She's trying to find solace at the bottom of a bottle, which never works."

"Oh, that's really sad," I murmured. "She was so quiet during dinner. I caught her staring off into space several times. Rach would ask her questions, and Darcy would answer flatly, but that was kind of it."

"Rach gets it. Gets Darcy, I mean. She lost her husband too."

My heart ached for them.

Darcy had mentioned that she was kid-free for the night, but I didn't know how many she had. "Darcy has kids?"

"Two. A boy and a girl."

I thought of losing my own father. How I was just starting to heal, three years later.

"There are things I'm ready to tell you," I said quietly. "But not here. Not in a bar."

He nodded slowly. "Okay."

"Follow me home?"

He nodded again.

"Let me say goodbye to Sutton," I said, looking around for her.

"Good luck finding her," Bones drawled. "Knowing Viper, he picked her up and carried her over his shoulder out of here."

"Seriously?"

"Seriously."

I was unable to hide my look of intrigue.

"You like that idea, don't you?"

"What? No." I shook my head. "Not in public anyway. In the privacy of my own home? Maybe…"

"I'll remember that." He kissed my forehead. "We can look for Sutton if you want."

"My jacket is at the table. I need to get it."

The table had been abandoned. It was clear the bachelorette party was over. No one else seemed that upset about it.

But Bones was right—I couldn't locate Sutton.

"You're leaving?" Logan asked as she and Smoke approached the table.

"Yeah. Aren't you guys?" I queried.

Logan shook her head. "A few of us are going to stay. Smoke wants to watch me ride the bull."

Smoke raised his arm and settled it over her shoulders. "I've got money on how long she'll last."

"If you see Sutton, please tell her goodbye for me," I said. "I had a lot of fun."

"It didn't last very long," Mia said as she came over with her husband in tow. "We can't go anywhere without our husbands following us around like lost little puppies." She looked up at her husband and flashed him a grin. "Am I right?"

"Sure, we can go with that," the man said. He looked at me. "I'm Colt."

"Nice to meet you."

"Okay, let's not do the Texas goodbye," Bones said. He shook Colt's hand. "Later."

I grabbed my jacket. "Oh. The bill."

"Handled," Mia said.

"Thanks."

Bones grasped my hand and tugged me toward the door. I looked over my shoulder. Mia gave me a thumbs up and a wink.

With a laugh, I turned back around and followed Bones out into the night.

∞

"You want something to drink?" I asked when we walked into the foyer of my house.

"No. I'm good." He closed the door behind us. "Did you have fun tonight?"

"Yes."

"You mad it didn't get wild and crazy?"

"How do you know it didn't? I might've been dancing on the bar before you got there," I teased.

"I don't think so." He leaned against the front door and watched me. "But I caught your moves on the dance floor. You're good."

I shrugged. "It's no ballroom dancing, but yeah. I'm okay."

He raised his brows. "You ballroom dance?"

"Cotillions, remember? I can teach you to fox trot, or even waltz if you want."

"Right." He pushed away from the door and stalked toward me.

"Bones," I began.

He leaned over and lifted me into the air and hoisted me over his shoulder. I squealed in surprise. "I didn't mean you had to do this tonight," I gasped.

"It's all I've been thinking about." He ascended the stairs, his hand settled below the curve of my butt.

My heart leapt with excitement.

"Did you bring a toothbrush?" I asked.

"Yes."

"Good."

He marched into my bedroom and flipped the light on. Bones brought me to the bed and gently dropped me. I bounced and then flopped back.

Bones looked at me as he slowly removed his leather cut.

"I care about your gums," I babbled.

"Oral hygiene is important," he agreed.

I nodded like an idiot.

He went to my walk-in closet and hung up his leather cut and then he sat down on the edge of the bed to take off his boots.

"I got carried away." He smiled at me. "Otherwise, I would've taken them off downstairs."

"I like that you got carried away," I said.

"Take off your boots. Get comfortable, Duchess."

I yanked off my boots and set them down on the other side of the bed. I debated on removing my tight jeans but decided against it.

Bones turned toward me. "Okay."

"Okay what?"

"Okay, I'm ready to listen. To whatever it is you want to tell me."

I was silent for a moment while I gathered my words and then I spoke. "My dad died three years ago—and my mother lost it. But not the crying and screaming and damning God kind of lost it. It was…" My hand went to my chest. "Inside. Like her heart was made of glass and it shattered into slivers too tiny to ever piece back together. After the funeral, she went to a *resort*."

"A resort," Bones repeated. "Like a spa or some shit?"

"Like Canyon Ranch but for…" I pointed to my head. "She came back from the resort and we didn't talk about my father's death again. My mother—she can't handle bad things happening the way normal people do. So, I don't tell her when bad things happen in my life. And up until someone trying to rob me at gunpoint, nothing bad has ever really happened in my life except my father's death. What I'm trying to say is, nothing bad ever happens because I won't *let* anything bad happen."

"You shut the world out to protect yourself, and your mother."

I nodded. "The world can't hurt you if you're not a part of it, you know?"

His hand snaked out and rested on my thigh. I covered his hand with mine.

"They were supposed to have forever, but forever was too damn short," I murmured.

"It's always too damn short. That's life, Duchess. You live it to the fullest while you've got it and when your time comes, you go out with a fucking smile and no regrets. You want to have regrets?"

"No. I don't want to have any regrets," I admitted. "The night I met you, Charlie had dared me to talk to you because she didn't think I would. She's been trying to get me to come out of my shell for a while."

"What made you talk to me? I mean, she dared you, but you didn't have to take the dare. You could've sat at the bar and sipped your drink and turned your back. But you didn't."

"Because she didn't think I'd do it. And for some reason I wanted to prove her wrong. Why were you going to approach me if given the chance?"

"Have you looked in a mirror?"

I rolled my eyes. "I'm flattered."

"No, you're not. But that wasn't all." He paused. "It was your laugh that set you apart."

"You heard my laugh?"

"Yeah. The way your face lights up, the way you throw your head back. You laugh with your whole body." He shrugged like it was nothing.

But it was everything.

Because it meant he saw me.

Not the me I showed the world. But the me I had tried so desperately to hide from the world.

"I'm frigid."

"Who the fuck told you that?" he demanded.

"No one."

"Bullshit," he said. "No woman thinks she's frigid unless some asshole puts that idea in her head. So, who's the asshole who said it?"

"My ex. Tyler. He's the only man I've ever…"

"Been with?"

I nodded.

"All right."

"All right?" I frowned.

"You're not frigid. You know how I know?"

"How?"

"Because I've kissed you. Because I've woken up with you." He lifted his hand to my face and held my chin between his fingers. "You need to hear me when I tell you, you're not frigid. And when you're ready, I'll prove it to you."

"You've been a saint."

"No one has ever accused me of that before."

"It wasn't an accusation." I laughed. "Do you have anywhere you have to be tomorrow?"

"Not until the afternoon. Why?"

"You want to see how I spend my time?" I asked.

"Yeah. I would."

"It means waking up to an alarm."

"I can handle that."

A yawn escaped my mouth and I hastily covered it. "By the way, I bought you a coffee maker and some coffee. I don't know if it's any good."

His eyes softened when they met mine. "It's perfect."

Chapter 26

"Where are we going?" Bones asked as I locked up the house.

"It's a surprise," I said. "We've got to take my car though."

"Fine." He took a sip of his coffee from the travel mug I'd given him. "This coffee isn't bad."

"Glad you like it."

"You know what else I like?"

"What?"

"Waking up in your bed."

"I kind of like that too."

The heaviness and truth of last night's conversation evaporated. This morning, it had taken all of my willpower to get up and not beg Bones to stay in bed with me all day.

He opened the driver's side door for me and after I got in, he walked around to the passenger side and did the same.

"You think we can make it a more regular thing?" he asked.

"We could," I said. "But if we do, that means I should probably have a talk with Charlie."

"About?"

"About her not coming over without calling first," I said with a smile. "She's known to walk in whenever she feels like it."

"Might be awkward if she does that and finds you laid out on the dining room table with my head between your thighs."

"You can't talk like that," I admonished.

"Why not?"

"Well, not when I'm driving. I don't want to get into an accident and then have to explain to the police that it was your dirty talk that caused it."

"My dirty talk is good enough to cause an accident? And just like that, my reputation has been restored. Are you really not going to tell me where we're going?"

I reversed out of the driveway. Bones' bike was parked in the second spot and a thrill of happiness went through me when I saw it. I was getting used to seeing it there, and I liked it.

I liked him in my house, in my kitchen, and in my bed.

"So, this thing I do, it happened by accident." I told him about the rescue dogs and pairing them with elderly people. "I pay the adoption fees and vet bills if there are any. People on fixed incomes in their older age can't usually handle the expenses associated with having animals."

"That's pretty cool actually. How do you know which dog and person belong together?" Bones asked.

"I don't know. I just have a hunch." I wasn't ready to tell him that Charlie and I were thinking about expanding it into something bigger. "You think it's weird."

"What? Following your gut? That's always a good idea. Do you do it with cats?"

"No. I'm not a cat person. I'm a dog person."

"And you haven't found a dog that's yours?"

I shook my head. "Not yet."

"But you're open to it?"

"Back to the dog thing, huh? They're a lot of responsibility."

"So are babies."

I frowned. "Babies? We weren't talking about babies."

"I'm just saying dogs are easier than kids. Do you like kids?"

"Sure." I was confused how we'd even gotten onto the topic of children. "Do you like kids?"

"Yeah, Duchess. I like kids."

My stupid little ovaries perked up at the thought of the brawny, tattooed biker holding a tiny infant.

Brain melted. Ovaries now in control.

We pulled into the parking lot of the animal shelter and I cut the engine. Bones held my hand as we walked toward the building.

"How do your magical powers work?" Bones asked.

I grinned. "I walk the rows. I look at the dogs. When I see one, I ask to spend time with it. I know everyone at the Rose Hill Retirement Community and it just kind of… merges. I don't know how to explain it."

"What if you pick out a dog for someone who doesn't want a dog?"

"Hasn't happened yet. You can literally see the moment a person falls in love with a dog."

Bones and I were silent as we walked down the shelter rows. The dogs jumped and put their paws onto the fence, their tails wagging, some of them vocally greeting us.

It tore at my heart. I hated that I couldn't save them all.

We came to the end of a row and there was a black Shepherd mix that was laying on the cement floor.

I crouched down and softly called to the animal.

It lifted its head and stared at me, but it didn't get up to investigate.

A volunteer I knew by name came around the corner and stopped when she saw Bones and I at the Shepherd mix's kennel.

"She came in a few days ago," Annie said. "We think she's about six months old. She should have more energy, but Dr. Henderson said there's nothing physically wrong with her. Best we can figure, she's depressed."

"She's the one," I said, rising. "Can I take her?"

Annie smiled. "Sure thing. Let me get a leash for you."

She disappeared around the corner and I heard a door open and close.

"Just like that?" Bones asked.

"Just like that," I said. "I've done this enough that they know the drill."

"Who's she going to? Do you have an idea?"

I nodded. "I have an idea."

~

I knocked on the apartment door and waited.

"Coming!" A voice called from inside. A moment later, the door opened. Jazz was wearing glasses, her dark hair in a loose braid and she was dressed in a pair of yoga pants and a purple sweatshirt.

"Bones," she said in surprise. "I didn't know you were coming." Her gaze dropped to the dog sitting serenely next to him. "You brought a dog."

"Who's there?" Brielle called from somewhere in the apartment.

"Hayden and Bones. And they brought a dog…"

I held up a bakery box. "And apple tarts."

A white, furry, wiggly body appeared at the threshold. He bent his front legs and lifted his butt into the air, his tail waggling furiously.

The Shepherd mix let out a low whine.

"I think she wants to play with your dog," I said.

"I think so. This is Fluffernutter," Jazz said. "I didn't realize you guys were at the stage where you were getting a dog together. Congratulations. First comes dog, then comes baby, then comes the wedding."

I frowned. "I don't think that's the way it goes."

"Hmm. No, she's right, Duchess. We don't follow the standard blueprint." Bones winked at me.

"Well, she looks like a sweet thing," Jazz said with a smile. "Let her off leash and come on in. I want to say hi to her."

Bones unclipped the dog's leash and she trotted into the apartment. We stepped into the loft after her and noticed the huge windows.

"Bones and Hayden got a dog together," Jazz announced.

"That was fast," Brielle said from her seat on the couch.

Bones leaned down to me and whispered, "Why did you let Jazz think that's our dog?"

"Trust me."

Brielle was covered with a fluffy blanket. "Sorry, I'd get up but I'm comfortable and I don't want to."

I held up the box of apple tarts. "Want one of these?"

"*Yes*, God, *please*," Brielle moaned.

"So, what's her name?" Jazz asked as she went to the cabinet to pull out plates.

"Haven't figured out a name yet," I said.

"Bones? You want some coffee?" Jazz asked.

"Sure thing."

The dogs were sniffing one another and both tails were wagging. Fluffernutter nipped at the Shepherd mix's hind leg, instigating a chase.

"Fast friends," Brielle remarked.

The Shepherd mix ran around the couch and then jumped up into Brielle's lap and began to lick her face.

"Oh," Brielle murmured, sinking her fingers through the dog's fur and fighting through the kisses.

I looked at Bones. "Three, two, one—"

"She's *adorable*," Brielle crooned.

"She's really sweet," Jazz agreed. She brought Bones his cup of coffee. "Cream is on the counter if you want it."

"Thanks," he said.

Jazz looked at the dog and it began thumping its tail against the couch cushions.

"Round two," I whispered.

"She has soulful eyes," Jazz said. "Doesn't she have soulful eyes?"

"Absolutely," I agreed.

The door to the apartment opened and the Shepherd mix lifted up in a defensive stance.

"That's a dog," the man rasped.

"Nothing wrong with your eyesight, is there?" Jazz sassed.

Brielle sighed. "Hayden, Homer, Homer, Hayden. My brother lives in our building. He time-shares Fluffernutter, and he and Jazz bicker every time they're in the same room."

"We do not," Jazz protested.

"Yes, we do," Homer stated.

"They even bicker about that." Brielle rolled her eyes.

"You let them name a dog Fluffernutter?" Bones looked at Homer. "Dude."

"Don't *dude* me. I wasn't consulted about the name. I wasn't even involved in deciding whether or not I wanted to time-share a dog in the first place. That was an accident."

Fluffernutter ran up to Homer and put his paws on his shins. Homer leaned down and scooped up the dog. The Shepherd mix must've realized that Homer wasn't a threat because she hopped down off the couch and went to sniff Homer. Her tail slowly began to wag and then she began to press against his leg.

He reached down to pet her. "Aren't you sweet…"

Bones looked at me. "Three for three, huh?"

"What's that mean?" Jazz asked.

I smiled. "She's a present."

"Who's a present?" Brielle asked.

"You wanted another dog, so I brought you the newest member of your family," I said.

"But she's *your* dog," Jazz said. "Yours and Bones'."

"You guys got a dog together?" Homer asked. "That's fast."

"She's not ours," I said again. "She's *yours*. Well, technically, she's Fluffernutter's. I got your dog a dog."

Homer set Fluffernutter down and then leaned over and snuggled up against the Shepherd mix. She looked up at him and licked his forehead.

"Fuck it," Jazz said with a sigh. "I'm not a monster. We'll keep her."

～

"Well?" I asked as I buckled myself in.

"That was kind of unbelievable," Bones said.

I grinned. "Do you have time to do another one? I'd like to take you to Rose Hill if you're up for it."

"I'm up for it."

He settled his hand on my thigh as I stuck the key into the ignition. "You didn't freak out."

"About what?" I asked as I started the car.

"When Jazz thought we'd gotten a dog together."

"But we didn't get a dog together. So, there was nothing to freak out about."

He paused for a moment and then said, "We could get a dog together."

"You're kidding, right?"

"You like dogs. I like dogs. I like you. You like me."

"Yeah, but getting a dog together implies commitment. A relationship. It's a huge step."

"So?"

"So, we haven't even slept together yet," I pointed out.

"Formality."

"We're dating, Bones. We're not even—"

His sudden smile had me stopping mid-sentence.

"*You jerk*," I said with a laugh.

"That was fun."

I snorted. "For you, maybe."

His phone rang and he reached into the breast pocket of his leather cut. "I've got to take this."

I nodded.

Bones pressed a button to his ear. "Yeah?"

He paused for a moment and listened. "Okay. I'll be there." He hung up and put his phone away. "Sorry, but I've got to bail. Club shit."

I tensed. "All right."

Even if I asked what that entailed, I knew Bones wasn't

going to give me an answer. The reminder that there would be things Bones would have to keep from me sprang up between us. Tension filled the car.

Our ride was silent and uncomfortable until my phone rang. It was a number I didn't recognize and I planned to ignore it, but I couldn't stand the strain.

I pressed a button on my steering wheel. "Hello?"

"Hi, is this Hayden?" came a male voice.

"It is."

"Hi, it's Walker Anderson. Your mother gave me your number."

Fuck. Fuck. Fuck.

Bones clenched his hand.

"Right," I said. "She mentioned that she did."

"I'm sorry it took me so long to call. I would've called sooner, but I went out of town unexpectedly. I know that sounds like an excuse, but it's the truth. Anyway, I'm back and I'd love to take you out to dinner. Preferably before the charity gala we're both attending next week."

"That's a really nice offer," I said. "But I think it's only fair to inform you that my mother kind of jumped the gun on giving you my number. She only told me about it after she did it."

"Ah, I see."

"Yeah." I took a deep breath. "I'm sure you're a lovely person, but I'm not interested. I'm sorry."

"Hey, no hard feelings. I understand the meddlesome parent thing. I guess I'll meet you at the event, then."

"Bye, Walker."

"Take care, Hayden."

I hung up with him right as I pulled into my driveway and cut the ignition.

"Why didn't you tell him you were dating someone?" Bones asked.

"Why does it matter? I said no to the date, didn't I?"

"You said you weren't interested."

I exhaled in annoyance. "Seriously? You're mad that I didn't tell a complete stranger I was involved with someone else?"

"Mad is the wrong word."

"Then what word would you use?" I snapped.

"We're more than involved. You know we are."

"I don't know *anything*," I stated.

"God damn it, Duchess. I'm ready to fuck the attitude right out of you just to prove a fucking point."

"Oh yeah?"

"Yeah."

The gauntlet was thrown down. We stared at one another and at the same time, reached for each other. His lips were on mine, his tongue was in my mouth, and I wanted him to prove what he'd just said.

I was done being patient.

I was done hiding.

My hand wrapped around the back of his neck as I strained to be closer to him.

He wrenched himself away, breathing hard. "Why do you always start this when I can't finish it?"

My gaze narrowed. "Bold accusation."

He held my stare. "Tonight."

I licked my lips. "Tonight."

Chapter 27

My hand trembled as I lit the last candle in the bedroom. And then I sat down on the edge of the bed and tried not to have a panic attack.

I grabbed my cell phone from the nightstand and looked at the screen. Bones had texted twenty minutes ago that he was on his way.

He would knock on the door at any moment.

And then…

I quickly dialed Charlie, hoping like hell she answered.

"Hey," she said after the second ring.

"I'm about to have sex with Bones for the first time and I'm terrified."

She was silent.

"Charlie?" I pressed.

"Let me take you off speaker phone," she said finally.

"*Speaker phone?*" I screeched. "Who are you with? Oh God, please tell me you're not with Savage."

"I'm not with Savage," she said. "That's done. Over. Kaput."

"Okay, we can talk about you later, right now we need

to talk about me. And who just heard me admit that to you?"

"Waverly," she said. "And Sailor. And Waverly's boyfriend, Dylan."

I groaned.

"I'm sorry, but I had Waverly answer my phone because my hands were occupied."

"Occupied with what? And why are you with Waverly and company?"

"Waverly's helping me with the dollhouse. Sailor and Dylan are here because—well, I don't know why they're here."

"We're always here," Dylan said in the background.

"I'm at Waverly's shop and we're restoring the dollhouse."

"Neat. Can you go someplace private? I need a pep talk. A pep talk I don't want them to hear."

"Let me go outside," Charlie said. There was rustling and the opening of a door and then she said, "Okay. I'm out of earshot now. So, you're going all the way with Bones. I think that's great."

"Yeah. Except, I'm sitting in my bedroom in a La Perla white lace body suit waiting for my biker to come over and…and…"

"Rip the white lace body suit off you with his teeth?"

"*Oh God*, I'm gonna faint."

"Now would be the time to have a glass of wine."

"I can't. You know I can't."

I heard the distant rumble of a motorcycle.

"Crap. He's almost here."

"Okay, I don't have a lot of time. So, here's what you're going to do…"

"I'm listening."

"You're going to pretend that you're one of the great

femme fatales of all time. You're going to get him on his knees and make him beg to let him pleasure you. You got that?"

"I got that." I swallowed. "But I'm more Audrey Hepburn than Marilyn Monroe."

"Not tonight. Tonight you're going to ruin him in the best way possible. You're going to ruin him forever."

"Love you for this," I said.

"Love you too."

I hung up and set my phone aside. I rose from the bed and picked up the white silk robe and put it on.

The doorbell rang.

"Showtime," I whispered.

As I walked down the stairs, I thought about Charlie's advice. I would be cool, confident. I wouldn't just be Marilyn Monroe, I'd be Marilyn Monroe, Jean Harlow, and Gene Tierney all rolled into one.

Only when I opened the door and saw Bones leaning against the doorframe, I crumbled. I gripped the door, praying it held me upright.

"Duchess," he greeted, his gaze slowly lowering. "You answered the door wearing *that*? I could've been the delivery guy."

"I'm not expecting a package."

"I've got a package."

I blinked and then suddenly I smiled. My smile turned into a giggle, my giggle into a laugh. It escaped through my mouth even as I tried to cover my lips to stifle the sound.

Bones let out a booming laugh of his own. "Jesus, you looked like you were about to faint."

I stepped back from the door and let him inside. I closed the door behind him and locked it, my laughter fading. "I was trying to channel my inner femme fatale. I don't think it worked."

"It worked. Damn, did it work," he said gruffly. He took a step toward me. "Hey."

I looked up at him. "Hi."

One of his hands settled on my waist, the other slid through the strands of my hair to cradle my head.

I placed my palm on his chest and met his lips.

Every worry drifted away.

He was tender.

Gentle.

And then his tongue slid into my welcoming mouth.

I whimpered and pressed closer.

Suddenly Bones wasn't gentle anymore. His hand skated from my waist to my lower back to pull me toward him.

He was hard everywhere.

"Bones," I whispered.

"I'm right here, Duchess."

"Take me upstairs."

He swept me into his arms and did as I bid. When we got to the bedroom, he looked around, clearly noting the low light and candles.

"You planning on seducing me, or romancing me?" he asked.

"Can't I do both?" I quipped.

"Yes." His lips caught mine and then he was lowering me to the bed.

He took a step back, his electric blue eyes on me as he slowly removed his boots and clothes. My breath caught in my throat as I watched his tattoos come alive across his rippling skin.

Bones reached for his boxer briefs, hesitating but a moment before sliding them down his muscular thighs.

His erection was massive and my eyes widened.

Bones gripped it in his hand and gave it a few strokes.

"Don't worry, Duchess. You'll be able to take me. I promise."

My throat was parched, and my heart drummed with nerves. Excitement swirled in my belly as I reached for my robe.

"What are you doing?" he asked.

"Getting naked?"

"No. You're all wrapped up like a present, and *I* get to unwrap my present." He grinned wickedly.

I leaned back against the pillows, watching as Bones settled onto the bed. He crawled up my body until he was hovering over me.

My fingertips glided across his shoulders, around his shoulder blades and down.

"Kiss me," I whispered.

Bones leaned forward and brushed his mouth over mine. He kissed me until I was delirious. He kissed me until I was writhing against him. He kissed me until the friction of my clothes between us was an unbearable obstacle.

He pulled back and opened his eyes to stare into mine. He sat back and looked down at me for a moment before reaching for the sash of my robe.

Bones ran a finger across my collarbone and then between my breasts, trailing lower.

"Jesus, Duchess. You're going to destroy me."

I bit my lip but didn't hold back my smile. "You're welcome to destroy my lingerie. With your teeth."

He let out a low laugh and shook his head. "There's plenty of time for rough. Plenty of time for quick. Not this time. This time, I'm gonna savor you."

His fingers danced across the delicate lace, gliding across my stomach and slipping between my thighs. He rubbed me lightly through the fabric and my back bowed off the bed as sparks shot through my veins.

I opened my legs wider.

"You like that," he growled as he continued to pet me.

I wanted to say yes, but my mouth didn't work.

He removed his fingers from between my thighs and reached for the straps of the body suit.

I lifted up so he could work them off my shoulders. He kissed the spot below my ear and drifted lower to my neck, my collarbone, the swell of my breast.

He tugged at the fabric until my breasts sprang free.

Bones took a nipple into his mouth, teasing it with his tongue.

My fingers plowed into his hair and I gasped when he gently bit my nipple with his teeth. He pulled it deeper into his mouth, sucking and licking.

And then he moved to the other breast and lavished it with as much attention as he had done with the first. While his mouth was occupied, his hand manipulated the lingerie down my body.

My ankles were trapped by the body suit and Bones reached down and removed it, flinging it away. His fingers delved gently between my legs, slipping inside me.

I was wet and ready.

He added another finger while his thumb brushed my clit.

I made a noise, a cross between a growl and a mewl.

Bones thrust his fingers gently at first, but then picked up speed. And when he pressed against my clit at the same time, my orgasm swept through me. My breast popped from his mouth as my back bowed, and I made noises I'd never made before.

He eased his fingers out of me as I caught my breath.

With hooded eyes, I watched him stick his fingers into his mouth and suck them clean.

I pressed against his shoulder and urged him to roll over. He settled onto his back and I lifted my leg over him and straddled him. I placed my hands on his chest and traced the ink marking his skin.

He gripped my hips.

"Take all the time you need, Duchess."

I leaned over and grazed his chin with my lips and then it was my turn to kiss him. I kissed his neck, and then lower. I gently tugged his nipple between my teeth, feeling it pebble against my tongue. My hand wandered between us so I could grasp him.

He was girthy and I gave him a squeeze.

Bones moaned.

"You like that?" I asked, smiling against his chest.

"Fuck yes."

I slid my grip up and down his shaft and my thumb stroked his crown. My mouth watered at the thought of tasting him.

Bones' hands glided down my outer thighs until he got to my ass cheeks, which he squeezed firmly. We touched and kissed, we stroked and toyed.

I felt a bead of moisture at the tip of him. He was ready, and so was I.

"Enough," he growled, grabbing me and flipping me onto my back. "I have to be inside you."

I nodded eagerly and gestured to the nightstand.

Bones leaned over and opened the drawer. He pulled out a new box of condoms. He ripped into it and pulled out a condom. He quickly tore into the package with his teeth and then he was rolling it down his straining shaft.

I flopped my legs open as he eased a hand beneath my

ass. Bones guided his erection toward my eager body. He slid the tip in, ever so slightly, and then he sank further.

Our eyes were locked on one another.

"You okay?" he whispered.

I nodded. I felt him everywhere. I was full of him, and I clenched.

His eyes rolled into the back of his head for a moment and then he opened them. "Can you take more of me?"

"I think so."

He glided all the way in and then ceased moving, giving me time to adjust to him. But then he slowly began to thrust, pulling back ever so slightly before sliding back in.

My body felt like it was on fire. The heat built in my belly, shimmering along my spine. It crept up my neck and prickled my skin.

I wrapped my legs around him as his movements picked up speed. He switched the angle of his pelvis, causing me to cry out, but not in pain.

"Fuck, I hurt you," he growled.

"No," I gasped. "It feels good. Do it again."

He did it again.

My clit throbbed as his shaft hit the exact spot inside me that had my toes curling, my back bowing, my release tearing through my body.

His hands slid beneath my ass and he lifted me up, thrusting deep and hard, elongating my orgasm as he had one of his own.

Bones gathered me in his arms as our breaths mingled and our hearts beat in sync.

We were still connected when he pulled back just enough to brush the hair from my eyes. He stared into them and said, "Told you. Not frigid. Not frigid at all."

Chapter 28

Bones grasped the back of my head and pulled me close for another drugging kiss. He released me and then gently eased out of my body.

I hissed in discomfort.

"Damn, I did hurt you," he said, sympathy splashed across his face.

"Don't feel bad about it. It was going to happen regardless."

He frowned. "What do you mean?"

"I mean, I haven't had sex in three years."

"Jesus, Duchess." Bones closed his eyes for a brief moment. "Why didn't you tell me?"

"Because I'd already told you enough. And I didn't need to stack all the reasons about why I was nervous to sleep with you and talk myself out of it."

"I could've been gentler—"

"You were plenty gentle," I interrupted. "Please, Bones. Don't feel bad about this. It was...*incredible*. Really."

"We're just getting started." He kissed the tip of my nose and then rolled away from me to dispose of the condom. He padded naked to the bathroom, giving me a glorious view of his backside.

I looked around for something to cover myself with and then realized a femme fatale wouldn't be shy. Not now, especially. So I got out of bed and stalked toward him. I placed my hand on his chest, stood on my toes and tilted my head back to receive his kiss.

"Give me five minutes and then join me in the shower," I commanded.

He smacked my ass as I sauntered away from him. I looked at him over my shoulder. "No one's ever done that before."

"How do you feel about it?" Bones asked with a devastating smile.

"I kinda like it," I admitted. Heat rushed to my cheeks and then I scampered off to the bathroom.

I did my business, wincing in discomfort. The soreness was a reminder of what we'd just done together.

Pleasure skated through me.

I got the shower going and then stepped into it. A few minutes later, the bathroom door opened and Bones came in. He stepped into the glass shower and without a word, pinned me against the wall and devoured my mouth.

"The lingerie…" he rasped.

"Yeah?"

"Fucking *hot*."

I grinned.

"I didn't take you for a lingerie kind of girl," he said.

"Next time I'll wear something a little less virginal and a little more sex pot."

"You're trying to kill me, aren't you? Death from permanent erection."

I grasped his shaft and massaged him. "You'll die happy then."

He raised his forearm and used the wall for support while I toyed with him. I didn't stop until he was coming again, splattering his release on my belly.

"You used to be shy," Bones said, breathing hard.

"Someone is making me fearless," I teased as I kissed him.

He pushed away from the wall and then grabbed the bar of soap. He lathered it in his hands and then he cleaned me.

"*The candles,*" I said in a panic.

"Relax, I blew them out."

I sighed. "Thanks. I wasn't thinking about them."

"No, you were thinking about me, and what we'd just done, and what we're going to do again and again…"

"You're filthy…"

He bit my earlobe. "You on top next time. Me behind you. You sitting on my—"

I cut him off with my lips.

When he pulled away, he looked down at me. "Shy again, huh? You weren't shy the other night when we were in bed at the clubhouse. You proved you were good at dirty talk."

"It was dark and I was facing away from you. Now, we're…the lights are on. It's different."

He smiled slowly.

"What?"

"My one and only goal now is ridding you of your shyness. It'll be fun. Practice makes perfect, you know."

I rolled my eyes and rinsed off and then I stepped out of the shower. I grabbed a white towel and dried myself before wrapping the towel around me.

Bones turned off the shower and grabbed the second towel I'd put out for him.

I strode into the bedroom toward the walk-in closet. I

opened the drawer of my dresser and pulled out my black silk camisole and matching sleep shorts.

Bones was already in bed by the time I was finished dressing. His bedside lamp was on and he flung back the covers and I climbed in next to him.

My hand crawled across the sheet to touch him. I encountered a warm thigh. "You're sleeping naked?" I asked.

"I always sleep naked."

"You didn't sleep naked the last few times we were in bed together," I pointed out.

He lifted up and turned off the lamp. "I was afraid it would make you faint."

"You arrogant bastard," I said with a laugh.

"Was I wrong?"

"I wouldn't have fainted," I assured him. "Hyperventilated, maybe. But not fainted."

He laughed. "Come here."

I rolled into his side and he settled his arm around me. "This okay?"

I snuggled closer. "It's perfect."

∽

One moment I was asleep, the next I was awake. I stared into the darkness, knowing it was sometime in the middle of the night. I also knew I wasn't going back to sleep because my brain was immediately on.

At some point, we'd changed positions. He was foiled around me like a candy wrapper.

I slowly wiggled from his embrace, pausing to see if he'd wake up. He slept on.

My robe was somewhere on the floor, and I felt around in the dark for it. I found it and put it on before quietly leaving the bedroom. I closed the door behind me.

I made my way to the kitchen and turned on the electric kettle. While I waited for it to boil, I got a mug and the loose-leaf tea Bones had brought me.

There was a sleeping biker in my bed upstairs.

My house suddenly felt full.

Full of laughter.

Full of emotion.

Full of life.

I cried in the kitchen as the water came to a rolling boil.

"Hayden?"

I tensed when I heard his voice. "Sorry, did I wake you?"

"Yeah. I thought you were coming back to bed, and when you didn't, I wondered what you'd gotten up to."

"I didn't even hear you," I said.

He placed his hands on my shoulders and I let him turn me around.

Bones stared down at me, his brow furrowed. "You're crying."

"Yes."

"Why?"

I swiped at my cheeks. "Lots of reasons."

"Tell me."

"It'll sound stupid."

"I doubt that."

I swallowed. "Haven't I bared my soul enough for one night?"

"Ah," he said, pulling me toward his chest. He'd put on his boxer briefs, but he was still on display.

I pressed my cheek to his warm skin and closed my

eyes, finding unexpected comfort, which only made me start crying again.

"Tell me," he urged. "Let me make it better."

"You already did," I blubbered.

He tightened his arms around me and dropped his chin to rest on top of my head.

"The last three years…it's all been bottled up with nowhere to go. You—released it. And now I'm crying all over you and I can't put it away and hide, which is all I want to do because if I don't, then you're going to think I'm an emotional mess who can't get it together."

"I think you've been carrying the weight of grief for a long time. And you've done it alone. Your mom hasn't been there for you. Not the way you needed her to be. And even though Charlie has tried, her world kept turning even when yours came to a grinding halt. Tonight, with me, you started living again."

"I'm in over my head, here." I sniffed. "I've never—"

"Felt this way about another person before," he finished for me. "I get it. It's fast. And it feels like you're on a freight train barreling toward a ravine on an unfinished bridge."

I looked up at him, my lips quivering. "I was going to say I've never come that hard."

He was silent for a moment. "I'm trying not to pound my chest like a Cro-Magnon right now."

"How's that working for you?" I teased.

"It's against every bit of my instinct, but I'm reining it in."

"Okay, seriously. What's wrong with you?"

"I'm going to need a bit more clarification on that." He released me and then pressed my hip to get me to move. He then poured the boiling water into my waiting mug.

"You just walk in on me crying and freaking out and all you do is hold me and tease me and make me feel better."

"Am I supposed to make you feel worse?" He looked at me in confusion.

"No, but…"

"But what?"

"My ex. He wasn't good at stuff like this."

"Your ex sounds like a douche."

I blinked. "Yeah, he kinda was."

"What would he have done if he'd walked in on you crying?"

"Gotten really uncomfortable and pretended it wasn't happening. He broke up with me two weeks after my father's funeral. He said it was too much and he couldn't handle it."

"You're shitting me."

"Nope. But I mean, he was twenty-three. Who can blame him?"

"He broke up with you when you needed him the most and now you're surprised when I do anything remotely sweet."

"I just wanted some tea and to cry in private," I joked. "Not a late-night therapy session."

He grasped my waist and hoisted me up onto the island counter.

"What are you doing?" I asked.

He urged me to lift up so he could slide my pajama shorts and panties down. "I know something better than tea at helping you sleep."

Chapter 29

"I COULD SPEND all day inside you." Bones took my lips in a ravenous kiss as he thrust into me.

As dawn streaked across the sky, I had another orgasm. I'd had so many, I'd lost count. I was sore and exhausted, and I didn't care.

Our skin was slick with sweat as I crested another wave, Bones' own release chasing mine. We collapsed onto the bed.

When I finally found my voice, I said, "I think you turned me into jelly. I can't move."

"You don't have to move." He cuddled me close. "At least not right now."

"You might want to take care of the condom, though," I remarked.

"Yeah. I'll do that."

He didn't budge.

"You didn't move." I laughed.

"Physically incapable."

"I knew we should've hydrated," I remarked. "And stretched."

"You can stretch now. I'll watch."

"Fiend."

He grabbed the back of my head and kissed me before releasing me. I got up from the bed and my vision immediately swam. I grasped the nightstand to ground me, but it didn't stop me from swaying.

"Hey, you okay?" Bones asked.

"Hmm. Yeah." I waited for my vision to clear and then I turned to look at him. I forced a grin. "I think it's low blood sugar."

Damned dirty liar.

"Well, let's get you fed."

Ten minutes later, we were in the kitchen.

"You sit," Bones commanded, pointing to the stool at the island. "I'll cook."

"What are you cooking?" I asked.

"You like eggs?"

"Yes."

"Okay. You have bread?"

"Yup."

"Then sit back and watch how hot I am with a spatula in my hand."

He was shirtless, moving around my kitchen, all rippled muscles and ink.

"What do your tattoos mean?" I asked.

He took a sip of coffee before he turned on the spider burner. "They mean what they mean."

"Okay, Yoda."

"Yoda?" He looked at me over his shoulder and grinned. "You're a *Star Wars* fan."

"No, I'm not," I said hastily.

"Oh, you *so* are." He let out a deep laugh.

"Okay, so I'm a fan. But not like I know all the rules and cannon of the *Star Wars* universe. And I'm a diehard for the original trilogy. I don't know how many movies there are total and I—" I paused. "What?"

"You're a nerd."

"I'm not a nerd."

"You're a secret nerd. You're a secret hot nerd," he said.

"I'm *not* a nerd."

"Oh yeah? What color is your light saber?"

"Green, obviously."

He raised his brows. "And what's the meaning of a green light saber?"

"Green represents wisdom and skill." I sighed. "Fine, I'm a nerd. I'll fly my nerd flag. What's your secret hot nerd trait?"

"I don't have one."

"Everyone has one."

"What's Charlie's?"

"I'm not spilling my best friend's secret nerd trait. So come on, tell me yours."

"I told you I don't have one."

"You're not secretly into Anime?"

"Nope."

"Legos?"

"Definitely not."

"I know what it is," I said with a smile. "You're a cosplayer and you go to conventions."

"You caught me," he said lightly. "I'm a cosplayer." He cut a hole in a piece of bread and then dropped it into the hot, greased pan. After a moment, he cracked an egg and dropped it into the hole. "I'm Gryffindor."

I gasped. "*Harry Potter*? That's your thing?"

With a sigh, he turned and came toward me. He pointed to a spot on his left upper arm that was part of his ink sleeve. I leaned forward to study what I was seeing.

"Oh my God, that's the Golden Snitch! You got a *Harry Potter* tattoo?"

He flashed a grin. "It's okay to admit you're totally into me now that I've shown you my boyish side."

"I'm *totally* into you," I said with a matching grin.

"Yeah?"

"Yeah."

"Feeling's mutual, Duchess."

"Bones," I said, lowering my voice.

"Yeah?"

"Your eggs are burning."

∽

"So for the wedding tomorrow," Bones said as I walked him to the door, "you want me to come over here and we'll ride together, or you want to meet me there?"

"Depends. Where is the wedding, anyway? I know nothing about it, not even the time."

"First Presbyterian. Four o'clock. Party is at the clubhouse so people can drink and crash."

"First Presbyterian? Really?" I wrinkled my forehead. "That feels…"

"Wrong?"

"Not wrong," I hastened to say. "Just, surprising. Sutton didn't seem the church wedding type."

"Sutton and Viper both had shit childhoods. Nothing was normal. Sutton wanted a church wedding. So here we are, a bunch of bikers going to a church wedding."

I grinned. "You wearing a tie?"

"The only woman I'll wear a tie for is you." He leaned down to kiss me. "Which I'm already doing."

"A black tie no less," I said with a smile. "Still can't wait to see you decked out in your tuxedo. Biker James Bond, maybe?"

"Hmm. Has a nice ring to it."

"So, I'll see you tomorrow," I confirmed.

"Yeah, tomorrow." He paused.

"Something else you want to say?"

"No." He drew me to him and gave me a proper goodbye. When he pulled back, I nearly slumped against him.

"You sure you have to go?" I asked, looking up at him through the sweep of my lashes.

"Yeah, I have to go. And I better do it now before I say fuck it all and take you back to bed."

The tenderness between my legs reminded me of the marathon of last night. I sighed. "I should probably give my body a break."

He grinned, a self-satisfied cat-got-the-canary-*and*-the-cream grin.

"Get out of here," I said with a laugh, pushing his chest.

"You own a pearl necklace?"

"Yes."

"Wear it to the wedding. And tomorrow night, I'm going to fuck you from behind while you wear nothing but your pearl necklace and heels."

I quivered. "Oh…"

"And then if you're good, I'll give you another kind of pearl necklace." He chucked me under the chin. "Later, Duchess."

I closed the door behind him and leaned against it for moment. I didn't move until I heard the rumble of his bike disappear into the distance. Then I went upstairs and grabbed my cell phone.

There were three missed texts from Charlie.

CHARLIE

Are you dead?

Did Bones' massive eggplant destroy you?

I need details

I called her and flopped down on the bed. The bed that smelled like me and Bones, and the unique perfume that two people made when they'd been intimate for hours.

"I thought I was going to have to send out a search party," Charlie said in way of greeting.

"I feel like I've been injected with a biker-lust serum," I said. "He's all I can think about. He just left and all I want to do is call him back and demand he ignore his obligations and service me again."

"Service you? You sound like the madame of a brothel."

"I sound like a client at a brothel." I snorted. "God, Charlie. Seriously, I've never experienced this before."

She sighed. "Yeah, that's the hormones talking."

"I hope so. Because it's making me all fuzzy and cloudy and…"

"Stupid."

"Stupid, yes. Totally stupid." I paused. "Is this how you feel with Savage?"

"Yeah. And I don't like that Savage makes me feel that way, which is exactly why I've ghosted him. Or tried to ghost him…"

"Tried?"

"He was pulling up to Willa and Duke's as I was leaving. One thing led to another…he asked me to go for a ride on his bike. Instead I went for a ride on his dick. I snuck out of the clubhouse this morning while he was still sleeping."

"Oh, Charlie."

"Don't *oh Charlie* me. I'm a woman and he's hot as hell. You try saying no to a biker that makes you feel alive and seen and understood."

"You poor bastard," I muttered.

"Tell me about it." She sighed again. "Willa warned me, you know."

"Did she?"

"Yeah. She said that Savage doesn't do repeats and to absolutely *not* fall in love with him."

"But he's slept with you more than once. Maybe that means he's falling for you too."

"No. It doesn't mean that," she said. "I'm not sure what it means that I'm apparently the exception to his repeat rule, but I know guys like him. He'll stick around for as long as he gets that dopamine hit and then poof, gone. I'm no better than some other vice. The minute I don't offer him a distraction from whatever it is that's eating him, then he's going to bail. And I'm not going to be left holding the bag. I'm not going to be left with a broken heart. I don't want to love someone who can't love me back."

"You might not have a choice in that," I said quietly. "We don't pick who we love."

"No, we definitely don't. But I have a choice if I decide to stick around hoping for scraps. I'm not a scrap girl. I'm a whole meal kind of girl." She fell silent for a moment. "That didn't make sense."

"It made sense to me," I said, smiling even though she couldn't see me. "And if he can't love you back, then there's something wrong with him. Not you."

"Maybe there's something wrong with all of us."

"Maybe there is. But there's still someone out there who will you love you, flaws and all."

"Yeah. I guess so."

"Charlie?"

"Yeah?"

"Want to come over and watch *Harry Potter*?"

Chapter 30

THE CHURCH WAS DECORATED with red and white roses, and the wooden pews were adorned with white satin bows. Viper stood at the altar with the minster. He had on a tie, but he was also wearing a leather cut. Raze was next to him as his best man.

Bones placed his hand at the small of my back and ushered me forward. We took the pew with Willa, Duke, Sailor, Waverly, and her boyfriend Dylan.

I slid in next to Waverly.

She looked at me and grinned. "Well, hey there, Hayden. How's it going?"

My gaze narrowed at her. "You be quiet."

"I'm not saying anything," she said with a smirk. She leaned forward and peered at Bones. "Hi."

"You don't have to be everyone's annoying little sister," I told her.

"Uh, yeah, I do. It's kind of my job. You know how I keep thoughts to myself?"

"How?"

"Bribery."

"I'm not paying you money," I said with a laugh.

"I don't want money, I want hard candy. Butterscotch," she said.

"I don't have any candy in my purse." I held up my teeny tiny clutch. "It wouldn't fit. Can I offer an IOU?"

She grinned. "Yes."

"You guys sound like you're making a business deal," Bones said. "What's all this about anyway?"

The string trio in the corner of the church struck a chord and the crowd fell silent. We turned to the back of the room and watched a girl with a mop of blonde curls wearing a pink dress throw rose petals as she walked down the aisle. Mia trailed after her. I saw Colt watch his wife. His eyes tracked her, and not even the baby smacking him in the face with her hands distracted him.

Sutton took her place at the back of the aisle, and then began to stroll toward her waiting fiancé. Though she was beautiful, I was much more interested in Viper's reaction to her, so I turned to look at him.

His face was stoic and he had no outward reaction to his bride. But in his eyes, I saw the truth.

This is forever.

Bones wrapped his arm around my waist and pulled me to him. I looked up at him and he was staring down at me, looking at me the way Viper was looking at Sutton; the way Colt looked at Mia.

My breath caught.

Maybe I can have forever too.

When the string trio ceased their tune, and Sutton met Viper at the altar, the moment between Bones and I was broken.

Everyone sat.

Boxer gestured to the flower girl and she ran to him and hopped up on his lap.

"We are gathered here today…" the minister began.

A baby cried and Brooklyn immediately stood up from the pew and hastened to the doors. Unfortunately, that set off another baby crying, and Joni quickly rose and all but ran in the direction Brooklyn had gone.

"The beauty of His creation. A reminder of why we enter into holy matrimony. Let us continue," the minister said.

"Where do babies come from?" the flower girl asked, interrupting the service again.

"Doc, you want to answer that one?" Kelp called from the other side of the aisle.

"Hmm, that's for Darcy to answer," Doc said.

"Great," Darcy said. "Foist it off on me."

"She's *your* daughter," Doc said with a laugh. "I could give her the clinical version if you want…"

"What's clinical mean?" the flower girl asked, looking around, completely oblivious to the ceremony, and instead hoping someone would answer her questions.

"Hush, Lily. You're interrupting the wedding," Darcy admonished.

Sutton pressed a hand to her mouth to stifle a giggle. Viper leaned in close to the minister and whispered something. The man nodded and began speaking again. I could see his lips moving, but he was being purposefully quiet.

"Waverly," the flower girl called.

Darcy groaned.

"Yeah, Lily Burger?" Wavery replied.

"Where do babies come from?" Lily asked again.

All eyes, except for the bride and groom, turned to look at Willa's younger sister.

"You wanna know where babies come from?" Waverly asked Lily.

"Yes." Lily nodded her head eagerly.

"*Waverly*," Willa warned.

"I'll tell you where babies come from." She gave a dramatic pause. "They come from Cleveland."

Lily frowned. "What's a Cleveland?"

"It's in Ohio," Sailor clarified.

"What's an Ohio?" Lily asked.

"Crisis averted," Darcy said. "Now maybe we can get back to the wedding—"

"You may now kiss the bride," the minister announced, loudly this time so all could hear.

∽

"That's the strangest wedding I've ever witnessed," I said as I washed my hands in the women's restroom. "We missed the vows entirely."

Brooklyn was sitting on a red couch nursing her newborn daughter, Palmer. Joni had just finished changing Everett's diaper.

"So did we," Brooklyn said.

"That's kind of how things go around here," Joni added. "Nothing goes according to plan. You should've been there for Doc's wedding. It was a riot." She quickly told me what had happened.

"Anyone else noticing that Lily is the center of all the shenanigans?" I asked with a laugh.

"Yeah, she definitely is," Brooklyn agreed. "But she's so cute no one can ever be mad at her."

"She's our little biker princess, and she knows it," Joni said.

"Now we rage," Brooklyn said. "And by rage, I mean I'll drink a mocktail, have some food, and pass out at seven thirty."

"Don't tempt me with a good time," Joni said, laughing.

Brooklyn sighed. "Come on, let's get to the clubhouse. Brielle and Jazz took care of everything and I want to see their splendor. They wouldn't let me help."

I met Bones in the sanctuary where he was talking to Smoke and Logan. When he saw me out of the corner of his eye, he reached his hand out to me. I slid into the spot next to him, and he wrapped his arm around me and tugged me close.

Logan's gaze darted between me and Bones and settled on me with a smile.

"We'll see you at the clubhouse," Bones said, slapping Smoke on the back.

Bones kept his arm around me and we began to walk toward the exit. When we were in the parking lot, he said, "Have I told you you're beautiful today?"

"Twice."

"Well, I'm saying it again." He slid his hand up to my neck and touched the pearl necklace. His promise from yesterday had been simmering in the back of my mind the entire day.

My dark hair was down and in big waves. The dress I'd worn was burgundy, with a full skirt, a lace bodice and open back. My heels were four inches tall, though they didn't do much to put me on an even playing field with Bones.

A dark-haired boy who looked on the verge of entering his teenage years loosened his necktie. He held Lily's hand as they walked with Darcy to her car. "Mom, can I ride with Silas?"

"That's fine with us, Cam," Mia said.

Darcy ruffled her son's hair. "Go for it."

"*Mom,*" the boy whined, trying to fix his hair that his mother had messed up.

"*Mom,*" Darcy parroted in the same tone, but she grinned.

"Cam no!" Lily yelled, squeezing his hand tighter and not letting go. "I want you to stay with me!"

"I'll see you in a few minutes," he promised. "We're all going to the same place."

"No! You can't leave me!" She let go of his hand, but then launched herself at her older brother, wrapping her arms around him like an octopus and refusing to let go.

Cam looked at his mother.

"Your choice," Darcy said to her son.

Lily whimpered.

"Okay, I'll ride with you, Lil," Cam relented. "Don't cry. I'm right here. I'm not going anywhere."

"Keys, please," Bones asked me quietly. "I'll drive so you don't have to drive in heels."

I fished my car keys out of my clutch and handed them to him. He unlocked the car and then opened the passenger door for me.

When the doors were closed, I said, "Wow. That was about so much more than Cam riding with Silas, wasn't it?"

"Yeah." He sighed. "Losing their father has been rough on the kids—especially Lily. She's got major separation issues now. Not really surprising, but even though she's seeing a kiddie shrink once a week it's not getting any better."

"And Darcy?" I asked as Bones started the car. "What about the brawl she almost got into two nights ago?"

"The Old Ladies are gonna stage an intervention."

"An intervention? I know you said she's been hitting the

booze hard since the death of her husband… Is she a full-blown alcoholic then?"

"I mean, it's going in that direction. So something's got to be done."

"Yeah," I agreed. "When is it happening?"

"This week. They're waiting until after the wedding. They didn't want to put a damper on the couple's happiness."

"Oh." I looked out the window as we drove out of the parking lot of the church.

"What were you and Waverly talking about?" Bones asked.

"Nah ah, no way. My lips are sealed. And that reminds me, I owe her butterscotch candies to ensure silence on her end."

"Come on, tell me, I have to know."

"Okay, but you promise you won't laugh at me?"

"No."

"Then I'm not telling you!"

"Fine. I won't laugh."

I looked at him. "You're lying."

"I'm not lying. I have no intention of laughing."

"No intention? So, you still might laugh?"

Bones' tone was light when he said, "You know what? It's not worth it. Keep your secrets, Duchess."

"Can I ask you a question?"

"I'm a tits man."

"Great, but that's not the question I was going to ask you."

"You've got a great ass too."

"Thanks."

"But your pussy… God damn, it's perfect. Pink, gorgeous. I just want to bury my head between your thighs and let you suffocate me."

"I'm game if you are," I said, breathless.

He shot me a wicked grin. A grin that shot straight to my core.

"It's hot in here," I said as I reached for the air conditioner controls, which only made him laugh.

"What's the question you wanted to ask me?"

"It's about Savage."

He raised his brows. "Throwing me over already? For someone younger?"

I rolled my eyes. "He and Charlie have been…"

"Playing Animal Planet?"

"Charming way to put it." I snorted. "But yeah. Has Savage said anything about her?"

"I don't know, Duchess. Want me to ask him when we have chemistry next period?"

"*Bones*."

"*Duchess*."

"He really hasn't said anything about her?"

"Not to me," Bones stated.

"Was he mad when he found out she wasn't with me even though she said she was?"

"I don't know. Third base," he quipped.

"Abbott and Costello? You're quoting Abbott and Costello?"

"You know Abbott and Costello?"

"I watch black and white movies. Of course I know Abbott and Costello. Why are you quoting Abbott and Costello?" I asked.

"Because you're not making a damn bit of sense."

"Was he mad when he found out she lied to him about where she was?" I clarified.

"No. He wasn't mad. He didn't care."

"He didn't *care*?"

"Savage never cares. That's what I'm trying to tell you.

He might've been intrigued by the mind games, but mind games never last with him. Women never last with him." He glanced at me. "Is she catching feelings?"

"No," I lied. "Charlie doesn't catch feelings either. I was just curious why he didn't invite her to the wedding."

"A wedding is a place to bring a date. Dates have expectations."

"What sort of expectations?" I asked.

He gave me another panty-dropping smirk. "I'll give you one guess."

"Weddings seem to bring out the dirty flirt in you."

Bones settled his hand on my thigh and began to hike up my dress.

"What are you doing?"

"Seeing if I can give you an expectation before we get to the clubhouse."

Chapter 31

"Those were great expectations," I said, my cheeks still flushed as Bones parked in the gravel lot of the clubhouse.

"Think about how great they'll be when I can fully devote my attention to them."

I cradled his cheek in my palm and skimmed my thumb over his lips. "It's probably all I'm going to be thinking about."

We got out of the car and Bones went to the back seat and picked up the small bag I'd packed. If I was doing sleepovers in a clubhouse room, then I wanted my own toiletries and comfortable pajamas.

Cars began to arrive, including the bride and groom. Sutton got out of the car and ripped at the skirt of her wedding dress which fell away to reveal a shorter skirt beneath it.

"I'll wear this dress the rest of the day," she said. "But I'm not dragging a train around. Where are my Converse?"

"I'll get them," Viper said with a wayward smile.

She sat in the driver's side seat as she changed her

white heels to a pair of bright red Converse. "Okay, I'm ready for food."

"Food?" Kelp asked as he got off his bike. "You need a drink. Preferably hard liquor. You did just legally bind yourself to Viper…"

"I don't think I'll be having a drink for the next nine months, give or take a few weeks."

It took a moment for her words to penetrate, but when they did, Viper's mouth widened in shock. "Seriously?"

She beamed up at him. "Seriously."

He swept her into his arms and held onto her, her legs dangling like a rag doll. Viper buried his face in her hair. I was witnessing what felt like a private moment, and hastily turned away, despite the fact that Kelp and Raze were seeing it too.

I looked at Bones but I couldn't tell what emotion was streaking across his face.

Viper finally put Sutton down and they were immediately swarmed by the Tarnished Angels.

"Why don't you look surprised?" Bones asked me once he'd offered his congratulations and stepped back.

"Because I already knew," I said with a smile.

Bones picked up my bag and took my hand, lacing his fingers through mine. "Yeah? How?"

"Sutton told us the night of her bachelorette party," I explained. "And she asked us to keep it a secret until her wedding day."

Bones led me toward the clubhouse and I glanced over my shoulder at the happy couple. Though they were surrounded by friends—friends they considered family— they kept stealing glances at each other, obviously sharing something that only they could share.

It made emotion leap into my throat.

We put my bag in Bones' room. When I turned to leave, Bones blocked the way.

"What are you doing?" I asked with a coy smile.

"Just looking at you," he said quietly.

"Yeah?" My hand reached for the zipper on the side of my dress.

"Leave the dress on," he commanded.

My hand stilled.

"If I get you naked now, we'll miss the entire party. Let's go celebrate my brother and his woman, and then I promise to satisfy your every need later tonight."

I flashed a grin. "Promise?"

"I promise. I'd grab a sweater. You brought a sweater, right?"

"I did. It doesn't match though," I remarked as I opened my bag and dug through it.

"No one cares."

"I care."

"You're hot when you're put together, Duchess, but I like it more when you're dressed down."

"Really?" I asked as I slid my arms into a black wool sleeve.

"Really. Come on, I'm starving."

We headed into the backyard and my breath caught at the sight. A white wedding tent had been pitched and there were several tables laden with white tablecloths and mason jar candle votives. Heat lamps graced the perimeter of the tent, waiting to be turned on when the temperature dropped in the evening.

There was a long table of chafing dishes with food, a pop-up bar catty-corner to the table, and then a separate area for the wedding cake and mini cupcakes.

Jazz, Brielle, and a few severs were standing at the

ready to help with the buffet. "Is there anything without red meat?" I asked.

"I have a plate for you inside. Let me get it," Jazz said.

Bones and I took our food to one of the vacant tables.

He set his plate down next to me. "I'm going to the bar. Want me to get you a drink?"

"Something non-alcoholic, please." I set the napkin in my lap and reached for my fork.

"Mind if we join you?" Doc asked just as I took a bite of fish. I waved to the empty seats and she and Boxer sat down.

"We didn't get much of a chance to talk at Sutton's bachelorette party," Doc said.

"A lot was going on," I responded.

"And then the menfolk crashed the party," Doc said, shooting Boxer an amused look.

"You weren't complaining later that night," Boxer drawled.

"Hush, you," Doc said as she began to blush. "Don't mind him. Our yellow lab is better behaved than Boxer."

"That's factually inaccurate. Last week, Monk ate a pair of your underwear and I just ate—"

Doc hastily covered Boxer's mouth with her hand. "Will you stop? We're trying *not* to scare the new girl."

"Don't hold back on my account," I quipped. "Bones has been attempting to desensitize me to his dirty mouth since the moment I met him."

"What have I been doing?" Bones asked, reappearing at the table with a bottle of beer and a martini glass. He set the martini glass down in front of me. "The bartender made you a Cosmopolitan without the booze, and he substituted sparkling water to make it fizzy. Whatever the fuck a Cosmopolitan is."

"Thank you," I said. "And never mind what you were doing."

"Apparently you've got quite the dirty mouth," Boxer said to Bones. Boxer swiped the bottle of beer from Bones and took a sip. "You might need another one of these."

"See? No manners," Doc said with a laugh.

"Guess I'm going back to the bar. Doc, can I get you something?" Bones asked.

"Same thing Hayden's drinking."

"You got it." Bones looked down at me. "Eat before it gets cold."

I took another bite of food and looked around the wedding reception. Sutton and Viper were talking with Slash and Brooklyn while Brooklyn held their newborn.

Everyone lent a hand where they were needed. Friends held babies while their parents ate and no one seemed put out by the fact that several children were at a wedding. Most of the weddings I'd attended were adults only.

I frowned.

"Hayden?" Doc asked.

"Hmm?"

"I asked you how your food is."

"Oh. It's great. Hey, Darcy isn't here yet. And she left when we did."

"She texted the Old Ladies group chat," Doc explained. "She had to run home for a second."

Bones and I chatted with Boxer and Doc, but once I finished my food, I got up and went to talk to Brielle and Jazz.

"Well?" Jazz asked. "How was the food?"

"Delicious," I said. "Thanks. I just wanted to know how it's working out with the new dog?"

"We named her Cuddle Bug," Jazz said.

"You," Brielle stated. "*You* named her Cuddle Bug. Homer and I voted for the name Millie."

Jazz rolled her eyes. "She has to be spooned at night, otherwise she doesn't go to sleep. She named herself, really."

"You should've seen the looks we got yesterday at the dog park calling for her." Brielle shook her head. "Downright embarrassing."

"How was the bachelorette party?" Jazz asked. "Brooklyn told us some stuff went down…"

"About the guys crashing the party because they couldn't stay away from their women?"

"No, about the fight Darcy nearly got into," Jazz said. "Good thing Bones stepped in when he did."

I frowned. "How did Brooklyn know about that? She left before it happened."

"Chain of command. Bones told Slash, Slash told Brooklyn, Brooklyn told us," Brielle said. "You must've had a front row seat."

"Yeah, I did."

"That's it? That's all you're going to say about it?" Jazz stated.

"It feels like gossip, and I don't want to gossip," I said. "I don't know her. I just know she's hurting, and we should all be there to support her."

"I didn't mean to—" Jazz sighed. "You're right."

There was an awkward moment of silence, but then Brielle asked, "Where *is* Darcy? And Lily and Cam?"

"Doc said she had to run home first, but she's probably on her way."

"It's been almost an hour," Brielle murmured. "Since you guys got here, I mean."

"Maybe I'll ask Mia if she's heard from her," I

murmured. I left Brielle and Jazz and headed for Mia's direction, but I was waylaid by Waverly.

"So, I was thinking," she said. "I know you promised butterscotch candies, but if you lend me those heels instead, I'll call it even."

I grinned. "My heels? How do you know we're the same size?"

"I'm praying we are because you've got amazing taste. Better taste than even Logan."

"I heard that!" Logan called, and then went back to talking to Rach.

"You don't think I have good taste?" Willa asked as she joined me and her sister.

"Nope," Waverly said unashamedly.

"I'm not really your style, am I?" I asked. Waverly was rocking the bad-girl-gothic-meets-80s-female-girl-band-legend. She wasn't wearing heels, but heavy motorcycle boots.

"I'm all about change," Waverly said. "Please, can I try them on?"

"You can absolutely try them on," I said with a laugh.

"I'd kill to see the inside of your closet." She batted her eyes at me.

"Actually, I have a dress that I bought even though it was completely wrong for me because I loved it so much. It would be perfect for you—and your red hair." I tugged on one of her curls.

"Really?" Waverly squealed and then launched herself at me, nearly knocking me over.

I laughed at her exuberance. She was so fifteen in that moment. Other moments I swore she was twenty.

I looked at Willa and she turned her head and wiped at the corner of her eye.

"You are the coolest person ever," Waverly said as she pulled back. "Now I'm gonna go eat three cupcakes."

"You didn't have to do that," Willa said once we were alone.

"Do what?"

"Treat her like she's your little sister," Willa said.

"Oh." I sighed. "Well, I don't have a little sister, but if I did have one, I'd hope she'd be just like Waverly."

"Crap, you're going to make me cry. Again." She let out a watery laugh. "I've been so worried about her."

"Worried? Why?"

"Our mom was hardly a mom. She officially bailed a few months ago, but I've been raising Waverly since I was a teen anyway. Duke and Savage helped because…they're family. But I was worried she was never going to open up. And now, she's like a different person. I'm just so grateful for this club. They've been here for us through the hardest time in our lives."

She squeezed my hand. "Anyway, I'm rambling. Now Waverly has so many older sisters she can count on. I just love that."

"Stop, now you're going to make *me* cry."

"We'll be sniffling in company."

I gave her an impromptu hug, my reserved nature giving in to the warmth of the moment. Willa, Bones, the club…they made it impossible to remain on the sidelines.

I pulled back, intending to take my leave and seek out Mia. As I did, I noticed the club president's wife was across the lawn talking on her phone. She lowered her cell from her ear and it slipped from her hand into the grass.

I saw the look on her face.

I knew that look.

It was the look a person wore when their entire world had just shattered around them.

It was the look my mother wore when she found out my father had died.

Chapter 32

Tragedy swept through the wedding reception, blanketing the celebration of life and the union of two people with the stark reminder that it was all temporary, and would end in death.

Darcy had lost control of her car and hit a cement barrier between the interstate and an exit lane going full speed. She died on impact. Cam was in emergency surgery due to a leg injury. The doctors didn't even have time to tell anyone what condition he was truly in, and Lily was in a medically induced coma with a punctured lung.

Boxer and Doc had already left for the hospital. Mia had asked Waverly to take care of Scarlett and Silas while she and Colt joined Boxer and Doc.

Now, Waverly was bouncing Scarlett on her hip, trying to keep her occupied.

As for the rest of us, we sat in the middle of the tent, surrounded by food and dessert. It was quiet except for the occasional noise of a baby, or someone crying in the background.

"It's our fault," Rach said quietly. "It's our fault this

happened. We all knew her mental state. We all knew her drinking was a problem. It's our fault our friend is dead and her children are in the hospital, fighting for their lives." Rach stood. "I'm going home. I can't—I can't sit here waiting for more bad news."

"Rach," Logan murmured, reaching for her friend's hand.

Rach pulled her arm away. "It's too much. And I'm as guilty as any of you."

"You're not driving home," Raze commanded.

"I only had one drink, and I had it an hour ago," Rach stated.

"I don't care. You're not in a clear frame of mind. You're not driving home. End of discussion."

She glared at him.

"Give me your keys."

"Fuck you, Raze," she spat, turning and marching toward the clubhouse.

Raze made a move to go after her, but Logan shot up to stop him. "I'll go. I'll make sure she stays."

Logan jogged after Rach, the two of them disappearing into the clubhouse.

"She's right," Joni said softly. She looked around the group of men and women. "We're family and we let this go on for too long. We all knew what was happening and we did nothing."

"That's not fair," Sutton said. "I saw what was happening before anyone else did. I told Rach. She was handling it because they shared a common experience."

"So, you're blaming Rach in all of this?" Joni asked.

"No. I'm just saying we were trying. I mean, how do you help someone who doesn't want to be helped?" Sutton asked.

"I agree with Joni," Brooklyn said. "We were all

wrapped up in our own lives. We didn't do enough for our friend. We shouldn't have waited to do the intervention."

"Were you going to be the one to tell her she couldn't order tequila at the bachelorette party? Or drink at a girls' hang out?" Willa asked. "Embarrass her in front of everyone? She's an adult for God's sake. You can't just tell someone what to do."

Tavy and I glanced at each other, sharing a look of awkward commiseration. We weren't Old Ladies; we weren't part of the club. And now we were witnessing them air their dirty laundry.

Hurtful words started to fly, people began speaking over each other, hurling accusations. Guilt permeated the entire conversation and anger began to brew.

I stood up and grabbed my clutch.

"Where are you going?" Bones asked me.

"I don't belong here," I said gently. "This isn't—I shouldn't be here."

His eyes softened. "Stay."

I looked at the Old Ladies who were facing off with each other, their men attempting to intervene, but it didn't seem like they were able to.

He rubbed the back of his neck. "You belong here."

I shook my head. "I don't, really. I'm not an Old Lady, Bones. My heart aches for those kids—losing not just a father, but a mother, too? And so soon? I can't listen to them blame each other. I won't. And what if the kids don't make it? That will destroy the Old Ladies."

"What do you need right now? This is rough."

"I need to leave. Spend the night with me. At my place. Your motorcycle is still there, anyway." I looked again at the group of people. The accusations had ceased, but now men were holding their wives, offering them comfort as they cried for their friend.

I turned away, not wanting to see the devastation on their faces.

Caring about people hurt. It hurt so much.

"Bones," Zip called. "Church."

Bones nodded. "Be right there."

"What's church?" I asked.

"Brothers meeting to discuss club matters."

"Go," I urged. "I can see myself out."

He sighed. "Fine." He cradled my cheek and kissed my lips. "I'll see you later."

Before I left, I stopped by to see Brielle and Jazz.

"You're taking off?" Jazz asked.

I nodded. "It doesn't feel right. Witnessing their grief."

She didn't have a response to that, so I hugged them both and then moved along.

Just as I came into the clubhouse, Logan was closing the door of Rach's room, a set of keys in hand.

"Hey," she greeted.

"Hey." It felt stupid to ask Logan how Rach was doing, so I didn't bother with the platitudes. "You got her keys. She didn't want you to stay with her?"

Logan gestured with her chin toward the living room and we walked down the hallway away from Rach's door.

"She wanted privacy to call my brother," Logan explained.

I frowned. "Brother?"

"Yeah. They're...complicated. They used to date when they were younger. They reconnected about a month ago."

"Wild."

"Yeah. Don't know how that's gonna shake out. She lives here. He lives in Idaho." She shrugged. "Not my circus, not my monkeys."

"Right. Well, I better get going..."

"Why are you leaving?" she asked.

"You're missing the brawl out there. It's not pretty."

Logan's eyes widened. "They're throwing punches?"

"What? No! Figure of speech, sorry. The Old Ladies, I mean. They're throwing words and it's getting ugly."

"And it's making you uncomfortable."

"I'm not an Old Lady."

"You want some tea? I'm going to make some tea."

"I'm leaving."

"Take the tea, Hayden."

I sighed. "Guess I'll have some tea."

I sat on one of the kitchen stools and watched her fill the electric kettle and grab two mugs. "How do you feel about chamomile?"

"Love it."

"Great."

While we waited for the water to boil, she stood across from me. We were divided by the kitchen counter.

"They're blaming each other," I said quietly. "They're blaming each other for Darcy's drinking and I just can't be there and listen to it."

"This was a no-win situation," Logan said. "Just because you intervene and tell someone they have a problem doesn't mean they're ready to deal with it. Unchecked, you have this—two kids with no parents who are in the hospital. If they even…"

"No-win situation indeed." I shook my head. "Look, these are just my opinions and I have no right to judge, but those kids are the ones who are losing. Maybe she wouldn't have listened. But they don't have parents now. Those kids are the ones who are going to have to live with the fact that there were people around them that knew what was going on at home and didn't stop it in time."

A voice came from behind me. "You don't know what the hell you're talking about!"

I turned on the stool. Rach stood in the living room with tears streaking down her cheeks. "Do you know what it's like? Do you know what it's like to have everything you love ripped away from you? If I hadn't been pregnant when my husband died, do you think I wouldn't have found solace in a bottle? Sometimes people break and there's not a damn thing you can do to put them back together."

My face drained of color. "I know exactly what it's like to have everything ripped away from me. I know what it's like to lose someone who loves you so much that you don't know how you're supposed to go on breathing. And I know what it's like to have a mother who isn't strong enough to be there for you. So yeah, Rach. I know exactly how it feels."

I stood up. "You know who was there for me when I lost my dad? My best friend. My best friend who sat with me on the bathroom floor during my father's funeral, holding my hair back while I cried so hard that I vomited. *That's* what it means to be family."

Without waiting for a reply, I grabbed my clutch and marched out of the clubhouse. I didn't look back.

Chapter 33

THERE'S a moment in your life so crystal clear that it's undeniable; it's the moment you become an adult. For me, it was the day my father died. It was the day I realized my mother wasn't strong enough to handle the hardships we all had to live through, and that I was on my own.

Maybe I was too hard on her. I didn't know what it was like for her or for Rach, losing their husbands, losing the love of their lives.

Children lose parents. It's a rite of passage. It's natural, no matter how grueling it is to live through. There's nothing you can do to prepare for it. There's no blueprint on how to get through it. You just put one foot in front of the other and take one breath after another. And one day, it's the anniversary of his death or his birthday, and it doesn't hurt quite as much as it used to. It never goes away completely, but instead becomes bearable because it has to become bearable. Otherwise, you'd just stay the sad curled up crying mess on the floor.

After I got home, I kicked off my heels and laid on the

couch. I covered myself with a blanket, including my head, and cried.

I cried for myself. I cried for those children I'd only recently met. I cried for the Old Ladies, who didn't know how to mourn their friend because of their guilt. I cried for the cruelty of a world I didn't understand.

My phone rang, but it was in my clutch by the door. I had no interest in getting up to see who was calling. Not even when it rang repeatedly.

It was only when there was a knock on the front door and I heard Bones yelling out that I realized I had to get up.

"Duchess, open the door or I'm gonna kick it in!" he shouted.

I flung off the wool blanket and sat up, but aside from that, it was too hard to move.

"Duchess! I'm giving you until the count of ten. One, two…"

I forced myself to rise and then I padded to the front door. I unlocked it and opened it.

Bones stopped mid count. His eyes swept over me, lingering on my face. "Duchess?"

I flung myself into his arms, the tears coming fast and hard.

He wrapped me in his strong embrace while we stood in the foyer, the front door open for everyone to see what was going on inside.

"I miss my dad," I whispered.

His arms tightened around me. He backed us up just enough so that he could close the door.

"I talked to Rach and Logan," he said into my hair.

"You did?" I hiccoughed.

"Well, they talked to me, actually."

I paused. "They told you what I said, didn't they?"

"Yeah, they did." He released me and pulled back so he could grasp my face in his hands and drew my attention to him. "What do you need? Tell me what you need and I'll get it for you. Do you want me to call Charlie? Are you sure you don't want some sort of sugary dessert? I hear that helps."

"I don't need—I have everything I want right here." I turned my head ever so slightly so I could kiss his palm.

He dropped his hands.

"Any news from the hospital?" I asked.

"Cam is out of surgery. He's stable, but still unconscious. His leg was badly broken but they're saying the surgery went well. He should be awake soon. They're slowly weaning Lily off the drugs used to keep her in a coma, but she still hasn't woken up yet. She had a punctured lung and they had to put her out until she could be stabilized."

I churned over the information and nodded. "The club? The Old Ladies?"

"A fucking mess. Some of them aren't even on speaking terms at the moment."

"I said some pretty awful things to Logan and Rach," I admitted. "I wouldn't be surprised if they're not speaking to me either."

"They came and told me what went down. I think you underestimate them."

"I guess I underestimate everyone," I murmured.

"Tell me about your father," he said.

"The biggest heart you can imagine. Always willing to lend a hand or stop for someone in need. His smile lit up his entire face."

"I'm sorry I never got the chance to meet him."

I looked up at him. "I'm sorry too."

And I was. Bones might not have been the man I

thought I'd want, but he was the man I needed. And the way he cared for me…my father cared for my mother the same way. Bones and my father were cut from the same cloth, even if they walked different paths in life.

"Some days, the grief is hardly there," I said softly. "Like an annoying toothache that won't bother you much if you don't touch it. Other days, it's like a heavy, wet blanket that makes it hard to get out of bed."

"How many days is it the annoying toothache versus the wet blanket?"

I thought about his question. "Most days it's like the toothache. Today it's the wet blanket. The wedding was supposed to be this joyous, beautiful celebration. Darcy's death turned it into a tragedy."

"Hmm."

"You don't think it was a tragedy?"

"Of course it's a tragedy. But it's also a reminder. Live your life. Be happy. Because one day, it all ends."

Be happy.

"If only it were that easy." I waved him toward the living room. "We don't have to keep standing here in the doorway having an existential crisis."

"But it's so fun," he mocked.

I rolled my eyes. "Fun. Right. Sometimes it would be nice to be able to turn my brain off."

"Good luck with that."

I ran my hands up and down my arms. "I can't get warm."

"Take a hot shower," Bones said. "I'll make you tea and turn on the fireplace."

"It's fifty degrees outside," I remarked.

"But if you're cold, you're cold."

"Okay."

"God, I wish you didn't look so haunted. It's killing me, Duchess."

"I'll be okay. I just need some time." I headed for the stairs.

Twenty minutes later, scrubbed free of makeup and hair product, I was dressed in a pair of sweats and a thick sweatshirt.

Bones had turned on the gas fireplace and he was sitting on the couch. He set his phone down as I walked into the room. He looked comfortable in my space. He'd removed his leather cut and rolled up the sleeves of his button down.

"Cam's awake," he said. "I just got the call."

"Lily?"

He shook his head.

I sighed and took the seat next to him.

"You want some tea?"

"No."

He settled the blanket on top of me and then wrapped an arm around me.

"You want to watch one of your comfort movies? *Sabrina* the remake, with Julia Ormond and Harrison Ford?"

I looked at him. "How did you know about that?"

"I saw your Netflix queue."

I smiled. "Oh." I buried my head against his chest. "No, I don't want to watch a comfort movie. Even though that is a good one. Way lighter than the original."

"You want to sit here in silence and let me hold you?"

I closed my eyes. "Yeah, I'd like that."

Chapter 34

My lids cracked open and I blinked. Bones' face was on the pillow next to mine, and his eyes were open, staring at me.

It only took me a moment to realize I was in bed—Bones must've carried me at some point. I had no recollection of falling asleep.

"What time is it?" I asked, my gaze darting to the window. It was daylight, and I deduced that it must've been late morning.

"3 PM," he said.

"What?"

"It's 3 PM. You fell asleep and I moved you to bed. You slept the night through." His brow furrowed.

"What?"

"You had me worried," he said. "I called Charlie. She told me you do this sometimes."

"Do what sometimes?" I asked carefully.

"When things get stressful, you check out and sleep for fifteen, eighteen hours."

"Oh. Yeah, I do that. I'm sorry you were worried."

"You hungry?"

"I am—wait, did you say it's 3 PM?"

"Yeah."

"Shit, I have dinner at my mother's house in two hours."

"Hold on a second, Duchess," he said.

"I have to shower," I replied, throwing off the covers. My head swam and I had to brace myself.

"You shower and you're going to fall over. You're not going anywhere. Call and cancel. Tell her you've got the flu."

"If I tell her I've got the flu, she'll insist on coming over here to take care of me."

He raised his brows. "She will?"

"Fine, she won't come over herself. She'll send Stanton with chicken soup. I'd rather not have to explain you to Stanton."

"Huh."

"I don't mean it that way," I hastened to say. "I just mean if Stanton knows about you, he'll report back to my mother. That's why I didn't tell Walker I was dating someone. It would've gotten back to her. And I'd rather have the element of surprise when I show up attached to your arm for the gala."

"I'm still not letting you go over there. Not when you need to rest."

"I just rested for eighteen hours," I commented. "I need to get up."

"You're allowed to go as far as the couch," he said.

"Have you been keeping vigil the entire night?"

He shook his head. "No. But when you didn't spring out of bed at 7 AM, I started to get worried. And then when it was past eight, I knew something was wrong."

I reached out and cradled his cheek. "I'm okay."

He grabbed my phone from the nightstand and handed it to me. "Cancel dinner with your mother. I don't care what you tell her, but you're in no shape to go over there."

Bones climbed out of bed and headed for the door.

"Wait," I called after him.

He turned and looked at me.

"How's Lily?"

"You've been asleep for eighteen hours and she's the first thing you ask about?"

"Bones. Tell me."

"She's awake."

"Thank God," I murmured.

"There's more. I'll tell you when you're settled on the couch."

"Where are you going?" I asked.

"To get you chicken soup," he said with a soft smile. "Call for me when you're ready to come downstairs."

"Why?"

"Because I'll carry you."

"I'm perfectly capable of—"

"*I'm carrying you*," he repeated. "No arguments."

He left the room before I could argue anymore. There was a glass of water on the nightstand. I grabbed it and downed it in a few huge swallows. Some of the fog was clearing from my head as I got up and went to the bathroom.

I climbed back into bed and thought about what I could say that wasn't an outright lie. I had a low-grade headache so when I called my mother, I fibbed and told her I had the start of a migraine.

"I'm just going to rest," I told her.

"Of course, darling. Whatever you need to do. I'll see you Wednesday."

"What's Wednesday?" I asked, searching my brain, trying to remember if we had plans I'd forgotten about.

"You're helping me finalize the seating chart," she said. "Don't you remember?"

"Oh, right," I lied.

"You forgot."

"No, no, I didn't forget." I was pretty sure she'd never told me she needed my help.

"You've been so absent from helping plan this event— normally you're in the thick of it with me."

"Migraine," I reminded her.

"Right. I'm sorry. Feel better. Should I send Stanton over there to take care of you?"

"Ah, no. I'm fine. I'm just going to put a compress on my eyes and close the shades and take a nap. Hopefully that kicks it."

"Well, just call if you need me."

"Thanks, Mom. I'll see you Wednesday."

I hung up and rubbed my third eye. I checked my other messages and found a few from Charlie. I messaged her back.

ME
I'm awake.

A few minutes went by and she replied.

CHARLIE
How are you feeling?

> **ME**
> Better.

> **CHARLIE**
> Bones was worried.

> **ME**
> Yeah.

> **CHARLIE**
> You should tell him the truth.

Not wanting to go down that rabbit hole, I tossed my phone aside. "Bones!" I yelled.

A few minutes later, he appeared in the doorway of the bedroom. "You bellowed, Duchess?"

"I don't bellow."

"Sounded like a bellow."

"You told me to call for you when I was ready to be carried downstairs."

"Hmm. The nickname Duchess feels pretty fitting right about now." He pushed away from the doorframe and walked to the bed. I grabbed my phone before he scooped me into his arms.

"How'd it go with your mother?"

"Fine. I told her I had a migraine, which isn't a complete lie."

"You have a migraine?"

"A headache," I clarified. "Don't worry, it'll go away after I eat and hydrate."

"I've got a prospect bringing over chicken soup. Your job is to sit and let me take care of you. I've got to make a call to Raze and get him to cover me tonight so I can stay—"

"Cover you tonight?" I frowned. "Cover you for what?"

"Security at Chaos." He set me down on the couch and swaddled me with a blanket.

"Really? I'm fine," I said. "Don't take off work for me."

"I don't want you to be alone," he stated. "I'm taking off."

"That's ridiculous."

"It's not ridiculous. If I'm at work, all I'm going to do is worry about you."

"Okay, don't take this the wrong way, but you're kind of…"

"What?"

"Smothering me," I blurted out.

He raised his brows. "Smothering? I'm *smothering* you?"

"I just need some space," I stated. "I didn't get a chance to process everything that happened yesterday. And I know you're worried and you want to take care of me, but I just…"

His stare was unwavering. "I'm not leaving you alone. So, either I stay or you call Charlie to hang out with you."

"I'll call Charlie," I said. "You can go."

He sat down on the coffee table and faced me. "I'll wait for you to call her."

"Wait for me to—do you think I'm not going to call her?"

"That's exactly what I think. You know what? Never mind." He pulled out his cellphone from his breast pocket. After unlocking the screen, he scrolled and pressed a number. He put the phone to his ear. "Charlie, can you come hang out with Hayden? I don't want her to be alone and she won't let me cancel work and stay with her." He paused. "Cool, see you in twenty."

He hung up with her and looked at me.

"Unnecessary."

"Entirely necessary," he rebutted. "I'm bringing you orange juice."

He got up off the table and headed for the kitchen. I stared after him. It was clearly useless to tell him no. I was surprised he was actually going to leave me with Charlie. He didn't seem the type to trust anyone else.

"You were going to tell me what else was going on," I said as he came back into the living room.

He handed me the glass of orange juice and sat down at the end of the couch. "Doc and Boxer have legal guardianship of the kids. When they're able to be discharged, they'll go home with them to live. They're both awake now, but it's rough. They're going to need to sedate Lily for a while so she doesn't re-injure herself during the hysteria. Cam is doing a little better."

"How's everyone else doing with the news?" I asked. "Emotions were running high."

He sighed. "The Old Ladies aren't talking to each other. Well, correction. Some are talking to each other. Others are not."

"Battle lines drawn," I said quietly.

"Yeah." He ran a hand across his stubble. "None of us know how to handle this. We feel like shit."

"So, was she inebriated?" I asked. "Do they know yet if she caused the accident?"

"It looks that way, but we don't really know. The doctors are going to wait until Cam is no longer under the influence of so many pain meds before they start to ask him questions."

"Jesus."

"Yeah…sip your juice."

I took a drink.

The doorbell rang and Bones got up to answer it. He

spoke to someone for a few seconds and then closed the door. He returned with a brown paper bag. A delicious aroma emanated from it and my stomach moaned.

"Let me put this into a bowl and get you a real spoon."

While I was in the middle of eating, Charlie showed up and relieved Bones of babysitting duty.

Bones leaned down and pressed a kiss to my forehead. "I'll check in on you later. Don't argue."

He left, and after I heard the rumble of his motorcycle disappear into the distance, I said to her, "You can go. You don't actually have to sit here with me."

"Are you kidding? If he finds out I bailed, there will be hell to pay."

I rolled my eyes. "He's over-reacting."

"You were comatose for nearly eighteen hours. What's he supposed to think? I'm surprised he actually left."

"He's overbearing," I muttered.

"He's not," she protested. "This is what it looks like when a man cares for the woman he loves."

"Love? Did you say *love*?"

"Oh please." She rolled her eyes. "He's got like, cartoon hearts in his eyes when he looks at you. Ten bucks says he's picking out your kids' names already."

Chapter 35

I ASKED Bones if we could have a few nights apart and his easy text of *Sure* had me frowning and questioning everything. Three days passed without him calling or making plans, and I walked into my mother's house in low spirits. But I put on a smile because the last thing I wanted was for her to know anything was wrong.

Stanton showed me into the dining room where my mother already had the seating chart splayed out across the long oak table.

"I'm glad to see you've recovered from your migraine," Mom said as she hugged me.

"Oh. Yeah. Nothing a little sleep couldn't help," I lied. Charlie had stayed the night just to ensure that if I needed anything she could get it for me.

"Good." She gestured to the seating chart. "It's a mess."

I looked down at the names laid out on the chart. "It's not a mess."

"Liar," she said with a laugh. "There are so many people that decided to RSVP late. There are only a couple of empty seats at the tables, which is wonderful, but Don Moriarty will be bringing his new wife and it turns out Sheila is coming, too."

"*Oh no*…second wife and half-her-age third wife are going to be in the same room together?"

"If we're not careful, they're going to be at the same table."

"We either need to put them on the opposite sides of the room or see if we can change the decor to medieval suits of armor. I'd pay good money to see Sheila chase the new toy around the room with a claymore."

Mom laughed. "You're terrible."

An hour later, we had it all sorted.

"Now that that's finished," Mom closed the binder, "I can ask you why you turned down Walker."

I blinked. "How did you know that?"

"I called him and he told me," she said.

"Mother," I said with a sigh.

"Don't *Mother* me. Tell me why you didn't accept his offer for dinner."

"Because I already told you I wasn't interested," I explained.

"Not that excuse again."

"It's not an excuse. It's the truth." I leaned in and kissed her cheek. "I'll see you Saturday at the event."

"Do you want to ride with us?" Mom asked.

"No, I'll take my own car."

As I was driving home, I realized I didn't want to go there. I missed Bones.

I called him.

His phone rang and rang. I thought it was about to roll to voicemail when he finally answered.

"Duchess," he greeted.

"Hey," I said, suddenly feeling embarrassed. "What are you doing?"

"Working on my motorcycle."

"Oh."

There was silence on the other end, as if he was waiting for me to say something.

"I was wondering if I could take you to lunch," I said.

"Yeah, I could eat."

He sounded casual. Almost aloof.

"I'm at Charlie's Motorcycle Repair. The bike's apart so I'll need a ride. I'll see you in a few."

Bones hung up before I could reply.

I drove to the commercial district and pulled into the driveway of the garage. I cut the engine and climbed out of the car. Kelp and Raze were working on a motorcycle, but I didn't see Bones.

"Hayden," Kelp greeted. "Hey."

"Hi," I said. "Is Bones around?"

"Yeah, he's washing up," Raze explained. "He'll be out in a bit. You want coffee or something to drink?"

"No, I'm fine. Thanks." I stood there awkwardly, unsure of what to say.

A side door opened leading into the garage and Rach stepped out. "I've got Mitch Landry on the phone. There's a problem with the order."

"I'll handle it," Raze said, stalking toward her.

Rach nodded and then her eyes met mine. "Hey."

"Hi."

"I'm gonna pick up lunch," Logan said, appearing behind Rach. "Then I'll be back. Oh. Hi, Hayden."

Nerves skated through my belly. Everything was wrong. I hadn't seen them since the deeply personal blowout we'd had and I wasn't even sure where to go from here.

And where the hell was Bones? He was taking forever.

Though I wasn't even sure I wanted to see him either since he'd been so cold to me on the phone.

"What are you doing here?" Logan asked.

"Bones and I have lunch plans," I explained.

"Ah." Logan nodded.

"You guys are being weird," Kelp said from the corner of the garage. He was rooting around in a red tool chest. "Work out your shit. It's making me uncomfortable."

Rach glared at him. "Not all of us get the luxury of going to The Ring and wailing on each other to vent our frustration."

I frowned. "Wailing?"

Kelp turned around, a tool in hand. His left eye was bruised.

"Wailing," I repeated in understanding.

"It's not wailing," Kelp stated. "It's sparring."

"You guys beat the shit out of each other and laugh it off like weirdos," Logan stated. "At least Smoke didn't get involved."

"Because we refused to spar against him," Kelp remarked. "He's barely recovered from…you know."

"I'm sure he loved that," Logan said with a shake of her head.

A door on the other side of the garage opened and Bones came out. He was wearing a white shirt with a streak of grease across the chest.

"Hey," he said.

"Hey," I replied.

"Jesus Christ, not you two as well," Kelp muttered. "Colder than a witch's tit in here."

Bones glared at him.

"Are you coming back?" Rach asked me.

"I have to drop Bones off, so yeah, I'll be coming back."

She nodded. "Can we talk? Later?"

"Sure." I looked at Bones. "You ready?"

"My shirt is stained with grease and I don't have a clean one. I'm not really restaurant appropriate."

"We can figure something else out," I said.

We headed toward my car. Bones didn't say anything as he opened my door for me. I climbed in and he shut it. He walked around to the other side and got in.

"Okay, what the hell is this?" I blurted out.

"What the hell is what?" His tone was calm, his expression impassive.

"You're acting like a stranger."

"Duchess, you pushed me away and I haven't heard from you in three days. How the fuck else do you want me to act?"

I blinked. "Phone works both ways."

"You said I was smothering you. So I backed the fuck off."

"Oh." I frowned. "I did say that, didn't I?"

"Yeah, you did." He rubbed the back of his neck in frustration and then lowered his hands. His knuckles were raw.

"You were sparring too?" I asked.

"How'd you know?"

"Logan mentioned it." I shrugged.

He paused for a moment and then said, "Everyone's still reeling."

"When's the funeral?"

"Tomorrow."

"Would you have told me? If I hadn't asked?"

"Why would I have told you?" His eyes met mine and the coldness evaporated, replaced by burning emotion. "You said it yourself. You're not one of us."

I tried not to flinch from the sharp blade of his words.

"I didn't belong at the wedding either, but I came with you. Do you really think I wouldn't come with you to a funeral?"

"I don't know. I thought I was beginning to know you. But you left the wedding. And you wouldn't let me take care of you. Why won't you let me take care of you, Duchess?"

"And why do you want to take care of me?" I asked. "Why, Bones?"

"Jesus Christ, do I have to spell it out for you?"

"Yes!"

"I love you, God damnit!" he roared.

"Well, I love you too, you arrogant, overbearing—"

I didn't get the rest of the words out because Bones reached across the car, grabbed my face in his hands, and kissed the breath out of me.

When he pulled back, we were both breathing hard. He pressed his forehead to mine. "No more bullshit."

"No more bullshit," I agreed.

A smack landed on the hood of my car, instantly pulling my attention.

"Fornicate somewhere else!" Kelp called out.

Bones looked at me and raised his brows.

I shot him a grin. "I didn't really want lunch anyway."

~

"I was supposed to go back to the garage," I said as I snuggled closer to Bones.

He moved the pillow behind his head to get more comfortable and then settled again. "Why?"

"Rach wanted to talk. I got the feeling she and Logan wanted to patch things up."

"Text them," he said.

"I don't have their numbers."

"I have them."

"What am I even supposed to say?" I asked, forcing myself up.

"Maybe you don't say anything. Maybe you give them a chance to speak first."

I threw him a glare over my shoulder.

"Did you tell Charlie what happened?" he asked.

"I gave her the highlights," I said with a sigh.

"What did she say?"

"She didn't say much," I admitted. "She wasn't sure how to even process everything that's happened. Between the wedding and the call about Darcy, my blowout with Logan and Rach—it feels like I shouldn't even have had a blowout, you know? Like, I *just* met them. I shouldn't have weighed in. I wasn't in the thick of it. I'd just met Darcy. I had no right to—"

"Fine, don't talk to them. But you'll see them tomorrow at the funeral and you'll have to deal with it then. Now, you promised me lunch, so what are we going to do about it?"

"Tell you what, why don't we head to the clubhouse so you can grab a few of your things, including a clean shirt. I'll take you to lunch and then we can come back here and do more of what we just did."

"You want me to keep shit at your house?"

"I have stuff in your clubhouse room already," I reminded him.

"You do," he agreed. "We gonna talk about it?"

"Talk about what?"

"The yelling of the feelings in your car?"

"Why do we need to talk about it?" I asked.

"Because it means something."

"Well, obviously." I rolled my eyes. "It's why I'm giving you a drawer like, a minute and half after meeting you."

"It's been longer than a minute and a half."

"Fine, two minutes."

"Brat," he said with a laugh.

I grinned. "Can I feed you or what?"

His eyes darkened and he pulled me toward him. "Or what."

Chapter 36

Darcy was buried next to her husband. Their son stood with crutches, his left leg in a bright blue cast. His expression was somber and in that moment, he looked far older than thirteen. His sister had a gash across her head that had been stitched, and other than sitting in a wheelchair, if you hadn't known she'd been in a coma recently with a punctured lung, you never would've guessed how close she had come to death. She looked dazed though, utterly shell shocked by the weight of it all.

Apparently, she hadn't spoken since Doc told her that her mother had died.

The Old Ladies stood with their men. Rach gripped her son tighter and buried her face in his hair. A man I didn't recognize stood next to her and put his arm around her.

Cool air brushed my cheeks and I shivered. Barren trees waved their naked branches. As the coffin was lowered into the ground, Lily came out of her stupor. She tried to scream but it came out more like a panicked wheeze and tears streamed down her face.

Boxer grabbed the handles of her wheelchair, turned her around and wheeled her away.

Doc placed her hand on Cam's shoulder and took a step closer to him. He made no indication that he felt her presence.

Instead of looking at the faces of the Old Ladies, I focused on Boxer and Lily. He'd parked her wheelchair a hundred or so yards away, and I watched as he crouched down in front of her and grasped her hands. Whatever he said made her lean into his arms as best she could and hug his neck.

I thought about my own father's funeral. I'd quickly escaped the crowd, swiped a bottle of my father's favorite scotch, and drank it in the privacy of my bathroom alone. Charlie had found me, but instead of partaking, she let me get stinking drunk and then held my hair back when I cried so hard I'd began vomiting.

"Hayden," Bones murmured. He squeezed my cold hand.

"Hmm."

"Time to go."

I blinked as I shook off the past. Nodding, I walked with him to my car. Women carried their babies, securing them into car seats as people began to say goodbye to each other.

"Where to?" I asked as I buckled myself in.

"The clubhouse," he said.

We drove in companionable silence. I appreciated not having to speak. Bones' cell phone rang. He reached into his leather cut and pulled it out. He pressed a button and put it to his ear. After a moment he said, "Yeah."

And then he hung up. "Prez is calling a meeting when we get to the clubhouse."

"I guess that means I have to face Rach and Logan alone."

"He's calling a meeting with the brothers *and* the Old Ladies. He wants you there, too, Hayden."

Though I wasn't technically his Old Lady, I let it pass. We'd just said *I love you*. I wasn't ready for a conversation about becoming his Old Lady, if that was something he even wanted. Love didn't mean a long-term commitment.

It was a caravan to the clubhouse and we all arrived in succession. We parked and got out of the car. Bones slung his arm around my shoulders as we walked up the steps.

The mood was solemn and quiet. Platters of food and bottles of alcohol were already set out. I guessed Jazz and Brielle had taken care of it, but they weren't around. No doubt they were giving the club privacy.

"Church," Colt announced.

Waverly and Sailor ushered the older kids toward the stairwell that led to the basement theater room. The women with toddler-aged children followed them downstairs.

Cam stared at the direction they were going. It was hard enough getting around flat ground on crutches, let alone taking the stairs.

"Need some help, buddy?" Boxer asked him quietly.

Cam nodded.

"I need my nursing blanket," Brooklyn said to Slash. "Palmer's getting fussy."

"I'll get it," Slash said. "You go out to the shed and I'll be there in a minute."

Rach turned to the man who'd come to the funeral with her and handed her son to him. "This shouldn't take long."

He put the baby to his chest and held him.

Leather & Lies

"Tavy will keep you company," Logan said. "Won't you, Tavy?"

"I'll keep your brother company," Tavy said. "And help him with Cash."

"You can change Cash's dirty diaper," the man said.

Tavy snorted. "No way. You're courting Rach, you change her son's diapers."

Bones placed his hand at the small of my back and ushered me toward the backyard. The dainty clop of high heels was pierced only by the heavy clod of motorcycle boots.

Colt Weston, President of the Tarnished Angels, opened the door to a shed-like building and flipped on the light. The Old Ladies went in first and I was last. Before I could turn to ask Bones where I should sit, the door promptly shut.

"What the hell is going on?" Mia demanded.

"You're not coming out until you guys talk," Colt shot back.

Joni marched to the door and pounded on the wood. "Zip! Let us out!"

"Prez is right," her husband replied through the door. "If you don't make amends, the club is finished."

"Brooklyn," Allison cried. "What are you doing?"

Brooklyn raised her brows. "I'm sitting down so I can nurse my daughter. She's got a set of lungs on her and I know there's about to be a lot of yelling. At least with her, I can put a cork in it."

"My morning sickness is becoming afternoon sickness," Willa yelled at the door. "You really want me to throw up in here? Duke? Answer me!"

"There's a bucket in the corner for you, babe," Duke called back. "I suggest you use it."

"There are bottles of water for everyone in the cooler," Smoke said. "Along with deli meat."

"Hayden's a pescatarian." Sutton looked at me and then called through the door. "You didn't think about that, did you?"

"There's cut up carrots and celery, cheese, and apples," Bones said.

"You knew about this?" I snapped.

"Damn right I knew about it," Bones replied. "It was my fucking idea."

"I'm going to murder you," I seethed.

"Just as long as you all make up," Bones said, his tone easy.

"We could lie, you know," Joni stated. "And get you to let us out of here."

"You really don't want to do that," Zip said.

"Why not?" Joni asked.

"We're on a sex strike," Zip stated.

"*What?*" Sutton screeched.

"Yep, we're not putting out until you guys are friends again," Savage stated.

"You don't even have on Old Lady in here," Willa bellowed. "Why are you on strike?"

"Solidarity," Savage commented.

"Well, we're fucked," Willa moaned. "And not in a good way. Savage never gives up sex."

The women began to speak all at once, throwing accusations and words of anger at each other.

"She wasn't drunk!" Doc raised her voice to be heard over the cacophony of various fights.

Rach turned to look at Doc as the room got suddenly quiet. "What?"

"She wasn't drunk," Doc repeated.

"How can you know that?" Mia asked.

"They drew her blood after the accident and there was nothing in her system. When you got the call they should have told you. I don't know why they didn't, but I called today and confirmed it. Blood test was clean."

Mia blanched. "I dropped my phone as soon as I heard she was gone. I didn't even think…I just assumed."

Doc continued, "Cam told me what happened when he woke up. The kids got into an argument and Darcy turned around to stop them from fighting. When she did, she must have turned the wheel and—and they crashed into the barrier between the exit and the interstate. Besides, the night before the wedding Cam got up in the middle of the night and went to the kitchen for a drink of water. Darcy was standing at the sink, pouring out the bottles of liquor. They're going to run a full tox screen to see if anything else was in her system, but those results could take a while."

The room was silent.

"Is it possible?" Rach whispered. "That she'd turned the corner and none of us knew?"

Doc ran a hand through her hair. "Can't we give our friend the benefit of the doubt? Can't we forgive each other for not being the best versions of ourselves? Can't we move forward and promise that nothing matters more than each other?"

Rach broke down in tears and Logan immediately wrapped her in her arms. The other Old Ladies moved closer to each other, embracing one another and crying, spouting words of apology and absolution.

I was the only one who sat by, unsure of where I belonged.

But then Rach looked up from Logan's shoulder and they both reached their hands out to me. I was pulled into the group and became one of them.

"Is that why you don't drink?" Rach asked. "Because of what happened at your father's funeral?"

"Yes," I lied. It was one reason, but not the only reason—and I didn't feel like sharing yet. I picked up a cube of cheddar from my plate and placed it in my mouth.

Though it was a wake, the oppressive heaviness had lifted, if only marginally. At least the Old Ladies had reknitted the bonds of sisterhood.

I sat with Logan and Rach at the picnic table. Bones and Smoke were talking to Logan's brother, Chase.

"Your brother looks like he's holding his own," I commented.

Logan nodded. "Yep."

Cash reached for a grape on Rach's plate. She picked it up and bit it in half before giving him a piece.

Chase paused in his conversation and looked at Rach. Their eyes met and she gave him a little finger wave. He smiled back.

"It looks like it's going well between you two," I commented.

"It's going slow," Rach said.

"He flew down for your friend's funeral to be with you," Logan said. "That's not slow."

Rach's brow wrinkled. "Well, I'm trying to take it slow. I've got a son. We live in different states. There's a lot to consider."

"My brother has been in love with you forever," Logan said. "Kinda hard to take that slow."

"He lives in Idaho. I live here," she reiterated. "I don't want to live through harsh winters. I've done that before. But he hates the weather here. My life is here."

"Sounds like an excuse to me," Logan said.

"Hey," Rach said. "Go easy on me."

"Have you asked him? If he'd consider moving here?" I asked.

"He'd have to change his entire life," Rach said. "He works with his father and brothers in the family business."

"Contractor family business," Logan clarified. "Chase is the numbers guy. But if he moved here, maybe that would get my parents to move here. And if my parents moved here, maybe the rest of my family would move here."

"Oh, I see how it is." Rach smiled. "You want your whole family near you. Can you imagine your brothers just walking into your house while you and Smoke are making breakfast."

Logan chuckled.

"How many brothers do you have?" I asked.

"Four," she said. "All older. All a pain in the ass. But I miss them. The club is attempting to break into real estate. Might be nice to have a reliable contractor to do business with."

The two of them started gabbing about the possibilities. I quietly excused myself and took my empty plate to one of the garbage cans.

I grabbed a sparkling water from a cooler and wandered around the side of the clubhouse to momentarily escape.

Doc was leaning against the siding like she wanted a moment of privacy, too.

"Sorry," I said, turning around to head back the way I'd come.

"You had the same idea," she said. "You needed some space. Some quiet."

I nodded. "I can go inside."

"No, it's fine."

"You sure?"

She nodded.

Making a snap decision, I decided to approach and took the spot next to her and mimicked her position.

"This must be a lot for you," I said.

Doc sighed. "I don't know what the hell she was thinking."

I frowned. "Who?"

"Darcy." She ran her fingers through her blonde pixie hair. "What was she thinking giving me guardianship of her kids?"

"Not just you. You and Boxer."

"Boxer makes sense. Boxer is Lily's favorite person. But me?" She shook her head. "I'm not maternal. I work sixty-hour weeks. I love my career."

She looked at the ground. "I'm not ready to be a mom. And now I'm responsible for two kids. Two amazing kids who lost their parents, and now they're stuck with me. Darcy—she makes—*made*—Lily's ballet tutus. I sew skin for a living. I can't sew tulle. And Cam? He needed a very complex surgery on his leg. He loves to play soccer. What if he'll never be able to run as fast again? What if it bothers him the rest of his life? What if…"

Her hand crept across her stomach and rested there.

It clicked immediately.

"What if," I said quietly, "they think they don't belong in your family because of the new baby?"

Her head whipped to mine and her sharp gaze softened. She swallowed. "Yes. That."

I took her free hand and gave it a squeeze. "If there's anything I learned about the people at this funeral, it's that they're family. You're not alone. And you won't have to do this alone."

"I'm good at being a doctor. What if it's the only thing I'm good at?"

"It's not. You'll figure it out, Doc. You don't have to make Lily's tutus. You're never going to be Darcy. You're never going to replace her. But you can be their…Doc. And you can be there for those kids the way they need someone now. Darcy chose you for a reason, remember that. She knew if anything happened, you'd be there for them. She chose *you*."

She shot me a look and smiled. "Yeah. I can be there for them."

Chapter 37

"An anonymous donor bought the seat next to yours," Mom said over the phone.

I held in a smile. "Oh yeah? That's fascinating."

"I hope he's a handsome billionaire who sweeps you off your feet."

"He's not a billionaire, but he is handsome," I replied.

Bones sat next to me on the couch, his hand settled on my thigh while I spoke to my mother. He grinned and shook his head.

"You know who it is, don't you?" she asked.

"Of course I know who it is," I said. "I'm the one who bought the seat."

She paused. "*Oh my God*, you're bringing a date."

"Yes, Mom. I'm bringing a date."

"Well, tell me everything about him! Who is he? What's his—"

"You'll meet him tomorrow night—like everyone else."

"You mean you don't want to give me his name so I won't have time to find out all I can about him."

If my mother knew Bones' real name, she'd take it to

my stepfather, who would then do a background check. It was going to be enough of a shock for me to show up to a charity gala on Bones' arm. What would my mother do when she found out he was a biker?

"Tell you what," I said. "You'll meet him tomorrow night at the gala and then we'll have Sunday dinner with you. You can quiz him to your heart's content, in person."

"I won't quiz."

"Hmm. Right."

"No wonder you said no to Walker. You were dating someone all this time, weren't you?"

"Yes."

"How long has this been going on?"

"A few weeks."

Only a few weeks…

How had it been such a short period of time?

"Does Charlie know about him?" Mom inquired.

"She knows about him. She's met him. And she already knows not to tell you anything about him," I added.

"You're choosing the night of my charity gala for me to meet your boyfriend for the first time? You sure he's up to the scrutiny?"

"I have complete faith in him." I reached out and stroked Bones' freshly shaven jaw. By tomorrow night, it would look like he already had three days' worth of scruff. The picture I had in my mind of Bones in his expertly tailored tux sporting scruff had me momentarily distracted.

"Hayden?"

"Sorry, what did you say?"

"I asked if he's someone special?"

I looked at Bones when I replied. "Very special."

"Well, I think that's wonderful," Mom said. "I look forward to seeing you both tomorrow night."

We hung up with each other and I set my phone aside.

I ran my fingers along his cheek and then slipped my hand into his newly styled hair. "I like the haircut."

"Yeah?"

"Yeah."

"It was the most expensive cut and shave of my life," he joked. "I'd better look good."

"Devastatingly handsome," I quipped.

"So, when I introduce myself to your mother, I'm guessing you'd rather I not say anything about the Tarnished Angels…"

"She'll find out the moment you give her your real name because my stepfather will do some digging. He'll corner you at Sunday dinner with the information and there's a chance it won't be pretty. But tomorrow night, you're Royce Dalton, and you're involved in the security business for a private client with an NDA."

"That's not really the truth."

"It's not really a lie," I pointed out. "PR 101. It's all about how you spin it."

"Sunday dinner," he stated.

"What about it?"

"You didn't ask me if I had plans Sunday, or if I wanted to be scrutinized up close by your butler and your mom and stepdad."

"You have plans Sunday." I smiled. "You're having dinner at my childhood home. Besides, my mom and stepdad will scrutinize you tomorrow night anyway. It's just that by Sunday they'll actually know who you are."

"Hmm, and what will you give me for having to suffer through Sunday dinner?"

"What do you want?"

"Depends how painful it is."

"If you can survive the night of the gala, you can survive Sunday dinner."

"Is this what our life is going to look like together?" he drawled. "You dragging me to black tie events and then dinners with your mom?"

My heart lurched in my chest at the thought of a life with him. "I guess so. Yeah. Probably."

"You guess so, probably?" he parroted. "You haven't thought of what life is gonna look like for us, have you?"

"There hasn't been a lot of time to think about it."

"Okay."

"Bones, don't."

"Don't what?"

"Don't do that. Don't think this means anything. We said I love you. Can't that be enough?"

"No, it can't be enough, because I'm already thinking about our future together."

"You haven't even unpacked the bag of clothes you brought over yet."

"Because you mauled me the moment we got home."

I gasped. "I didn't *maul* you."

"Not only did you maul me, Duchess, but you were feral."

"Feral!" I screeched.

"Your greedy pussy clamped down on my dick and refused to let go. And I've got nail marks on my back to boot."

I playfully smacked his shoulder and then buried my flushing face against his chest.

"Don't get shy on me now," he quipped.

I lifted my head and met his gaze.

"Good girl." He brushed hair away from my face.

"I'm still prudish, I think. Yeah…prudish for sure," I said.

"You want to remedy that?"

"How do we remedy that?"

He flashed a grin. "I'll show you tomorrow night at the gala."

∽

My dark hair was twirled up to show off the diamonds and sapphires winking in the light at my throat and ears. They had been part of my inheritance from my grandmother and screamed old money through and through.

They complimented the black gown I'd chosen for the event. It was floor length, strapless, and cinched at the waist. It was classic and elegant, but for the evening, I'd decided on a heavier eye and red lip than I'd normally choose to wear.

I was showing off Bones, and I wanted both of us not to shy away from the limelight. It wouldn't be possible anyway—he was an outsider. He deserved to have someone on his arm that wasn't afraid to be seen. It was the only way we would look like a couple instead of like I'd brought someone by accident that didn't fit.

I was done hiding in the shadows.

A knock resounded on the door, momentarily causing my heart to cartwheel in my chest in excitement.

It took all of my willpower not to run to answer the door, but somehow, I managed to walk calmly to greet the man I'd fallen desperately in love with.

I opened the door and exhilaration flitted around in my belly.

"Oh," I breathed.

Bones' slow smile dawned across his face—his face that

was once again sporting stubble. His dark hair was expertly mussed, making him look roguish and youthful.

His electric blue gaze slowly drifted down my body. "*Wow*."

I couldn't stop my answering grin. "Wow yourself."

I yearned to slide my hands across the broad expanse of his shoulders, which filled out the custom tuxedo jacket perfectly.

He held up a single white peony.

I took it from him. "Thank you."

After I grabbed my clutch, I locked up the house and then took Bones' offered arm. We walked down the steps to the driveway where a limousine was waiting with a driver standing outside to open the door for us.

I grasped my skirt and climbed in the back of the limo. Bones followed, sliding in next to me and then the driver closed the door.

Without a word, Bones pressed a button and slid up the divider between us and the driver to give us privacy.

I'd suggested Bones bring over his tuxedo and get ready with me at my house, but he'd surprised me by saying he would get ready alone and pick me up. He'd been secretive though, and I couldn't figure out why.

"Now will you tell me where you got ready?" I asked. I reached out and touched his expertly donned tie.

"I got ready at Smoke and Logan's," he explained.

I frowned. "I don't understand."

"Smoke knows how to tie a tie," he admitted with a dapper grin. "He grew up in the same world you did. I asked him to help me out for the evening, so I wouldn't look like a rube."

"You definitely don't look like a rube," I murmured.

"Logan styled my hair." He grimaced. "It's got some weird hair gum crap in it. I have no idea what it does."

"Well, you look perfect," I admitted. "Effortlessly perfect."

"So do you." His eyes drifted down my body and his finger touched the necklace around my neck and then drifted lower to graze the swell of my breast.

My nipples hardened immediately.

"Thank you for the peony," I said, my voice breathless.

"I thought you'd like it." His voice was husky. "I brought you another gift too."

"You did?" I asked with a raise of my brows. "What is it?"

He dropped his finger from my skin and then leaned over to grab a small black gift bag with gold tissue paper.

Bones handed it to me and I took it. I dug into the gift bag and pulled out a black velvet bag cinched at the top.

With a frown of confusion, I opened it. My mouth gaped. "This isn't what I think it is…"

"It's *exactly* what you think it is," Bones said easily. "And you're going to wear it tonight."

"I'm *not* wearing this tonight!" I hissed as I held up the small steel butt plug. "We're going to a charity event! Are you out of your mind?"

"Probably."

"I'm going to be talking to people. I can't—"

"We have forty-five minutes until we get to our destination," he said. "You want to spend it arguing, or are you going to lay across my lap like a good girl and let me put it in you?"

"Bones, *no*, this is—"

"You asked what I wanted in exchange for a dinner with your mom and stepfather. Well, I want this. I want to look at you from across the room and know it's inside you. Know that every time you walk, you feel it stretch and tease you, knowing I was the one who put it in you."

He gently grasped the back of my neck with his muscular hand. "I want you to be thinking about me fucking you with this still inside you. I want you to think about it the whole night until it's actually happening."

I swallowed. "This is insane."

"Time's a tickin', Duchess. Hike up your dress and lay across my lap."

"The driver—"

"He can't see or hear us unless you get really loud, so you'd better be quiet."

"How do you know I'll even like this?" I asked.

"I don't. Guess we'll just have to see, won't we."

"I'm wearing panties," I muttered.

"So, pull them down," he commanded.

Dear lord. What am I getting myself into? And why am I so turned on?

I handed him the butt plug so I could hitch up my dress. I pulled my black lace thong down my legs and then leaned across Bones' lap.

He slid the metal butt plug into his mouth, his eyes watching me.

My skin crackled with need and I flushed from his heated gaze.

"I'll go slow," he whispered.

One hand caressed the curves of my ass. I sank into his touch and immediately began to relax.

The head of the butt plug was cool against my back entrance. I flinched at the foreign feel of it.

"Easy." He continued to tease me with the device, slowly gliding the head of it in before pulling it back out.

My muscles unclenched as pleasure bloomed between my legs. Excitement swept through me.

"Such a good girl," he murmured. "Taking this plug like you're going to take my cock in your ass."

I shivered at his filthy words. I closed my eyes as he put the plug into my back entrance again and slipped it in. There was a slight pinch as the toy breached my tight muscles and then it went all the way in.

"Beautiful," he whispered.

He lifted his hands from my body and helped me sit up.

"How do you feel?" he asked.

"Full," I admitted, trying to adjust to the feeling of something inside my body that hadn't ever been there before.

I put my panties back on and lowered my dress, thanking God I hadn't stained the fabric of it with my desire.

Bones took my hand in his and we were silent the rest of the ride to The Rex Hotel.

Chapter 38

The Gold Ballroom was enchanting. A crystal chandelier that had once graced a European palace winked with golden rays.

I scanned the room, searching for my mother. No doubt she was looking for me as well.

"Well, hot damn," Charlie said as she sauntered toward us, holding a glass of champagne. She turned to Bones. "You clean up good."

Bones grinned down at her. "Glad to see a friendly face."

"I'm not a friendly face?" I asked.

"Another friendly face," he clarified. He held out his hand to Charlie. "Royce Dalton, pleasure to meet you."

Charlie shook his hand and batted her eyes. "The *pleasure* is all mine."

"You're not hitting on my boyfriend, are you?" I asked.

"Boyfriend?" Charlie raised her brows. "That's new. And I'm not hitting on him. I'm preparing him for all the divorcees and cougars who are going to swoop in and try to seduce him."

"Hmm. Have you seen my mother?" I asked.

"Yes, she's standing with my mother," Charlie said. "You've said nothing about my dress."

It was a red confection that hugged her curves and matched the color of her lips.

"You look stunning, as always," I remarked. "I'm surprised you wore a gown that didn't show off your new shoulder tattoo."

"I thought about it," she stated. "But then I realized it wasn't worth the fight with my mother."

"You're playing nice?" I asked.

"Trying to. Come on, I want to be there when your mother meets your new *boyfriend*."

I was mindful of the plug with every step. And each step kept me on the brink of arousal. By the end of the night, I was going to be a puddle of hormones and greedy demands.

I glanced at Bones who shot me a knowing smirk. I bared my teeth. He winked.

We garnered several looks as we trekked across the ballroom. People stared with avid curiosity at Bones. He wore a tux like he'd been born in one. Part of me had worried that he'd feel uncomfortable. It wasn't like a tuxedo was his everyday wear. He wasn't James Bond.

My mother was holding court, laughing and conversing with my stepfather and godparents. Three carat diamonds winked at her ears. Her blonde hair was still shiny and bright and hadn't yet begun to fade due to the inevitable passage of time.

"Hayden," she greeted, a wide smile blossoming across her delicate mouth.

"Hello, Mom." I dropped my hand from Bones' elbow so I could lean in and brush my cheek against my mother's.

My stepfather enveloped me in a quick hug and then I

turned to Charlie's parents and exchanged a greeting with them.

"Mom, I'd like you to meet Royce Dalton." I gestured to Bones and watched my mother's eyes light up.

"Mr. Dalton." Mom held out her hand. "It's a pleasure to meet you."

"Pleasure's all mine, Mrs. Walsh."

"Please, call me Marilyn." Mom dropped her hand and gestured to my stepfather. "My husband, Arnold."

My stepfather's gaze that had been warm moments before was suddenly cooler, but he took Bones' offered hand.

"And my godparents," I added. "Dina and Patrick Sutherland. They're Charlie's parents."

"Where have you been hiding him, Hayden," my godmother teased.

"I'm afraid that's my fault," Bones said with an impish smile. "From the moment I met Hayden, I've been doing everything in my power to monopolize her time."

Charlie choked on a laugh.

"Are you all right, darling?" Dina asked her daughter.

"Fine," she said. "But I'm in desperate need of another glass of champagne."

"Royce, can I interest you in a glass of scotch?" Patrick inquired.

"Only if it's a glass of SINNERS," Bones quipped. "It's all I drink when I come to The Rex."

I raised my brows in surprise. How could Bones possibly know about the hotel owner's unique and ultra-expensive small batch single malt scotch? I filed the question away to ask later.

"Good man," Patrick said. "Arnold, you want to join us?"

"Sure," my stepfather replied. "We'll be back in a few

with drinks." He kissed my mother's cheek and then I watched my godfather, my stepfather, and my boyfriend all head in the direction of the bar.

When they were out of ear shot, Dina said, "I'm pretty sure your boyfriend has the power to reverse menopause."

"Dina!" I laughed.

My mother giggled. "Well, darling, based on looks alone—and how he fills out a tuxedo jacket—I think you did very well."

"Wait until you get to know him," Charlie said. "You'll like him even more. Plus, he treats Hayden like a princess."

"How did you two meet?" Mom asked.

Bones and I had agreed to stick to the closest version of the truth we could without telling outright lies that would burn us later. "We met the night I went to Chaos with Charlie."

"And it was lust—I mean *love* at first sight?" Dina joked.

"Lust," Charlie stated. "Definitely lust."

"Charlie," I warned.

She held up her hands.

"That sounds like a good story," my mother pressed.

"That's basically it. We met at Chaos and then he pursued me until I finally gave in."

"Hoops. There were so many hoops," Charlie added.

I glared at her.

"Oh stop, you know there were hoops," she stated.

"Hoops are good," Mom said. "Hoop jumping proves that he wants to be with you. That you're not just a conquest."

"Nothing wrong with being a conquest," Dina murmured, staring off in the direction of the bar.

"Stop ogling my boyfriend," I said with a laugh.

"Darling, it's impossible to do that," Mom said. "He's so…so…"

"Masculine," Dina supplied. "*Virile*."

"Ew, Mom, please never say that again," Charlie muttered.

"There's a rascal quality to him, isn't there? It's in the twinkle of his eyes," Mom said with a sigh. "I'm happy for you."

"Thanks, Mom." My heart lifted.

The men returned and Bones handed me a glass of sparkling water with a lime. He took a sip of his scotch and then wrapped his arm around me, pressing me against his side.

"They make a beautiful couple," Mom said. "Don't they, Arnold?"

"Beautiful," my stepfather agreed, though his tone belied what he was saying.

"Think of their children," Dina said, causing me to choke on my drink.

"They'd be gorgeous," Bones said easily. "But they'd get all of that from Hayden."

"Oh my." My mother placed her hand on her heart. "Already talking about children. It must be serious."

"Actually," I began.

"As serious as it gets," Bones interjected, looking down at me. "I'm crazy about this one."

"Hayden's a hard sell," my stepfather stated. He shot Bones a lofty stare. "It'll take more than just a pretty face to make her fall in love."

"I guess I've got my work cut out for me then," Bones joked, causing the ladies to laugh.

Arnold downed half his glass of scotch in one swallow.

"I don't know. I think Hayden might be sold," my mother said thoughtfully as she looked at me.

"Let's stop talking about my relationship," I suggested. "There are so many other things we could talk about."

"Like what?" Dina asked.

"Yeah, like what?" Patrick parroted.

"Oh, uh, how beautiful the room looks, the delicious food that will be served, the exorbitant donations being made tonight," I suggested.

My stepfather reached into his breast pocket and pulled out his cell. He looked at the screen. "Excuse me a moment, I have to take this."

"You promised," Mom whined.

"I won't be gone long." He flashed her a strained grin and strode from the room.

Mom's gaze wandered to Bones' arm which was still tightly wrapped around me. He didn't look at all concerned that my godparents and mother were openly examining him.

They began to talk to each other and for a moment they were so caught up in discussing us that I was able to whisper to Bones, "We could escape now, and I don't think they'd notice."

"They'd notice, and then give us hell tomorrow at dinner."

"Tomorrow at dinner?" Mom asked as she turned to look at us again.

I sighed. "We're both coming to Sunday dinner."

"This is serious," Mom said. "You never invite men to Sunday dinner."

"Mother," I warned.

"Anyone want to take bets on when they get married?" Patrick asked.

"A year out at least," Mom said. "We'll need time to plan the wedding, which would be nearly impossible in that time anyway."

"Okay, that's enough," I stated.

"Royce doesn't look like the type who wants to wait," Dina said. "I give it six months."

"Dina!"

"You're both wrong," Charlie interjected. "Hayden's gun shy so it would take some time for Royce to convince her…"

"Traitor," I snapped. I looked at Bones. "You want to say something?"

He smiled. "No. I'm enjoying the conversation."

I elbowed him in the ribs, causing him to grunt and release me.

"Darling, if you married him sooner rather than later, you'd be able to take your rightful seat on the board," Mom said.

I shot Charlie a panicked look.

"Okay, enough talking about them," Charlie stated. "Who wants to see my new tattoo?"

~

As Charlie expertly diverted the attention of my godparents with her announcement about her tattoo, a server approached my mother and pulled her away.

Bones took the opportunity to sweep me to the other end of the room.

"Slow down," I muttered. "I can't walk as fast as you right now."

He immediately slowed as I reminded him of the toy currently nestled in my body.

"I'm sorry about that," I said when we had a moment of privacy. "I should've warned you that's how they were going to be."

"I'm not upset by that," he said. "I think your family is hilarious—and they obviously love you very much."

"Okay, but can you ignore all the marriage stuff?" I begged.

He took a sip of his scotch. "What did your mother mean?"

"About what?" I averred.

"You know what. What board? What seat?"

I sighed. "My father was the President and CEO of Spencer Pharmaceuticals. When he died, his trust was clear…in order to inherit my seat on the board, I had to wait until I was thirty years old or be married."

He frowned. "Why those stipulations?"

"Not sure, really. I think because he thought if I was married, it would mean I was more stable."

"But you're not thirty or married," he pointed out. "So, who's in control of the seat?"

"My stepfather," I said. "He and my father were business partners."

"I see," Bones murmured.

"It's been a lifesaver, really," I stated. "I haven't been in a head-space to even contemplate taking my rightful seat on the board. It's still too painful to think about my father's company. Everything about it reminds me of him. It was his legacy."

He took another swallow of his drink but didn't reply.

"Your turn to answer a question for me. How did you know about SINNERS scotch?"

A smile swept across his face. "Prez is long-standing friends with Flynn Campbell. I know all about The Rex and SINNERS. Surprised?"

"Completely," I said with a laugh.

"I heard Ramsey Buchanan is supposed to make an appearance here tonight," Bones drawled.

"You know Ramsey?"

"I haven't met him, no. Do *you* know Ramsey?"

"I've met him a few times. My parents' circle overlaps with his."

"I'm surprised your mother didn't try to marry you off to Ramsey—what with him being the most eligible bachelor in all of Dallas."

I sniggered. "She tried."

"You're not serious."

"Well, sort of. I mean, she kept inviting him to events, but he was out of the country for a while. Always sent his condolences that he couldn't be there." I placed a hand on his chest and stared up at him. "Who knows how my life would've turned out if I'd met him."

His gaze darkened. "Are you trying to make me jealous?"

"Maybe. Is it working?"

He covered my hand with his and then leaned close to my ear and whispered, "You deserve to be punished. I'm going to spank that ass and then fuck it. How about that?"

My breath hitched and I nearly shuddered from the primal, raw possession in his voice.

"Hayden?"

I whipped back so fast I nearly toppled on my heels. My mouth was suddenly dry and my face leeched of color when I realized who'd interrupted my private moment with Bones.

"Tyler," I said, my tone shaky.

My ex-boyfriend was tall and thin, built like a runner, with sandy blond hair. His pale blue eyes shifted to the man standing behind me, the man who was currently wrapping a possessive arm around me.

I instantly relaxed into the solid wall of Bones' chest.

"It's good to see you," Tyler stated.

When I didn't reply, he took a step forward and held out his hand toward Bones. "I don't think we've met."

"We haven't," Bones said, his tone clipped.

Tyler stood straighter and dropped his hand.

Years of manners bred into me forced the words from my lips. "Tyler Armstrong, Royce Dalton. Royce is my—"

"Boyfriend," Bones interjected.

"Boyfriend," Tyler repeated. "Your mother didn't mention you were dating anyone."

I clenched my jaw so hard, I worried I'd crack my teeth. "Well, I am. Excuse us."

When I tried to take a step forward, Bones' arm tightened around me even more.

I glanced up at Bones who wasn't even looking at me. He was staring at Tyler. Without taking his eyes off my ex, he lifted his glass of scotch to his lips and took a drink.

"I'd like to get some air," I said pointedly.

Bones finally looked down at me and cracked a smile. "Whatever you want, Duchess."

He released me and took my hand, linking his fingers through mine.

We strode past my ex. I slapped a smile on my face as I met gazes of guests who I recognized but didn't stop to greet.

Bones ushered me from the room with a sense of urgency. We didn't speak as we walked across the marble lobby floor toward the elevators. He pushed the button, and a carriage came almost immediately.

I didn't ask where he was taking me, I just enjoyed his command of the situation.

Bones kept his fingers linked with mine, even as we stepped out of the elevator to the Whiskey Room, the hotel's sensuous rooftop bar with glass walls that showed off the Dallas skyline.

The fireplace roared with giant flames. Customers sat

on leather couches and enjoyed after-dinner drinks and conversation.

Bones led me to the doors and we stepped out onto the roof terrace. I gulped a breath of fresh cold air and immediately shivered.

He stripped off his tuxedo jacket and wrapped it around my shoulders. I hugged it tight, a whiff of his cologne hitting my nose.

"That was your ex, wasn't it?"

"Yeah." I shook my head. "I had no idea he was going to be here tonight. My mother didn't say anything—"

"I'm not mad."

"No?"

"Well, not at you." He shot me a lopsided smile. "I was ready to punch his face in. But I don't think your mother would've appreciated that at her event."

"Definitely not," I agreed. "But it might've been fun to watch."

He grasped the lapels of his tuxedo jacket and pulled me close. "I need to touch you."

I swallowed. "Touch me how?"

He gently backed me up until I hit the stone wall. Even though the city lights illuminated the sky and there were terrace lights, he'd moved me into the shadows at the side of the bar, discreetly out of view for anyone unless they walked a very specific path around the corner.

"Spread your legs, Duchess."

I immediately spread my legs.

He caged me in with one of his hands pressing against the stone wall. The other hiked up the skirt of my dress.

Bones grazed a finger over the lace of my panties, causing me to shudder.

"I'm going to slide my fingers inside you, Duchess. I'm

going to make you come and you're not going to make a sound. Do you understand?"

I nodded eagerly.

He continued to play with the scrap of fabric shielding me from his complete touch.

I bit my lip to stifle my demand that he hurry up and make me explode.

His eyes were on me, watching me, gauging me.

Finally, he slid aside my thong and rested his finger at my warm entrance. He glided in the tip and stopped.

I glared at him, wanting to shout at him and beg him to continue.

He sank his finger all the way inside me.

I shuddered around him, clenching, the plug in my ass shifting as I did.

"Bones," I whispered.

"Not a word, Duchess," he growled.

I nodded so he knew I'd heard him.

He pumped his finger in and out, changing the rhythm until I was biting my lip to stifle my cries.

Bones added another finger as his thumb swiped across my clit.

My knees collapsed, but his arm was suddenly there to hold me up. His fingers were inside my body and I was clamping down on them like my life depended on it.

"You're gonna come for me, Duchess. You're gonna come all over my fingers while that plug is in your ass and you're going to beg me for more. Aren't you?"

I nodded as his fingers picked up speed. He knew just the way to curl them, just the amount of pressure to use.

The idea that anyone could walk by and see us and guess what we were doing had me clenching around him, squeezing until I was coming hard and fast.

Something clanked against the terrace stone as I grabbed his bicep and rode out my orgasm.

When my tremors began to subside, Bones gently slid out of me and I watched him lick my desire from his fingers.

I suddenly felt empty.

My eyes widened in horror when I realized what had fallen to the ground.

My orgasm had been so furious that my body had pushed out the butt plug.

I shoved against him and hastily looked around. It was laying on the stone near my feet. I hastily reached for my clutch that I'd set on the terrace wall and pulled out a white handkerchief. I urged Bones to move so I could lean down and wrap the butt plug in the handkerchief and then hastily slid it into my clutch.

"You're bright red right now," he commented.

"How can you tell? It's dark out here."

"Not that dark." He gently grasped my chin and lifted my gaze to his. "You were perfect." His lips barely touched mine.

"I probably look a mess," I muttered. "We better get back to the ballroom before people start noticing we're missing."

"Duchess," he drawled, a smile blooming across his face. "They see us coming back into the room, they're gonna know. No way to hide it."

I groaned. "Then let me find a bathroom so I can fix my appearance."

Chapter 39

I was just coming out of the ladies' room as Bones put his cell phone away.

"Everything okay?" I asked, taking his offered hand.

"Everything's fine," he said. "I'm starving. You never did tell me what I'm eating for dinner."

"Quail in a red wine reduction with garlic mashed potatoes and haricot vert and shallots," I stated.

"Doesn't sound bad," he remarked.

"It won't be," I assured him.

"So, if I'm eating tiny, weird birds tonight, what are you eating?" he asked.

I chuckled. "They've prepared another dish for me."

We re-entered the ballroom and I was glad to see that no one paid us much attention.

"Another drink?" I asked.

"Sure," he said as we headed for the bar.

An all-American blond man was standing at the bar, waiting for his drink when we approached. He turned when he saw us.

He smiled. "Hayden."

I paused. "You must be Walker."

"That's me." Walker looked to Bones, his pleasant expression remaining.

"Walker, this is Royce Dalton, my boyfriend."

"Boyfriend." Walker laughed and shook his head. "No wonder you said no to dinner. Nice to meet you, Royce."

"You too," Bones said. I looked at his face to determine if he was being authentic. There was no tension in his shoulders or jawline.

"I came here without a date. Thanks," he said to the bartender who offered him his drink. "But I'm kind of glad because there's a gorgeous woman in a red dress that I want to meet. You wouldn't by any chance be able to introduce me?"

"Gorgeous woman in a red dress," I repeated with a smile. "She's my best friend, Charlie. And I'd be glad to introduce you. Actually, there's a spot open at our table. I can do some last-minute re-arranging so you can sit next to her if you'd like?"

"Absolutely. I don't think my father will miss me," he said with a rueful smile. "He's in his element. Shop talk, you know?"

"I know. Believe me, I know."

"Well, great. I'll see you both in a bit," Walker said as he left the bar.

We stepped up to order.

"Nice guy," Bones said. "For a politician's son, anyway."

I grinned. "I appreciate you reigning in the jealousy."

"Nothing to be jealous about," he said easily, taking his scotch from the bartender.

"But you were jealous of Tyler," I said. "Why? That was years ago."

"I was jealous," he admitted, wrapping his arm around

me and pulling me toward him. "But it was more of wanting to flatten his ass for how he treated you. Two entirely different things."

"I think you're turning me into a heathen," I quipped. "Because I kind of like the possessive alpha thing. Just don't club me over the head and haul me over your shoulder. Oh, well, actually…you could throw me over your shoulder if you wanted."

His booming laughter turned heads and I enjoyed that people saw us happy together.

If I had Bones at my side, how many of these events could I live through? The idea that he'd get to wear the tux more than once had my insides cartwheeling.

"I have to speak to my mother real fast about inviting Walker to sit at our table," I said.

Bones' phone buzzed in his trouser pocket. He let me go to pull it out. "I have to take this. I'll come find you in a bit."

I nodded and watched him put the phone to his ear and walk toward the exit.

My mother was in the middle of a conversation with Imogene Oglethorpe, a wealthy socialite who'd recently married an even wealthier cattle rancher.

I smiled and sidled up to my mother's side. "Sorry to interrupt," I said. "Hi, Imogene."

"Hayden!" She beamed. "You look incredible! You're positively glowing."

Mom examined me and raised her brows. I shot her a warning look and smiled.

"It's good to see you," I said, embracing Imogene.

"And you," she said. "I just got a new thoroughbred. You should come out and ride him. And see the solarium I just had remodeled."

"Love to," I said. "How's married life treating you?"

She waved her left hand, flashing an extravagant ring that didn't look at all too big for her finger. "Pure bliss."

"I'm so glad," I said.

"Hayden is actually dating someone. Where is Royce, darling?" Mom asked.

"He had to take a phone call," I said. "Actually, I need to talk to you about the seating arrangements. Do you have a moment?"

Mom looked at Imogene. "Excuse us?"

"Of course," she said with an understanding smile. "A hostess's job is not done until the caterers are paid."

"You understand it well," Mom said.

Imogene took her glass of wine and whisked away, leaving me alone with my mother.

"That empty seat we left open at our table? Walker Anderson is going to join us."

"Fabulous."

"Next to Charlie," I specified.

"Well, isn't that interesting," she said with a wide grin.

"Don't say anything to Dina, okay?" I said. "You know she'd support it and once that happens Charlie will do anything to sabotage it."

"You're right."

I had my own reasons for wanting Charlie and Walker to hit it off. She wasn't going to forget about Savage until a new man entered her life. As much as Charlie claimed she wanted a bad boy, I knew she'd get tired of her rebellious stage and eventually settle down.

"Where's Arnold?" I asked.

Mom frowned. "I don't know, actually. The last I saw him he was taking a phone call, but he hasn't come back yet."

"When were you going to tell me Tyler was coming?" I asked.

"Tyler's here?" She looked around. "I had no idea. You were there with me when we finalized the seating chart. He wasn't on the list."

"Maybe he's crashing the party."

"I can get security," Mom insisted.

"No, it's fine. I don't want your event ruined with scandal. Leave him be."

"I would've told you if he was coming. I never would've clobbered you with that out of the blue." Her expression clouded. "I've never forgiven him for how he treated you after the funeral."

"It's done now," I said. "I don't want to think about that time in my life. Not when I'm…"

"Happy?" she supplied for me.

I nodded.

"I'm happy that you're happy," she said, squeezing her hand.

Tears prickled my eyes. "Thanks, Mom."

"Let's find our seats. And watch Walker fall head over heels in love with Charlie."

We strolled to our table. Patrick helped us with our seats since Bones and my stepfather were both MIA.

Charlie waved off her father and took her seat. She drank from her champagne flute, looking bored and in need of a distraction.

Walker Anderson swooped in, not taking his eyes off Charlie.

Charlie couldn't take her eyes off Walker, either.

"Walker, I'd like you to meet my best friend, Charlie. Charlie, this is Walker."

"Nice to meet you," she said, boldly perusing him.

"Nice to meet you, too," he said. His eyes lingered a little too long and Patrick cleared his throat.

While my mother was making introductions, Charlie met my gaze and fanned herself and pretended to swoon.

I bit my lip to stifle my grin. Walker took the chair next to Charlie and the two of them immediately jumped into conversation.

I looked at Dina and held up crossed fingers.

She blew me a kiss.

Bones returned to the table and slid into the chair next to me. "Have I missed the weird, tiny bird yet?"

I shot him a grin. "They haven't even served the salads."

He set his arm on the back of my chair and leaned closer to whisper, "How long do we have to stay before we can leave? I want another taste of you."

Shivers danced down my spine. I turned my head to reply, pitching my voice lower. "There's a break between dinner and dessert. We can slip away then."

My stepfather returned to the ballroom just as they were serving the salad course. His face was chalk white and when he reached for his newly poured glass of white wine, his hand shook. I tried to catch his eye, but he never met my gaze. He was quiet, letting my mother direct the flow of conversation.

At some point during the main course, Bones placed his hand on my thigh and let it wander toward the juncture of my legs. I glared at him in warning, but he looked remarkably composed as he ate his food, like he wasn't tracing circles on my thigh and tantalizing me.

Dina and Patrick were regaling us with tales of their early courtship.

"He was a complete and utter ass," Dina said with a laugh. "There wasn't anything he wouldn't do to get my attention."

"Like streaking across the football field at Notre

Dame's homecoming game with her name painted on my behind," Patrick said with a wide smile.

"I could've been happy never knowing that story," Charlie said, causing a round of laughter at the table.

"Kellen tried to talk me out of it, but I wouldn't be deterred," Patrick said. "We were roommates at Notre Dame. Thick as thieves."

The words were out of his mouth without any thought and a pall fell over the table. I glanced at my mother to see how she felt about my father's name being mentioned.

"It was one of his favorite stories to tell at Christmas, after one too many glasses of sherry," she said with a fondness I rarely heard from her. Not because she didn't love my father, but because the mere mention of his name usually made her clamshell.

"How did you two meet?" Bones asked my mom, gesturing to her and my stepfather. He took his glass of wine and held it to his lips while he waited for the story.

My mother looked to Arnold, waiting for him to explain, but he was lost in thought, not paying attention. He lifted his drink to his mouth and downed half of it.

I frowned. My stepfather was a social drinker, but tonight he seemed to be hitting it hard.

"Kellen and Arnold went to the University of Chicago Booth School of Business together, and he's been a longtime friend of the family," my mother finally expounded. "And he was my rock after Kellen died. After a while, it turned into more."

"Hmm." Bones took a drink and then set his glass of wine down.

I looked at him, but he just picked up his fork and began eating his meal again. I glanced at Charlie. She gave me a strained smiled and shrugged before turning her attention back to Walker.

The servers cleared away our plates as Dina and Patrick started talking about where they were going to spend Christmas.

My mother picked up her glass of wine and said, "I need to make the rounds."

"I'll join you." Arnold wiped his mouth on his black napkin and rose, placing a hand on the small of her back and ushering her away.

"The Selzinks just bought a place in St. Moritz. I want to ask them about it," Dina said. "See you kids in a bit."

"Don't get into any trouble," Patrick said, pinning a stare onto his daughter.

"Why are you looking at me?" Charlie asked. "I'm an angel."

"More like a fallen angel," I muttered under my breath, which caused Bones to laugh.

Once Charlie's parents left the table, Charlie turned to Walker and said, "I just got a tattoo. Do you want to see it?"

"Yes," he said, not taking his eyes off her. "Should we get some fresh air?"

"That sounds perfect," Charlie said.

They rose from the table and without a backward glance, left the room.

"And then there were two," I said.

"Let's get out of here." Bones downed the rest of his red wine and rose.

He held out his hand to me and I grasped it. He hauled me up, his hand going to my waist as we walked toward the exit.

We were stopped along the way by friends of my mother's. I introduced Bones, we shared a few jokes, and then we politely extricated ourselves. When we were finally in the limousine on the way back to my house, I breathed a sigh of relief.

"I wasn't sure we were going to make it out of there," I said with a laugh. "Everyone was so curious about you. No doubt they're gossiping now as we speak."

"Let 'em." Bones pressed a button and raised the partition between us and our driver.

He undid his tie and set it aside and then he removed his tuxedo jacket.

Then he crouched on floor of the limousine in front of me.

"What are you doing?" I whispered.

His hands inched up my calves, raising my dress as he went. Bones' grin was wicked and full of promise.

He tugged at my thong.

I lifted up and allowed him to ease it down my legs.

And then he spread my thighs. "I'm going to eat this pussy the entire way home. Keep count of how many orgasms I give you."

He bent his head to his task.

I lost count after four.

Chapter 40

The mattress dipped and my hand immediately felt for him.

"Go back to sleep," he whispered.

"What time is it?" I murmured.

"Late. Or early. Depending on who you ask."

I was exhausted, my body limp and sated from all the orgasms. Not just from the limousine ride home, but from the one in the entrance hallway.

The moment we'd closed the door to my house, Bones had pulled a condom from his pocket, sheathed himself, and then he'd lifted me against the wall to fuck me into oblivion. I'd barely managed to take off my dress and heels before tumbling into bed; makeup and jewelry still on.

I sat up, the sheet falling off my naked body. I reached for the clasp around my neck and set the heavy thing aside. My earrings followed. No doubt my pillow was stained with makeup.

With a sigh, I threw my legs over the side of the bed.

"Where are you going?" he asked.

"Bathroom. I've got to wash my face."

I padded naked to the bathroom and quietly closed the door before turning on the light. I immediately dimmed it.

My hair was a rat's nest. Bones had plowed his fingers through it and removed the pins that held it up all night. After I cleaned my face, I brushed my hair out, wincing at the snarls.

When I was finished, I quietly trekked back to bed. As I climbed in, Bones reached his hand out and urged me toward him.

I snuggled into his embrace. His heart drummed heavily in my ear. I waited for his breathing to even out, but I waited in vain.

"You're awake," I stated.

"Yeah."

"I thought you went to sleep when I went to sleep."

"I did. Got a phone call that woke me up."

"Everything okay?" I asked quietly.

He paused for a moment and then he said, "It was an interesting night."

"I guess."

"I heard a lot of things. Things that made my antenna go up."

"Such as?"

"For starters? I had no idea your father was the founder of Spencer Pharmaceuticals."

"Oh, back to that, are we? You already know I have money—"

"Hayden, you're a fucking *heiress*."

"What's that supposed to mean?"

"It means you're not just rich, you're fucking ultra-rich. Your father's company is worth—"

"One point two billion dollars. That's public knowledge, and I thought you already knew that."

"How would I know that? You didn't tell me you were *the* Spencer, of Spencer Pharmaceuticals."

"Okay, maybe I should've told you about my father's company, but I didn't because I have no interest in taking a seat on the board."

"Even if you don't take the seat on the board, you're still worth over five hundred million dollars."

"And why do you think I've kept you at arm's length for as long as possible? Hm? You don't know what it's like having this much money. People will do *anything* to get it."

"Hayden, I'm not that guy. I don't care that you have money. Honestly it would be easier if you didn't. But our worlds don't have to be the same for me to love you."

"I grew up how I grew up. There's nothing wrong with that," I said.

"I didn't say there was. And I didn't grow up poor. I grew up…normal."

"Okay, normal."

"And this isn't even what I was getting at." He sighed, his hand plowing through my loose waves.

"Then what are you getting at?"

"When you were in the bathroom and I was waiting for you, Tyler found me and we had a talk."

"Tyler? He talked to you? About what?"

"Actually, it wasn't so much a *talk* as it was a statement. He told me it looks like Arnold hasn't sat me down yet and told me how it's going to be. When I asked what the fuck that meant, he said Arnold spoke with him a few weeks after your father's funeral. Arnold told Tyler there was no way in hell he'd let him marry you. That he might as well give up then because he wasn't getting his hands on your money or your company. Hayden, your stepfather—before he was even married to your mother—all but threatened

Tyler into dumping you. If he didn't, he was going to destroy Tyler and everything he was working for."

I blinked. "Wait, are you telling me—"

"That Tyler didn't dump you because he wanted to. He was *made* to dump you. Your stepfather was directly responsible for that."

I shook my head. "But why would he do that? And why wouldn't Tyler tell me?"

"To protect you, I'm sure. You said Tyler was only twenty-three when you broke up. He was young enough to be swayed then. But he's never gotten over you. He's still in love with you."

"How do you know that?" I demanded.

"Because he told me that was why he was at the gala—to win you back."

My head was reeling. "Win me back?"

"That's what he said. He wasn't expecting me to be there, though. He planned on leaving after he saw us together, but before he did, he sought me out to warn me about what I was getting into."

"Bones, I don't love him. I love you."

"I know."

"All this time," I murmured. "I thought Tyler didn't have a spine. I had no idea… And what the hell was Arnold thinking? Ruining my relationship on the heels of me losing my father? What the hell?"

"I can't believe I'm even saying this, but Tyler actually seems like a decent guy. He saw me with you and didn't try to break us up just so he might have another chance with you."

"I don't want Tyler," I insisted. "Even knowing what I know. I want *you*."

Bones cracked a smile. "I know that too. Are you gonna be okay?"

"I will be, but when we see Arnold tomorrow night, I'm ripping him a new one."

∾

I wasn't sure what had startled me awake, but my heart jumped into my throat and my eyes opened.

Something's wrong.

Bones curled his hand around my hip, as if he was silently telling me not to move.

A noise in the room had the hairs on the back of my neck standing up, and just as I was about to ask Bones what was going on, the sound of his pistol going off rang in my ears. A flash of light from the gunshot illuminated a man in all black wearing a ski mask.

He scuffled in the darkness and ran off down the hallway into the night.

"*Stay here*," Bones commanded as he jumped from the bed with his pistol still in hand and sprinted from the room.

I flipped the bedside light on and curled my legs up to my chest as my eyes scanned the room. Drops of blood were on the wooden floor at the threshold of the door. Bones had wounded the intruder.

I lived in a high-end, safe neighborhood, and I had a professional security system. How had this happened?

I was still naked, and I felt exposed. I got out of bed and quickly threw on a pair of sweats and a sweatshirt while I waited for Bones to return.

He came back to the bedroom, a scowl marring his handsome face. Bones marched over to the nightstand and grabbed his phone. He quickly unlocked his cell and pressed a button. He put the phone to his ear and waited. "I'm at Hayden's. Someone just broke into the house...

yeah, we're okay." He paused for a moment while someone on the other end of the line spoke. "No signs of forced entry so far as I can see. Security system didn't even go off." He paused again. "Wounded, but he's gone. I didn't want to leave Hayden so I'm back in the room with her. We're safe. Right. See ya."

He hung up. "Pack a bag." When I didn't move, he barked, "*Hayden, pack a bag.* We're not staying here anymore."

I jumped off the side of the bed and grabbed my jewelry. I went to the walk-in closet and unlocked the hidden jeweler's safe behind one of the drawers in my custom-built closet.

"Bones," I called out, my voice hoarse.

"Yeah?"

"Bones, I—we set the alarm."

He appeared in the doorway of the walk-in closet as I put the jewelry inside and locked the safe.

"We set the alarm before we went to bed," I repeated. "That means—"

"I know, Duchess."

I swallowed. "Then you think—this wasn't—"

He stalked toward me and grasped my cheeks in his hands. "Pack your bag, Duchess. We'll talk at the clubhouse."

"The clubhouse? We need to call the police first and tell—"

"*No.* No police. We're going to the clubhouse and staying where I can protect you."

I closed the drawer over the safe, hiding it from sight and then ran my hands up and down my arms which were covered by my old, faded sweatshirt. "I don't need to pack a bag. I have a bag of clothes already in your room."

"Right. Then let me get dressed and let's get out of here."

"Who did you call?"

"Colt. He's sending a few guys to come clean up."

I swallowed. "There's not much to clean up. I mean there's a little…blood. But no broken glass or anything."

He didn't reply as he came further into the closet to the drawer with his clothes. He pulled out a pair of jeans and a long-sleeved black shirt. "I didn't think to bring a pair of spare motorcycle boots. I'm gonna have to wear my dress shoes."

I grabbed my fluffy, comfortable boots and took them to the bed. My hands shook as I put them on.

"Hey…" Bones crouched in front of me and grasped my cold hands, holding them in his. "You're okay."

"I'm okay." I nodded. "Because of you."

He pulled me to him and wrapped me in his strong embrace. I buried my head against his neck and whispered, "I'm glad you sleep with a pistol on the nightstand."

Bones paused for a moment and then said, "I never thought I'd actually have to use it."

"What's happening, Bones?" I asked, rearing back to meet his eyes. "First the gunman outside Leather and Ink, and now this? Is it just a coincidence?"

His jaw clenched. "I don't believe in coincidence."

Chapter 41

Bones drove us to the clubhouse in my car. We were silent the entire ride there. The gates opened and we passed through. I let out a deep exhale once we were in the perimeter of the clubhouse.

He reached over and settled his hand on my thigh.

"I keep thinking about what would've happened if you hadn't been there," I murmured.

"I know, Duchess. I know." He parked the car and cut the engine. "I'm trying not to lose my shit, but it's not working so well."

I unclipped my seatbelt but made no move to get out of the car. In the car, I was safe. Out there, I was exposed.

"Come on. Let's get inside."

My home. My sanctuary. It had been violated. Would I ever sleep soundly there again? Even if Bones slept by my side every night, would that be enough?

I closed the car door and the sound of it slamming echoed in the night. Bones came to me and wrapped an arm around my shoulder and hauled me close. We walked up the front porch steps.

Savage and Duke were drinking beers and talking quietly. They stopped when we approached.

"You all keep late hours," I said.

"Goes with the job description," Savage drawled. "How are you, honey?"

"I'm...okay. I think."

"You've had a rough go of it, haven't you?" Duke asked as he took a sip of his beer.

I nodded.

"Should we get you a drink?" Savage asked. "Just a shot to thaw the moment?"

"No thanks."

"Colt and Zip are in the office," Duke said.

Bones grabbed my hand and all but dragged me inside. The oven read 4:14 AM. "Did you wake Colt up out of a sound sleep?"

"Yep," he said.

We walked down the hallway and he knocked on a door before opening it. The president of the Tarnished Angels sat behind a wooden desk and his vice president perched on the edge.

"Come on in," Colt said. "Get comfortable. We're gonna need a minute."

Unease trickled through me as I took the chair. Bones closed the door behind me.

"Start talking," Colt said.

"Who, me?" I asked.

Colt gestured with his chin to Bones.

"I think it was a hit on Hayden," Bones said.

I flinched even though I'd been thinking the exact same thing.

He looked at me. "We set the alarm. There was no forced entry. No struggle. No broken glass. Someone knew how to get in. And a few weeks ago, someone stuck a gun in her face before Willa shot him dead. Cops said it was some tweaker looking for an easy mark. But now I'm not buying it."

I nibbled my lip, my mind churning.

"Okay, so someone's trying to kill her," Zip said. "Why?"

"Because I'm worth a lot of money," I stated baldly.

"Not just that, but she's set to inherit a seat on the board of her father's pharmaceutical company when she either gets married or turns thirty," Bones said.

"Father's pharmaceutical company?" Zip asked.

"Spencer Pharmaceuticals," Bones clarified.

"Shit. You're *that* Spencer?" Colt asked.

I nodded.

"God damn, you hooked up with a rich bitch," Zip stated. "No offense, Hayden."

While the three of them discussed my wealth like I wasn't sitting right there, my brain went haywire. And then all at once the picture came together and I finally admitted the truth.

Tears began to prick my eyes.

"Duchess?" Bones asked. "What's wrong?"

"I think," I croaked, "I think we both know who's behind all this." I met Bones' blue eyes. "Arnold."

"That's the same conclusion I got to," Bones said.

I looked at Colt. "The board seat I'm set to inherit was set up by my father in a trust. It's a controlling seat with a huge percentage of the company shares. It would make me the largest single shareholder and put me in control of Spencer Pharmaceuticals in full. No one would be able to challenge it unless the seat is voluntarily forfeit and the trust revoked by me once it goes into effect…or if I die, in which case the shares revert to my mother. Right now, there are only two things standing in the way of me being on the board; I'm not thirty, and I'm not married. And I had a boyfriend I was set to marry, but yesterday Bones told me that it was actually Arnold who forced Tyler to leave me after my father died. Why would he do that? There's only one reason. He's trying to prevent me from gaining my seat on the board and taking control of the company."

"Who is Arnold, and why wouldn't he want you in control?" Colt asked.

"Arnold is my stepfather. He was my father's best friend and married my mother shortly after my father died. He was the senior most manager in the company and the board elected him as interim chair until I could take his place as was set forth in the trust."

"He'd benefit from your death," Colt said, nodding in understanding. "Because he'd remain in control. So the board seat goes up for a vote if you die?"

"Yes," I said. "I'm an only child and my mother has no interest in running the company. She still has enough shares for a seat on the board, but she votes how Arnold tells her to. If I die, she'll be the majority shareholder and Arnold will get voted in as permanent chair. If that happens, Spencer Pharmaceuticals all but belongs to him."

"And you have no husband and no children, so you can't leave the seat to anyone if something happens to you, right?" Colt asked.

I nodded my head. "Exactly. In fact, until the trust executes upon my marriage or turning thirty, I can't alter or revoke it in any way. At this point I can't even choose a new trustee if I want. It's completely set in stone until it executes."

Colt rubbed his jaw. "So then killing you is about that board seat and controlling the company, not just the shares.

What's been going on with the company since your father died?"

"Patents are getting approved; medications are selling well. There were some major ups and downs right after Dad died. Speculation went wild after his death about the direction of the company. But things settled down when Arnold took over…until recently. Arnold wants to take the company in a different direction and the shareholders are spooked. The board has been split with Arnold as the tiebreaker."

Bones and Colt exchanged a look and then Bones asked, "How did your father die, exactly? You never did tell me the full story."

"Ski accident," I answered absently. "But he was an expert skier. It never made any sense. He was always so careful. Wore a helmet and everything."

I hadn't remembered much about the details of his death. I'd been grief-stricken and nothing really registered, especially those first few days and weeks after he died.

Suddenly, I jumped out of my seat, feeling the blood drain from my cheeks.

"Arnold was with him. He was the *only* one with him. Oh my God, what if he…"

The room fell silent as my words lingered in the air.

Arnold killed my father.

And now he's trying to kill me, too.

"That's some heavy shit. So, what's the plan?" Zip asked. "You've got a plan, right?"

Bones nodded slowly.

My hands went cold. "You can't, Bones. You can't do it. I won't let you endanger yourself."

He looked at me and raised his brows. "I can't do what?"

"You can't kill him," I blurted out.

Bones smirked. "I wasn't planning on killing him."

"Oh?" My brow furrowed. "Then what's your plan?"

"To marry you," he said. He might as well have been talking about a dentist appointment for all the emotion he delivered with that loaded statement.

"Get a new plan!" I commanded.

"Don't want to," Bones stated.

"You can't marry me," I protested.

"It could work," Colt said. "It protects you, Hayden. It's an immediate solution until you have time to invoke a new trust. If you delay, it could be the end of *you*."

I shot a glare at Colt. "*Do not* encourage this crazy idea."

"It makes sense actually," Zip added. "Marry Hayden, and she gets control of her board seat immediately. If her stepfather is in fact trying to kill her, he'll then have to come after both of you, which puts him in a bind and would draw attention to him. And it stops him from fucking up the company. Gives you some time to sort things out on paper."

"And it'll make Hayden your Old Lady," Colt said to Bones. "So she'll be one of us, officially."

Hysteria rose in my chest and clawed its way up my throat, but I forced it down. "What does that have to do with anything?"

"If you're part of the club, it's another layer of protection. If anyone fucks with you, we fuck with them." Bones' grin was feral.

"We can't get married," I stated again.

"Why not?" Bones asked. "Your family was taking bets on when that would happen anyway."

"That's not enough of a reason."

"Your mom wants grandbabies." Bones shrugged. "I'm happy to oblige."

"*Oh, are you?*" I screeched.

Zip let out a laugh.

I glared at him. "You mind giving us some privacy?"

"I mind," Zip said. "We're not leaving this room until you cooperate."

"*Cooperate?*" I seethed.

Bones pushed away from the door and came to me. He grasped my hip and turned me around to face him. He cradled my face in his hands and forced me to look up at him.

His thumb swiped across my lips. "Trust me, Duchess."

"But I can't just…we can't."

"We can," he insisted. "We will. You love me."

"Love doesn't have to mean marriage."

"Argue all you want," he said. "But you know this is the only way. Let me protect you, Duchess. Let me protect what your father built for you."

His words lanced my heart and I let out a breathy sigh. His eyes were earnest, his touch was firm, and I bent to his edict like an aspen tree bending in a storm.

"This is crazy," I whispered.

"But it's right. You know it's right."

I stared at him, this man who wanted to protect me and bind his life to mine. And even though it was insane, my heart eased. I would not have to do this alone.

"All right, Bones. I'll marry you."

He kissed me softly and then pulled back, refusing to take his eyes off me.

"We can leave now and let you guys consummate right here on this desk if you want," Zip offered.

"Not on my desk," Colt growled.

I hid my face against Bones' chest.

Holy hell. I'm engaged.

"We have to iron some things out though," I stated.

"Sure," Bones agreed.

"*Legal things*," I stated.

"Prenup. I get it," Bones said. "You're an heiress. You have a lot of money. I don't hold that against you."

"Thanks," I drawled. "A blanket prenup can be drawn up and finished in a day. So far as protecting the company…that's going to take some time. Right now, as crazy at this sounds, you guys are going to have to keep me alive."

"We will. But the sooner you get married, the better off you'll be," Colt said.

"I'll call Vance's emergency number in a few hours," Bones said. "What about you, Duchess? You got a lawyer on retainer?"

I snorted. "Of course. But not for something like this. I need someone I can trust, and I know someone I can call to get the name of someone like that."

"Your mother," Bones said.

"Not my mother." I sighed.

Bones looked at Colt. "We done?"

"For now," Colt said.

Bones took my hand and pulled me from the room. My feet dragged as we headed up the stairs. I was both wired and exhausted.

My brain wasn't functioning. What was I supposed to tackle first? The thought that my stepfather—my father's business partner and supposed best friend—was behind his death and the attempts on my life? Or the fact that I was about to marry a biker?

Bones opened the door to his bedroom and flicked on the light.

I groaned at the garish brightness of it and quickly went to the nightstand to turn on the lamp. He turned off the overhead light immediately.

I flopped down onto the bed with my legs still hanging off the sides.

Bones sat next to me, but he didn't say anything. He just removed his dress shoes and then stood to strip out of his jeans.

Finally, he spoke. "Give me your phone."

"Why?" I asked.

"Because I need it."

With a sigh, I sat up and pulled it out of my pocket. I handed it to him. He took his cell phone and left the room. A few moments later he returned, closing the door.

"The conversation I want to have can't happen if there are phones around."

"That's terrifying," I muttered.

He shrugged. "That's the world we live in. You gotta think ahead. So, the next time you ask me if I'm going to kill someone, do me a favor and make sure we're not around any electronics."

I flinched. "You're offended that I asked that."

"Offended?" He shook his head slowly. "No."

"No?"

He scratched his jaw. "I've done shit, Hayden. I've done shit for my club. Don't ask me what because I wouldn't tell you even if I thought you could handle it."

Bones strode toward me. He knelt down and placed his hands on my thighs. His penetrating stare held my gaze captive.

"There's nothing I wouldn't do for you, Hayden. *Nothing.*"

I knew what he was saying. This man, on his knees in front of me, would kill for me—and he'd have no remorse about doing it.

The tightness in my chest eased.

I placed my hand on his heart. "I love you, too."

He crooked a smile at me. "You know what this means, don't you?"

"What?"

"You just became my Old Lady."

"You didn't ask me to be your Old Lady. And you didn't ask me to marry you, either."

"You're going to marry me," he commanded.

"Am I?" I asked.

His hands slid from the top of my thighs to the underside of my legs, close to my butt. And he hauled me toward him. My legs naturally opened to accommodate his presence.

"You're going to marry me," he said again. "You're going to be my Old Lady. You're going to take my last name."

"Bossy," I murmured.

His look was charged. "And you're going to have my babies. And I don't want to hear any argument from you. Got it?"

"Any other stipulations?" I asked.

"Our babies have to look like you."

I cradled his cheeks and skimmed his lips with my thumbs. "I'll see what I can do."

Chapter 42

My phone alarm went off a few hours later. It was early Sunday morning around 8 AM. Bones reached for the nightstand, and then blessed quietness enveloped the room.

I hadn't fallen asleep fully the entire night. My nerves were frayed and I'd bounced in and out of consciousness for hours until the alarm went off.

"You ready to get up and face the day?" Bones rumbled next to me.

I rolled over and curled into him. "No."

"That terrified of marrying me?"

"That terrified that my stepfather really is behind all this and that everything I thought I knew is a lie." With a sigh, I forced myself to sit up. "I don't know how I'm going to make it through the day without caffeine. And we're going to have to figure out how to bail on dinner tonight. There's no way we can go after what happened."

"We'll come up with something. For now, have a cup of coffee."

"Hm. No. It'll give me a headache. And will probably make me nauseated."

"Not worth it then." He threw off the covers and sat up. Bones scratched his bare chest and reached for his phone. "I'm gonna call Vance now. Let him know about the situation. He's going to want to meet with us and go over a few things."

"Like the prenup?"

He handed me my phone. "Among other things."

"What other things?"

"Things," Bones said evasively. He leaned over and kissed me. "I need coffee before I call Vance. Meet me downstairs when you're done."

He quickly pulled on a pair of jeans, a long-sleeved shirt, and his boots before leaving the bedroom.

I sat for a moment and then I opened my phone and found Oliver's number. He answered on the first ring. "You're calling me this time."

"I am," I said.

"You never call me."

"I didn't see you last night at my mother's charity event," I said.

"You know I never attend those things. How was it?"

"Beautiful. Am I disturbing you?"

"No, I just sat down at my desk and I'm finishing my cup of coffee. What can I do for you, Hayden?"

"I need to talk to you about something, but I need your promise of discretion."

"You have it."

I took a deep breath. "I need the name of an attorney you trust. Someone not tied to Dad's company. Someone who specializes in family law."

"Family law," he repeated slowly.

"I need a prenuptial agreement," I stated honestly. "And while I'm at it, a will and testament drawn up. And after I'm married, I'm going to need to alter the trust for

Spencer Pharmaceuticals, and it's going to take some time."

He paused for a moment and then he said, "I can get you a name of someone I trust with my life."

"Thanks, Oliver."

"You'll tell me the good news? When you're ready?"

I smiled even though the older man couldn't see me. "I'll do you one better. You'll get to meet him soon. How about that?"

"I'd like that. Your father…he asked me to look out for you. I wish you would've let me."

"I'm letting you now."

I hung up with Oliver and then I went downstairs to see my fiancé.

My heart melted when I thought of the man I was marrying. The man who wanted to do the exact same thing for me.

∼

"This is the least romantic engagement in the history of the world," I muttered Monday morning. "I can't tell people this story."

Bones wrapped his arm around my shoulder as we stepped out of the courthouse with our marriage license. We had to wait three days before we could officially tie the knot. "I guess this is a bad time to talk about your ring."

"I already have a ring," I said.

He looked at me as we headed toward the car. "I'm supposed to get *you* the ring. You get that, right?"

I threw him a look. "There's a tradition in my family. The engagement ring is always an heirloom, but the wedding band is new."

"So…"

"So, I've had my engagement ring picked out since I was sixteen years old. It's in a safety deposit box."

"You want to talk about unromantic?" he asked. "So let me get this straight. I'm off the hook from buying you an engagement ring and I'm permanently moving into your house. Is there anything I get to provide as the man?"

I looked up at him and flashed him a devilish grin.

He unclipped the sunglasses from the collar of his shirt and slid them on. "I know what's on your mind, clearly."

"Does it bother you? Really?" I asked, my smile slipping.

"That you come from money? No, Duchess. It doesn't bother me. If your money dried up tomorrow, I'd still be able to take care of you. Not at the level that you've clearly grown accustomed to, but you'd be fine." He smirked.

My phone rang and I dug it out of my purse. "Hold on a sec." I pressed a button and put it to my ear. "Hi, Helen."

"There are two men in your house!" my housekeeper screeched.

"Two men?" I asked, shooting a look at Bones.

"They say they're friends of your boyfriend. By the way, when did you get a boyfriend?"

"Hang on a second." I pulled the phone away from my ear and put it on mute. "There are two men in my house?"

"Prospects," Bones clarified.

"Why are there prospects in my house?"

"They're standing guard."

"But why?" I asked.

"In case there's trouble. I doubt anyone is dumb enough to try and break in twice, but better safe than sorry."

"Oh." I paused. "It would've been nice if you'd told me."

"Didn't think it mattered." He shrugged. "I didn't know Helen was going to be at your house. By the way, who the fuck is Helen?"

"My housekeeper," I stated.

"You mean *our* housekeeper."

I rolled my eyes and unmuted the phone. "Helen?"

"Yes, I'm here. I don't trust these guys," she whispered. "*They're looking at me.*"

"Looking at you, how?"

"I don't know, they're just looking at me."

"You can trust them."

"They have tattoos," she stage-whispered.

"I know," I whispered back. "I guess now is the time to tell you that you'll see a second toothbrush in the bathroom, along with some shaving stuff because my boyfriend is moving in."

"Fiancé," Bones said as soon as he overheard. "Call me your *fiancé*."

I rolled my eyes at him.

"Wait, your boyfriend, who you've never even mentioned is moving in?" she asked.

"Yes," I said. "It happened really fast. I get that, but I'll bring you up to speed. I promise."

"Hmm. I don't like this, Hayden."

"I love that you're protective, but he's a good man and you'll like him."

"Does he have tattoos?"

"Yes."

"We'll see."

I hung up with her and couldn't stop a laugh from escaping me despite the exhaustion and terror of the unknown.

"She doesn't like men with tattoos?" Bones asked as he opened the passenger door for me.

"She's old school, sorry about that." I shook my head.

"Just as long as you like my tattoos, we're good."

"I like your tattoos just fine," I assured him.

He shut the door and then climbed into the driver's side. "Why do I have this vision in my head of a stuffy British housekeeper just on the younger side of sixty?"

"She's fifty, and not British. But I adore her, so you'll just have to win her over somehow."

"I can be pretty charming, Duchess. Won you over, didn't I?"

I nodded. "On that thought, we might need to get her tipsy."

"Brat." His phone beeped and he pulled it out of his pocket. "Vance just got your attorney's paperwork."

"Excellent."

"And he wants to see us in his office in an hour."

"Good." I looked at him. "You seem really composed for a man who's about to sign a prenup."

"You seem really composed for a woman who's about to marry a biker."

I grinned. "That sounds so weird."

"What? That you're marrying a biker?"

"No. That I'm getting married." I shook my head and looked out the window.

He reached over and placed his hand on my thigh, drawing my attention back to him. When I was looking at him, he said, "I'm sorry we couldn't do this the way we were supposed to do it."

"How were we supposed to do it?" I asked softly.

"We were supposed to go to Florida," he replied, looking away from me to stare out the front windshield. "I was gonna ask you to take a trip on the back of my bike. Just you and me and we'd go to this place that I used to visit when I was a kid. There's this beach, on the gulf side, where the water is warm. Warm like you're taking a bath. And it's so clear that if you look down you can see your feet. The sand is white and soft. Powdery. Not like that harsh shit on the New England coast. We'd sit on the sand, watching the sunset. Only I wouldn't be watching the sun set, I'd be watching you watch the sun set. The sky is always so beautiful there. Oranges, pinks, and reds, and shades of color you can't imagine until you see it for yourself. And as the sun faded into the never-ending ocean, I'd pull out a ring box and hold it out to you. I wouldn't say a damn thing. When you pull out a ring, you don't need a bunch of words, or speeches. You're not trying to convince someone to share a life with you. When you pull out the ring, you already know the answer. And if you don't, you're asking the wrong person."

He paused and I waited for him to go on. He painted such a clear picture, a picture so full of yearning I could almost taste it. Almost feel the ocean spray on my face, the salt on my tongue.

"You'd look at the ring and smile. You wouldn't say anything, you'd just lean in and kiss me and that would be your answer. And then I'd slide it onto your finger and then we'd walk along the beach, barefoot, hand-in-hand, back to the little cottage that's been there since the 50s. That little cottage that's withstood I don't know how many hurricanes and tropical storms. But it's still standing. We'll be like that cottage, Hayden. We'll withstand all the hurricanes."

I sighed and gently reached out to cup his face so that he could see my expression when I gave him the answer, the answer I could see he still wasn't quite sure about because the way we were getting married was all wrong. Not our feelings for each other, but the circumstance of it all. Circumstance had robbed me of that beautiful, quiet proposal that was both poignant and perfect. What I got instead wasn't fancy. It was stripped bare of all but raw emotion.

Which was what I had to show him now.

"I love you," I said quietly. "I love you when you're Royce Dalton, and I love you as Bones. I love you when you have to be both of those men. I love you when you can't be either. I love you for what you're offering me. I love you for offering me yourself because it's more than enough. Yes. I'll marry you."

He looked at me, his expression filled with tenderness. And then he leaned in to kiss me like a husband who'd kiss his wife for the rest of their lives.

Chapter 43

"Nice to see you again, Hayden," Vance said as he held out his hand in greeting.

"You too." I shook his offered palm and then let go.

"I wish it was under better circumstances," he said.

"Same," I agreed.

Vance led us to his expansive office. Though his furniture was clearly expensive, there was none of the dark hardwood usually prevalent in an attorney's office. Vance was all modern convenience, a mix between Japanese design and the lightness of a Scandinavian aesthetic.

There was no clutter here.

He gestured to the chairs in front of his desk and both Bones and I took our seats.

"Your attorney sent over the prenup he had drawn up," Vance said. "If you're okay with it, I'd like to go through it point by point. That way we're all on the same page."

"That's fine with me." I looked at Bones. "You?"

"Same." Bones leaned back against the chair, looking completely at ease despite the fact that we were talking the legalities of our marriage.

"Great." Vance picked up the stack of papers. "Basically, it's as follows. Hayden's trust will execute and all assets and ownership remain in her name and under her full control. You'll never have access to any of it."

"I don't want access to it," Bones defended.

I reached over and placed my hand on his thigh. "Please don't take any of this the wrong way. I don't for a second think you're marrying me for my money or to gain access to anything. We just have to make sure we're both protected in case something happens."

"I'm not an idiot," Bones said lightly. "I just hate attorneys." He looked at Vance. "No offense."

Vance raised his brows. "None taken."

"Be nice," I warned. "You never know when you're going to need a good attorney."

"Listen to your smart and beautiful fiancée," Vance stated.

"Stop flirting with her," Bones said.

"He wasn't flirting with me." I rolled my eyes.

"Yes, he was," Bones insisted.

"Yes, I was." Vance shot me an amused grin. "Mostly to piss him off. Anyway, let's get back to it. So, we've covered the trust. The same goes for all assets, including the properties she currently owns."

"Properties?" Bones asked. "What properties? Just the house, I thought."

I shifted in my seat. "There's a few more."

"A *few* more? How many more?" he asked.

"The apartment in Venice, which belonged to my grandmother," I said. "The house in Snowmass."

"Snowmass?"

I sighed. "Aspen."

"Jesus," he muttered.

"And then there's the, ah, French chateau." I looked at Vance. "That's all of them, right?"

"That's all of them," Vance agreed.

"You had to ask an attorney if there were any more properties? Like you just have so many you forget they exist?" Bones asked, his mouth all but dropping open.

"You knew I was wealthy," I muttered.

"Yeah, but Jesus, Duchess." He shook his head and sighed. "So, any properties she already owns, remain in her name. Got it."

"Any assets you acquire after marriage, and any properties you buy together, should divorce occur, you'll either sell the asset and split it, or one party may buy out the other."

"Divorce isn't happening," Bones said. "This is all about protecting Hayden."

"I appreciate the optimism, I really do," I said. "But better to discuss these things now before emotions get involved."

He looked at me.

"What?" I asked.

"The only thing that can separate me from you is death."

"Bones…" I whispered.

"So, what happens if I die?" Bones asked Vance.

Vance didn't look away from him when he replied, "Well, as we discussed when you had me draw things up, you don't own any property and you have a retirement fund courtesy of the club. That reverts to her as you requested."

He nodded. "And what happens if she dies?"

"Once Hayden marries, she gains control of the company as soon as the trust her father made executes. At that point, she'll own fifty one percent of the shares. Her seat is the controlling seat on the board. With that position, she can override decisions of the rest of the board in full, even if it's not a tie. Basically, she's it. Now for the changes we're going to make the moment you two are married. If Hayden passes away after you're married, the company is going to be dissolved, the patents will all be sold to the highest bidder, and all proceeds will be donated to charity. It's important to understand by doing this, we're protecting her. There's no incentive for Arnold, or anyone for that matter, to do anything to Hayden beyond that point. Properties in her name will transfer to her mother if her mother outlives her. If not, then they will be sold as well. If she dies or you divorce," Vance looked to me and then to Bones, "you will get a monetary sum to be determined at a later date."

Vance stared at me, his brow furrowed. "Your company's share prices will most likely tank when the public becomes aware that you married a biker."

"I discussed that with my attorney. I'm solvent enough that I'll be able to buy back any shares that hit the market. I'm not worried about that. Is that all? Can we sign these and get out of here?"

Chapter 44

"I don't know the first thing about pharmaceuticals or my father's company. How am I even qualified to have a seat on the board?" I asked as I got into the car.

"Your mother has a seat on the board. Is she qualified?"

"Point."

"You're your father's daughter. You care about his legacy and his vision. You don't have to know all the steps of how to accomplish what he wanted to accomplish—that's why you have lawyers, scientists, and other experts. What is it you want?"

"I want to stop hiding my head in the sand because it's been too painful to have anything to do with my father's company. And now I'm worried that it's too late."

"It's not too late. We're getting married in a couple of days…we're stopping Arnold in his tracks."

"We'll never be able to prove what he did, will we?" I asked quietly.

Bones didn't reply.

"He won't be there." A tear slipped out of my eye and

rolled down my cheek. "My dad, I mean. He won't be at our wedding. My mom won't be there. Charlie won't be there. No one can know we're doing this and that means we'll be alone. We're not even having a real *wedding*."

I burst into tears just as the prospects opened the gates to the clubhouse. Bones drove through and parked the car. He turned off the ignition, unlatched his seatbelt, and then moved to wrap me in his arms.

He let me cry all over him.

"I'm sorry." I hiccoughed. "I'm just exhausted. And when I'm exhausted, I can't think straight."

"It's okay," he crooned, brushing his lips across my head. "Cry it out."

I heaved out a sigh and attempted to burrow deeper into his neck.

"I'll make it up to you," he said. "You want to have a real wedding with me in a top hat and coat tails, then I'll do it."

I grinned and lifted my head. "You really would, wouldn't you?"

He brushed the tears from my cheeks. "Yeah, Duchess, I would."

"Well, there's no telling what will happen when my mom finds out we got married without her."

"She'll understand when we tell her why it had to be this way."

"You don't know my mother. My wedding was what she's been training for her entire life."

"She won't care when you tell her we're having kids."

"Yeah, but that's not for a while."

When he didn't reply, I cocked my head to the side. "Bones. Not for a while, right?"

"What's a while?"

"I don't know. A few years?"

"A few years? You really want to wait that long?"

I raised my brows. "Hold on, sir. When were you thinking we were going to have kids? Because we like, *just* got together, and now we're already getting married. I was hoping we could settle into our relationship before bringing kids into the mix. You know, practice for a bit. Practice, practice, practice."

"Why do you want to wait?"

"I just told you. Can't we enjoy each other and the settling in phase before that all changes?"

"Changes that include a piece of you and a piece of me?"

"Stop," I said, my insides melting.

"A piece of you and a piece of me with your attitude and my charm? Kid'll be unstoppable."

"Bones…"

"And when we can't possibly think about shit getting any better, we'll have another one."

I sighed. "You're holding my ovaries hostage with your words and it's not fair."

He cradled my face in his hands. "A year."

"What?"

"We'll wait a year, but I don't want to wait too long. I've waited long enough and now that I've found you, I want to make a life with you. I want to make a home with you. I want to make a family with you. Okay, Duchess?"

"Okay."

He leaned in close and brushed his lips against mine. "What were you saying about practice?"

∽

I woke up to a dark room and a cold spot in the bed next to me. I reached out to touch his pillow, but the indent was long gone.

With a sigh, I rolled over onto my back. I stared at the ceiling though I couldn't see. I didn't need a clock to tell me it was the middle of the night. My throat was dry and the back of my neck felt hot.

I closed my eyes and prayed that I wouldn't have one of my spells now. I couldn't afford the time wasted when my body took me out of the world for several hours at a time.

"Please," I begged the dark. "Not now."

My feet hit the floor and I sat for a moment and then I finally switched on the bedside lamp. Bones' pistol and phone were gone. I picked up my cell from the nightstand and glanced at the screen. Three thirty in the morning.

There was no way in hell I would be able to go back to sleep. My mind had kicked on, occupied with the several mountainous problems that had fallen into my lap.

I quietly crept from the room. As I passed closed bedroom doors, I heard the unmistakable sounds of shared pleasure.

My stocking-clad feet were quiet on the stairs as I descended. The lights were on in the living room and kitchen, but it was devoid of people.

I moved around the kitchen and made myself a cup of tea. I texted Bones asking where he was, and when I got no immediate reply, I set my cell aside.

In a few days, I would be married.

In a few days, I would be standing in front of the board, my father's legacy weighing heavily on my shoulders.

For the last couple of years, I hadn't been ready to take charge, to take my rightful place within my father's company as his heir. I relished in the fact that I wasn't old enough yet and that I wasn't married. Both those things had felt like protections from the weight of the burden I knew I'd soon have to carry. Now I feared it was the opposite—it would be my body that failed me. Perhaps I was more like my mother than I realized; we both collapsed under the weight of stress. Hers was a mental battle, mine physical.

My body rebelled against me. No matter how much I tried to cater to it. It was frustrating, not being able to rely on something that was supposed to function properly. No matter what I did, no matter what I fed it, even limiting the amount of stress in my life didn't solve the problem.

It was unsolvable.

I finished off my tea and then laid down on the couch and spread a blanket over me. My eyes drifted shut of their own accord, and not even my overactive brain could go toe to toe with my body. I sank into oblivion.

∼

I floated awake, encased in a warm cocoon. A heavy arm was slung across my waist and I smiled with my eyes closed and wiggled back against Bones.

His erection pressed against me.

"Duchess," he growled.

His hand delved into my pajama pants and slid into my panties. His fingers explored and then they dipped into my body.

I gasped at the pleasure. The back of my neck crackled with heat and shivers danced down my spine.

"Open for me, Duchess," he rasped against my ear.

I grabbed his wrist and gently urged him out of me, but only so that I could slide my clothes off.

A drawer opened and I heard the crinkle of a foil wrapper.

"No condom," I murmured.

He stilled behind me. "That's playing Russian roulette."

"I know. But I don't want anything between us."

He paused for another moment. "You sure, Duchess? We do this, there's no going back."

"I'm sure."

Bones grasped my thigh and pushed it higher toward my chest. "You want my cock."

"Yes." I gasped when I felt the crown of him teasing my swollen flesh.

"You want me buried deep."

"Yes," I all but begged.

He slid the tip of him inside me and stopped. "You want me to fuck you until you're biting the pillow so you don't scream."

"*Yes.*"

"And you want me to come inside you. Fill you completely. Mark you as mine."

"God, yes. Bones," I nearly whined.

He slipped all the way inside me, stretching me wide, making me moan with pleasure. I felt him everywhere.

His hand came around to settle between my thighs. And while he ground into me, his fingers masterfully played with my clit until I was grabbing the pillow and biting into it, just like he said I would.

"I'm going to fuck you like this every day, Duchess," he rasped against my ear. "I'm going to start my day by sliding into this pussy and owning it. I'm going to fill you with so much of me that it'll be running down your leg. I'm going to fuck you so good and so hard you'll feel me with every step. I'm going to remind you who you belong to. And when you're pregnant with my baby, the world will know it too."

His filthy words pushed me over the edge. I screamed around the pillow in my mouth as my orgasm blasted through my body.

"I want to see your face." He pressed a kiss to the spot below my ear. "I want to see your face when I come inside you with nothing between us."

He eased out of me and then he was rolling me onto my back. Bones spread my legs wide and then he was inching inside of me again. I quivered around him as I felt every hard ridge of him.

"You love my cock. Say it."

His blue eyes were lit with fire as he watched me. I licked my lips. "I love your cock."

He buried himself inside of me and slid his hand beneath my ass and changed the angle of my body. And then he fucked me like a man possessed, a man determined, a Viking with the need to spread his seed so his progeny could live on long after he was gone.

I took every inch of him.

I squeezed his shaft.

I welcomed him home.

With a curse and a guttural moan, Bones came with the force of a hurricane. But he didn't stop until I was crying out again. He wrung every last bit of pleasure from me and only then did he nearly collapse on top of me.

He pressed his forehead to mine. "We might've just made a baby."

"We might have, yeah."

He shifted and I gasped.

"Does that scare you?" he asked.

"If it does it's a little too late." I smiled.

"Duchess…"

"Yeah, Bones. I'm scared, but it's okay. I don't want," I

swallowed, "I don't want life to pass me by because I'm scared."

He was propped up on his elbows, but then he lowered himself, covering my body with his. He rolled us to the side. We were still connected, and I wrapped a leg around him to keep him close.

"You don't have to be scared anymore," he said as he stared into my eyes. "I'm here."

Chapter 45

"The shower isn't big enough for both of us," I protested as Bones closed the door to the minuscule bathroom.

"We'll fit." He winked at me and leaned closer. "You didn't think I'd fit inside of you, but we made that work, didn't we?"

A flush stained my cheeks, which only made him laugh and steal his arm around my shoulders and haul me toward him. "Still shy, huh? Guess we have some more work to do."

He let me go and bent to turn on the shower. I watched him fiddle with the knobs, a frown marring my face when I saw his raw knuckles. I scanned the rest of his body—the part that I could see anyway—and noticed the light discoloration marring the side of his ribs.

"What the—" I grabbed his arm and urged him to turn so I could give him a full examination. "What is this?"

"What's what?" He rubbed his stubbly jaw with his rough hand.

"Don't," I snapped. "You know what. Have you been

fighting? You have been fighting. Your knuckles are red and in a few hours, you're going to have some wicked bruises."

When he didn't reply, I shook my head. "Wait a second. I woke up last night and you were gone. I fell asleep on the couch. This morning, I woke up in your bed. How did I get there?"

"Get in the shower, Duchess. I'm running down your leg."

"You don't get to distract me."

"I'm not trying to distract you. I'm trying to embarrass you, so you stop asking me questions."

"Royce Dalton, *answer me*."

"You're hot when you're scolding me."

I crossed my arms over my chest. It was hard to look fearsome in a towel, but I tried anyway.

"I went out last night," he admitted.

"Uh huh."

"I came back and you were asleep on the couch. I carried you up to bed."

"And in between you leaving and coming back, where did you go?"

He raised his hand and gently placed it on my chest, in the spot between my collar bones. Bones inched his hand up to my neck and gently wrapped his fingers around my throat and gave it a light squeeze.

My breath hitched and my heart fluttered in my chest. "Bones…"

His head dipped as he was getting ready to kiss me. "Yeah, Duchess?"

"Tell me where you were last night."

His grip remained, a hand necklace around my throat. My stomach summersaulted with the idea that he could overpower me.

Take me.

Make me his.

"I was at The Ring and I was sparring with Raze."

He paused, waiting for me to speak.

"Why didn't you just tell me that?" I asked. "Why the big show of not wanting to tell me?"

"I wasn't sure how you were going to react. I left in the middle of the night; you woke up alone. I knew you were safe here, but I just—I was going out of my mind. I had to channel that rage somewhere. And I didn't want you to see it. So, I took it out on Raze at The Ring."

My fingers brushed along his ribcage with his blooming bruises. "I'd say he gave as good as he got."

"Can't ask a brother to vent and not fight back." Before I could say anything else he captured my lips with his and squeezed his hand around my neck. Desire fluttered through my body, and I was hungry for him again. "Let's shower," he murmured, pulling back. "And then I'll find a way to occupy you for the next two days so you don't go crazy."

"I can't have sex for two days nonstop," I stated. "I need to be able to walk."

He grinned. "You sure about that?"

I rolled my eyes. "Yes."

"Well, lucky for you, I have some other things on the agenda."

"Such as?"

"I'm gonna teach you how to handle a pistol."

My hand shot out to palm his erection over the towel. "I can handle one just fine."

Bones grasped the back of my neck and hauled me toward him. "Prove it."

∼

"Hot damn, Duchess," Bones said, looping his arm around me as we headed back toward the clubhouse. "You're badass."

I looked up at him and grinned. "Impressed you with my marksmanship, did I?"

"Regular sniper in the making." His grin suddenly lost its sparkle.

"What?" I asked.

"Nothing. Well, not nothing. Darcy's husband was a sniper. Just a reminder that he's gone. Fuck, he's gone and it hasn't been long since we buried him."

We tromped across the autumn grass, the sun shining down on us as he talked about loss. That was the way of it, apparently. People died, seasons changed, the world moved on even if you were still stuck in it.

"How are the kids doing?" I asked softly. "I feel terrible not asking about them but there's been so much going on."

"Lily's still not talking," Bones said. "Boxer doesn't know what to do. Cam's angry at the world and pissed that he's on crutches. Just a shit time for them."

I bit my lip, not wanting to mention Doc's news that she was pregnant, unsure if she'd even told her husband yet. "And Doc? How's she doing?"

"She took a step back at the clinic," Bones stated. "Which is probably killing her. It's her pride and joy, you know? But she doesn't want Lily and Cam to feel even more abandoned with her working all the time. Boxer said she burnt a batch of cookies and then begged Brooklyn for help."

He shot me an errant grin. "She's trying. They're all trying to find a new normal."

"It takes time," I said.

"How long did it take you?" he asked.

I held up my hand and crossed my fingers. "Any day now."

He hugged me tighter.

"So, I'm a good shot, huh?" I asked, wanting to steer the conversation in a lighter direction.

"Damn good shot."

His compliment warmed me from the inside out. Bones made me feel far more capable than I thought of myself being.

"How do you see me, Bones?"

"What do you mean?"

I sighed. "I mean, we all have our self-image, don't we? But it rarely matches how other people see us."

"Why does it matter how I see you?"

"You're marrying me. You want kids with me. But how do you *see* me?"

He stopped walking, forcing me to stop too. Bones placed his hands on my shoulders and turned me toward him.

"I see a woman who is coming out of her shell. I see a woman who is stronger than she gives herself credit for. I see a woman who loves fiercely, but who takes her time to open up and allow others in. I see a woman who loves with her whole heart. I see a woman who shut out the world because her heart was so soft she didn't know how to protect it. I see a woman who laughs with her whole body. I see a woman who's scared, but no longer wants to hide. I see a woman who's ready to face the truth, even if it means her entire world comes tumbling down."

I swallowed. "And if it does come tumbling down? What then?"

He cradled my face in his hands and stared into my eyes. "Then I'll be there beside you to help you pick up the pieces."

I sighed. "I'm not alone."

"You're not alone."

"Bones!" a voice called.

We turned in the direction of the sound. Raze stood at the fence line. "Prez called church."

"Be right there!" Bones called back. He dropped his hand and then grasped my palm, and we tromped the rest of the way.

"Oh my God!" I gasped when I saw Raze.

"What?" he asked.

"Your eye!"

"Oh, yeah." Raze shrugged.

I whirled to Bones. "You hit your friend in the face? I thought you guys were just venting."

My gaze bounced from Bones to Raze and back to Bones.

"It's all good." Bones said. "Isn't it, Raze?"

"Absolutely. It's not even a thing," Raze said.

I glared at him and whirled to look at Raze, who hadn't taken his eyes off Bones even as he'd spoken. "Raze?"

Raze's attention slid to me. "Yeah?"

"You really okay?" I asked.

"We're brothers," Raze stated, and then looked at Bones. "Come on, man. Prez is waiting."

"See you in a few, Duchess," Bones said as he followed his brother toward the shed.

I went inside the clubhouse and heard the smattering of conversation coming from the living room. Mia and Sutton were sitting on the couch, but they both stopped talking when they saw me.

"Hey," Mia greeted, shooting up from her seat. She came to me and enveloped me in a quick hug. "How are you?"

I frowned. "Why do you ask?"

Mia and Sutton exchanged a look. "Colt told me you and Bones are getting married—and why."

"That wasn't his business to tell," I stated.

"Don't be mad," Sutton said. She turned toward me but didn't get up.

"You know too?" I asked.

"Yes, but only because we want to help," Sutton said. "We want to give you a wedding. If you'll let us."

"And there's a code among us," Mia said. "We help our own. And you're an Old Lady now, so sometimes that means knowing things we probably shouldn't know. Bones thought you might want a wedding, even knowing it won't be the one you had in mind."

My defensive posture softened. "Sorry. I'm so used to keeping stuff to myself—or only telling Charlie. I'm not used to having people know about my life. I didn't mean to—"

"Forget it. So, will you let us throw you a wedding?" Mia asked.

I smiled gently. "Will you be offended if I say no?"

"Kinda, yeah," Sutton pouted.

"I know you're trying to help, and God, I can't even begin to tell you what it means to me. But my best friend can't be at my wedding, and neither can my mother, so I'd rather not have one."

"Can we at least throw you a party?" Sutton asked. "It's not every day a brother makes a woman his Old Lady."

Mia snorted. "Lately, that's not really true. In the last few months, we've had Duke and Willa, you and Viper, Logan and Smoke, and now Hayden and Bones."

"Okay, but it's still something to celebrate," Sutton pointed out. "And God knows we need more reasons to celebrate."

"If I say yes, can we please keep it mellow?" I asked.

"Just a bonfire with a barbecue," Mia promised. "It's easy to put together. Nothing fancy."

"That would be okay with me," I said.

"Good, now that that's settled, did your men leave in the middle of the night too and not tell you where they were going?" Sutton asked.

I frowned. "I woke up to Bones gone. He told me he went to The Ring to work out some of his anger. I got a good look at Raze's face—he took a beating from Bones, apparently."

Mia didn't reply.

"You know something," Sutton accused.

"I might know something," she said slowly.

"And you're not supposed to tell," Sutton stated. "This isn't the first time you've known something and kept it to yourself."

Mia glared at her. "I'm the president's wife. Sometimes I know things that you don't get to know. Not until it's the right time, anyway."

"Now's the right time," Sutton stated. "Viper came home and fucked me into oblivion when I tried to ask questions. I'd like to know why—and what he's keeping from me."

An image of this morning flashed through my brain. My cheeks instantly heated.

Mia looked in the direction of the hallway, as if she was waiting for Colt and the other bikers to appear. When it was clear we were still alone, she looked at the two of us. "You keep this to yourselves, okay?"

Sutton and I nodded.

Mia sighed. "Those bikers you saw at Spurs the night of Sutton's bachelorette party? Well, they've been showing their faces on Tarnished Angels turf. The boys went to... investigate."

"Investigate," I repeated. Understanding dawned. "You mean they went looking for a fight?"

Mia nodded. "Yeah. Viper, Raze, Bones, Kelp and Colt went to deal with them."

"Run them out of town, you mean?" Sutton guessed.

"Yes. But also to find out what the hell they're doing here," Mia explained. She looked at me. "There are two prominent MC clubs in Waco. We stick to our side. The Jackals stick to theirs. These guys...they aren't from here. The boys found out they're scoping out the city to see if they can move in and set up shop."

"Who are they?"

"Hopeless Souls MC, from Nebraska."

"Why didn't Bones just tell me the truth? Why would he tell me he was working out his anger at The Ring?" I asked.

"Old Ladies aren't supposed to know about club business," Mia said slowly. "Though that's been changing over the past few months."

"Guess the brothers becoming family men isn't the only change," Sutton stated. "It still doesn't make sense why Viper wouldn't tell me."

"Probably didn't want to upset you—in your condition," Mia said. "I don't know. Sometimes I want to know everything Colt talks about in church. Other times, I wish I could stay in the dark. But with the club direction changing..." She shrugged.

"You don't think the Hopeless Souls are going to come back, do you?" Sutton asked.

"I hope not," Mia stated. "Our club is just getting out of the thick of it. I don't want us involved in that kind of business anymore."

"The thick of what?" I asked.

"Things we want distance from," Mia averred. "Now what food are we going to have at this wedding barbecue?"

∼

"Hey," Bones said, taking a seat next to me on the far side of the bonfire.

"Hey," I greeted, not taking my eyes off the dancing flames.

The sky was overcast and we couldn't see the stars. It was chillier than I would've liked, but the fire had been roaring for hours and kept the nip at bay.

Without another word, he reached over and took my hand in his. He lifted his bottle of beer to his lips.

The kids had been put to bed and the rest of us were celebrating my union with Bones.

Earlier that day, we'd met with Vance who'd had a justice of the peace marry us after our mandatory three-day waiting period. We'd signed our marriage license in front of two brothers from the club as witnesses, and then I'd called Oliver and asked him to inform the board about an emergency meeting tomorrow morning. Vance had sent a copy of our marriage license to the company attorney and Oliver, and both of them had been instructed not to tell anyone what the meeting was about.

My mother hadn't stopped texting since she'd met Bones at the gala. After bailing on Sunday dinner, I'd lied and told her that Bones had surprised me with a quick romantic getaway out of town for a few days. She would find out it was all a lie when she saw us at the board meeting tomorrow morning.

That's when I would inform the board about a changing of the guard.

"The cupcakes were good," Bones informed me. "Especially the chocolate ones."

"Hmm."

He squeezed my fingers before letting them go. "You're thinking about tomorrow."

"Tomorrow my entire life changes," I stated.

"It didn't change today?" he inquired.

"Today? You mean when I became Hayden Spencer Dalton?" I shot him a tender smile.

"I like you with my last name."

"I haven't even practiced my new signature." I shook my head. "It's going to be insane tomorrow, isn't it?"

"Yes." He placed his hand on my thigh. "But tomorrow, we move in together. Tomorrow, we get to celebrate."

I touched his face. "I hope you don't take this the wrong way, but I'm not in the mood to celebrate."

He turned his head to kiss my palm. "It's my wedding too, you know. I wanted to have a celebration with my wife."

Wife.

I looked down at my ring finger. Bones had pulled out a thin gold band and slid it onto my finger while we said our wedding vows.

"I thought men hated weddings," I teased.

"I got off easy," he quipped. "But I want to take you out tomorrow night. We deserve that, at least."

"All right. We'll go out."

"Good, because I already made reservations at Holliday's."

"The steakhouse?"

He leaned forward and grinned. "They've got other things too. But just in case, I already called and informed the chef I'd like something special made just for you."

"Aren't you sweet." I scooted my chair closer and leaned my head against his shoulder. "I'm sorry I'm so sad."

"Don't be," he said quietly. "I know why you are."

"My wedding was always going to be bittersweet after losing my father. But I didn't expect it to feel…like this."

"You have regrets."

I lifted my head so I could stare at him. Flames from the fire cast shadows along his jaw. "Yes, I have regrets. So many regrets. I regret that you never got a chance to propose to me the way you wanted. I regret that we didn't get to stand up in front of friends and family and have a real ceremony. I regret that I didn't get to wear my grandmother's veil or shop for my wedding dress with my mother and Charlie. I regret that my dad isn't alive to walk me down the aisle. I regret that it all turned out this way."

His tone was vehement as he said, "Your stepfather did this. Him, and no one else. If you want a wedding, a real wedding, I'll give it to you. We can have a do-over. Whatever you want. I just wanted to protect you. Even if that meant signing paperwork in my attorney's office like it was all business. Sometimes that's how it's gotta be. But we're together now. And I'm not sorry about that part. Not at all."

My eyes filled with tears. "You're just so…"

He smiled gently. "What am I?"

"The one that I need," I said simply.

We stared at one another for a moment. He swallowed. "Hayden, there's something that I should tell—"

"Fuck yeah! Are you serious?" Boxer yelled in excitement.

Bones and I looked in the direction of Boxer and Doc. She nodded.

He grabbed her face and kissed her on the lips.

"What's that about?" Bones asked in curiosity.

Boxer pulled back, but only so that he could lift Doc into his arms and hug her tight. He buried his face in the crook of her neck.

I smiled. "Doc just told Boxer she's pregnant."

Chapter 46

"You can do this," Bones said, taking my hand and kissing the back of it.

"I know," I stated. I glanced out of the town car window and looked at the building I was about to walk into. It was going to be brutal, but I'd strut into it with my head held high and face the board…and my stepfather.

This morning, I'd woken up in bed next to my biker husband. Instead of letting anxiety and panic get the best of me, I'd slid off my panties and straddled him. I needed to take control and get what I wanted. I needed to know I could enter the arena like a fighter ready for hand-to-hand combat, and that I deserved to take what was rightfully mine.

While I was showering, Bones had knocked on the bathroom door to let me know the clothes I'd had delivered from Folson's department store were waiting for me.

My dark hair was swept back away from my face. I wore a crisp white button-down shirt, a black suede knee-length skirt and leather boots that stopped at my calf.

I looked over at Bones who was dressed as Royce

Dalton—dark trousers and a gray cashmere sweater that made his blue eyes pop. He hadn't argued when I told him I'd arranged for clothes to be picked out for him too. He knew the persona he'd have to adopt when we entered Spencer Pharmaceuticals, even if everyone was going to know who he was before the day was over.

"Okay," I said with an exhale. "Let's do this."

The driver opened my door, and I climbed out with a folder of documents in my hand. Bones wasn't far behind me.

We entered the glass revolving door of the building and stepped into the lobby. I waved to the security officer behind the reception desk who'd been alerted earlier that I was coming and that I'd have a guest.

Bones pressed the elevator button and the carriage doors opened. We both stepped inside. I pressed the button for the floor with the executive conference room. As soon as the doors closed, I took a step toward him.

"You've got this, Duchess," Bones said.

A smile tugged on my lips. "Now I know everything is all right because you called me Duchess, not Hayden. You only call me Hayden when it's something serious."

My heart drummed in my chest. The words felt like a lie on my tongue. This was serious. I was facing my fate; I was embracing my legacy.

Love you, Dad.

The doors to the elevator opened and Bones placed his hand at the small of my back, urging me to step out first. Oliver stood by the receptionist's station, a smile blooming across his wrinkled face when he saw me. I walked to him and embraced him quickly before stepping back.

"They're all in there," Oliver said. "No one has any idea what's going on. Arnold is blustering something fierce." His gaze darted to Bones and then back to me.

I nodded. "That's to be expected, I think. My mother?"

"She's in there, too. She's as confused as your stepfather—she has no idea you're behind this meeting."

"It's probably better that way," I stated. "Oliver, I'd like to introduce you to my husband, Royce Dalton."

Bones held out his hand to the older man. "Pleasure to meet you, Sir."

"And you," Oliver said, immediately taking his hand. "I apologize, but only board members are allowed to attend meetings."

"I have no problem occupying myself," Bones said. He shot me a smile and dropped Oliver's hand.

"Margot will be happy to get you anything you need," Oliver said. "Shall we, Hayden?"

"Yes, I think we shall." I looked at Bones one last time for moral support.

"Give 'em hell," he whispered, loud enough for Oliver to hear.

"I will," I assured him.

Oliver and I headed toward the double mahogany doors of the board room. "I approve."

"You don't even know him," I said with a smile.

"I'm a good judge of character. And Hayden, before you go in there you should know it's going to get ugly. Stand your ground. You've got me and a couple of other board members as allies. We'll go to bat for you, but the rest is up to you. Be strong."

Oliver pulled opened one of the doors and gestured for me to enter first. The board members of my father's company were already sitting at the table, and they were talking in low voices. One by one, attention turned toward the door to see who'd arrived.

Surprise lit several of their faces. A few of them openly

smiled at me. I didn't smile back. My gaze went to my mother, who sat at the far end of the table looking confused. Her gaze bounced from me to my stepfather who stood next to her.

"Hayden?" my mother asked. "What are you doing here?"

"Only board members are allowed at emergency meetings," Arnold stated.

"Thank you for being here on such short notice," I said, addressing the entire room and ignoring Arnold completely. "Yesterday morning, I got married."

There was a rumble of surprise, followed by some cursing and at least one *congratulations*.

I waited for the room to calm. "As board members, you know exactly what this means. You've all known this day would come since my father died. Well, the day is here, and as of this moment, I'm the new majority shareholder and Chair of the Board of Spencer Pharmaceuticals."

"*Married?*" my stepfather spat as his face darkened with annoyance. "We're just supposed to take your word that you're married all of a sudden?"

"No, you're not." I set the folder I'd carried into the room on the table in front of me and opened it. I pulled out my marriage license and a copy of the trust my father had set in stone and handed it to Oliver. Oliver immediately took the documents to Joyce Lynwood, the company's General Counsel.

"It's her marriage license and a copy of the trust," Joyce announced. "I received an official copy of the license as soon as it was done. It's been reviewed, and you can be assured that she's satisfied the legal waiting period and the marriage is bound and filed with the county clerk. It's official, and the requirements to execute her father's trust have been fulfilled."

"Who the hell did you marry?" Arnold snapped.

I met my mother's stupefied gaze. "Royce Dalton."

"Let me see that." My stepfather jumped from his seat, but Joyce was already passing the marriage document to the next board member.

My stepfather nearly ripped it from Bruce Allentown's hand. He stared at it in disbelief.

"I've also updated my personal will and testament." I didn't take my eyes off my stepfather when I delivered the final piece of news. "As of this moment, in the unlikely event that I die, Spencer Pharmaceuticals will be dissolved, the patents sold to the highest bidder and all proceeds donated to charity. Shareholders will of course be compensated for any shares held at the market stock price at the time of my death. Do I need to point out that would not be good?"

Arnold's face morphed into a picture of rage. His eyes bulged like a cartoon character and his nostrils flared.

"This was my father's company," I said. "And his vision was always about affordable medication for patients in need of drugs that work as well or better than anything else on the market. He wasn't interested in maximum profit. It's why no one believed he'd ever amount to anything, and how he was able to maintain control of the company during its rapid growth before he died. No one was interested until the patents started getting approved and the money began to flow. And then, in the last few years after his death, the company has diverted sharply from his original vision. I intend to rectify that effective immediately. And in order to do so, my first act as Chair of this board is to fire *you*, Arnold."

"You can't fire me!" Arnold bellowed. "You need a unanimous vote. Marilyn, stop your daughter from doing this. She's a *child*. This is insane!"

"I can't," Mom murmured. She looked confused. Hurt. And completely unsure of what was going on. "The trust has executed. The moment Hayden assumed her rightful seat on the board, I became nothing more than a minority shareholder. My vote is null. Actually, *all* of our votes are null if she wants you gone."

Joyce Lynwood nodded in agreement but didn't say a word.

"You planned this! You planned a coup," my stepfather raged. He swept his hand across the table, scattering the papers to the floor.

Oliver went to the door of the boardroom and opened it. He stuck out his head and asked the front desk to call for security.

Arnold marched across the room toward me. He looked like he wanted to wring my neck. "You stupid fucking *bitch*," he hissed. "Do you have any idea what you've done? They're going to come after—"

A hand reached out and clamped Arnold's shoulder hard enough that it ended his tirade.

It wasn't security—it was my husband. His expression was furious and he looked ready to tear Arnold's head off his body.

"You're done, asshole." He met my gaze as he grabbed Arnold, ready to carry him out of the room if necessary. "I'll make sure security escorts him from the building."

"Thank you," I said to Bones.

Before Arnold left, I leaned in close to my stepfather and whispered, "I know what you did to my father."

I watched his expression; his eyes narrowed and color bloomed across his cheeks. "You'll never be able to prove that."

Bones roughly escorted Arnold from the room.

Oliver closed the door behind them.

A few board members rose from their chairs and left without saying a word, and others began coming up to me, congratulating me on my marriage and expressing their excitement that I was finally Chair of the board. I couldn't help but notice it was all men who'd known my father.

Joyce surprised me when she came up to me and hugged me. "We've been waiting for this for a while, Hayden. Your father's passing was hard on all of us who knew him, and we want his vision to succeed. With you at the helm, that can happen now."

"Thank you," I murmured, taking her hand and giving it a squeeze.

My mother hadn't risen from her chair. Instead, she'd swiveled it and was now staring out the window as the last of the board members left the room.

I looked at Oliver. "Thank you. For everything."

"My pleasure," he said. "I'll ensure Mr. Dalton has no trouble coming back up. And I'm sure there are things you want to speak to your mother about…alone."

I squeezed his hand and then watched the elderly man stand erect and nearly skip to the door. "Feels good to clean house, doesn't it?"

I smiled. "It does."

The door shut quietly behind him. I turned back toward my mother and slowly approached her. I pulled out the chair next to her and took a seat.

"What just happened, Hayden?" she asked, rotating the chair to look at me.

"There are some things I need to tell you. Things I've purposefully kept from you." I paused. "I need you to be strong for me, okay? I need you to hear me."

"For the love of—I'm listening, Hayden. Just tell me why you got married and didn't tell me, and why you went behind Arnold's back—just tell me everything."

I'd doctored my life for so long when it came to my mother, but I realized what a disservice I'd done to us both.

Time for the truth.

"A few weeks ago, a man pulled a gun on me," I began. "We thought it was just an accident—the police said he was a tweaker looking to rob someone and get his next fix. But a few nights ago, a man broke into my home. There was no sign of forced entry and the security alarm had been disarmed."

My mother's face paled.

"He was there to kill me, Mom. Bones shot him and then went after him, but he got away. Then we started to put the puzzle pieces together. Bones didn't believe it was a coincidence and the more we discussed it, the more it became apparent they were both attempts on my life. There's a lot going on here, but it all pointed to Arnold. Mom, he was the one *with* Dad when he died. The only one…and as soon as Dad was gone, he took control of the board and married you. And then Bones found out that he's the one who scared off Tyler. He was preventing me from getting married and taking my seat on the board. With Arnold's shares, plus yours and the interim Chair position, he gained full control of the company."

The look of shock let me know she'd heard every word.

"He killed my Kellen, didn't he?"

"Yes, but we can't prove it." I paused, and then tried to put myself in her position for a moment. "This is a lot to dump on you." I took her hand. It was warm in mine.

She gave my hand a squeeze. "I don't know how to process it. I'm so sorry, darling. I had no idea such a monster lurked beneath the surface. I feel like a fool."

"He fooled us all," I said quietly. "This isn't your fault."

"It's my job to protect you. It's a mother's job to protect her children." She clenched her jaw. "Why did you keep me in the dark? Why not tell me you were getting married and you were going to take over the company? Wait, who's Bones?"

The door to the office opened and Bones strode inside. He marched over to the end of the table, pulled out a swivel chair and maneuvered it so it was next to me. He placed his hand possessively on my thigh, immediately drawing my mother's attention.

"Mom," I began. "I'd like to introduce you to Bones. He's a member of the Tarnished Angels Motorcycle Club."

My mother's expression didn't change, and it wasn't because of the delicate work she'd had done. "You married a biker."

I angled my chin. "Yes."

She looked from me, to Bones, to the hand on my thigh, and then back to Bones. "Thank you for protecting my daughter."

"It's my honor," Bones said, his voice low.

"I could kill you both for depriving me of attending your wedding," Mom said. "And now with Arnold ousted, this will be a publicity nightmare. Not to mention the press is going to have a field day when news spreads that my twenty-five-year-old daughter with no experience running even a small company just married a biker and then took control of one of the most profitable pharmaceutical companies in the country."

I winced. "The stock is most likely going to tank and people will flood the market with shares, but I'm prepared to buy them back. I'll use every penny Dad left me if I have to in order to keep the company alive."

My mother waved her hand away. "We can handle that together. That's not my concern. My concern is standing as a united front when the news about Arnold hits. It'll be messy. What with him being your stepfather and my... husband."

"You've got a plan to spin this, don't you?" Bones asked.

"I do." My mother smiled. "We're going to throw the wedding party of all parties. And if I recall, you look spectacular in a tuxedo."

Chapter 47

"Your house isn't safe," my mother said as we rose from the table.

"We've been staying at the clubhouse," I said.

My mother blinked. "The clubhouse? Right. It's going to take me a little while to adjust to the truth of his identity."

"We weren't trying to hide it from you," I began.

"Yes, we were," Bones interjected with a roguish smile. "Just long enough for you to realize I'm the right choice for your daughter. And then we were going to tell you the truth. Honest."

My mother laughed and shook her head. "Your father would've had a field day with this one. Can you imagine?"

I looked at Bones. "I can imagine, yeah."

"I'm just impressed that you held your own the night of the charity gala," Mom said. "You actually looked like you enjoyed yourself."

"I did," Bones stated.

"I hate to even bring this up, but I have to know the truth—did you sign a prenup?"

"Yes, I did," Bones said. "You have nothing to worry about. I'm not after Hayden's money."

My mother's expression softened at Bones' answer. "So, are you returning to the, ah, clubhouse?"

"I guess so," I said.

"No," Bones replied. "I've taken care of security at Hayden's house. We can go back there."

I shot him a look.

He winked.

"Besides, we're married now," Bones went on. "There's no benefit to hurting Hayden anymore."

"I'm still in shock that Arnold is behind all this," Mom murmured. "I mean, I believe you. Of course I believe you. I just wish we had solid proof that he did all this."

"There's no trail. Not really," Bones said. "Just deductive reasoning on our end, which isn't enough to actually do anything other than protect the company and Hayden."

Mom reached for her phone. "Hold on a second." She unlocked her cell and pressed the screen and put it to her ear. A moment later, she said, "Stanton, I don't have time to explain, but I need you to do something for me. Under no circumstances is Arnold allowed back into the house. I'll explain why later." She paused and looked at me. "All right. Thank you."

Mom hung up with Stanton. "We'll go through his home office and see if we can find anything incriminating. Though I'm not even sure what to look for."

"We'll meet you at the house," Bones said.

Mom nodded.

"What are you going to do about Arnold?" I asked.

"Call my attorney and begin divorce proceedings." Mom's face hardened. "I never should've married him so soon after Kellan's death, but he…"

"Said all the right things," I said.

"Yes. I did love him. Not like your father. Not anything like your father, but still…" She shook her head like she was trying to banish the thought from her mind. "Why didn't you tell me about the man who tried to mug you? You purposefully kept that from me. Why?"

When I didn't reply, she went on, "The truth, Hayden. I can take it."

"I wanted to protect you," I said quietly. "Daddy's death was so hard on you; I wasn't sure that you'd…"

"Be able to handle it?" She raised her brows. "That's my fault if you thought you had to keep something of this magnitude from me. You may think I'm fragile, but I'm your mother. I have the right to know these things. Don't hide them from me anymore."

"Okay."

"I'll head back home and then see you both in a bit, right?" Mom asked.

I nodded. "Before we leave, I want to show Bones Dad's old office."

Her gaze softened. "He'd be so proud of you for what you did today."

"I don't know about that," I said with a self-deprecating laugh. "I haven't done much to deserve the praise."

In a maternal gesture I was entirely too old for, Mom brushed a finger along my cheek. "I would have to disagree."

"Me too," Bones said as he wrapped an arm around my shoulder and pulled me toward him.

Mom smiled at him. "Normally, I'd be concerned at the speed of your relationship, but now I know I have nothing to worry about."

"Nothing at all," Bones assured her.

The three of us finally left the conference room and I

hugged her goodbye at the elevator. My mother turned to Bones and embraced him. "Welcome to the family."

The doors to the elevator opened and she stepped into them. She snapped her spine straight just as the doors closed.

Bones took my hand in his. "Show me your dad's office."

With a nod, I turned the other direction, and we walked past the receptionist.

"I can't figure it out," Bones said.

"Figure what out?"

"Your mother. You told her that her husband was behind the attempts on your life, and she hardly batted an eye."

We stopped at the door at the end of the hallway. "She's holding it together. Tonight, she'll have Stanton make her a drink and she'll sit and process. Until then, she'll bury it. That's just how she is." I gestured to the door. "Here we are."

I reached for the knob and twisted it. The office hadn't been touched. It looked the same as it did three years ago. It might've been a waste of an office, but neither my mother nor I had the heart to clean it out. Someone came in once a week to dust and vacuum.

The bookshelves were lined with leather-bound books, the brass lamp on my father's heavy, dark wood desk rested on the corner, and the high-backed leather office chair was just as I remembered it.

I walked over to the window that overlooked the courtyard. The stone fountain in the shape of an angel spouted water and dribbled into the pool. "When I was in high school, I used to meet him here after classes. He'd take me to get gelato and spoil my dinner."

I looked at Bones over my shoulder and smiled. "He'd get pistachio, and I always got mint chip."

"It's a nice memory," Bones said, shoving his hands in his trouser pockets.

"It is," I agreed. I looked around the office. "I haven't been in here in three years. I guess this is my office now. I thought…"

"You thought?"

I rubbed my sternum. "I thought it would hurt. Being in here." I closed my eyes. "I swear I can still smell his cologne."

I kept my eyes closed even as I heard Bones trek across the carpet. He wrapped his arm around me, and I buried my face in his chest.

"Duchess?"

"Hmm?"

"What the fuck is gelato?"

I leaned back to peer up at him. "Seriously?"

He shrugged.

I grinned. "Come on. I'm about to change your life."

∼

"There's nothing here," my mother said after two hours of digging around in my stepfather's home office. She collapsed into his chair and looked defeated.

"Did you really think we were going to find anything incriminating?" I asked.

"No, but I'd hoped." She glanced at her cell phone that rested on the desk. "Still no word from Arnold. I thought for sure he'd call so I could at least tell him I was starting divorce proceedings."

The door to the office opened and Bones entered. "Any luck?"

"None," I announced.

"The boys have finished changing the locks on the doors and I changed the front gate passcode for you."

"Thank you, Royce. Who knew having a son-in-law in private security would come in handy."

"Private security?" Bones repeated. "Is that the PR spin we're putting on my job?"

"Hmm. You catch on quickly," Mom teased. "Though, I have several friends that are always on the lookout for security detail as well as home monitoring. How are you with computers?"

"I can turn them on," Bones said dryly. "You'd need someone in the tech field to get involved for the level of security I think you're talking about."

"Well, something to consider." Mom shrugged her elegant shoulders. "Let me know if it's something you want to consider."

Bones' brow furrowed in pensive thought. "I'll think about it."

Mom looked at the dainty Rolex on her wrist. "I think it's time to take a break. We missed lunch. I can have Paula make us an early dinner."

"Oh." I bit my lip. "Actually, Bones is taking me out to dinner to celebrate our marriage."

Mom's gaze softened. "Of course he is. That reminds me…" She walked toward the door. "I'll be right back. Don't leave yet."

She left us alone in the office and Bones took a seat on the dark leather Chesterfield.

"Where'd she go?" Bones asked.

"I don't know," I admitted. "Your guess is as good as mine."

My mother returned to the office a few minutes later. "I wanted to give you this before you left." She handed

Bones a black velvet jewelry box. "I stopped off at the bank before I came back home."

Bones opened the box to reveal my grandmother's sapphire and diamond ring that I'd wanted as my engagement ring since I was sixteen years old.

Without a word, Bones plucked it from its velvet bed, picked up my hand and slid it onto my finger. He stared at me while he did it, a silent conversation passing between us.

My mother swiped the corner of her eye. "It's perfect." She hugged Bones and then embraced me. "Have fun tonight," she whispered. "Don't think about anything else except celebrating your marriage."

Stanton held the front door open while he glared at Bones.

"Be nice," I whispered to the aging butler. "He's my husband now."

Stanton harrumphed.

"Next time we come over, I promise he'll bring you a bottle of your favorite Courvoisier. All right?"

He harrumphed again.

I hugged the butler who'd been a part of my family for as long as I could remember. He'd been informed of the circumstances surrounding our sudden marriage but would remain protective of me and my mother no matter what. "Please take care of my mother. I'm sure she's waiting for the sun to go down before she starts in on the martinis."

"It's been a hard day," Stanton said. "For both of you. I'll keep an eye on her as best I'm able."

I nodded.

Bones placed his hand at my waist and guided me toward the waiting town car. I climbed in first and he followed.

I leaned my head against his shoulder and quickly fell asleep.

"Duchess," Bones rasped, his hand gently squeezing my thigh.

"Hmm?"

"We're home."

I reluctantly opened my eyes and lifted my head. "Sorry, I didn't mean to fall asleep."

He looked at me. "We don't have to go out tonight. We can order in."

I shook my head. "No. We have to celebrate. There's plenty of nights to stay in."

His gaze heated. "I'm starting to think going out is the worst idea in the world and I'm an idiot for even suggesting it."

I laughed. "Come on. Let's go have a beautiful meal. I promise you can ravish me later."

Chapter 48

"How's your dinner?" Bones asked as he looked at me across the table.

"It's good," I replied.

He arched a brow. "It's *good*. Don't let the chef hear that."

I smiled and reached across the table to caress his cheek. His scruff was rough underneath my fingers and a shiver worked its way down my spine. He looked glorious in candlelight, carved in shadows, his normally bright eyes dark and mysterious.

The sapphire and diamond ring on my left hand glinted in the light.

"It's good," I said, getting back to our conversation. "But your steak looks better."

"Well, Holliday's *is* a steak house." He reached for his glass of wine.

"Can I try a bite?" I asked.

He raised his brows. "You don't eat red meat."

"I know, but I was wondering if maybe I'm getting a taste for it again."

Bones cut off a piece of his filet mignon and set it on my plate. I cut it into a few pieces and then stuck one into my mouth. It nearly melted on my tongue. It was savory and warm, and it had been cooked to perfection.

I looked longingly at his plate.

"Trade with me," he said.

"What?"

"I'll eat your fish and you can eat my steak."

I shook my head. "I shouldn't. I mean, I haven't had red meat in years. I should go easy."

"Then go easy," he suggested. "But I'll give you my plate."

"You really do love me, don't you?" I teased.

"I really do," he said, his voice rough as he stared at me.

"How's the wine I chose for you?" I asked, once we'd traded plates.

"Perfect. You want to try a bit of that too? Live a little?"

I shook my head. "No. That, I'll pass on." I cut another small bite of steak, wanting to savor it, but also wanting to make sure it didn't upset my stomach. "Can I ask you something?"

"Sure. By the way, you're insane. This fish is amazing. And I'm not a fishy person."

I smiled. "It's not better than the steak, though."

"No. It's not. What were you going to ask me?"

"When my mother mentioned private security…you had this look on your face like you were seriously considering it."

"I am considering it. Actually, it's something I've been thinking about for a while. And I'm considering bringing it to Colt."

"Really?" My brow furrowed. "That seems so…"

"So what?"

"Tame. By the books. Not outside the bounds of normalcy," I stated.

A crooked smile painted his mouth. "The Tarnished Angels are kind of in uncharted territory right now. We've moved away from what we were involved with, but we haven't really figured out what will replace…the other things and still remain lucrative. You understand?"

"There's that PR spin," I said with a smile. "Well, speaking as your wife, I approve of the direction you're thinking of moving in and I'll do anything to support it—even fund it."

"Line drawn," he said. "Not happening."

I looked up from my plate. "What, you don't want to talk about it anymore?"

"Not if you're going to talk about money. Your money doesn't touch our club."

I frowned. "I don't understand. I have more than enough money. I love you. I don't want any of you struggling when there's no reason to struggle."

"It's not about the struggle. I didn't marry you to hit you up for cash. So, no, Hayden. If the club wants to get involved with private security, we'll fund it another way. Not from your trust fund. End of discussion."

I leaned back in my chair. "End of discussion? Why is me offering to help a bruise to your ego?"

"It's not a bruise to my ego."

"Then take it as a loan." I shrugged.

"*Enough*," he barked. His tone was loud enough that he turned customers' heads.

I clamped my mouth shut.

"We're supposed to be celebrating our marriage. Not talking about finances," he muttered.

"Fine. I'll shelve the discussion." I reached for my water.

I knew the man had pride, but it wasn't as though I was lording my wealth over him. At some point, he'd have to see how ridiculous it was not to accept my financial help. The club getting a bank loan at a terrible interest rate was just bad business.

And yet I knew he'd never ask me for help, which was why I had no problem offering it.

Silverware clanked against our plates as we continued to eat in silence.

"I didn't marry you for money," he repeated. "I won't ask you for it."

"You didn't ask, I offered," I pointed out. "If you want to shelve this conversation until we're in private, then we can. But we're not done talking about it."

He leaned forward. "Under no circumstances are you to go to Prez with this."

I frowned. "What the hell does that mean?"

"I mean, you don't go behind my back. I'm your man, and we'll discuss it between us. You won't go to my president and move ahead with this idea and cut me out."

"That's emasculating and I'd never undermine you like that," I said automatically. "But just answer this one question and then I promise to drop it for the rest of the night."

"Go on."

"Would Colt accept my money?"

"Yes," he said immediately. "Because his first thought is aways about the club. What's best for it as a whole. That's why he's president."

"And your first thought isn't the club?"

He paused. "It was, but it's…different now."

"Different."

"You made me different."

I frowned. "What are you saying?"

"I don't know, Duchess." He paused as he gathered his words. "Today made me see things in a different light. See my life—and my club in a different light."

"In a bad way?"

"No. Just different, I guess. I'm not explaining it well."

"No, you're not," I agreed.

"When I walked into that building with you, I was wearing a four-hundred-dollar cashmere sweater. I haven't been comfortable being called Royce in far too long. But hearing you introduce me as Royce… For the first time in a long time, I wanted to be Royce first and Bones second." He fell silent for a moment. "I'm not good enough for you, Duchess. I know that. No matter how your mother spins it. No matter if I go into private security or not. I'm still a biker with rough hands."

"A little late to be having this conversation, don't you think?" I asked softly. "Besides, we've already talked about this. You're both Royce *and* Bones. I love both sides of you."

"They'll drag you through the mud in the papers," he said.

"No doubt," I agreed.

"They'll say you're not fit to run Spencer Pharmaceuticals."

"Then let them say it—I've already thought that for far too long. And if they think that because of who I married, then fuck them."

He arched a brow and a slow smirk spread across his lips. "Didn't know you had it in you, Duchess."

"What? To be foul-mouthed?" I snorted. "I guess I better learn if I want to hang with you and your boys, hmm?"

"I like you just the way you are," he said, his eyes shining with pride. "Don't change on my account."

I smiled. "Same goes for you."

"You finished with your meal?"

"Yes."

"Then let me pay and let's get out of here."

I lifted my napkin and dabbed my lips. "I just need to use the restroom."

"Make it quick, Duchess. I want *dessert*."

"You didn't just say that," I said, feeling my cheeks heat.

"Yeah, I did."

"I'll be quick," I assured him.

I grabbed my black clutch and then turned and strode toward the bathroom. I didn't need to look over my shoulder to know he was watching me.

Holliday's' decor was designed to look like an old railway car. Leather booths, tablecloths with white napkins over heavy tables, and Edison bulbs in European sconces that added a bit of mystery and luxury. The women's restroom had a leather love seat and three stalls.

As I was washing my hands, a quick stab of pain shot through my temple. I closed my eyes and held on to the marble counter. My stomach rolled with nausea, and I swayed like I was on a yacht deck.

"*No*," I murmured.

Opening my eyes, the room kaleidoscoped as I tried to step toward the door and call for help. Another stabbing pain shot through my temple and I pitched forward, smacking my head against the counter on the way down.

I barely registered the pain as I fell to the floor.

"Bones," I whispered just as the vortex swallowed me and everything went black.

Chapter 49

"If you don't let me see my wife, you're gonna have a fucking problem!"

The bellow pulled me from the thickness of unconsciousness. The back of my hand stung as I tried to roll over onto my side. I blinked in realization that I was in a hospital bed and I was hooked up to an IV.

My hand went to my forehead and gingerly encountered a bandage.

The door to the room opened and Bones strode inside. His crisp white shirt was untucked and the front of it was stained with blood.

My blood.

His face was drained of color. He looked shaken. Bones never looked shaken.

With a deep breath, he came to the side of my bed and crouched down and gently took my hand in his. "You scared the living shit out of me."

"I—what happened?"

"What happened?" His eyes pinned me with an intense stare. "You went to use the bathroom and when you didn't come back, I went to find you. You were on the bathroom floor and your head was cut open. You didn't even wake up when they loaded you into the ambulance."

"Oh." I struggled to lift my hand, but I managed, and then I was touching his stubbly cheek.

"Yeah, *oh*." He sighed. "Tell me what's going on, Hayden. I know something isn't right. There was that day you slept eighteen hours straight, and all the dietary restrictions, and now this? They brought you here and immediately rushed you off to do some tests. An MRI, I think. Do you have some sort of neurological disease? Seizures? What's going on?"

I swallowed; my throat dry. "Can I have some water?"

He dropped my hand and stood. Bones went to the bedside table and poured a cup of water from the pitcher and brought it to me. I sipped from the straw and when I'd had enough, I lay back, exhausted.

"I don't know if I have a neurological disorder," I said quietly. "They don't know what it is."

He frowned. "I don't understand."

"This…whatever it is…started a few years ago. Whenever I get really stressed, my body sort of checks out. I faint, or I sleep for fourteen to eighteen hours. Usually, I can tell when these episodes are going to occur, but I was in the bathroom when I felt the stabbing pain in my temple. Before I knew it, my vision was winking in and out and then I fell. I must've hit my head on the way down."

"Stress," he said slowly. "Stress is what causes it?"

I nodded. "As much as the specialists I've seen can deduce, anyway. They've run a bunch of tests. MRIs and CAT scans are normal. Bloodwork, normal. Hormones, normal. The last specialist I saw recommended a strict diet —to see if that limited the episodes."

"Strict diet," he murmured. "It's why you don't drink."

"It's why I don't drink," I agreed. "And why I don't eat sugar or eat red meat…or have caffeine."

"Has it helped?" Bones asked.

"Apparently not," I said. "Limiting stress is the only thing that really prevents it. It's why…"

"Why, what?"

"Why I didn't go to business school. Why I didn't want to get involved with my father's company. Why it looks like I waste my days doing whatever I want instead of something useful."

He took a deep breath. "Christ, Hayden. Why didn't you tell me sooner? Why did you hide this from me?"

"What was I supposed to tell you? That I have this condition that's not really a condition? I had a few doctors tell me it was all in my head. They thought it was psychosomatic. One even told me to see a shrink."

"Well, fuck them. I'm not a doctor, I'm your husband. And you should've told me. I have to know these things so I can help you. So I can know what to do when an episode happens."

"You're right," I admitted. "I just…"

"What?"

"Didn't want you to look at me differently. When you're sick, people treat you differently."

"I know," he said quietly. "God, I know."

"You do?" I asked. "What do you mean?"

Bones looked down at the floor.

"Bones," I pressed.

He dropped my hand and then went to grab the chair and brought it to my bedside. He took a seat and rested his elbows on his thighs and interlinked his fingers.

"You might not want people to treat you differently, but do you know what it's like to find the person you love passed out on the floor? Do you know the terror, Hayden?"

I shook my head.

"It's fucking terrifying." His blue eyes bored into mine. "The blood…the pallor of your skin, the coldness of your hands…"

"I'm sorry," I whispered. "I should've told you."

"Yeah, you should've." He paused. "But while we're clearing the air, I haven't been completely honest with you, either."

Dread curled in my stomach like a rattlesnake waiting to strike. "Honest about what?"

"About my past." He clenched his hands together. "I've been married before, Hayden."

A gasp escaped my lips.

"I was nineteen years old and I married my girlfriend at the time. She was dying of a rare type of blood cancer. She died three days before her twentieth birthday. It was a gorgeous day. Not a cloud in the fucking sky. Birds singing, wind blowing through the trees. It was perfect, except…" He shook his head, his brow wrinkling at the memory.

He gestured to the spot on his arm where the Golden Snitch tattoo was buried underneath his clothes. "I got this for her. It was the only thing…it made her happy. Hours and hours, the first few movies on repeat while she grew thinner and sicker."

My heart drummed in my ears. Heavy, pulsing; carrying my life through my veins.

I reached my hand out toward him. He looked at it for a moment before unlinking his hands and taking my palm in his.

"We were at one of those traveling carnivals," he murmured. "I was standing in the hotdog line and she was standing in the lemonade line. Suddenly, someone yelled that a person had fainted. It was Iris. She told me it was heat stroke. But three weeks later, she told me the truth.

She'd been diagnosed with her condition and she was starting treatment."

Tears gathered in my eyes as I watched Bones relive his past.

"I drove her to doctor's appointments. I held her when she yelled at her body for betraying her. I slept on her parents' couch when she tried to break up with me—which she did pretty regularly." He looked at me, his blue eyes, normally so electric, so vibrant—dull and lifeless like the girl he'd lost.

"I shaved her head when her hair started falling out. I shaved mine, too. And when her father told me they were stopping treatment because it wasn't working, I asked her to marry me. Because everyone deserves to be someone's *everything*. And she was my everything. She was my future and my hope…my dreams and my only plan for the future was to love her. But all that went to shit when she got sick."

He swallowed. "Her getting sick changed everything. Changed the entire trajectory of my life. And I never thought I'd want that again—to feel so deeply for someone, knowing that life could throw me a curve ball and shatter what was left of me. But then I saw you laugh for the first time, and that was it."

Bones held my gaze.

"I laughed," I repeated.

"You laughed, and I thought *here we go again*. There was no stopping it, Hayden. Even if I'd wanted to. I think I fell in love with you the moment I heard that laugh."

It all made so much sense now. Why he didn't want to leave my side after I'd been asleep for eighteen hours, why he'd run headfirst into this relationship without slowing down over the speed bumps.

I tugged on his hand to bring him closer and then I

cradled his cheek. "A life with me never scared you. Did it, Bones?"

He turned his head and kissed my palm. "No, Duchess. It was a life without you that scared the shit out of me."

∽

"Bones," I whispered.

"Hmm." He hugged me tighter in the small hospital bed that he'd climbed onto to hold me.

"Were you ever going to tell me about her?"

"Yes."

"When?"

"I tried to tell you the night we celebrated our marriage with my club and their Old Ladies."

"You tried, huh?"

"Not hard enough, obviously." He sighed. "I wasn't sure how you'd take the news."

"Take the news that you'd loved someone before me? And lost someone before me?"

"Well, when you put it that way…"

I wiggled out of his embrace and lifted myself up so I could stare at him. "I'm sorry you had to live through something like that."

He nodded; his eyes hooded in the low light of the hospital room. The overhead light was shut off and there was just the dim glow from the lamp on the bedside table.

"I wondered, you know," I said, cuddling up with him again.

"Wondered if I'd ever been married before?"

"No. Not that. But I did wonder if you'd been serious with someone in your past. The way you treated me—from the beginning—you were very natural about it. The way you took care of me. The way you checked in with me when we weren't together. Part of me worried it was love-bombing. The other part of me thought that maybe you'd done all this before so you knew how to be."

"It was a good instinct."

I closed my eyes. "My mother isn't here. Did you call her?"

"I called the house," he said. "And I spoke to Stanton. Your mother...she..."

"Was already asleep, wasn't she?" I said quietly.

"Yes." He paused. "Did you know she's been taking sleeping pills?"

"What? I had no idea."

"Stanton shared that with me—as an explanation for why she was unavailable. He didn't want you to think she was purposefully staying away."

"I'm kind of relieved she's not here, actually. I just clobbered her with the truth about Arnold. Like she needs more to worry about."

"She doesn't know about your health issue?"

"No."

"Hayden..."

"Don't *Hayden* me. I'll tell her. I promise."

He was quiet for a moment and then he said, "I called Charlie and left a message."

"Oh."

"I thought she should know."

"She already knows. About my issue, I mean."

"Of course she does."

"She wanted me to tell you. She urged me to."

The door to the hospital room opened and the night nurse strode inside. She placed a hand on her hip and stared at Bones. "Visiting hours are long over, honey. It's time for you to leave."

"I'm not leaving," Bones said. "So, either you find the

doctor to discharge her so I can take her home, or I'm sleeping right here in this bed."

"I really want to go home," I said. "Please?"

"I'm not authorized to make that call," the nurse said.

"Looks like I'm getting comfortable." He gently removed his arm from underneath me and then he kicked off his shoes.

"You look pretty comfortable to me," the nurse said with a grin. "I'm a sucker for true love. Night, kids. Sleep well."

Chapter 50

THE NEXT MORNING, I was discharged from the hospital. I was sure Bones wouldn't let me walk on my own two feet, and I was correct. He commanded that I sit in a wheelchair.

"This is ridiculous," I argued. "The doctor told you my CAT scan and MRI came back clean. I'm hydrated. I slept great. I have no headache or vision problems. Let me walk."

"You let me push you in this wheelchair or I'm carrying you bride-style out of here. Your choice." His tone and expression brooked no argument.

With a sigh and crumbling resolve, I took the wheelchair and let him wheel me toward the elevators. It was overcast and gray clouds threatened to open up.

I was quiet on the ride home, checking my phone every few minutes to see if my mother or Charlie had called, but my cell was silent.

Bones reached over and placed his hand on my thigh and gave it a squeeze.

We pulled into the driveway and Bones cut the engine.

I reached for the door handle and he looked at me and said, "Don't you fucking dare."

I placed my hands in my lap and waited for my husband—*my husband*—to open the car door for me. He helped me into the house and he quickly disarmed the alarm before it blared to life.

"I want to shower off the hospital smell."

He nodded. "Okay, let's shower."

"Bones…"

"Hayden. No arguments. Not today. Tomorrow I'll let you do everything yourself, but for today, please give this to me."

I sighed and nodded. "You think I'm weak."

"I don't think you're weak."

"You look at me and you think about Iris," I stated. "Don't you?"

"I thought we talked about that already."

"Not enough. Not nearly enough. I don't know anything about her. What does she look like? Am I like her at all? You tattooed a Golden Snitch on your body because of her, but what about me? We're married. You want babies with me. And you don't have a tattoo of that commitment on your skin. Why not, Bones?"

"She was blonde," he said. "Sunshine blonde. Bright, you know? Her teeth were a little crooked, but it just made her approachable. And when she laughed, her nose scrunched. You're nothing like her, Hayden. You don't remind me of her. You don't look like her. You don't laugh like her. You don't love like her."

His words pierced my heart.

Bones took a step toward me and reached for me. He placed his hands on my shoulders. "You remind me of *you*. You look like you. You laugh like you. You love like you. I don't look for her in you. You're your own person, Hayden. And I love you for *you*."

"Oh," I whispered.

"And the reason I don't have a tattoo on my body that commits this thing between us in ink yet is because I haven't left your side long enough to get it done. But as soon as I can stand to leave your side, I'll get Roman to tattoo me. Okay?"

"Okay."

"Now let's shower and when we get in there, I'm going to wash your hair and you're going to let me love you. Got it?"

I sighed. "Got it."

∽

"Do you need another blanket?" Bones asked.

"No." I smiled. "Two is plenty. You've cocooned me."

He handed me the remote. "I have to call Prez. Will you be okay?"

"I'll be fine," I assured him. "My bladder is empty, my belly is full, I'm good."

He looked at me.

"I'm *good*. Now go deal with whatever it is you have to deal with." My cell phone rang. "See? I have to take this. It's Mom."

He nodded and leaned down to kiss my forehead. He then sauntered toward the dining room, looking far too delectable in a pair of grey sweats and a white T-shirt that showed off his muscular arms.

I picked up my cell and pressed a button. "Hello?"

"You were in the hospital?"

The doors to the dining room closed and Bones disappeared.

I held in a sigh. "Yes. But really, Mom, I'm fine."

"Where are you? Are you still in the hospital? I never should've taken that pill. Damn it."

Silence fell between us.

"It's okay," I said gently. "I know about the sleep meds. Stanton told Bones."

"I shouldn't have hidden that from you."

"Probably not," I agreed.

"I haven't taken them in eight months. But yesterday was…yesterday."

"I understand. And no, I'm no longer in the hospital. I'm at home."

"What happened?"

"I guess it's my turn to come clean about some things, too."

"More things, Hayden? Really?"

"Just listen, okay?"

I quickly told her about my condition, and when it had started. She was quiet the entire time and didn't try and interrupt me. "I had an episode for lack of a better term, last night at dinner. I was in the restroom. I fell and cut my forehead and Bones found me on the bathroom floor."

"Did they call an ambulance?"

"Yes."

"Did Bones ensure the restaurant kept your name confidential?"

"I don't know."

"I'll call and make the inquiries," she said.

"I appreciate that."

"So, they really don't have an explanation for why you have these episodes?"

"No. No clue," I said.

"Have you thought…"

"What?" I pressed.

"About seeing someone? A therapist, I mean."

"We don't talk to therapists."

"Maybe we should," she said. "Maybe a therapist will help you work through the things you're still holding on to."

"And what about you?" I asked. "Are you going to see a therapist to help you work through things you're still holding on to?"

"I'm thinking about it," she said. "Even though the idea of unveiling my private issues to a stranger without a vodka gimlet in hand is borderline terrifying."

"Maybe we should do the terrifying things, Mom."

"I'm not sure I'm ready for that level of self-awareness." She chuckled.

"Has Arnold returned any of your calls?" I asked.

"No. I thought for sure he'd attempt contact by now, but it's been silent."

"Do you think he left town?"

"It's possible. Who knows, though. It will make trying to serve him divorce papers more difficult if I can't find him. But right now, I'm so angry that if I see him, I'm liable to do something completely out of character."

The front door burst open, and I heard the clack of high heels on the wooden floor before Charlie appeared in the living room. She glared at me in anger.

"Mom, I gotta go," I said suddenly. "Charlie just showed up. And she looks pissed."

"She probably saw the marriage announcement," Mom said.

"What marriage announcement?" I asked.

"Bye, darling. I'll be in touch when I have news about the restaurant."

She hung up and I set my phone aside. "Hey, Charlie."

"*Hey, Charlie?*" she snapped. She marched around to the

couch and waved her phone in my face. "Why am I reading about your marriage announcement after the fact?"

"Charlie, none of this was planned," I said simply. "And for your information, I had no idea my mother was going to put out a public announcement about my marriage."

"You got married without me and didn't even have the decency to let me know? I was supposed to be your maid of honor."

I looked her up and down and couldn't fight the smile. She was wearing a man's white button-down shirt that was cinched at the waist with a tie—and a pair of black heels. "Maid of honor? Or maid of *dishonor*?"

Her eyes bugged out of her head. "You're not seriously cracking jokes at my appearance right now."

I patted the couch. "Sit. And I'll explain everything. And then you're going to explain why you're dressed the way you're dressed. And before you continue ranting, you should know that Bones called you last night and left a message."

She sighed. "I dropped my phone. Again. I had to get a new one this morning."

"Well, that explains the radio silence," I said. "And I won't hold it against you that you didn't visit me in the hospital last night."

"Hospital?"

"Sit down, Charlie."

She all but collapsed onto the couch. I held out my hand and she gave me her phone. The website she had open was the society section of the local paper where major announcements about prominent or wealthy people were listed. There we were—Bones and I—a picture from my mother's charity event that I had no idea had even been taken. Bones was looking down at me and smiling and I was unaware of the camera on us.

It was a beautiful photo. Unposed. Unfiltered. I quickly scanned the announcement itself.

"Uh oh," I muttered.

"What?" Charlie asked.

"My mother was very creative when explaining Bones' background."

"Oh, yeah. The private security spin. I wondered about that. Guess she really couldn't say biker in a motorcycle club, though."

"Correct," I agreed.

"So, what happened in the last several days since I've seen you? Because apparently, you've had a full schedule what with getting married and all."

"Buckle up," I muttered. "It's going to be a bumpy ride."

Before I could even begin to explain, the double doors to the dining room opened and Bones strode in.

Charlie launched herself up. "You!"

Bones frowned. "Me what?"

"You did this," she accused.

"I did what?" Bones asked.

"You and your dick sorcery somehow got my best friend to marry you—without even inviting me," Charlie accused.

"My dick sorcery in no way influenced your best friend to marry me," Bones argued.

"It had a little bit to do with it," I said with a shrug.

Bones raised his brows and Charlie glared at me.

"Call off your dog," Bones said. "She's about to rip out my throat."

"Charlie, sit," I commanded again. "And let me explain everything."

With a snarl at Bones, Charlie finally sat again.

The story came out quickly and a bit disjointed, with Charlie constantly interrupting to ask questions. But by the end of my explanation, she had a decent grasp on the situation.

"So like, you're really married? Not like, *get a handle on your dad's company and get through the publicity and then divorce* kind of married?" she asked.

"We're *married*, married," Bones ground out.

He was still standing next to the couch, and I reached my hand out to him and he took it. Charlie's eyes took note of it.

"Where's Arnold?" Charlie asked. "That fucker has some explaining to do."

"That fucker hasn't even contacted Marilyn or tried to come home. My guess is he's laying low, licking his wounds and trying to figure out just how much we know."

"Or, he's worried about you going Bad to the Bones on his ass," Charlie said. "For hiring a hit on your woman. You *are* going Bad to the Bones on him, aren't you?"

"Charlie, stop. Bones isn't going to do anything to Arnold."

Bones' hand tightened around mine.

"But he has to!" Charlie insisted. "You can't let him get away with this. And you're clearly not going to the cops with this. Why not, by the way?"

"Because we have nothing substantial on him," Bones said. "Her father's death was already ruled an accident. Arnold was legally elected to the board and his marriage to her mother…everything was legal. Everything seemed above board."

"And if you did have proof, you'd turn him over to the authorities?" Charlie pressed.

When Bones didn't speak right away, I looked up at him.

"We got married to put an immediate stop to it," Bones replied instead of answering her question.

"How the hell is marrying her protecting her?" Charlie asked. "He could still try and hurt her."

"He could," I agreed. "But he won't. Because if I die, the company will be dissolved, and the patents sold. Arnold doesn't gain anything by coming after me anymore."

"And you married her so she could have access to the controlling seat on the board, thereby neutering Arnold and all his power."

"Yes. That's why he married me."

"I married you because I love you, Duchess. The other shit was just a reason to push the timeline up."

I sent him a tender look and then I returned my attention to Charlie.

"I'm sorry we couldn't tell you what was going on. We didn't even tell my mother until after I'd already assumed control of the company yesterday."

"Has she forgiven you for usurping her right as the mother to watch her daughter get married?" Charlie asked.

"Enough, Charlie," Bones stated. "You've made your point. You're pissed you didn't get to see her get married."

"No." Charlie shot up. "That's not what this is about. I get why you had to do all the secrecy shit. You couldn't let Arnold know about your plan. That all makes perfect sense. I didn't get to do the thing that best friends are supposed to get to do."

"Wear an ugly dress and do the chicken dance?" Bones drawled.

She glared. "No, I didn't get to have my one-on-one

talk with you about how you should treat my best friend, *or else*, talk. And for the record, Hayden never would've made me wear an ugly dress."

I nodded. "It's true. I would've let her pick her own dress. Despite the headache it would've caused."

Bones let go of my hand and walked to the other side of the room to the chair. He took a seat. "Okay."

"Okay what?" Charlie asked in confusion.

"You want to have the talk. Let's have the talk."

"I'm not having the talk with you while she's present," Charlie said, snapping her spine straight. "I'm going to sound bloodthirsty, and I might go feral goblin on you. I don't want her to see that side of me."

"I've already seen that side of you," I said with a smile. "I can handle it."

Charlie shook her head. "Nope. I will not budge on this. Bones and I are having this conversation in private, or I won't come to the party your mother is throwing for you."

"How do you know about the party?" I asked in surprise.

Charlie rolled her eyes. "Please. That woman was deprived of a society wedding. She's throwing you a party."

"Name the time and the place," Bones said. "And you can give me your best friend speech."

"Noted." Charlie sat up straighter. "Now can you give me and my girl some alone time to talk?"

Bones rose. "You know she's just going to tell me everything you talk about, right?"

"She will not," Charlie stated. "We have an iron pact. Layers of secrecy."

"But she's married to me now. And I know how this all works."

"I'm not telling you anything that Charlie says to me," I said. "Girl code."

"Married code trumps girl code."

"*Like hell it does*," Charlie fumed.

Bones looked at me. "You want to know why everyone in the club knows each other's business? Because you tell an Old Lady, they're gonna take it back to their man. Before you know it, the entire club knows your shit."

"Is that really true?" Charlie asked, her gaze flitting from me to Bones and then back to me.

"I knew Doc was pregnant before everyone else," I pointed out. "And I kept that to myself."

Bones looked at Charlie. "You're wearing a white button-down shirt, so I know it's not Savage's and last I knew, you were trying not to be in love with Savage."

"You told him!" Charlie gasped.

"I told him nothing." I glared at Bones. "How did you know that?"

"Willa was scolding Savage. I overheard."

"So, it wasn't Hayden," Charlie pointed out. "See? She keeps my secrets. And I keep hers. You're not breaking up the dynamic duo. I don't care how much sorcery is in your dick."

Chapter 51

Bones left for the clubhouse, but not before leaving a pistol for me within reach on the coffee table. He also stated there were prospects standing guard and keeping their eyes and ears open in case there was trouble.

"He left you a pistol," Charlie commented. "Is that, like, his love language?"

I sniggered. "I think so. He took me to the gun range that's on club property to make sure I could handle it."

"Bet that's not the only thing you handled."

"Hmm, another dick joke. How quaint. Okay, your turn. Please distract me from all the crazy shit in my life."

"And the fact that you have a husband?"

"And the fact that I have a husband."

"It's like you went to the animal shelter one day and adopted him." She smiled. "He protects you, and I love that. You know I'm happy for you, right? I mean, aside from the crazy circumstances that kinda forced you to get married so fast, I'm happy for you."

"Yeah?" I asked. "Because you are my best friend, and I would've had you there if I could've."

"I know."

"So, the shirt?" I asked. "You gonna tell me about the shirt?"

"I stayed at Walker's last night."

"That's all?"

"Well of course that's not all." She rolled her eyes. "We did stuff."

"Dirty stuff?"

"Yes. Of course." She was thoughtful.

"What?"

"I like him. But I liked Savage too and we saw how that went. I just don't want Walker to get hurt because I have the emotional bandwidth of a raisin."

"Did you tell him that?"

"Kinda," she said. "I mean, I told him I was getting over someone and didn't want Walker to become wreckage in my quest to move on. He appreciated that. He's not pressuring me for anything, but he still calls, and he still makes plans, and he still feeds me, so I'll see where it goes."

"Hmm."

She frowned. "What does *hmm* mean?"

"Not sure you want to hear it," I said.

"Now you have to tell me."

"I think Walker is playing the long game."

"No. No way." She shook her head. "He can't be."

"Why not?"

"Well, because we just met."

"Uh huh."

She rolled her eyes. "Just because you married Bones like five minutes after you started dating—and you don't seem freaked out, by the way—doesn't mean the rest of us operate on that timeline."

"Let's look at the facts," I said. "I saw you guys lock eyes when you met, so…"

"I don't believe in insta-love."

"Okay." I shrugged. "But you told him you were hung up on someone else and instead of walking away, he decided to stick around and be what you needed."

"Lots of men would do that. For the promise of easy sex? Please."

"But you haven't said you've slept with him yet."

"I implied it."

"No, you purposefully said you did dirty stuff, but that's a blanket statement of avoidance, not an *of course*, or something that confirmed it."

"That bump to the head has you addled," she griped. "Speaking of which, it's not gonna scar is it?"

"Don't know. I'm not sure who stitched me up, I was unconscious. It could've been anyone from a first-year intern to a plastic surgeon. But if it does scar, I'll look like a pirate and I can enter my swashbuckling fashion era."

"I'm here for that."

"Nice try changing the subject." I grinned. "You care about Walker's feelings. I can't remember the last time that happened."

"It happened with the guy *before* Walker," she said. "Savage."

"No, it didn't. You and Savage were like two wrecking balls, swinging at each other. You hit a few times before realizing it would end in nothing but destruction for you both."

"I didn't tell you much about my time with Savage," she said.

"You never volunteered," I pointed out.

"He's like chasing a high," she said quietly. "And when you get it, you get it for a few hours and then it all wears off and you feel worse. I had to go cold turkey if I had any chance of surviving him."

"Maybe he's not surviving you, you ever think of that?"

"I try not to," she stated. "He's not good for me. It doesn't matter that I was finally able to feel something for someone after years of not wanting that, but Savage is chocolate cake."

"First he's a drug, now he's chocolate cake?"

"Chocolate cake isn't bad for you in small quantities," she said. "Every once in a while. But he's the human equivalent of a chocolate cake that you eat in its entirety in the middle of the night in a single sitting."

"Oh, I see." I nodded. "Poor Savage. I feel for him, actually."

"Poor Savage? You mean poor Charlie…"

"No, I mean poor Savage. Charlie has someone in her life who is sticking around. Savage is still Savage. He's alone."

"And that, right there, was why I had to walk away and ghost him. No matter how much I hoped he'd come around and want something real, he didn't. He can't, I don't think."

"You still heartbroken over him?"

"A little," she admitted. "But it was such a foreign feeling. He slipped through my defenses effortlessly. I'm not even sure how he did it."

"That's the kicker, isn't it?" I asked, thinking about Bones and how he'd done the same thing with me. Only he'd wanted to stick around and build a life with me.

"It's his loss, you know. Savage's, I mean."

She shook her head. "I don't see it that way. Mostly, I'm just kind of sad for him. Have you ever been with someone who's sitting right in front of you, but they're a million miles away? They're trapped in their own head, their own memories, and they don't even care to clue you in? No one deserves to be in a partnership like that. I'm not even sure if Savage knows how to be by himself, much less with someone else."

"Probably why he fills his time with booze and different women."

She chewed her lip. "And fighting."

"What?" I frowned. "Fighting who?"

"This has to stay between us," she said. "Marriage code or not. You can't tell Bones this."

"All right, I swear on our history. What are you talking about?"

"Savage came to me one night in the middle of the night. He was busted up. Split lip, black eye. His body was nothing but bruises. I refused to let him cross the threshold of the pool house. I told him I didn't want trouble brought to my doorstep."

"Smart," I said. "So, you turned him away?"

"No." She sighed. "He said he had nowhere else to go. And that tugged on my stupid heart and I let him in."

"He couldn't go to the clubhouse?" I asked.

She shook her head. "I got him inside and doctored him as best I could. I wanted to take him to the hospital, but he said no."

"So where was he?" I demanded.

"He said he'd been in a fight. Only it wasn't like, a bar brawl or whatever. He said it was an illegal fight. Underground."

"Stop it."

She shook her head. "He swore me to secrecy. And that's when I ghosted him. I wasn't going to be a part of whatever he was into."

"An illegal fight? Why?"

"Hell if I know. But he clearly didn't want the club to know about it, which means the club wouldn't approve." Charlie's expression became pinched. "The bastard used my feelings against me. He knew I would keep his secret because I was in love with him."

"I'm sorry," I said.

"Don't be. It's not your fault. I'm a grown woman. I chose to get on the back of his bike. I chose to continue seeking him out for that damn dopamine hit that only a bad boy can give you." She sighed. "Anyway, thanks for not telling Bones. I'm sure it wouldn't be good for Savage."

"Or maybe it would be," I said.

She shook her head. "Savage does what Savage wants. No amount of talking to him will change that."

"Yeah, you're probably right."

It weighed on my mind—I knew I could trust Bones. But trust Bones to tell me the entire truth about everything the club was involved in? I knew he wouldn't.

"I'm surprised Bones left you alone. What with his overprotective nature," Charlie said.

"He only left because he knows you'll stay until he gets back. Plus, there is the matter of private security patrolling the streets."

The doorbell rang and Charlie shot me a confused look as she rose. "You expecting anyone?"

I shook my head.

"I'll answer it," she said.

Charlie walked out of the living room into the foyer and began to laugh.

"What?" I asked. "Who is it?"

"The fleet," she said as she opened the door. "Come on in."

Willa, Mia, Logan and Doc entered the living room.

"We brought food," Mia said, lifting a casserole dish in her hands.

"You brought food?" I asked. "Why?"

"Why?" Logan repeated. "Because you're recovering and this is what we do."

The other Old Ladies nodded in agreement.

"It's all vegetarian," Doc announced.

"And nothing sugary," Mia added.

"Okay, that's really sweet, but how did you know I was recovering?" I asked.

"Bones called Smoke," Logan said. "Smoke told me, and then I group texted the Old Ladies with the news. Everyone wanted to come at once, but I thought it was better to come in shifts. There's a lot of us."

"Speaking of which," Doc said. "It's time to add you to the Old Ladies' group chat."

"Aww man, you guys have a group chat?" Charlie whined. "That sounds fun."

"It's mostly for informational purposes," Mia said.

"And dirty memes," Logan said. "You don't know how many I get on any given day."

"Well, come on in," I said, about to throw the blanket off me and get up.

"You, stay," Doc commanded. "Let me get a look at those stitches."

"Charlie, why don't you show them to the kitchen and get them something to drink?" I suggested.

"Good idea." Charlie waved at the Old Ladies to follow her.

There was a murmur of conversation as they trailed after her like little ducklings.

Doc sat down on the couch and inched closer to me. "You mind?"

I shook my head.

She leaned forward and examined the stitches on my forehead. "Must've been deep if they had to sew it. We use skin glue for most things these days. Ah, yep. Looks like you lost a bit of flesh during the fall. It's not bad, but stitches were the only way this was going to hold back together. They did a good job. Really good, actually. You'll scar, but it won't be bad."

She paused for a minute, but when I didn't say anything, she asked, "So, what happened?"

I frowned. "I thought you all knew?"

"We know the watered-down version. I want to hear it from you."

"Why?"

"Why? Because I'm a doctor. And your friend."

"I don't want to have to tell the story again," I said. "Shouldn't we wait until they come back?"

Doc's grin spread across her face.

"What?" I asked.

"If Charlie knows the whole story, I'm sure she's telling them what happened as we speak."

"Before you interrogate me," I said with a laugh, "can I ask how you're doing?"

"Barely any morning sickness so far, but I don't expect that to last. Boxer is over-the-moon excited. The timing of this pregnancy, though, with Darcy…" She shook her head. "Not that I can really be surprised. I mean, I got my IUD out a few months ago. I just didn't think it would happen this fast, you know?"

"How are Lily and Cam?"

"Pretty listless. Shut down. Cam…he just doesn't care about anything. Not that I fault him, but because he's in a cast, he has nowhere for his emotions to go. He's just… angry. All the time."

"Question for you," I said. "You have a dog, right?"

"Yes." Doc nodded.

"Would you be willing to get a second one? For Cam?"

"I don't know. Life is already crazy."

"What's one more?" I asked. "I think Cam needs an animal to just be there for him. Keep him company. Something for him to focus on instead of his own situation. You know?"

"It's a great idea. I wish I'd thought of it," she said. "I'll take him to the shelter so he can pick the dog of his choice."

I shook my head.

"No? Is that a bad idea?"

"Not bad at all," I assured her. "But I'm guessing you haven't heard that I'm something of a savant when it comes to animals."

"What do you mean?"

"I mean, I have this way of matching people with their animals. It's a gift, or something."

"What's a gift or something?" Charlie asked as she came back into the living room. She was holding a plate with several servings of each of the dishes the Old Ladies had brought. "For you."

"I'm not hungry," I said. "Bones just fed me."

She grinned. "Perfect. Then I'll eat this." She sat down on the floor and set the plate onto the coffee table. "So, what's a gift or something?"

"My animal-people match making skill," I said.

"How does it work?" Doc asked.

"I don't know how it works, it's just something I can do. I spend time at Rose Hill Retirement Community as well as the animal shelter and I just *know*. I'll meet a dog and immediately know who it's for—but only if I've already met its owner."

"It's kinda spooky," Charlie said. "But it's really true. We've been talking about starting a non-profit around the idea. Though, Hayden probably won't have time now that she's Chair of the Board of Spencer Pharmaceuticals."

"Spencer Pharmaceuticals," Doc repeated. "Wait, you're *what?*"

"I'm Hayden Spencer," I said. "It was my father's company, and as of yesterday, I'm now in control of the company."

"*Holy fuck,*" Doc said. "Sorry, I just…holy fuck."

The Old Ladies returned with dining room chairs and began to take seats near us.

I smiled. "I guess this wasn't a drop and run."

Willa shook her head. "We pitched in and got you a little something. We didn't get to throw you bachelorette party, so this'll have to do." She handed me a brown paper bag with Leather and Ink's logo on it.

I peeked into the bag and pulled out a delicate, crotchless lace body suit in jet black. I hastily shoved it back into the bag, my face flaming with heat.

The Old Ladies cackled.

"Sorry, darlin'," Mia said with a huge smile. "Guess we should've warned you."

"Yes, you should've," I agreed. "Warning: *will cause supreme embarrassment.*"

"Warning: *will make your biker get on his knees and worship you,*" Logan said.

The Old Ladies nodded in agreement.

"I want one of those," Charlie said.

"A biker, or the lingerie?" Willa asked.

"The lingerie." She looked at me. "Walker's been such a good boy. I think it's time for a reward."

Chapter 52

"What are you doing?" Mia asked.

I stood. "Going to the bathroom."

"Let me help you," Mia said.

"I don't need help," I protested.

"Bones told us we weren't allowed to let you out of our sight," Logan said.

"No, we are *not* doing this," I stated.

"Not doing what?" Willa asked.

"I'm not letting you treat me like I'm constantly on the verge of fainting," I stated. "Bones is already overprotective. I can't handle that from you guys too."

Doc pointed to my head. "Are you forgetting about your stitches? Of course he's going to be overprotective."

I doubted any of them knew Bones' history. And I wasn't going to share it with them. I knew why he was overprotective, but I wasn't going to live my life having the people close to me constantly watching me.

"We care," Mia said. "Don't take it as anything more than that."

I nodded.

"I'll stand outside the bathroom," Charlie said as she got up off the floor. "And if you feel like you're going to faint, you yell."

"This is ridiculous," I muttered, but I stopped protesting.

The only way I was going to get Bones to back off and stop hovering—and to get him to stop including the Old Ladies in his desire to keep me in a bubble—was to prove to him that I wasn't going to collapse at any minute.

After I did my business, I opened the door. Charlie stood by and shot me a lopsided smile. "Be grateful you have so many people in your corner. It's a good thing."

"What's he going to do when we have kids?" I asked.

She blinked. "Kids? You've talked about having kids?"

"Yes. We've talked about having kids."

"Like, soon?"

"Like, if it happens it happens," I said slowly.

She placed her hand on my arm and stopped my trek back toward the living room. Charlie pitched her voice lower. "What are you saying—that you're trying to get pregnant?"

"I'm saying I'm not, *not* trying," I said. I stared at her. "You think I'm crazy."

"As a fox," she agreed with a nod. "This is like the worst time in the world for that. You just got involved with your father's company. Your stepfather tried to have you killed—*twice*. You've been with Bones for a hot minute. And you want to add *more* stress to your life? When you have a condition that is brought about by stress?"

She stared at me in confusion. I didn't blame her.

"I know it's crazy," I said. "I know how it sounds. But I…what am I waiting for, Charlie?"

"I don't know, maybe for your life not to be in danger?"

"I'm always going to be in danger," I said quietly.

"Don't you get it? That's life. One minute you've got your entire life ahead of you, the next you die in a ski accident. None of us are safe. None of us know when the timer is going to go off. I don't want to waste any more of my life hiding or being scared. I don't want to waste any more time worrying about things I can't control."

I shook my head. "I don't know the intricacies of how to run a billion-dollar company. But so what? There are people all around me at Spencer Pharmaceuticals who do. Dad made sure of that. And you know what I *do* know? I know what his vision was. We talked about it for years while I was growing up. And now I'm in a position to direct the people who know how to make it work that way. The rest? I'll figure it out. I'll figure out the life stuff too. I just—for the first time in three years—I *want*, Charlie. I want it all. I want to live, and I want to live with Bones."

She took my hand and gave it a squeeze. "Then live."

I smiled.

"I don't get it," she admitted. "Not the living part—that I get. The baby part. That I *so* don't get. They're messy."

"Yep."

"And loud."

"Yep."

"Did Bones like, hotwire your ovaries or something?" she asked.

"Oh, absolutely." I grinned.

We finally made it back to the living room and I took my spot on the couch.

"What were you doing in there? Writing a novel?" Mia teased.

"So, what are we talking about?" Charlie asked.

"Mia and Boxer's new bar," Doc said. "It's coming together."

"With Logan's help," Mia said. "She's a design genius. We were supposed to have a cocktail night. I have all these recipes I want to try, but my pool of loyal tasters are off the sauce."

"Sorry, we're growing humans," Willa said with a laugh.

"What about mocktails?" I asked. "I'm always happy when restaurants include mocktails for us non-drinkers."

"That's a great idea," Mia said.

My phone buzzed with a text.

BAD TO THE BONES
Old Ladies still there?

ME
Yes.

BAD TO THE BONES
Good. I'll be home in a few hours.

"I know that look," Logan said.

I glanced up from my screen. "What look?"

"The look that says you are planning on seducing your husband." Logan grinned. "Aren't ya?"

"I might be," I agreed. "He won't be home for a few hours though. Just enough time to spin my web and trap him like a fly."

"Hmm. I think he's happy to be trapped." Willa winked.

"We should go," Mia said.

"Thank you for coming over," I said to them.

"The rest of the reserves will show up over the next few days," Mia said. "Hope that's okay."

"That's more than okay," I assured her.

One by one, they leaned down to hug me. They all left, but Doc stayed behind.

"I'll call you about the dog for Cam," I said.

"Perfect," she said. She shuffled from one foot to the other, her brow wrinkled.

"What?" I asked.

"I've just been mulling over your…condition."

"Yeah? What about it?"

"You said it started right after your father passed."

"Yes. It did." I nodded.

"And stress brings on the episodes."

"Uh huh."

"And they can't find anything in your MRI or CAT scans."

"Correct again. Doc, what are you getting at?"

She glanced at Charlie. "Can you give us a second?"

"Ah, sure." Charlie took her phone and headed for the dining room. Without asking if we wanted privacy, she shut the doors and gave it to us anyway.

Doc sat down on the couch. "I don't think your condition is related to anything physical."

"What do you mean?" I asked.

"I mean, I think you went through something really traumatic, and your body hasn't released it yet. I think your body is still holding onto it. The body stores things."

She was silent for a moment and then she spoke again. "I had something bad happen to me. Something I don't talk about unless it's in therapy." Doc cocked her head to the side. "I was seeing a therapist for months, but I wasn't getting any better. Talking about what happened wasn't helping me process—it was just keeping me stuck in that place. That dark place. I had to take sleep meds and I could see how this was going to go."

When I didn't say anything, she quickly went on, "I started doing some research. Looking for an alternative path because the traditional path wasn't working. I saw an acupuncturist, an osteopath, and a reiki practitioner to start."

"And did any of those other avenues work?" I asked, intrigued.

She nodded. "Yes. They helped immensely. I sleep without the meds. I'm down to one therapy session a week. And," she held up her hand that was riddled with angry scars, "it's helped this."

"Oh, wow," I murmured.

"I'm not telling you what to do," she insisted. "But I just thought, well, if what you've tried isn't working, maybe it's time to try something else."

"Thanks, Doc," I said.

She squeezed my hand and then stood up and headed for the front door. "Oh, question for you."

"Shoot."

"I know you said Cam needs a dog. But does your talent include cats?"

"I'm not a cat person, so I've never really tried. Why?"

"Lily." She smiled. "She's been begging for a kitten. Even before Darcy died."

"I'll see what I can do," I promised.

~

After the Old Ladies had left, Charlie had stuck around for another hour, but then I'd urged her to go live her life. She'd resisted, but I was adamant. Eventually, she relented.

"If Bones tries to yell at me for leaving you—"

"I'll handle him," I assured her with a smile.

"You'll *handle* him?" Her grin was devious. "You mean distract him with sex."

"Tried and true method. It's worked for women for eons. It'll work for me, too."

"Especially if you wear that new lingerie the Old Ladies got you." She winked and flitted out the door.

I locked up after her and set the alarm.

And then I took the pistol Bones had left upstairs with me so I could get ready for him.

Now, I was sitting on my heels in the middle of the bed as I waited. My hair was curled, the candles were lit, and I was wearing my new lingerie.

I'd texted him to warn him the house was empty and that the alarm was set.

He left me on read.

No doubt he was angry that I wasn't sitting on the couch, surrounded by people who could take care of me if something happened.

I heard the front door open, followed by the disarming of the alarm.

"Duchess!" Bones called, his tone laced with anger. "Where the hell are you?"

"Up here," I yelled back.

I heard the heavy tromp of his motorcycle boots that he hadn't bothered taking off. His steps were slow on the stairs and my heart tripped in fear.

He pushed the bedroom door open and came to a stop. His gaze traveled from the top of my head down my body, eliciting shivers as he went.

Bones placed his forearm on the doorjamb and leaned against it. "You want to tell me what's going on?"

"I thought it was obvious." I rose up on my knees.

"You decided seducing me was more important than worrying about your own health?"

When I didn't reply, he went on, "You could've passed out—by yourself—and no one would've known."

"I'm fine, Bones."

"Are you?" he demanded.

I nodded.

He pushed away from the doorjamb and stalked toward the bed. "How am I supposed to believe that?" His gaze skittered across the stitches on my forehead. There was no way to hide them. Not unless I'd wanted to give myself bangs.

"I'm not going to let you steam roll me on this," I stated. "Otherwise, you'll never let me be alone again. And I can't live my life with you hovering. I've got to live, Bones."

"I'm pissed."

"I see that," I said lightly. I thrust my breasts forward. "So, what are you going to do about it?"

"Punish you."

His tone was dark and gravelly, and it made my nipples pebble against the lace. It drew his attention.

Bones slowly removed his leather cut and set it on the back of the chair in the corner of the room. And then he took a seat. He leaned forward and placed his forearms on his thighs and stared at me.

Stared at me for so long I grew nervous.

"Bones?"

"Crawl to me."

"What?"

"You heard me. I want you to crawl to me." His stare was unyielding. In our short time together, Bones had never given any indication that he was into something like this.

"Duchess," he rasped. "Get on your knees and crawl to

me. Show me how sorry you are for scaring the shit out of me."

My chest filled with understanding. This wasn't about me kicking the Old Ladies out and wanting to be alone. This was about him finding me on the bathroom floor, forcing him to relieve the terror of finding Iris in a similar state.

I slid off the bed and got on all fours. And then I crawled toward him. I kept our eyes locked as I came to him. He might've commanded me, but I came willingly.

The soft rug slid against my skin as I crawled toward him.

His expression didn't change, not even when I was within reach.

It was on the tip of my tongue to ask *what next*, but something told me to remain silent.

"Turn around," he commanded. "Stay in that position."

My breath hitched as I slowly did as he bid. I looked at him over my shoulder.

"Eyes front."

I whipped my head around.

"Spread your legs. I want to see my wife's gorgeous pussy."

I shivered at his crude words, even as I spread my legs.

"More," he commanded. "And place your head on the floor."

The position angled my body so that he could see all of me. I closed my eyes and breathed through the rapid beating of my heart.

I heard him rise and then felt the heat of his body behind me.

"God, this really is the most beautiful thing I've ever

seen," he murmured as he dragged a finger through my folds. "And it's all fucking mine."

He slid his finger inside me and I quivered around him. He thrust it gently for a few beats before pulling out.

I lamented at the emptiness.

His hand smacked my ass. I whimpered in surprise more than pain. And then his hand smacked my other cheek.

"My wife likes that," he stated. "You know how I know?"

He teased my entrance again.

"You're fucking drenched. I bet I could slide right in. Should we find out?"

"Yes," I gasped.

"Hmm. No, I don't think so. I don't think you've been punished enough."

He grasped my cheeks in his huge hands and gently pulled them apart, baring me to him. And then his tongue was lavishing my clit and I curled my fingers into the rug.

I couldn't see him, I couldn't watch him, all I could do was feel the pleasure he chose to give me. And it wasn't enough, so I leaned back into his mouth. My stitches began to throb, but I didn't care. I couldn't let him stop.

"My wife is so fucking greedy. Aren't you?"

"Yes. Please, Bones…"

"Please, what?"

"Please make me come."

"Not yet." He slipped a finger inside me, but then he didn't move.

"*Bones*," I snapped.

"Hmm?" He added another finger, but still didn't move them.

"I'm going to kill you."

He smacked my ass with his other hand while his fingers were still inside me and I clenched around him.

"Yeah, Duchess. Just like that."

He clapped my ass again.

"You know what I can't stop thinking about?" he asked as he finally—*finally*—began to thrust his fingers.

My moan was my answer.

"I can't stop thinking about fucking this ass."

He squeezed my cheek as he continued to tease me with his fingers.

"I can't stop thinking about you taking all of me, inch by inch. And while I'm buried in your ass, you've got a toy inside you. So fucking full you can't think straight. Would you like that?"

When I didn't answer, his fingers stopped. "Would you like that?"

"Yes, you bastard," I huffed. "I want that."

He slowly dragged his fingers out of me, so achingly slow, I choked on a sob from the pleasure.

I heard the sound of his zipper and then the crown of his shaft was teasing my swollen flesh.

"You want my cock inside you, Duchess?" he asked.

"Please."

He slid inside me and we both moaned.

Bones was big, and from this angle I wasn't sure I could take all of him, but he inched inside me until he was buried to the hilt.

His hands clasped my hips as he began to thrust, pounding into me until tears of pleasure slid down my cheeks and coated my lips.

When I began crying out my release, he pulled out quickly.

"No!" I yelled at the absence of him, my orgasm disappearing.

He flipped me over onto my back and while I stared up at him with languid eyes, he quickly removed his clothes. Bones palmed his erection and then guided it back inside me, keeping his gaze locked on mine.

Bones tugged the lace over my breasts to free them. He grasped a nipple between his fingers and tweaked it.

I arched my back, trying to get closer.

Oh, God.

"Eyes on me, Duchess," he growled. "We're coming together. I want to see you come."

He let go of my nipple and slid his hands beneath my ass and angled my body, his shaft hitting the perfect place inside me.

"Bones, I'm going to—"

"I know."

He ground into me and my orgasm raged through my body.

My veins filled with fire and I combusted around him, squeezing him tightly inside me.

"Fuck," he roared as he filled me with his seed.

We didn't speak for several seconds as our hearts and breaths calmed. Finally, Bones lifted himself off me, his tender expression morphing into one of concern.

"What?" I asked, looking up at him.

"You're crying." He cradled my cheeks and swiped the tears away from my eyes.

"Because it was so good."

His mouth met mine in a torrid kiss. "I didn't hurt you?" he asked when he pulled back.

"No."

"Did I scare you?"

I took a breath. "A little. But I kinda liked it."

"It wasn't too much?"

"I would've told you if it was too much."

"You sure about that?"

"Yes."

"Okay. I believe you." Bones nodded and then lifted himself off me. He gingerly slid out of me, causing me to tremor in his wake. "I'm a fan of the lingerie."

"You can thank the Old Ladies for it," I quipped.

"I'll send them each a fruit basket." He grabbed his T-shirt and handed it to me.

I stuck it between my legs and then climbed off the floor. "Are you still mad at me?"

He sighed. "I wasn't mad at you."

"I know you weren't mad at me."

"Then why did you ask if I was still mad at you?"

I shot him an amused look. "I wanted to know if *you* knew you weren't really mad at me."

He grabbed his boxer briefs and pulled them on. "I don't like that I can't protect you all the time. Even from your own body."

"I know," I said softly. "But we won't have much of a life together if you're always watching and waiting for me to collapse."

"I know that. On some level, I know that."

"But the other level, the primal, alpha male, *I must control everything* level, it doesn't register. Is that about right?" I asked.

"Hmm. Yeah, something in my lizard brain stops functioning." He shot me a boyish grin. "Be patient with me, yeah? While I work through this."

"I'll be patient," I said. "If you promise to punish me like that more often."

"You know what I love?"

"What?"

"That you're no longer shying away from your kinks. And that you feel safe enough to explore them with me."

"Hmm. I think that's what we call true intimacy."

Chapter 53

"You cannot keep me in the house bubble for a moment longer," I stated. "I have a billion-dollar company to run. I have to make an appearance in the office or everyone's going to think I'm running scared."

"Oliver has been calling you non-stop. You're getting a lot of shit done from the couch."

"But I can't keep taking meetings from the couch," I insisted. "It's been three days. Three days of wasting away, eating through the food the Old Ladies brought me, and then you carrying me up to bed."

"You like what I do to you after I carry you up there," he pointed out. "Several times, in fact."

I glared. "I've recovered. I need to get back to my life. I promised Doc I would do my witchy voodoo trick and find Cam the perfect dog. And a kitten for Lily. Besides, don't you have to meet up with Colt?"

"Yeah." He sighed. "I do."

"This'll be good for both of us." I handed him the car keys. "You can drive."

"Damn right, I'm driving."

We locked up the house and remotely set the alarm and then Bones was opening the car door for me.

He looked at me for a minute.

"What?" I asked.

He brushed my hairline. "I hate to even say it."

"Say it."

"I think you might have a scar."

"Then I have a scar." I shrugged. "Doc already warned me. I'm not worried about it."

"Hmm. Still. There's gonna be photographers at your mother's party, right?"

"Yes."

"You sure you want your stitches on display? It'll invite questions. Questions you probably don't want to answer about your health so soon after you taking over your father's company."

"My mother called you, didn't she?"

"She called me," he agreed with sigh.

"She wants me to cover it up."

"Yeah. For your own protection."

I sighed. "I'll make a hair appointment. Looks like I'm getting bangs."

After we stopped off at Spencer Pharmaceuticals so I could show my face, Bones drove us to the shelter and I walked the aisles until I found a white, wiry-haired terrier mix whose tail would not stop wagging.

"That one," I said immediately. "That's Cam's dog."

"If you say so," Bones said. "Now let's see if your superpowers work on kittens."

An hour later, I was sitting with the dog on my lap and Bones had a grey kitten with tan splotches on her back nestled in his shirt.

"Are we sure this is Lily's kitten?" Bones asked. "She's purring."

"I never would've believed it," I said with a laugh. "You want to keep her, don't you?"

The dog yipped when we started driving and Bones let out a hiss. "Cat got scared and clawed me. Fuck that. This is definitely Lily's kitten."

"Easy come, easy go," I said.

We drove to Darcy's. Boxer and Doc had temporarily moved in after discussing it and concluded that the kids had gone through enough upheaval. They needed to stay in their home for a short while until they could come to grips with their new reality.

"I don't know if I could do it," Bones said as he parked on the street out front of the house.

"Do what?" I asked as I unbuckled my seat belt and clipped the dog's leash to his collar.

"Do what Boxer and Doc are doing."

"What? Raising someone else's children?"

He shook his head. "Not that. I meant living in Darcy and Gray's house."

"Yeah. Well, we're here to make it better," I said.

When Bones made no move to get out of the car, I looked at him. He was staring at me with a tender expression across his brow.

"What?" I asked.

"Just thinking."

"About?"

"Your dad. I'm sorry I never got to meet him. But…"

"But?"

"I have a suspicion you got the best parts of him. You've got a good heart, Hayden. I'm glad I got to marry you."

Emotion filled my throat.

"Hold onto that dog, he's gonna get excited," he said gruffly.

Nodding, I waited for Bones to open my door. The moment it opened, the dog shot out with such force I nearly dropped the leash. Luckily, I was able to cling to it as we headed to the front door.

I rang the bell. Boxer answered the door. "Hey guys," he greeted, a cheery smile across his face. His gaze lowered. "That's a dog. You guys got a dog?"

The dog yelped in excitement, its tail still wagging furiously.

I looked at Bones and then back to Boxer. Before I could reply, Doc and Boxer's yellow lab showed up at the door. He immediately lowered his front legs and stuck his butt in the air, his tail flapping with enthusiasm.

"I feel like I've seen this before," Bones said to me.

I laughed. "You mind if we let him off leash?"

"Have at it," Boxer said, stepping back.

I unclipped the dog and he immediately ran after Monk into the house.

"Come on in," Boxer said, waving us forward.

We stepped into the house and followed him through the hallway to the kitchen. Lily and Cam were sitting at the table, their sandwiches in different states of completion.

Monk chased the white-haired mutt around the kitchen table until the mutt got to Cam and then he jumped up onto Cam's lap and immediately began eating the crust off his plate.

"Hey, that's mine," Cam said, trying to wrangle the food away from the dog.

"A little late, bud," Boxer said with a laugh. "He devoured that in two bites."

The mutt turned around and faced Cam. Cam stared at the dog for a moment and then the dog leaned forward and licked Cam's nose.

"I guess it's okay," Cam said. He looked away for a moment, but not before I saw him swipe at his eye.

"How are you doing, Lily Burger?" Bones asked.

The seven-year-old looked up at him and shrugged.

"Where's Doc?" I asked.

"Shower. She'll be down in a second," Boxer replied.

Lily pointed at Bones' leather cut. "Somethings moving under your shirt."

"Is it?" Bones asked, feigning innocence.

She nodded.

"It's your present," Bones said.

"Present? I get a present?" Lily asked, excitement replacing the somberness in her eyes.

A furry little head popped out from Bones' shirt collar and let out a soft meow.

"I get a kitty?!" Lily screamed.

Monk lifted his head from his water bowl. Tongue hanging out of his mouth, he went to investigate the furry creature barely bigger than Bones' fist.

Bones lifted the kitten out of his shirt and introduced them.

"You got her a kitten?" Boxer asked.

"Doc said it was okay," I hastened to say. "She said Lily's been wanting one."

"Yeah, she has been," Boxer said. "I just planned on surprising her with one myself. You've spoiled it."

Bones handed the kitten to Lily, who cuddled it close.

"Sorry, brother," Bones said. "I didn't know."

"Wait, if she gets a kitten, who's dog is this?" Cam asked. "Is he yours?"

I shook my head. "Nope. He's *yours*."

"Hold on," Boxer interjected. "No one said anything about another dog. Monk just ate a pair of Doc's panties, I don't need any more of that shi—"

"I don't see why that would upset you," Doc said as she strode into the kitchen, dressed in a pair of sweats and a sweatshirt.

"They were my favorite pair," Boxer muttered under his breath.

"It was Hayden's idea to get Cam a dog," Doc said. "But I thought it was a good one."

"A very good one," Cam said. "Please, Boxer? I'll take care of him. You know, when I can walk without crutches, I mean. I promise."

"And I'm taking my kitten to school," Lily announced. "She can hang out in my backpack."

"Lily Burger," Boxer began.

Bones stood up and ruffled Cam's hair. "Well, it looks like our work here is done. Ready to go, Duchess?"

"Fuck you," Boxer said. "You're not running out of here after dropping those bombs."

"Language," Doc stated.

"Please." Cam rolled his eyes. "We've heard worse."

"Hell yeah, we have," Lily said.

Doc groaned. "We're epically failing."

"Why don't you take Boxer out to the car so he can help you with kitty stuff," I said to Bones.

"Kitty stuff? What kitty stuff?" Boxer asked.

"We brought you all the things you'll need," I said. "Automatic feeder. Litter box. A bunch of toys."

Boxer sighed. "There's no way out of this, is there?"

"Nope," Lily said. She held the kitten out to Boxer. "How can you say no to this face?"

"The kitten's face or your face?" Boxer asked.

"Both."

"Give in, brother," Bones said. "It'll be easier for you."

∼

Bones' fingers trailed down my naked spine. I was sprawled across him, my cheek pressed to his inked chest. The candle flames bathed him in a warm glow, turning his skin the color of burnished honey.

I traced the tattoo along his pectoral. "Can I ask you something?"

"Sure."

When I didn't reply right away, he said, "This is the part where you ask your question."

"I'm trying to form my words."

"Did I render you speechless again. Like earlier?"

And by earlier, it was clear he was referring to when I had him in my mouth and he came down my throat. I shivered at the raw pleasure he'd taken from the act, but then had so generously reciprocated after he was done.

"Kind of hard to talk with your cock in my mouth," I replied dryly.

"God, I love it when you're crass."

"This conversation is not going the direction I want it to go." I sat up and dragged the sheet to conceal my breasts.

He raised his brows but otherwise said nothing.

"The night you came back covered in bruises…"

"Yeah?"

"I don't know how to ask what I want to ask without opening a can of worms and potentially getting someone in trouble."

"Who would you be getting in trouble?"

I closed my mouth.

"Can't answer the question if you don't ask me,

Duchess." He lifted his arm and placed it underneath his head as he waited for me to continue.

"If I ask this, this has to stay between us," I intoned. "I'm invoking the marriage card over the club card."

His expression hardened. "You can't play that card until I know what this is about."

I shook my head. "That's not how this works." I made a move to get out of bed, but Bones' hand shot out to gently clasp my wrist, forcing me to stop.

"All right," he said. "Marriage card trumps club card. Now tell me what's on your mind."

"Have you been fighting in an illegal ring? You've come to me several times with raw knuckles and I want to know the truth."

Bones' expression didn't change, nor did he let go of my wrist. "I'm guessing you're asking that question because you found out about the illegal fighting ring. How?"

I bit my lip.

"Marriage card," he reminded me.

"Charlie. Charlie told me about it."

"How did she find out about it?" he asked. Understanding swept across his face. "Savage. Savage told her."

"He went to her one night. She wouldn't let him in until he told her the truth."

"You didn't ask any of the Old Ladies about this, did you?"

I tugged my wrist from his grasp. "No. I didn't. I wanted to come to you first."

He sat up and swiped a hand across his face. "If I tell you the truth, you can't repeat it. You can't ask them about it, you can't say a word. Understand?"

"I understand."

He paused for a moment and then he said, "There are some brothers who aren't…content with the direction the club is going. We're adrenaline junkies. We like danger. Since the club has changed course, some brothers are pissed off. They're broke and bored, and went from dumping adrenaline and making tons of money to bookkeeping and standing around all day doing nothing. It's not working for some of us."

"Us? Are you bored?" When he didn't reply right away, I sighed. "You're bored."

"Bored is the wrong word," he said. "I'm restless."

"That's the same thing as bored."

"Maybe," he allowed.

"It's my fault," I stated. "I'm the reason you're bored."

"What the fuck? No. You're the least boring thing in my life." He placed his hand on my thigh. "But you gotta understand. To go from crazy shit with the club to a more stable existence, I'm still trying to find the rhythm of it. My entire life changed. A month ago, I was living in the clubhouse. Now I'm living with my wife. *My wife*."

"So, it *is* about me, a little bit anyway."

He ran a hand along his jaw, his whiskers rasping against the pad of his thumb. "I know what the club is about. I've been a Tarnished Angel for years. I know what that meant. I was committed, every step of the way, every direction. But you're you, and you live a different life. And for the first time in a long time, I'm thinking it's not such a bad idea to have a more stable existence."

"I forget sometimes that we've only known each other for a little while," I said quietly. "It feels like I've known you forever."

I covered his hand with mine.

"I know about the illegal ring, but no, I'm not fighting in it." He pinned me with a stare. "Something else is weighing on you."

"You're astute."

"I watch you all the time. I'm learning your expressions."

"Creepy," I teased.

He grinned. "What else is going on, Duchess?"

"It's about my stepfather."

"What about him?"

"I want him to pay for what he's done," I stated baldly.

"I know."

"I wish I had proof." I shook my head. "He's just going to get away with what he did to my father."

"Okay, let's say there was proof. You know how this would go? An exhausting trial with your entire family's dirty laundry on display—not to mention the company's dirty laundry on display. At best, he'd get convicted and probably strike a deal to go to some white-collar prison where he could play pool and watch TV. And it wouldn't feel like a prison at all for him. And in a few years on good behavior, he'd be out again, because that's the world we live in now. And you'd know he was still alive, even if day to day you could forget about him, you'd never forget that he was alive and your father is dead. Or, if you want real justice, I can give you real justice."

His offer hung in the air between us.

"And you won't lose sleep over it?" I asked.

"I wouldn't regret it for a minute."

"Do you have any regrets at all?"

"What's the point of regrets, Duchess? Can you change the past? No. All you can do is move forward."

"I wish I didn't know," I murmured. "I wish I didn't know what he did to my father. Because that's not something I'll ever be able to rectify, even if Arnold pays for what he's done."

Bones pulled me into his arms, and I fell against his chest. I buried my head into the crook of his neck.

There wasn't anything Bones wouldn't do for me. The man would kill for me. He'd stain his soul in the name of justice.

Arnold's death wouldn't bring my father back. It wouldn't replace the last three years. But maybe it would bring me peace. And that had to be enough.

Chapter 54

My phone trumpeted on the nightstand, startling me out of a sound sleep.

"What the fuck," Bones muttered. His face was pressed into the pillow. "Who the hell is calling so early?"

I glanced at the alarm clock. "It's just past eight, it's hardly early."

"It's early when you go to bed at 2 AM," he pointed out.

I grabbed the phone and quickly silenced it, but not before glancing at the screen. "It's my mother." I set the phone aside and snuggled back down into bed. "I'll call her in a bit."

Bones threw an arm across my waist and crushed me to him.

My phone began to ring again.

"It must be important," I said.

"Important like what flower arrangements you want at the party she's throwing for us, or important like which jewels should she get out of the vault important?"

"Be nice," I chastised. "The fact that my mother adores you after such a short time speaks volumes."

With a sigh, Bones removed his arm from across my body so I could rise. I picked up my phone and pressed a button before putting it to my ear. "Good morning."

"Did I wake you?" Mom asked.

"Yes, but it's okay," I assured her. "And peonies are fine."

"Peonies are fine for what?"

"The party flower bouquets." I shot Bones a smirk. "That's why you're calling, isn't it?"

"Hayden," Mom said, her tone low. "Your stepfather's body was found this morning. Arnold is dead. They found him in a seedy motel about forty-five minutes away. There was a suicide note."

All good humor fled, and it felt like someone trekked a cold finger down my spine. "A suicide note?"

"Yes." Mom's voice sounded strained. When I didn't say anything, Mom prodded, "Hayden."

"I'm still here," I croaked. "How are you—are you okay?"

She sighed. "I guess I have to be. I was on my way out this morning to have a breakfast meeting with my divorce attorney. I should call him and... None of this feels real, Hayden. Nothing's felt real since I found out the truth about him. I think I'm in shock."

"Yeah, I've been feeling that way myself," I admitted. "Let me throw some clothes on and I'll come over."

"You don't have to do that."

"Mom."

"All right. I appreciate it, Hayden."

"See you in a bit."

I hung up with her and turned to Bones. "Something you want to share with me?"

"You start," Bones stated. "A suicide note?"

I frowned. "Arnold's body was found in a motel with a suicide note. And since you were here with me last night…"

"Shower. Now." He flung off the covers and strode to the bathroom. He closed the door and I spent a moment staring at my phone, wondering what the hell was going on.

I got up to join Bones and once I was in the shower, he placed his hands on my shoulders and turned us so that the hot spray washed over me.

"We just had this conversation last night. How did this happen so quickly?" I asked.

"It wasn't the club," Bones announced.

"You sure?"

"Yes. My brothers knew I was going to talk to you about this. It was mine to carry out. We were supposed to find him and I was supposed to…"

"Do what you were going to do." I nibbled my lip. "So, this is the end of it, then, isn't it? He took care of it for us?"

"Yeah. Close your eyes for me."

I closed my eyes. Lavender suddenly wafted through the shower and a moment later, Bones' hands were on my head. I let him wash my hair and sank into his touch, breathing in the soothing aroma. He gently guided me underneath the spray and then I took over rinsing my hair.

He got out first and was dressed by the time I was coming into the bedroom wrapped in a towel.

"I gotta make a call," he said.

"Who are you calling?" I asked.

"Colt. To let him know about the situation."

"Oh, right." I nodded. "I'll meet you downstairs?"

He walked up to me and grasped the back of my neck and kissed me. "Take your time."

I was not in the mood to go through the whole rigamarole of an outfit, so I went with a pair of leggings and a sweater and my comfortable boots that felt like slippers. After blow drying my hair and swiping on mascara and lip gloss, I was ready to go.

Bones was sitting on the couch with a cup of coffee when I came downstairs.

"You had time to make coffee," I stated. "That means I took a long time."

"Don't worry about it, Duchess." He stood up and finished off the rest of his coffee before setting the empty mug down on the coffee table.

"How was the call with Colt?"

"Fine. Ready?"

"Yeah." I grabbed my coat from the closet. He picked up the ring of car keys and twirled them around his finger.

A few minutes of silence into the ride, Bones said, "Talk to me."

"About what?"

"How you're feeling."

"I'm sick to death of talking about my feelings," I admitted.

"That's fine. We don't have to talk about that. We can talk about something else."

"Like what? All the crazy going on in my life?"

He shot me a look. "What are you and Charlie going to do about this charity you guys want to start?"

I rubbed my brow. "I don't know. My plate just got really full. And I don't want to juggle two big things and fail at both of them. I need to focus on one thing—and that thing has to be Spencer Pharmaceuticals."

"Yeah, but what do *you* want to do?"

I looked at him. "What do you mean?"

"What do you mean *what do I mean*? Do you really want a controlling seat on the board of your father's company? Or do you want to do this thing with Charlie?"

"I don't know, Bones."

The rest of the drive was quiet as I was lost in thought.

Stanton answered the door and in a brief show of outwardly affection, he embraced me. "I'm glad you're here."

"How is she?" I asked.

"She's in the sitting room," Stanton said.

I arched a brow. "You didn't answer my question."

"She's…your mother," he said, pitching his voice lower.

"So she's completely fallen apart?" I asked.

He shook his head. "On the contrary, she's holding it together. Go in and see her. I'm getting the tea."

"Can I change my order from tea to a coffee?" Bones asked.

Stanton stared at Bones.

Bones stared at Stanton.

"Is espresso satisfactory?" Stanton finally said.

"Make it a double, bring a lot of sugar, and I'll suck it down. Please."

"Please? We're on our way to making you a gentleman."

"Don't hold your breath," Bones remarked.

I swore I saw Stanton's stoic mouth flicker with a smile.

As Stanton headed off to the kitchen, Bones and I went to the sitting room. Mom was standing with her back to the door, staring at a massive oil painting of my father. When Arnold and my mother had gotten married, it had suddenly disappeared. No doubt Arnold hadn't liked my father staring down at him. But now it was in its rightful place over the mantle.

"Mom," I voiced.

"You're here." She turned slowly, her brows rising as she looked at Bones. "And so are you."

"You didn't think he'd come?" I asked.

Mom shook her head. "No, it wasn't that. It was—sorry, Royce. I forgot for a moment that I had a son-in-law."

"Normally, I'd be offended that I was so forgettable, but under the circumstances, I understand. How are you holding up, Marilyn?"

"Better now that you're both here." She waved us to the couch and then she took the high-backed chair on the other side of the fireplace. "I was on my way out to have a breakfast meeting with my divorce attorney when the police showed up on my doorstep to tell me about your stepfather. I admit I didn't hear much after they said they'd found a suicide note. It's going to be horrible when the reporters start calling."

"Do you have a statement prepared?" I asked.

Mom sighed. "There's what I want to say versus what I'll *have* to say. I'll remain vague and say I wish for privacy to be respected and for their understanding during this difficult time."

"Funeral?" I asked.

"Quiet and small," she said. "They'll understand that."

Stanton entered the sitting room carrying a heavy silver tea tray. He set it down and immediately began serving, starting with my mother.

"Dina and Patrick will be there, of course. Charlie. The two of you. And me."

"Have you told Dina and Patrick the truth?" I asked.

"Yes. I called them after I called you," Mom said.

"They wanted to come over, but I asked them to wait until this afternoon. I wanted time with you. Alone."

Stanton quietly retreated from the room.

Her cheeks suddenly flushed with anger. "Your stepfather disgraced himself in front of the board. And then for him to disappear for days without a phone call, only for him to take his own life in a seedy motel. It's a scandal and I should cancel the party. A party on the heels of Arnold's betrayal and death? It would send the wrong message."

"You're right," I said. "It's bad form."

"Hmm." Mom's gaze slid to Bones. "What do you think I should do, Royce?"

"Honestly?"

"Honestly."

"It's a shit situation any way you look at it, so I think you should say *fuck it* and show your face. I think you should tell the reporters that you're thrilled your daughter has taken her rightful place in the company and that you want to celebrate her marriage. And when they ask about Arnold, you tell them the truth; it's a tragedy. But no one knows that he went after Hayden, so you put on a brave face and let them know the Spencer family will survive, and the way to do that is to move forward."

My mother's expression softened. "You really are a wonderful son-in-law."

"Yes, you're very lucky," Bones said with a wink, causing my mother to laugh.

She pressed a hand to her chest. "Oh, that felt good."

"You should laugh more often," Bones said gently.

Stanton entered the sitting room and stated, "There's a phone call for you, Mrs. Spencer. A reporter from the *Waco Sun* is on the line. Should I tell them you're unavailable?"

"No, Stanton." Mom rose and lifted her chin. "I'll handle it."

Chapter 55

I SAT UP SUDDENLY, my eyes flipping open in the darkness.

"Duchess?" came Bones' sleepy voice. "You okay? You have a bad dream?"

I fumbled with the lamp on the nightstand until the light came on.

"Jesus, warn a guy," Bones grumbled as he threw an arm over his eyes.

I jostled his shoulder until he was forced to look at me. "What?"

"I don't think Arnold's death was a suicide," I blurted out. When Bones didn't say anything, I rushed on. "He was incommunicado for days. No one saw him or heard from him. And then suddenly, he's found dead in a seedy motel room with a suicide note? My stepfather is rich. He would've licked his wounds at a five-star hotel. You only go to a motel off the highway if you don't want to be found."

Bones still hadn't reacted.

"You think I'm crazy," I accused. "You think I'm overreacting."

His hand crept over to my leg and he gripped my thigh. "I don't think you're crazy or overreacting."

"Then why aren't you—Oh my God, you already had the same idea, didn't you?"

"Yes."

"Why didn't you tell me?"

"Because I wasn't going to give you something more to worry about. I'm looking into it."

"What do you mean you're looking into it?"

"I mean, the club has some connections we're using to find out the whole picture. Because I agree. Your stepfather's disappearance was because he was afraid. He said something to you in the board room, remember? *Do you have any idea what you've done? They're going to come after*—And then I cut him off. I think whoever *they* were caught up with him."

"Is my life still in danger?" I asked.

"I'm not sure, Duchess. But I'm taking all the precautions necessary. Why do you think I have my boys guarding your house? Why do you think I refuse to let you go anywhere without me?"

"My own private security," I murmured. "What the hell did my stepfather get into?"

"I'm not sure yet. But we'll find out."

I let him pull me into his arms and I buried my head against his chest. A dark sense of foreboding settled in my body. I eventually fell back asleep, but my dreams were murky and unsettling.

∽

The news of my stepfather's death hit the tabloids. And while I was having breakfast with Bones, Oliver called to tell me the stock price of the company had plummeted. I had made a call to Spencer Pharmaceuticals' general counsel a few days prior and had confirmed that I could legally buy back as many shares as I wanted. We'd expected the shares would tank. So upon hearing the news from Oliver, I picked up my phone and immediately contacted my private attorney, James, and instructed him to purchase all the shares that hit the market.

I set my phone aside and picked up my fork and dug into my omelet. When I was halfway finished, I looked up to find Bones watching me.

"What?"

"Nothing. I'm just impressed. All that accomplished before 9 AM."

I grinned. "Maybe I am cut out for this business."

"Maybe you are," he agreed.

The flower deliveries started an hour later. The dining room table was soon covered, and eventually there was no more room. My housekeeper Helen began putting them on the kitchen table.

Mom called with the time and place of the funeral. We'd bury my stepfather a day before the wedding celebration.

"How'd she sound?" Bones asked.

"Resolved," I said with a sigh. "What are we going to do with all these flowers?"

"No idea."

"Ah, I've got an idea. Let's donate them to the hospital. Fresh flower bouquets always bring a smile."

"Great idea." Bones pulled out his cell.

"What are you doing?"

"Texting the prospects to get a van and get over here. They'll take care of it."

"Then what are we going to do the rest of the afternoon?" I asked.

He raised a brow.

I rolled my eyes. "Is that all you think about?"

"Yes."

He strode toward me. I put a hand up to stop him, but my hand settled on his chest and my fingers curled into his shirt of their own volition.

Bones slid his thumb underneath my eye. "You didn't sleep well."

I shook my head.

"You're still worried about it, aren't you?"

"It's all I'm thinking about," I admitted.

"You're not alone in this, Duchess. Remember that. I'm here."

"Right. You're here. But what if you're in danger now too, because of me?"

"Then I'm in danger." He shrugged. "I'm used to danger. But now I have more than just my club to protect. So, take a deep breath and know that I'm here with you."

My brow furrowed. "You know what would take my mind off this?"

"Sex?"

"Bones," I warned.

"What would take your mind off this?"

I grinned. "I'll grab the keys and show you."

Chapter 56

"Thanks for that," I said, tilting my face up to Bones.

He grasped the back of my neck and kissed me soundly. "You don't have to thank me." He made a face. "Don't take this the wrong way, but you smell like horse shit."

I sniggered. "You don't smell much better."

He removed his leather cut and hung it up in the front closet before sitting on the stairs to take off his boots. "Guess that means we gotta shower."

"Guess it does," I agreed.

"Seriously, though, Duchess," his gaze found mine, "thanks for sharing that with me."

"You're welcome," I murmured.

I'd taken Bones to the stable where Dad and I had ridden together. I hadn't been there since he'd died, but today, with all the worries and concerns swirling in my head, it was the only place I could think of running to.

Bones and I hadn't actually ridden any of the horses, but we'd spent time brushing and feeding them.

"Next time, I'll get up on a stallion," I stated.

"Trading one stallion for another?" he quipped.

"The horse would give me less trouble." I flashed a grin.

"Don't tell Stanton you took me to the stables. He's going think I'll want to take tennis lessons soon."

"Not tennis," I said. "But what do you think of golf?"

"No way in hell."

"You can drink scotch and smoke cigars."

"And become an unofficial member of the Rat Pack."

"You know about the Rat Pack?" I asked in surprise.

"There was a Rat Pack movie marathon on one of those classic movie channels. Frank Sinatra is one dapper mother fucker." He grinned.

"Hmm. You're pretty dapper too. Come on, let's shower off the stables."

As we headed up the stairs, my phone rang. I frowned. "I have to take this."

"Who is it?"

"My private attorney," I said.

Bones nodded.

"James," I greeted. "How's everything going?"

"Fantastic," he said. "I've been doing exactly as you instructed. I've been buying up shares of the company all morning. I've gotta say, you really put your money where your mouth is. Limit prices twenty-five percent over ask was genius. Every share is coming straight back to you. In fact, selling has slowed down and the price is beginning to stabilize. I've seen some interesting things in the past but overpaying to buy back more of the company even though they're not preferred shares is a new one. Anyway, congratulations, you now own another six percent of Spencer Pharmaceuticals."

My stepfather's funeral was quiet. Unfortunately, a reporter had discovered the location. Bones confronted him, and the reporter snapped a few pictures and then jumped into a waiting car and left.

By the night of my mother's party, my mood was in the toilet, and I had no desire to put on a pretty dress and smile.

"We should've canceled the party," I said to Bones as I looked out the window of the limousine.

He took my hand and laced his fingers through mine. "But then you wouldn't have gotten to see me in my tux again. You look gorgeous, by the way."

"Thank you," I murmured.

"I wish I could make all of the horrible things that have happened the past few weeks go away for you, Duchess." Bones' gaze met mine. "But I can't. All I can do is be here for you."

He brought my hand to his lips and kissed the back of it.

The limousine pulled up to the entrance of The Danbury Hotel.

"You ready, Duchess?" Bones asked.

"Yeah."

He got out first and beat the driver around to my side and opened the door for me. He held out his hand to me and I took it.

His palm went to my waist as he guided me up into the hotel. Security stood at the hotel doors. Anyone not on the guest list wasn't getting in.

The Danbury Hotel was smaller than The Rex by orders of magnitude, but I appreciated my mother's attention to the warmth of the space. She was an immaculate party planner and moreover, she enjoyed doing it.

The intimate ballroom was all golden light and cream

tablecloths. My mother held a glass of champagne and stood with Dina and Patrick.

Charlie was nowhere to be seen, but I knew she'd turn up eventually. A server passed by with a tray of salmon puffs. I was starving and I took one and popped it into my mouth.

"You almost lost a finger eating that thing so fast," Bones said with a laugh.

"Rude."

He draped an arm around my bare shoulder and pulled me into his side. "Let's say hi to your mom, and then I need to find the bar."

In fact, Bones didn't need to find the bar, because a server approached him and took his drink order and brought it to him while we were talking.

He kept stealing glances at me, his hand tightening at my waist as he stood next to me.

"What?" I whispered.

"Nothing."

"Not nothing. You keep looking at me like…"

"Like?" He raised his brows.

"Like you either want to get me into a coat closet or you're worried about me."

"Your mother would skin me alive if I disappeared with you for a while in a coat closet." He took a sip of his drink. "How are you feeling? Physically, I mean."

"Ah, so you *are* worried about me," I said.

My mother and godparents had left us to speak to other friends, leaving me and Bones to have this conversation in the middle of ballroom.

"You barely ate all day. The last several days have been really stressful. I'm just concerned about you."

"You mean you're waiting for me to have one of my episodes."

"Yeah, I am," he admitted. "Sue me."

"Bones…"

"I've tried not to smother you or hover," he stated. "But, Jesus, Duchess. A lot of shit has gone down in the last two weeks. I just want to make sure you're okay."

"Well, I'm not okay!" My voice had risen, and unfortunately that had drawn a few curious eyes. I flashed a socialite smile at them, hoping they couldn't see my brittle expression.

I grasped Bones' hand and dragged him to the corner of the ballroom in hopes for some measure of privacy.

"You promised," I accused.

"Promised what?"

"That you wouldn't treat me differently because of my condition."

"Treat you—for fuck's sake, Duchess. I've held back what I've really wanted to say."

"Well, say it now," I commanded.

"Here?"

"You brought this up."

"Fine, you want the truth? The truth is, I think you took on too much and for someone who has a stress triggered condition, I think it's a bad idea."

"I'm not letting my condition stop me from doing what needs to be done," I said, lifting my chin.

"So what happens? Huh? You go to the office one day and you pass out from stress? And then you're out of commission for days? What then?"

"I'll deal with it."

Bones sighed and dropped his hand. He shoved his fists into his pockets. "We shouldn't be having this talk here."

"No, we shouldn't," I agreed.

"But we need to have this conversation," he insisted.

"I know." A pit of anxiety settled in my stomach. "I need to use the ladies' room."

"I'll go with you. I'll wait outside."

"No, Bones," I protested. "I need just a few minutes to myself. Please."

He clenched his jaw but reluctantly nodded.

I kissed his cheek, enjoying the slight five o'clock shadow along his skin. I slipped out of the ballroom and wandered through the lobby. I asked the front desk agent to point the direction of the restroom.

As I wandered down the hallway, my mind churned over everything Bones had said. I'd never once been angry at myself for my condition. It was what it was. But for the first time since my episodes began to occur, I resented the hell out them. I hated that my body wouldn't cooperate. I hated that I was weaker than everyone else. I watched what I ate, I didn't drink alcohol or caffeine. I limited my stress —what I could control, anyway, and still my body failed me.

Was having a baby even a good idea? Not only would it put stress onto my body—my weak, insufficient body—but would Bones ever trust my capability as a mother? He didn't want to leave me alone even now, afraid that I might have an episode and faint.

Will he ever trust me with our child?

The restroom was empty, and I plunked down onto the black couch as my thoughts continued to swirl out of control.

Maybe I was selfish. For wanting to have a baby with Bones. For wanting to take on this role in my father's company. But I meant what I'd said. I was tired of sitting on the sidelines, watching my life pass me by. I'd already lost too much time to grief.

It's time to live.

With a sigh, I stood up and went to the sink. I was rummaging through my clutch for my lipstick when I heard the restroom door open behind me.

I turned to smile at the newcomer.

My face froze when I saw a pistol pointed directly at my head.

In a flash, time stopped and I noticed so many things about him.

He was tall, with short, cropped blond hair. His eyes were blue like winter's ice—and his cheekbones were sharp and angular. He wore a cater waiter's uniform.

This man wasn't at all like the men who'd tried to kill me before. This one was calculated and calm.

Determined.

Professional.

All the thoughts that had been swirling in my mind suddenly evaporated.

I stared down the barrel of his gun, wishing that I hadn't left Bones. Wishing that I'd been able to say all that I wanted to say to him. But I'd need a lifetime with him for that. And mine was about to be truncated.

The door to the restroom opened again, this time hitting the man in the back as Charlie tried to enter.

His grip slipped and he pulled the trigger.

A bright flash erupted from his hand and my skull felt like someone hit me with a sandbag. I didn't hear a thing, and my knees went out from under me.

I fell to the ground.

Regret.

I thought it in a flash of time.

Such a stupid, useless emotion.

And then the world winked out.

Chapter 57

My eyelids fluttered, as if they were attempting to open. They were heavy and steadfast against me, but somewhere in the depths of my soul, I willed them to do as I bid.

I gazed at a stark white, texture-free ceiling that I didn't recognize.

Anxiety at not knowing where I was assaulted me, causing my heartbeat to skyrocket.

The machine at my bedside began to beep incessantly.

An alarm went off.

Heavy leather boots hit the floor and suddenly Bones was there—at my bedside.

"*Hayden*," he whispered.

His eyes were bloodshot, and though he had the healthy sprout of a beard, his skin was wan. Dark hair fell across his forehead. He didn't bother pushing it away.

I moved my tongue in my mouth, and slowly the feeling began to return to my face.

"You look like hell," I croaked.

The plaster of his face finally gave way and he smiled. A smile so bright it was nearly blinding.

Questions filtered through my wool-stuffed head, getting trapped as they attempted to rise to the surface.

"Water?" I asked.

He walked slowly around the bed to the nightstand and poured water from a pitcher into a plastic cup with a straw. He brought it to my lips and I greedily sucked down the cool liquid.

It tasted stale and overly chlorinated, and yet it was the best thing I'd ever tasted.

When my thirst was quenched, I leaned back and stared at him.

"Nurse is on her way," he stated. "You set off the alarm. She'll be here in a minute."

I blinked but said nothing.

"Where the fuck is she?" He grimaced and ran a hand through his dark hair and then he marched to the door. He almost yanked it off its hinges in his haste.

I stared at the ceiling and waited for him to return.

My mind played over the last thing I remembered. The gunman cornering me in the bathroom. Charlie opening the door and hitting him by accident. The gun going off—

And then nothing.

Charlie.

I struggled to sit up as I looked around for my phone. Panic swelled in my chest. I needed to know what had happened to Charlie.

The door to the hospital room opened and Bones returned with a blonde, middle-aged nurse. "Easy, sugar," she crooned.

"Where's Charlie?" I asked, my pulse spiking, causing the alarm to go off again.

"With Walker," Bones replied. "She's been by your bedside the last four days—Walker finally convinced her to leave the hospital and go home and get a few hours of sleep in her own bed. She's okay."

I took a deep breath.

The kind nurse gently placed her hand on my shoulder and urged me to lean back. She checked the monitors, tapped out some notes on her device, and then said, "Your anxiety is off the charts and I need you to try to relax. How's your pain?"

"Pain?" My body wasn't registering pain. "I don't feel much."

"Good. If you start to feel pain, you press the call button. I've paged the doctor to let him know you're awake. He should be here soon."

"Thanks, Janet." Bones took my hand and laced his fingers through mine.

Janet left and I looked at Bones.

"Four days?" I asked softly. "I've been out of it for four days?"

"No, Duchess. You've been out for a whole week. We didn't know if…"

"If what?"

"If you were going to wake up." His eyes filled with anguish. "Your mother's been here constantly. They brought in a cot for her to sleep on, and she's stayed by your bed. Charlie and I slept in the chairs. The Old Ladies and brothers have stopped by. Oliver, too."

"Oliver," I murmured. "A week? Really?"

He nodded.

"Tell me what happened," I insisted.

"You were shot," he said, his hand tightening. "The fact that you're alive is a miracle. The bullet didn't hit dead-on. The angle…it came in shallow and slid underneath your skin instead of punching through. It zipped around underneath your scalp and then shot out the side of your head. If Charlie hadn't opened the door when she did…"

"And that's why I was unconscious for a week."

"No, you were unconscious for a week because you hit the floor so hard your brain swelled. They put you in a medically induced coma to give your brain a chance to heal and relieve the pressure. You were intubated. They removed the tube this morning and you breathed on your own just fine." He paused for a moment. "After that, they began to wean you off the drugs so you could wake up."

I sat with the information for a moment. It felt like it had happened to someone else.

"And Charlie…she's okay?" I frowned. "He didn't go after her?"

"No. She was focused on you, and he used the chance to get away."

"He got away?" I whispered, fear striking a heavy chord in my chest.

The door to the hospital room opened and a doctor in a white coat entered.

"Mrs. Dalton," he greeted with a wide smile. "I'm glad to see you're awake. I'm Dr. McCullough. I'm going to ask you a few questions, and while I do, I'm going to need to check your pupillary response. A little light coming on. Open your eyes for me…"

Mrs. Dalton. Right. I'm married.

I wanted to shout at the doctor to leave. I didn't care about anything else except getting an answer from Bones about the man who'd shot me in the head.

Bones squeezed my fingers in support and then he let go. He moved back to give the doctor room.

"You were lucky," Dr. McCullough said after he finished my exam. "No memory loss that I can tell. No permanent damage. You just need time to heal and recover. And may I suggest counseling. You've been through a lot."

"When can she be discharged?" Bones asked.

"In a few days," the doctor said. "I want to monitor her a bit longer. Just to be safe."

Safe. I wasn't safe. None of us were safe. There was a gunman still out there who hadn't finished the job. No doubt he was waiting for the perfect time to come back and finish it. And kill anyone who stood in his way.

Dr. McCullough left the room and the door closed behind him.

"Bones," I said. "The gunman? He's still out there?"

"I need you to stay calm," he said. "I need to tell you some things, but not at the risk to your health. You have to promise me you'll breathe and keep your heart rate low."

"Not knowing is causing my heart rate to spike," I stated. "So please. Just out with it."

Bones reached into his pocket and pulled out his cell phone. He turned it off and then took it into the small bathroom in my hospital room. Bones turned the sink on and left it running, and then he shut the bathroom door and came back to my bedside.

"My brothers have been on guard duty outside your room since you were brought to the hospital," Bones said. "You haven't been alone. But we found out who he is…"

I frowned. "You found him?"

"Not me, personally. I haven't left your side. Until I knew you were going to wake up, I couldn't leave you. The club…outsourced it."

I closed my eyes as my head swam. "You outsourced *what*, exactly?"

Bones sighed. "We got the security tapes from the hotel. And with the help of several…acquaintances, we found out who he is and grabbed him. It wasn't long before he gave us the name of the man who hired him. Pyotr Novikov."

"Russian?"

"Yes. We didn't have the full picture. Novikov was behind all of it, including your father's death."

I stared at him. "None of this makes any sense."

"It will. Novikov found Arnold several years ago and made a deal with him. Novikov was going to use Arnold to get rid of your father and take over Spencer Pharmaceuticals. The plan was to get control of the board and tank the company so Novikov could buy up shares for pennies on the dollar. After he'd acquired the shares, he was going to have Arnold begin to sell off the company patents one by one to fund the company again and cook the books. That kind of cash inflow would send the stock price to the moon. Then Novikov would sell everything he'd bought and make out like a bandit with clean money. It was in the works—but our marriage put a stop to it."

"It screwed Arnold completely," I murmured. "But why would Novikov still come after me if the plan was already ruined?"

"Because instead of letting the share price fall, you started buying up stock over market value. While you and I were at breakfast, Novikov's plan was crumbling. A plan that had been in the works for years. Tens of millions of dollars vaporized, for him at least."

Dread filled my stomach. "And Novikov and his hitman are still alive?"

"For now."

I frowned. "What does that mean?"

"It means they're being held somewhere that no one

will ever find. It means I'll deal with them." He gripped my hand. "I'll end this for you, without mercy. No one will ever know what was done."

"Will you tell me? How you plan on…handling this?"

"Duchess…" His eyes softened. "You said you loved both Royce and Bones. But if you find out what Bones is truly capable of, you might not be able to lie to yourself anymore. You think you want to know that side of me, but be careful what you wish for." His look was solemn. "I'll leave it up to you. If you really want to know, I'll tell you."

I knew he was capable of violence. I knew the lengths he'd go through to ensure I never had to look over my shoulder again. But he was offering me the truth, if I was strong enough to handle it.

"Would you think I was weak if I said I didn't want to know?" I asked softly.

"No. I wouldn't think you were weak."

"You'll have blood on your hands. I'll know that much. That's enough for me. I don't need details."

"All right." He squeezed my fingers. "There's just one thing…"

"What is it?" I asked.

"Novikov is Bratva."

My eyes widened. "Bratva? You mean Russian mafia?"

"Yes."

"But if you kill him, won't that just mean more violence?" I asked. "Won't they come for you? For me? And everything we love?"

"No. Pyotr Novikov is the younger brother of Alexei Novikov. Pyotr was planning a coup to supplant his older brother. Everything he was doing was part of that plan. It was a power move to gain the funds to hire mercenaries to kill his own brother and prove he could pay his allies. Alexei doesn't want it known by his men or his enemies that his own brother was planning to kill him. We have an agreement with him now; we take out Pyotr and there will be no retribution from Alexei, even though we're technically engaging directly with Bratva."

I frowned. "And how did you get Alexei to agree to that? It's his brother, and things like that are usually dealt with internally, aren't they?"

"Ramsey Buchanan," he said quietly. "Ramsey has ties to a very powerful Russian who has sway despite living in Europe. Ramsey's…*friend* parlayed on our behalf."

I swallowed. "When are you going to…"

"When you're safely home. When I can stand to leave you for longer than five minutes."

"Will you ever let me out of your sight again?" I asked with a quivering smile.

"Doubtful," he said, his tone gruff. "It's my fault this happened."

"What? No. No, it's not."

"If I hadn't left you alone, he wouldn't have tried anything."

"How did he get into the hotel?" I asked. "There was security."

"He went to the worker's entrance, dressed as a cater waiter."

"He was determined to find me," I said. "Where there's a will, there's a way."

"I could've lost you."

"But you didn't," I said gently. "And you were by my bedside when I woke up."

"I didn't leave the hospital for the first three days," he admitted. "They gave me a pair of scrubs to change into because of…"

"Because of…oh, the blood. My blood."

"There was a shit ton of blood," he mumbled. "You're

not allowed to scare me like that ever again. I can take a lot of shit, but I can't take that again. I love you, Hayden."

I looked at the man I loved. The man who'd kill for me to ensure I was safe. Tears threatened to spill down my cheeks.

"Then hold me, and never let me go."

Epilogue

BONES

I sat in the private office at Chaos with four powerful men.

Colt Weston drank rye.

Elijah Padgett drank Irish whiskey.

Ramsey Buchanan drank SINNERS single malt scotch.

Sasha Petrovich drank *Krasnyy*, his own personal brand of vodka.

Chaos was Elijah's wine bar, and the private office had been built into a military-grade faraday cage where no electronics were allowed. I didn't know what kind of deals Elijah had made from this room, and I didn't ask, but nothing that was said here could ever be recorded.

The Tarnished Angels handled security for his wine bar and our relationship was professional.

Elijah kept shooting glares at Sasha Petrovich, who calmly sipped his vodka.

Sasha turned his head, and in a Russian accent said, "I

might be blind in one eye, but I could still be out of my chair and snap your neck before you knew what was happening."

"I'd like to see you try," Elijah stated in a thick Irish brogue. "And with a mouth like that, you're lucky that Ramsey calls you a friend."

"Before the fists fly," Colt drawled. "Maybe we can get down to business."

"I'll give you the location of the warehouse where the Russians are being held," Elijah said. "But you and your club clean up the mess. And if there's any blowback, I'm not involved."

"Fine," Colt said.

"I'll call Alexei personally when the deed is done," Sasha remarked. "And that should close out the matter."

"There's just one thing," I said, looking at Colt. "The club isn't involved in this."

"We're involved," Colt said. "Because Pyotr came after your woman."

"Brother, the club just went legit. There's no way in hell I'm jeopardizing your families for this. I'll take care of it on my own."

"Like hell you will," Colt stated.

"He doesn't have to do this alone. I'll go with him," Ramsey interjected.

I looked at him. "Why would you do that? Get yourself involved in something that has nothing to do with you?"

"I have my reasons," Ramsey said. "And I'll explain them to you after it's done, if you let me."

I looked at Elijah. "Works for me. I'll have the location now."

Elijah rattled off the address. "Everything you asked for is there."

Ramsey and I both stood and Sasha handed me a set

of keys. "There's an unmarked black Sedan in the back. It's bulletproof, not that I expect you'll need it, but you can never be too careful."

"Thanks," I said, turning away from the scarred man. Even in the dim light of the room, I could see that half his face had been badly burned.

I looked at Ramsey. "It's time."

Ramsey threw back the rest of his scotch and nodded.

We stepped out into the night. Those awake at this hour were either looking for trouble, or trouble was looking for them.

Nothing good happens in the night.

I climbed into the driver's side and Ramsey got in on the other. He shut the door and then latched his seatbelt.

"You sure you want to do this?" I asked.

"I'm sure."

"And you won't tell me why you're doing this until after?"

"No."

"All right, then."

I put the car into gear and we drove off. Adrenaline hummed in my veins and my attention narrowed. Anticipation coursed through me as I thought of the two men waiting for my retribution.

Forty-five minutes later, we pulled up to a warehouse surrounded by barbed wire. Several pieces of specialty machinery sat quietly in the dirt. I waited for Ramsey to get out and open the gate for me to drive through. He closed the latch behind me and then he jumped into the passenger side again. We drove around to the back and parked.

Even though we were far enough away from the city that there was hardly any light pollution, and we were in the middle of nowhere along a stretch of highway, there was no use drawing attention to what we were doing.

The back door was unlocked and I flipped the light on as we walked inside. Harsh fluorescent lighting illuminated the entire space—a giant square cement room without any windows. There were unmarked crates stacked along the wall, along with a few oak barrels—liquor, no doubt. Guns, maybe.

There were two men in the center of the warehouse. Their wrists were cinched tightly with ropes that had been thrown over the rafters in the ceiling and pulled tight so that both men's feet barely touched the ground. They were clearly exhausted, and there was no possible way they could escape.

Pyotr Novikov lifted his head. He glared at me and spewed angry Russian words.

"He called you a cock sucking son of a whore," Ramsey translated.

"You speak Russian?" I asked in surprise.

"A bit," Ramsey said.

I walked up to Pyotr and slapped his cheek, hard enough to turn his head.

"You slapped him?" Ramsey asked in surprise. "Like a man slaps a woman?"

"Can't have him unconscious for what I'm about to do to him."

My grin was feral.

The other man made a noise, turning my attention. "I haven't forgotten about you, Gregor Kuzmin."

I walked to the oak barrels and took off my leather cut, and then I looked around for the supplies Elijah had left for me. I found them next to an empty crate with the lid off and plastic lining the bottom.

Next to the crate, there was a pile of folded blue tarps, a hammer, a hand saw and a blow torch.

I picked up the hammer and looked at Ramsey. "Ready to learn how I got the name *Bones*?"

∽

By the time the sun came up, the screams of the dead men had finally begun to fade from my ears. We placed their bodies in the tarps and then put them in the crate Elijah Padgett had left for us. When we hammered the lid on, I noticed the crate had a shipping order attached to it with an address for a fish processor in Romania. Those bodies would leave the country and disappear forever.

Ramsey called Sasha to let him know it was done.

"I'm meeting Sasha at The Rex," Ramsey said. He looked me up and down. "You should probably shower before going home to your wife."

"Drop me off at the clubhouse," I said. "It's on the way to The Rex. And then you can take the car and return it to Sasha."

I'd been running on fumes since Hayden had been brought to the hospital, but now that she was safe, I allowed Ramsey to drive. I closed my eyes and leaned my head against the seat. I slept the entire way to the clubhouse, only waking when Ramsey turned off the main road onto the dirt one that lead to the clubhouse gates.

The prospects opened the gates and we drove through.

"Sure you don't want to stay and have a drink?" I asked. "You've earned it."

"Can't," he said. "Have to get to The Rex. And if I stay and have a drink, I'm liable to fall asleep for a few days."

Leather & Lies

I clapped his hand in mine. "Thank you for your help. Are you finally ready to tell me why you offered?"

Ramsey explained what he needed.

I nodded. "I'll be in touch when I have some information."

"Appreciate it."

I climbed out of the car and headed up the front porch steps. I was running hot despite the cool autumn temperature. I was covered in blood, my knuckles were bruised, and I was in desperate need of a shower.

My phone beeped. It was a message from Charlie telling me that Hayden slept through the night and had no nightmares. Marilyn had taken first watch and then Charlie took the second. Hayden was on some heavy painkillers that had knocked her out—but I was glad she'd slept soundly. She'd had enough real-life nightmares. She didn't need them in her sleep, too.

I opened the front door of the clubhouse, expecting to find it empty at this hour, but Raze was sitting on the couch having a cup of coffee. He took one look at me and nodded.

"It's done, then?" he asked.

"Yeah. It's done."

"Why don't you look relieved?" he asked.

"Aside from the fact that I'm covered in this shit?" I moved past the couch toward the stairs. "I'm gonna shower."

"What aren't you telling me, brother?"

I paused and looked at him over my shoulder. "What wouldn't I be telling you?"

He shrugged. "Don't know. But I do know you're keeping something to yourself when you have that look on your face."

"You wouldn't understand."

"Fuck you," he said lightly. "What wouldn't I understand?"

When I didn't reply, his expression cleared.

"Oh. You think it has to go down like that?"

"Yeah Raze, I do."

Raze rubbed a thumb along his jaw. "You sure that's what you want to do? I mean, really sure?"

"I'm sure."

"You don't think you can have both?" he asked. "It has to be one or the other?"

"One or the other. You gonna try and talk me out of it?"

He frowned. "We've been through it. You, me, Smoke, Kelp…Viper. Does that not mean anything to you?"

"It means everything," I said quietly. "But there's something that means more."

∼

It was late morning when I pulled my motorcycle into the driveway. My steps were heavy with exhaustion as I punched in the door code. I quickly silenced the alarm and waited to hear movement from the living room. But no one came to greet me.

I didn't want to yell in case Hayden was sleeping. But then I heard laughter from upstairs and my chest immediately eased.

The sight that greeted me brought a smile to my face. Hayden was in the middle of the bed, Charlie and Marilyn flanking her. They were propped up against the headboard, the three of them tucked underneath the covers.

I'd never seen my mother-in-law without a face full of makeup. It was unlike her to dress comfortably, but the last week had clearly taken its toll.

"Hi," Hayden said, her smile bright when she met my gaze. Her eyes asked a thousand questions—questions I couldn't answer with Charlie and Marilyn in the room.

"What are we watching?" I asked, my eyes sliding to the TV.

A black and white sitcom played across the screen and Hayden laughed again. The sound warmed my cold insides.

"*I Love Lucy*," Marilyn said. "Charlie bought the anniversary DVDs and we've been watching them all morning."

"Have you seen it?" Charlie asked me.

"No."

"Classic," Hayden said. "The chocolate factory episode is the *best*."

"No way," Charlie negated. "Vitameatavegamin wins, no contest."

"You're both wrong," Marilyn stated. "It's the one where they're in Paris and Lucy goes on a hunger strike until Ricky buys her a designer gown."

"Clearly I'm going to have to sit and watch this show and see for myself," I stated.

Marilyn lifted the covers off her and she got out of bed. "Now that you're home, I can go."

"Me too," Charlie said, getting up.

"Thank you," Hayden said.

Marilyn leaned over and kissed her daughter's forehead. "We'll come back tomorrow." She walked toward me and brushed her cheek against mine. "We can show ourselves out."

I gave Charlie a side hug and then the two women left the bedroom. Hayden and I were quiet until we heard the front door shut.

"You look tired," Hayden murmured.

"So do you," I stated.

"I slept the night though, apparently."

"I know. Charlie texted. But it's pain meds sleep. It's more like it knocks you out, but I don't think it's all that restful."

She patted the bed. "Come here."

I sat on the edge of the mattress and stripped down to my boxer briefs. I slipped into bed next to her and gently cradled her in my arms.

Her warm breath fanned my skin and I was careful not to slide my fingers through her hair to avoid accidentally grazing the stitches at the back of her head.

"It's finished," I said.

She inhaled sharply but didn't say anything; she only hugged me tighter.

"There's something else."

"What is it?" she asked.

"I'm leaving the club."

She slowly pulled out of my arms to stare down at me. "Say that again?"

"I'm leaving the Tarnished Angels."

"But why?" she asked. "You've been part of the club for twenty years. You can't just walk away. They're your family."

I brushed a strand of hair away from her cheek. "You're my family now."

"I didn't ask you to do this," she said, her brow wrinkling.

"I know. But I have to. You've been through too much."

"I don't understand. You're just not going to be a biker anymore? Just like that?"

"Just like that," I said.

"I still don't understand."

"You and I come from different backgrounds."

"We've established that."

"Yeah, but we haven't established how we're going to overcome that. We could go on this path for a while. Me in my life, you in yours, but eventually, what will we have? Two people who might love each other who haven't built a life *together*. I don't want that."

"You'll resent me," she said quietly. "You'll resent me at some point. You'll blame me for giving up your life just so you can live in my world."

"I'm not giving it up. Raze, Smoke, Kelp, Viper, and everyone else…they're still family. But I can't pretend that I can still be part of the club and also be your husband. I can't go to galas with bloody knuckles and black eyes. I can't be involved in strip clubs—"

"*Strip clubs?*" I screeched.

"It's not even worth talking about. Because I'm choosing. I'm choosing you and the family we're going to make together."

She turned her head away, but I gently grasped her chin and forced her gaze back to mine. "I want you to be able to stand by me and not have to lie about what I do for a living. I don't want to have to tell you it's *club business*. I don't want to have to keep those kinds of secrets from you. I haven't wanted to be Royce Dalton in a long time. But Duchess, you make me want to be a better man. You make me want to be Royce again."

Her lips quivered and her brown eyes shone with tears. "You promise you won't resent me?"

"I promise."

"You promise this is your choice and that I didn't pressure you into this?"

"I promise," I said.

"Do you promise to love me forever?"

My mouth softened. "I promise."

She leaned forward and gently brushed her lips across mine before pulling back. "I guess it's my turn to tell you something."

I arched a brow and waited.

"I want to go forward with my charity with Charlie. It's where my heart is."

"What about your father's company—"

"It's still my father's company," she said. "I'll still have voting rights, I'll still be active. But I don't want the daily responsibility. I've never wanted that. My father would want me to be happy. And after everything that's happened…there's no more time to waste. I'm going to make my dreams come true. I'm going to live a happy life."

"I'm proud of you for coming to that conclusion, Duchess," I said gruffly. "Who's going to take over as Chair?"

She beamed. "My mother."

"Yeah?"

She nodded. "It was her idea. She wants to do something more than just organize events and go to Pilates. She needs a purpose. I think this will be good for her. Good for me—and us—too. Does that make you happy?"

"I'm happy if you're happy."

"I'm happy." She ran a thumb across my lips. "Just one teeny, tiny, little problem."

"What's that?"

"Do I have to change your name in my phone? I kind of like that you're in my contacts list as Bad to the Bones."

I laughed hard. It was deep and joyful and came from the depths of my soul.

"You don't have to change a damn thing," I said.

"You don't have to change a damn thing either," she

quipped. "Especially not the tattoos. You can keep those, right?"

"Normally, I'd have to remove the club's logo. But the brothers held church and voted. After twenty years, they've decided I can keep mine. I'm still their brother in flesh and blood—but I have to give up the cut."

Her fingers began tracing along my body, wandering, and dipping. "You still haven't gotten a tattoo for me, yet."

"I will." I closed my eyes. "Duchess, you gotta stop touching me."

"Why?"

"Because if you keep that up, I'm going to want to do things. And you need to rest."

"I've rested enough." She wiggled against me. "We can do things."

I opened my eyes and stared down at her, my woman, my wife, and one day soon, the mother of my child.

"We can't," I protested.

"We can," she insisted. "We're trying to start a family. Do you know how that happens?"

I let her push me onto my back and then she draped herself across me. I smirked. "No, I don't know how that happens."

She grinned and kissed my chin. "Lay back, Bad Decision, and I'll show you."

Additional Works

The Tarnished Angels Motorcycle Club Series:

Wreck & Ruin (Tarnished Angels Book 1)
Crash & Carnage (Tarnished Angels Book 2)
Madness & Mayhem (Tarnished Angels Book 3)
Thrust & Throttle (Tarnished Angels Book 4)
Venom & Vengeance (Tarnished Angels Book 5)
Fire & Frenzy (Tarnished Angels Book 6)
Leather & Lies (Tarnished Angels Book 7)

SINS Series:

Sins of a King (Book 1)
Birth of a Queen (Book 2)
Rise of a Dynasty (Book 3)
Dawn of an Empire (Book 4)
Ember (Book 5)
Burn (Book 6)
Ashes (Book 7)
Fall of a Kingdom (Book 8)

Additional Works

Others:

Peasants and Kings

About the Author

Wall Street Journal & USA Today bestselling author Emma Slate writes romance with heart and heat.

Called "the dialogue queen" by her college playwriting professor, Emma writes love stories that range from romance-for-your-pants to action-flicks-for-chicks.

When she isn't writing, she's usually curled up under a heating blanket with a steamy romance novel and her two beagles—unless her outdoorsy husband can convince her to go on a hike.

Made in the USA
Columbia, SC
03 May 2024